I want Everything

Roland DeCarra

I want Everything

Roland DeCarra

Other titles by Roland DeCarra

I WANT (2016)

I WANT MORE (2018)

Acorn Independent Press. 82 Southwark Bridge Road, London SE1 0EX, England

his book is the work of fiction. All characters within are the imagination of the author.

Acorn Independent Press

Roland DeCarra was born in Epsom, Surrey, England.
After leaving school he worked as a draughtsman for various
engineering establishments, Government agencies and the
Metropolitan Police.

He currently lives in Dorking, Surrey, England.

This is his third published book.

In memory of all my girls - Suzie, Cagney, Lacey and Heidi.

Contents

Acknowledgements

Many thanks once more to Acorn Publications, London, England for having faith in me and my work.

Also to Traudl von Scheidegger for trying to keep me sane and giving me a means of escape, Emma Tilley, Debbie Coombes (Party Popper), Eva Longoria, Nina Hagen, Perrie Edwards, Jesy Nelson, Zee Nix (my No.1 fan!), Adam Russell for his technical assistance, Michelle Lisle, Nikkolette Day, Nancy Weppler, Monique Gortzak, Gemma Smith for her special love, Jenhams Clinic (Dorking) for fixing me, Annuschkatz (Annette Reuner), Kim Proulx, Debora Esposito, Natalie Jay, Isla Fae, Janis Nelleman-Gotan, Gina Nt, Tish De Graff, Riley Steele, Locks Velvet, Lucero Luna, Maggie Bell, Grace Kiss, Elena Nolan, Alejandra TorARTE, Lady Nicole Banshee, Vanessita Bohorquez, Sofia Sanders, Raquel de Leon-Rey, Jillian MSex, Brittany Pettibone, Kalena Rios, Alissa White-Gluz, Kanae Izumi, Ramona Kaur, Emily Qvortrup, Mia Ping Ping, Lili Ardat, David Evans, Amber-Jayne, Cataline Guzman, Amanda Blackmore, Melly Greenall, Ioana Mihai, Mary Whitehouse, Avi Frankel, Evelyn Self, Maggie Chajek, Autumn Hammond, Isabella Della Porta, Lily von Trapp, Brittany Elizabeth, Stella Del Piro, Louella Mason, Betty Starfighter, Chris Bromley, Dave Smalldick, Alexandria

ACKNOWLEDGEMENTS

Ghinzani, Susan Cocksucker, Slutty Potato, Jacqueline Del Mar, Gudrun Schmauch-Schulte, Plum Sauce, Fanny Michau, Bridge von Burg, Alex Cooper, Laaura Perolla Muniz, Fanny von Perignon, Sara Kroft, Heather Weatherypoo, Raquel Esprit, Allegra Spinnetti, Gwendolyn Dora Bates, Maya Rozini, Nicolette Shea, Giovanna Isabella Deghetti, Jen Gamble, Latina Shana Cheim, Crystal Lavender, Tatiana Tchalabaeva, Katrin Gajndr, Rebecca Crow, Nina Milano, Cloud DeDevil, Mini Boom Boom, Agnes Pulut, Linda La Milf, Hannah Claydon, JJ-Jenny, Ruth Carrillo, Almendrita Luna, Crystal Riesett, Emilie Barbie DiPace, Jenna Bella Rose, Kaelyn Jaye, Roxy Shizzl, Ivana Alonso, Liliput Du Chapelet Enchante, Danielle Bathory Lobishomen, Alexa Scout, Samantha X, Domino Presley, Adriana Michele, Piper Jackson and Amber-Jayne.

Thank you also to iStockphoto.com for usage of the front cover photo.

1

Solitary Confinement

My only friends. You find me in solitary confinement, languishing in extreme mind-numbing boredom as I sit here writing this for you. My life is so bleak it's unbearable. My time now is mostly spent being introspective, lost in dreams of yesterdays future. There are many days, and some weeks also, where I do not speak or even see anyone - nobody. I have too much time but I also have so little, incarcerated in this shell swallowing vacuum, a pathetic existence of fetid and oblique visions. I am at the foot of my stairs. I have taken myself off the grid. I no-longer exist.

I will always relish in my anonymity and I am a misanthrope even to myself. I have to subjugate and close myself off to the outside World otherwise I'll go completely fucking insane. I am not open to anyone, I am always distant. Life has made me this way. I think that maybe I've had too much experience of life, and that has made me hard, cold and bitter. Of course I'm supernaturally perceptive of my surroundings, particularly when it comes to sussing-out other people, like all those idiots I've ever had to work with for instance. They're already dead, every one of them, they always were - they just don't know it themselves yet.

I am constantly perplexed by this planet and everyone on it, even myself. I'm like a jar with no lid. One minute I'm on cloud number-9 and the next I'm fucking suicidal, spending my time waiting for the next disappointment to rear its ugly head. The oppressiveness is almost unbearable. What is the sodding point of it all? I have to carry-on with the joke that is my life, the life that is one big fucking lie. My prurience is always there, constantly lurking under the surface in my mind. This is the terror of my inner angst. Where is it all going to end?

My anxieties are not a fantasy, it is the endless pain of being alive. My happiness and contentment is followed by the onslaught of despair and darkness. I try to face my demons but they're all around me all the fucking time and I don't know how to pull out of it. Even you my lovely reader are one of my demons.

Hypo-mania follows depression. This in turn leads to further depression and then another bout of hypo-mania and so the cycle continues on. Misery loves company and I've got it in abundance, whereas solitude multiplies my independent existence but also leaves me incarcerated.

It's hard work being a sociopath but even so I wouldn't want it any other way. I operate best from the shadows, especially as my motives themselves are always shadowy. My idealism is a rare breed, although fortunately I'm not alone in this, there are others out there like me. This is my life as I see it.

I've never really been a part of anything in my life, I've always been the outsider, as I still am to this very day. It will never change. People frighten me.

I wish to remain pure - not in the virginal sense of course, that ship sailed years ago! - but pure in the sense of freedom and individuality. Pure to seek out new experiences and run with them to their limits and beyond. I continuously seek peace and freedom away from those around me. I seek a time of pure stratification from the human race and all its evils. My reluctance to engage in human contact remains paramount, except when it comes to fucking of course, which I can do anytime I choose with the aid of my looks and my wealth.

I am alone and I dream alone.

My financial situation has fortunately insulated me further from my fellow humans. Any interaction with them is now minimal, with the only connections being limited to when I'm out on the road driving, shopping, or as I've said - fucking.

My privilege, bestowed upon my by my late husband and lover Andy, is mine to use and abuse as I WANT. Material possessions are all very well and all that, but there is a lot more to life than a big house, lots of money and loads of cars. Although I revel in the power of my wealth and natural beauty, both can be a hindrance. Wealth has bought me pure independence but also loneliness, whilst my beauty has given me an air of confidence - bordering on insanity! - but also jealousy and vitriol from other women.

I am a beautiful woman trapped inside a beautiful woman's body. I am the paradigm of the perfect female and I fucking know it. I am a Goddess in human form. I have become more like a deity than a human. This is the cross I have to bare. There are no real winners in whatever one does, that's the way life is. My beauty and my fortune are a double-edged sword.

I am the inescapable image of the past, present and future all rolled into one perfect creature. No-one can touch me. I am not here nor there and yet everywhere at once. I belong to no particular place in time, stuck in perpetual unreality.

I see things that other people can't, or don't want to see. I know that I'm a complex girl, made up of many different facets, each of which contributes to my whole being. And if I didn't have Eva, the house, the cars or Andy's money I don't think that I would be alive today - the World would have destroyed me for sure. Either that or my latent paranoia. As ever though, my resilience is super-strong and I will survive.

I do miss the companionship of being with someone though, someone like Andy or Amanda, and I really miss them both. They were both a slice of Heaven and I cherish the moments we had together. I just hope that in the not too distant future there will be another someone for me to love and who will love me back, although I'm not entirely sure that I have any understanding of what love means any more. At this moment, with me, love is sex and sex is love - nothing more.

I will never give myself to anyone totally though as I really don't think that it's natural, or healthy. Having said that, I'll continue to indulge myself in anything I like - with a man or a woman, I don't care either way - I have freedom and material happiness to exercise my eccentricities and desires, although I seem to have forgotten what happiness is as well. I'm always searching for peace and harmony but never seem to find it. I am dark and I'm lonely. I'm also bored and scared. It's all a bit sad really.

I'm so scared of the future. Not even millions in the bank can save me. Why do I have to keep pushing myself harder and harder just to survive? This is what I have to do, I have to push it, push it further. There is no point in being alive if you don't push.

Polarities of life are forever changing. The Devil and his demons within me push me to carry on and have banished me from my former life. I've certainly been savant enough to survive this far so I have to be hopeful of going the distance. I'm not going to follow the herd, that's not my vocation at all and never has been or ever will be. This year is going to be different, I just know it. Something has changed in the atmosphere and freed my path. As one phase of my life ends, another is about to begin.

I do not exist in the same dimension as everyone else, I'm on a one-way ticket to oblivion and no-one can stop me. Bring it on!

***

I've had no-end of fucking hassle off of all and sundry ever since Andy died and left me the house, all his money and all the cars. It seems like everyone is trying to take a little slice of me and I hate it, I am completely bloody sick of it all. The money has been like Heaven and Hell all rolled into one.

Andy's bitch of a sister Angela has also been a fucking nightmare, forever sending me poisonous letters via her stupid solicitor about the contents of Andy's Will, the house and yet again the fucking money. Give it up you stupid old cow!

The financial side of things has been a fucking nightmare generally anyway. I've had the sodding Tax people on my back whinging and whining about inheritance tax and all that crap, not that I really give a shit about them of course! There's no fucking way I'm going to let the fucking Government get their hands on my assets!

I've also got the Taxman chasing me for money as I haven't paid any tax or National Insurance since the day I got the sack from that shithole last job of mine and I've no intention of doing so either - they can all go and kiss my perfect arse! So too can the local Council, as they're also chasing me for non-payment of Council Tax as I haven't paid that either since the day I moved-in with Andy - my love. Now I've got the bloody TV licensing people after me as well as I haven't paid that either! They've all been threatening me with legal action for months and unless I pay up they said they will take me to court. At first I just sent all the letters back with a big "FUCK OFF" scrawled across them in red but now I've just been shredding them as soon as I receive them - fucking BBC twats! Who do they think they are telling me what to do?

I've also cancelled my private pension that I had built-up over the last 10-years or so. There was absolutely no point in keep paying into it any more with all the money I've got behind me now. The amount I cashed-in was shit anyway, barely enough to keep me in vodka for a year!

Mr. Simpson - Andy's solicitor and now mine - has helped me a tremendous amount - bless him - what with all the aforementioned crap and with sorting out the deeds to the house and stuff. Getting the titles to all the cars and bikes changed over to my name was also a right pain in the arse but at least that's all been taken care of now. A lot of the cars and all the motorbikes have subsequently been sold off, leaving me with the cream of the crop. I had to keep the Lamborghini of course - who wouldn't? - as well as the Aston, the GT40, the Willys, the Lister, the Mini, the Ford Hot Rod, the Mustang, the Morgan Aeromax and a couple of the other "toys". I did feel kind-of sad getting rid of the others as they were a big part of Andy's life. But time moves on and so must I, Andy has gone and the cars also had to go, that's just the way it is.

I also sold my orange Focus ST as well as Andy's green RS as there was no point in hanging on to either of them. It was a shame to see them go but life moves on as I've said. To replace them I treated myself to one of the new RS's, a white one with a 2.3-litre 400bhp engine and 4-wheel-drive. It's super-fast and I love her with all my heart. All the bikes were sold off as well, I can't ride the things so there was no point in them just sitting there gathering dust. I did keep the Penny Farthing though, purely as an ornament. I think if I ever had a go at riding that I would probably break my bloody neck!

It was Andy's old car club friend Craig that took everything off my hands. He didn't even charge me commission, although I think he was expecting some other kind-of payment, like in kind for instance! That obviously wasn't going to happen, despite his continuous amorous advances, and I had to tell him to: "Back Off" and send him away with his tail between his legs - that's guys for you! With some of the money from the sales I treated myself to one of those Ferrari La Ferrari's - a red one of course! - to replace the Italia that I sold. It's absolutely beautiful and turns heads wherever she goes - just like I do! I know it was an indulgence but I don't care, I can do whatever I fucking like. I bought it as a joint Birthday/Christmas present to myself. I can't believe that I turned 36 last November, doesn't time go quickly? This past year has disappeared into nowhere. I didn't spend my birthday alone however as I hired a couple of fucks for the day as a special treat to myself. I booked a male escort at lunchtime to fuck me and a female one for the evening and to stay with me overnight. Both of them were really good and I thoroughly enjoyed myself thank you! Christmas time though was very lonely, just me and Eva and that was that. I ate and drank too much as per bloody usual but what the fuck, it was Christmas!

My Eva, she's like a mixture of all different things - Heidi, Suzie, my Guardian Angel, my Mum, Abigail, and of course myself. She is so painfully beautiful. She's such a typical cat though, all she ever does is eat, sleep, wash and poo! There is an unbreakable bond between us, she is mine and I am hers, a kindred spirit that is beyond love. Of course I really do love her to bits, although I still keep calling her Lacey - I just can't seem to help it - she was such a special cat and I will never forget her, not ever.

***

Oh come on, fuck me, fuck me. I WANT your cock in me. Come on, fuck me. Cum in me, cum inside me, come on, oh fuck me. Fuck me harder, oh harder, oh more, more, come on. Harder. Fuck me, aw aw aw. Cum in me. Fuck my arse, come on, you can do it, fuck in me. Cum in my ass, you can do it my love, fuck it, fuck it harder. Fuck me and cum in my face. Ah ah oh uh oh oooo ah aw aw ah ah uh uh oh yeah oh ah ah ah ah ah ah ah ah ah ah eeeck ooooooh.

I cum.

And I laugh.

***

I am constantly dismayed at the state of my England. This is the pleasure and pain of being xenophobic. Why can't things be better? It's hard I know, but all it takes is balls and guts and we can win our country back and reclaim our freedom. It won't happen of course, the so-called "Right" are the new Left whilst the Left are now genuinely insane. The cracks in the country are now too big to breach and there is no going back. Things will only get worse. We haven't even got much of a country left any more anyway let alone an Empire.

All our past history and heritage is being wiped-away by the Left, race traitors and so-called political correctness - and if you play their game you really are fucked. In the not too distant future we will have nothing left and England will cease to exist, replaced by Mosques and Temples and a barren wasteland full of immigrants and the scum of the Earth. The whole World is up-side-down.

The population of this country - MY England, this island race - has increased to an intolerable level. The infestation of immigrants from the shit-holes of the World has disaffected the indigenous population, they in turn being lied to and cheated by the hypocrisy and subterfuge from successive blind Governments - particularly by that delusional Left Wing race-traitor Blair with his arrogant, spineless, contemptible, elitist, smug, egomaniac negligence when he opened the gates to this country and purposely flooded it with uncontrolled Slavic scum, simultaneously causing irreparable damage whilst also lining his own pockets at the same time - CUNT. He should be hanged - slowly.

I'm sick to the back-teeth of being treated like a second-class citizen in my own country. Don't you fucking people understand, I've had enough of it all, I can't fucking stand it any more. The World drags me down. Everything is oppressive, the stresses of life and this environment. What have we done to ourselves, our lives, we humans? Why do we destroy everything we have created? We have a beautiful World so why do we have to fuck it up? Am I the only person on this planet with eyes? Can you see this?

Everything has fallen apart - yet again.

Now, how do I get off this bloody rock?

***

I prance around naked in the garden without a fucking care, why fucking should I? No-one can touch me. I touch myself. I am out of reach of every fucker that dares to attack me and I laugh in the faces of my so-called "humans", they are pathetic beyond any words.

I am completely naked apart from the beautiful silver pendant that hangs around my neck, the one from Andy with the words of Aleister Crowley etched on the reverse, hidden against my perfect skin. I am the embodiment of the perfect female.

I climb upon one of my garden sculptures - the glass-fibre one in the shape of a giant white penis that measures nearly 2-metres in length - and straddle its girth. Placing one-hand on each of its balls I begin to shuffle my body back and forth along its veiny length. My labia quickly starts to love itself and in under a minute I cream myself and cum, my juices feeling so fucking good as the wetness eases my sliding motion along the smooth surface of the artwork. I hug and kiss my massive cock as I love it, spinning myself around 180 to lick my honey in ecstasy and fuck.

Running through the grass and between the trees I skip and jump and laugh myself stupid. I am so deliriously fucking happy that even my tears of despair are smiling.

What is wrong with me?

How have I ended up like this?

Why am I so fucking twisted?

I fall down onto the grass and make an angel in its wetness and lay there looking up at the stars. I wonder to myself if there is anything out there, in outer space? There must be, there has to be something better than this shitty fucking planet? This can't be all there is in the universe - can it?

I lay there for ages just staring at the stars and the moon, wondering what the Hell it's all about - life and stuff? I wonder to myself if I've had too much life and that it's that that has made me the way I am?

I know things that no-one else does on this life and that sets me apart from the rest of humankind. I understand that I'm controversial, but that's what makes me ME. Not that I really care what you think, I gotta get on.

Under the illumination of the moon I prowl the garden in search of my life and my future - I find nothing.

I'm followed by the spirit of my Guardian Angel, his presence so deeply embedded in my subconscious that I cannot escape him. As always I have to keep fighting. I have to keep pushing-on before it's all too late. One day we will all be extinct and then what are you going to do, look back from the Spirit World and weep of missed opportunities and regret?

Talking of which, I gave up reading my horoscope in the paper ages ago. I was sick and tired of them keep winding me up with their false predictions and promises, I've had enough. I'm not wasting any more of my precious time stargazing. Whatever will be will be and no crackpot with a crystal ball will make any difference to that.

BANG THE DRUM - PULL THE STRING

That night - when I eventually get to bed that is! - I have a strange dream about Mum. We're whizzing along in her little grey Ford Ka and we end up in a quaint little old village miles from anywhere. It's also pissing down, and I comment to her about some of the other drivers driving along without their lights on in poor visibility, the arseholes and clowns in their BMW's and Audi's, all thinking that they're immune to danger. What is wrong with these fucking people? Arrogant twats!

We stumble upon an evil-looking church with big pointed spires with devils and gargoyles adorning its facade. Mum spots a sign on the churchyard gate that says: *"TEA ROOM"* and so she pulls into the small car-park and stops the car.

"Would you like some tea?" She turns to me and says.

"Well, no, not really. Do we have to stop here?" I question her back.

"I fancy a cup of tea." She informs me, already half-way out of the car door.

"Well, I guess so do I then!" I quip back.

For some weird reason we have to queue-up for a ticket in order to be allowed into the tearoom - fuck knows why? - and we then have to stand there like lemons at what looks like an old train station kiosk when suddenly I get a strange tickling sensation under my right-arm. I quickly spin around to see what or who it is that's causing it. Behind me stands an old creepy guy - tall, thin, old, creepy, and dressed all in black.

"WHAT THE FUCK DO YOU THINK YOU'RE DOING?" I scream at him as he then looks straight at me, straight into my eyes and says:

"I've got 6-heads. Which one would you like me to put on?" He says in a sinister tone that freezes my spine solid.

"JUST FUCKING KEEP AWAY FROM ME YOU FUCKING CREEP." I fire back at him.

Mum and I go and sit ourselves down at a table for 2 in the tearoom and natter-away about nothing for the next 20-minutes or so. The old creep sits by himself over the other side of the room, just by the exit-door, staring at me with his big, round glaring eyes.

We soon finish our tea and go to leave, heading over in the direction of the creep and the exit. As we pass I stab the old bastard in the eye - his left - with a fork and he screams in blinding agony and goes to pull it out. Blood spurts everywhere but it's all too late, I've already left the building. I'm in Mums car. We drive away. It's raining. The dream is over.

* * *

It's Monday 11th January 2016. I'm off to Horsham today for a mooch around the shops, nothing more. It's been pissing-down for most of the night and it's still drizzling a bit now and is quite overcast, as well as being a tad chilly. Because of this I'm wearing a white pure-wool v-neck jumper from Monsoon, a pair of pale-blue skinny-jeans from Topshop, a pair of tan-coloured ankle-boots from Schuh, and my old white leather biker-jacket that was a Christmas gift from "What's-his-face" way back when. My clutch-bag today is my beautiful white leather one from Hermes. My hair and make-up are both done to perfection - my usual style and razor-sharp - whilst my perfume is *Poison* by Christian Dior.

Once again I'm taking the Lamborghini out for a spin, my regular car of choice.

From my driveway I turn right onto the A272 and put my foot down with plenty of sweet sounds from the triple-exhausts. The traffic is really light for 10.35am and so fortunately I don't encounter anything in my way for a bloody change. I pass a cop-car going in the opposite direction out on the duel-carriageway, noticing the 2-pigs inside looking across at me and I laugh at them as I tear-along doing 140 in a 50-zone. There's nowhere for them to turn around at this point and chase me so they can fuck-off - Ha! The sound of the engine screaming its beautiful music though the exhausts brings tears to my eyes. I can't really describe why I feel this way. I guess it's the feeling of freedom and of being independent, of being at one with this beautiful machine.

For some inexplicable reason, as I approach another large sweeping roundabout, I decide to turn the radio on in the car, something I never do as it interferes with my concentration. The voice of the DJ from BBC Radio Sussex automatically emits from the surrounding speakers with her going-on about David Bowie and how inspirational he was. What does she mean "was", he's not dead so why is she talking about him in the past tense? She starts going-on about the fact that his latest album *BLACKSTAR* was only released last Friday - not that I bought it, I've always found his later work far too morbid and depressing - and now he's not around to see its success.

I slow right down to 50 as I come up to the roundabout and turn the sound up on the radio. It's David Bowie. He's dead. He died yesterday at home in New York of cancer at the age of 69.

NO, THIS CANNOT BE REAL? NO, HE CAN'T BE DEAD, HE JUST CAN'T?

I screech to a halt in the middle of the road, not believing what my ears are hearing. This cannot be true. He can't die, he's David Bowie.

All of a sudden some fucking idiot in a white van sounds his horn at me as he passes me on the right-hand lane of the road. I quickly snap myself out of my nightmare and move myself up the road further, pulling over to the left into a lay-by out of everyone's way and sit there in complete shock. My World has stopped and a part of me dies. My memory transports me back to when I was living at the "Family" home, locking myself away in my bedroom trying to escape the mental torture and all the fucking abuse from the "Old Man" and the rest of the World and all that shit, contemplating the hopelessness of my life, and how the music and words of David Bowie - and alcohol - saved me from certain suicide, both elements drowning the ugly things in my life to fade away.

He gave me my independence.

He taught me how to be me.

And now he's gone.

David Bowie has gone.

The tears come flooding out and I can't hold them back.

I am destroyed.

I can't stay sitting here like this all bloody day and I don't feel like going shopping now that's for sure. I click the paddle-shift into first and move off, traversing the roundabout and head back home to Foxhill. I have to switch the radio off, I can't listen to any more words about the death of my saviour, it's just too painful.

I drive back to the house on autopilot, not even bothering to park the car in the garage, I can't, I don't want to waste time getting inside my cocoon.

I slam the front-door behind me and head straight for the living-room, still in tears, pouring myself a large neat vodka to drown my sorrows. I down it in one go and pour myself another. I switch on the TV and Bowie's image is everywhere, on every news channel and more. The outpouring of grief from his fans and those who had worked with him over the years is heartbreaking to watch and I can't take it any more. I switch the

TV off, swap my empty glass for the bottle and make my way upstairs in devastation.

I find Eva dozing on my bed and I sit down next to her and cry my eyes out once again. They are tears of total and complete loss and I weep like I did at the passing of my poor old cat Lacey. I feel the soft hairs of Eva's fur as she brushes against me as she tries to comfort me but it's too late - I am gone.

I cry like a baby, just like I used to when I was being tortured by "Him" as a little girl and then as a young woman, sobbing wails of pain as I locked myself away in my bedroom, just as now. I guzzle-down the vodka until I can take no more and then make my way back downstairs with Eva in tow to protect me - my little love.

I put *Heroes* on the stereo and crank up the volume, making the whole house shake with the sound of Bowie's voice and Robert Fripp's wailing guitar as I sing and cry along to my favourite Bowie song as tears roll down my face. I still cannot believe this is happening, not "my" David Bowie. Who is going to save me now?

The song comes to an end and I can't take another, I can't listen to his voice or hear his inspirational words or even to see his face - I just can't do it.

I sleep on the sofa for most of the afternoon as I try to disperse my inebriated state. That evening I eat light - some chips with salad and pickles - as I watch one documentary after another on every channel but it's all too much, I just can't take it in.

I go to bed early that evening at 9.20pm and reflect on this day of sadness. And that's just what it is - a sad day for music, for art, for film and for England herself.

We have lost a true genius.

R.I.P. David Bowie.

I wonder what it was that made me turn the radio on in the first place?

***

It's another day of glorious winter sunshine as I sit in the rear section of the living room gazing out through the giant glass patio doors at my snow-covered garden amidst its inherent silence. The Sun beams down on the white blanket but has little effect as it's actually bloody freezing cold outside - it's early February.

Indoors though I'm all lovely and as snug as a bug in a rug, the underfloor heating warming me from my feet and toes upwards. Eva sits on my lap, curled-up like cats do, underlining the love and harmonious existence between us. I sit here in my empty nest, lost in my own little World, reading whilst contemplating my life and where its going - where is it going?

Yesterday I finished reading *Paradise Lost* by John Milton and today I'm starting on another classic book - *Dante"s Inferno* by Dante Alighieri. I'm reading these, and others, in order to try and get some inspiration and courage to continue with my own book, which all-in-all is going pretty well actually, but more of that later. With a hot mug of tea to comfort me I read on and absorb and dream for the following couple of hours or so.

At mid-day I break for lunch and fix myself something to eat - sushi today, with plenty of soy sauce - all washed down with several glasses of German white. For Eva I give her half a tin of duck in sauce with garden vegetables. It was poor old Lacey's favourite treat - my love. I go and sit my arse down in front of the TV and channel-hop from one shitty program to another. I've got over 200-channels on this box but still there's nothing on any of them, just crap, with "macaroons" and "donkey-drivers" in 9 out of 10 programs on every fucking side. Once again it's the Left that is to blame, infiltrating the media with their warped sense of life and the World, even rewriting history by including blacks and Asians into historical dramas and documentaries to make them "multiculturally acceptable". Well they're not fucking acceptable to me. I click onto BBC News-24 where there's a report on the lack of skilled labour in the Country but that just winds me up even more and I have to switch over yet again. Before I do, the camera pans-around a classroom of schoolkids sitting behind their individual computers. The footage has obviously been taken at some school in London somewhere as virtually every fucking kid is non-white with the white ones probably either fucking Slavs or of some other denomination. It's a fucking joke even though in reality it isn't - it's a fucking nightmare.

All this technology and the lack of teaching kids about the real things in life is just breeding a nation of morons who can't spell or even tell the bloody time - where is it all going to end?

My mind and my damaged brain plunge into another spiral of despair as I destroy the TV and then myself.

I don't want to be alive.

I'm not sure I have the strength to stay alive.

Even my anti-bodies are fighting amongst themselves, the red at war with the white. My life has become a joke, it's a farce from beginning to end. Most of it is pure bullshit so you should be in good company! What do you expect me to do, write a book about it?

I had no set plan to turn into a megalomaniac, I just became that way, life happens. We are all deconstructed into our simple base forms and act upon our inherent abilities - we love, we hate, we eat, we drink, we sleep, we fuck, we kill, we die. We all have our fantasies and I'm no exception as you well know!

As you're also well aware of by now I have no inhibitions and I'm fully aware of my sexual predisposition. I know exactly what men, and women, want from me. Sometimes I even let them have it! Sexual frustration boils-away within me 24/7 and I can't control it, not even with alcohol or masturbation. There is no-way of abating it, I need to fuck all the time, I'm constantly on heat and submissive into the red-zone. That in-turn obviously gets me into trouble and there I am - back to square fucking one again.

Why do I always run before I can walk? I want for nothing, only love. The time has now come for me to make a monumental decision. Everything must be in place for this next chapter in my life. Preparation is key to the success of this project and then vengeance will be mine.

I don't have the patience to write any more.

***

Remember that guy Craig, the creepy friend of Andy's, the one that helped me sell-off all the unwanted cars and bikes that I told you about earlier? Apparently there's some big do on that he's got 2-tickets for and has invited me to be his partner at the event scheduled for later-on today, some kind-of charity thing or whatever?

For several weeks now I've resisted his persistent begging to accompany him but now I've decided I'm going to go with him anyway - to the do that is, NOT to have sex with him, that would be beyond even me, I hope! The event is only down the road at Petworth House, so it's not like it's bloody miles away. Plus of course it's on during the daytime so hopefully I can keep myself safe and out of trouble as well as away from Craig's wandering hands!

Anyway, he's picking me up at mid-day so that gives me plenty of time for me to dress to kill. I'm going all-out on my image as it's supposedly quite a prestigious event, and so with that in mind I'm wearing a sexy white cross-over top from Maschino that exposes most of my front and side-cleavage - I'm not wearing a bra - as well as my abdomen and belly-rings. My skirt is a white leather mini from Prada that really shows-off my curves to the max, including my beautiful long toned legs. It was stupefyingly expensive at £1,600 - more than I used to take home in a month when I was working! - but times have changed, this is a different me now. My knickers are a sexy white lace pair from Triumph. On my feet I'm wearing a pair of white Lobita shoes from Manolo Blahnik that also cost me a bloody fortune - over £600! - but what the Hell, I've got shit-loads of money and I WANT, so I did! My clutch-bag is my faithful white leather one from Hermes. My perfume is *Poison* by Christian Dior. My hair is my own style and my make-up sharp and dark, featuring coal-black eye-shadow and cherry-red lipstick. I look like Death on a good day!

I down 2-large glasses of the evil Russian poison to help me chill before "Whats-his-face" gets here, the time now being 11.35am. No- sooner have I finished my second glass and go for number-3, the entry-gate buzzer sounds and he's here early - fuck it! I open the gate to let him in and watch him drive up to the front of the house in a beautiful silver Ferrari Daytona Coupé - it's gorgeous, just like me! We exchange the usual old pleasantries as he calls me "Darling" and "Lover" and says: "You look gorgeous" and kisses me on the cheek and all that shit even though I don't want him to - I have no interest in him whatsoever. I give Eva a quick kiss "Goodbye" and then we go, although I immediately notice that I have to open my bloody passenger-side door my fucking self - typical!

The Ferrari is pure class and sounds glorious as he starts it back up and then powers out the drive and along the A272 to Petworth. The house itself is situated behind a massive stone wall right on the edge of town, literally lining one side of the main access route and beyond. We make our way up the main drive to the impressive 17th-Century country-house, parking along the main thoroughfare between a brand-new green Bentley Continental GT and a red Jaguar F-Type Coupé. This goes to show what a stuck-up event this is going to be!

Once again I have to open my own bloody door as I then extract myself out from the womb-like confines of the car. Suddenly Craig goes to link his left-arm with my right as we make our way to the entrance but I move away from him and his manoeuvre is thwarted. What does he bloody expect? Just because Andy is no-more doesn't mean that I'm going to drop to my knees and suck his dick!

The interior of the house is just as you would imagine for a building of this status and grandeur - massive rooms with high ceilings, old paintings, marble floors and antique furniture. It's lovely in its own way but not really my cup of tea.

After handing over our entry-tickets to one of the stuffed-shirts on guard to the party, Craig and I head in. As we enter the whole room screeches to a halt and I'm surrounded by a million stares. Is it because I'm over-dressed? Or is it because I'm under-dressed? Either way I don't fucking care, it's not my bloody problem that they're all jealous of my supermodel looks. Maybe it's my tattoos and piercings that have freaked them all out? It's their tough shit if it is, not mine.

The ice is broken by a pretty waitress with a silver tray - real silver of course, no shit here! - full of glasses of Champagne. I pinch one from her and sink half in one gulp but Craig doesn't indulge himself. I really must remain sober - I really must. We're suddenly joined by another couple, he in his mid-50's and she - looking me up and down with daggers as well as claws! - much younger at about my age, maybe less? She's dressed in some fucking awful-looking ball-gown, as I notice are most of the other attending females, she smiling at me a fake smile full of hate. I don't bother returning the favour as what's the fucking point, she's nothing too me just like the fucking rest of them here or anywhere else for that matter so why should I fucking care?

Both Craig and his friend Robert shake hands - not a proper one you understand, one of those dodgy shakes where one has to stand in a bowl of custard beforehand - get the picture? I fucking knew it right from the very first moment I met him that he was a bloody Freemason, I just knew it. Didn't I bloody tell you? This is the limit, I'm out of here right now!

All of a sudden Robert's wife - Caroline, that's her bloody name! - starts to bitch at me:

"You're a bit underdressed for this event aren't you?" She whines like a cow.

"That's only your opinion. If I had been told I had to dress up like bloody Queen

Victoria I wouldn't have fucking bothered coming." I snap back at her. Stupid fucking bitch.

"Charming! I would have thought your husband would have told you that this was a Victorian-era themed women's event?" She bleats on.

"He's not my husband, he was a friend of my late-husband. And no, he didn't bloody tell me." I spit back at her.

She stands there perplexed at my reply, at my language, at my image, at my beautiful face, my perfect body and my sparkling blue eyes of horror and inner-suffering. She has no comprehension of me or my life, of the pain I have endured over all the preceding years. She and everyone else here are completely ignorant to what it's actually like to be both dead and alive at one and the same time. They don't have a fucking clue.

I turn on my heals and head out the door, ignoring Craig's questions of: "Where are you going?" and "Sarah, what's the matter?" and all that shit, I'm just not fucking interested at all. I ask one of the stuffed-shirts where I can find the nearest loo and he points me in the right direction. I hide myself away in one of the toilet cubicles like a moth in its chrysalis, like a baby in its womb, except I don't want to be born - I want to die. I want to go back in time to before life existed and start the World again, to make it right, to make it peaceful, to make it happy. I know it will never happen of course, I'm talking shit. I'm living in a nightmare/daymare dreamworld just as I always have done, trapped in non-reality, just surviving.

Andy's money, the house, the cars, all give me the freedom and independence I crave but that doesn't solve the problem within me - the problem of being ME, of who I am, the pain inflicted upon me and buried within me by the "Old Man".

I retch and puke my guts out, missing the toilet bowl completely as the liquefied vodka/Champagne sick splatters against and down the cubicle wall. I stand there and watch it slither and slide down its surface as it creates its own art, it's actually quite a nice pattern.

I hear the main toilet-door open as someone else enters. I try to clean myself up the best I can using plenty of toilet-paper, fortunately I haven't puked down my clothes or that would have sent me right over the edge and no mistake.

Exiting the cubicle I see a woman over at the basins washing her hands. She's way-older than me - in her 60's at a guess? - and similarly dressed as all the others. She turns her craggy face and stands there gorping at me, not quite believing that someone as beautiful and gorgeous as I am actually exists. I look back at her but I'm not really looking AT her, I'm looking right through her into her mind. Once again it's another one full of jealousy and dismay of the vision that is me. After at least 30-seconds pass I look away and spit into the basin next-door-but-one to hers. Although I'm not looking at her I know for a fact that she has an expression of disgust across her lined old face. I spit a couple more times before I reach down and take a mouthful of cold water, swill it around to try and cleanse myself and spit once more. I turn side-on to her and dry my hands under the warm air of the automatic dryer, all the while sensing the old bitch staring at my body, my legs, my perfect bum, my tattoos, my gorgeous hair, my firm and full breasts and my tight clothes and FUCK HER TO HELL!

Picking up my clutch-bag I leave the toilet and the building, emerging out into the invigorating open-air. I call for a cab on my mobile and spend the following 13-minutes wandering around the car-park looking at all the beautiful cars as I wait, with not a sight nor sound of Craig or anyone else coming to my rescue or to even check if I'm still alive.

Back home at the house I smash myself to pieces on evil Russian liquid, English gin and German white as I fuck myself along to high-class blonde lesbian fisting porn on my computer. I cum as I cry and laugh at the same time as I try to work out what the Hell is wrong with me?

I fail yet again.

***

I'm going to get that arrogant old fucker John Fitzherbert, the lazy bastard I used to "work" with at the last company I was employed by, those bunch of deadbeats in Horsham - remember that lot?

It's 2.30am on a Monday morning and I'm on the A29 heating South towards Pulborough in West Sussex to where the ignorant old tosser lives. I got his address ages ago after he had accidentally left a letter on his desk at work regarding a dental appointment. Obviously I made a mental note of it at the time for future reference, just in case of times like now. I'm driving along in the new RS, minding my own business and trying not to get involved in racing anyone or having any antagonism from the pigs.

Naturally I'm dressed all in black to disguise myself as I know for a fact that there's CCTV cameras guarding the flats where the miserable old fucker lives as I recall him saying so.

I'm wearing a black jumper, a pair of black jeans and boots and a black nondescript jacket with black gloves. I'm also wearing a black wig that I stole off a Paki-run market-stall in Chichester a couple of weeks ago. It's funny the way it makes me look - somehow plainer? My make-up I've left plain and simple as again I don't want to draw attention to myself. Also I'm not wearing any perfume as there's no real point is there? For protection I'm carrying one of my super-sharp Japanese kitchen-knives, just in case someone decides to get smart with me.

Once in Pulborough itself I transverse the 2-stupid mini-roundabouts and then head past the antiques shop on my left, over the small bridge spanning the River Arun and continue along the A29 a short way where there's a small lay-by hidden behind some trees. I park easily as there's no other cars to be found there and switch-off my engine. From the boot of the car I remove the small green plastic can of petrol and an old rag. With the car secure and the coast clear I make my way on foot back to the last mini-roundabout and walk left towards the Rail

Station, I know the old cunt lives in one of the flats opposite to my left and so I home-in on them.

There's not a soul about and the night-sky is as black as a black man's bum. The air is full of tension and feels slightly creepy but nothing and no-one is going to stop me as I near my target. I spot the block of flats before me and my heartbeat goes into overdrive at my impending attack. Scanning the long lines of cars parked outside the block I quickly spot the old fuckers shitty silver Jap-crap car. I squat-down beside it on the offside and remove the cap to the petrol can, inserting the rag about half-way into its orifice. I place the can under the car as far as I can reach and carefully light the end of the rag with a lighter.

I run like fucking crazy to get away from the inevitable fire and explosion, hiding myself around the corner of one of the numerous garages on the opposite side of the road. The burning rag seems to take forever to catch but then in an instant I'm rewarded with a sudden burst of blue and orange flame and then a deep whoosh from under the Mazda, it taking me by surprise and lighting-up my beautiful face and my smile. I laugh a muted laugh at the vision before me as I don't want to give my position away to the inevitable congregation of people all coming to gorp at the flames. The fuel-tank of the rice-burner then erupts with an echoing boom that makes me jump off my feet and this time I really do laugh out loud - LOL! I decide to make my exit before I get caught as already a phalanx of humans are quickly gathering around the bonfire.

I make my way steadily but swiftly back to my car and restart the engine with a roar. I pull out from behind the shielding trees and head back over the small bridge to the roundabout, although just as I approach the junction a Police car with sirens and flashing blue-lights suddenly appears from behind the building to my right and cuts right across in front of me, making me start. I watch it disappear into the distance to my left and then turn into the old wankers road but I have to go, I have to get away from here.

Once again I take it easy on the roads back to Foxhill, trying not to draw attention to myself. I drive through my entrance gates and watch them shut themselves in my rear-view mirror, the time on the RS's clock now reading 3.37am. Safely indoors I breath a sigh of relief that the "Hit" was successful and LOL at the destruction of the old bastards car. I bet that will give him something to fucking moan about! He'll be milking that one until his dying fucking day - fucking lazy old cunt.

I strip naked in the living-room and swig on a bottle of the evil Russian fluid as I hold Eva in my right-arm. I kiss her with my vodka-soaked lips and she sticks her pert little nose up in the air to smell its vapour - she's so funny! After half-a-dozen mouthfuls or so of the nasty - I wasn't actually counting! - I release her and slowly drop her down onto the white fluffy rug in front of the fire. I insert 2-fingers into my vagina and masturbate myself, pushing them harder and deeper into my lover. I fuck my bean as I wank and in no-time I have myself, my legs start to shake uncontrollably and my breathing becomes more erratic as I bring myself to the perfect ending and I orgasm, scream and cum. I pant like a steam-engine as I slowly ease off and I'm finished. I roll over onto my back and lay there with my legs apart, my vagina hot with my love, as I lick the honey from my fingers.

What a rush!

What a hit!

What a fuck!

I sleep a lovely sleep and lay in bed until 1.25pm that very same Monday. The stupid Police are absent from my door as the old cunt is so bloody ignorant there is no-way he would even comprehend that it was me that torched his shitty fucking car - fucking old bastard.

***

I'm sitting in Andy's old office on the computer. I'm completely naked. I've been doing some more research and writing for the book this morning, followed by some porn - bisexual bukkake licking featuring one guy and 2-girls, all 3 of them horny and obviously drugged out of their skulls. The guy was fucking one girl up the rear-end as she was positioned on all fours with the other girl straddling her back cowgirl-style and every now and then taking the guys cock out of the other girls bumhole and sucking on it. After he had cum up the girls rear-end the other girl then proceeded to lick it and swallow the bukkake. It was precisely at this moment that I cum.

I'm now checking through my Emails, all but 2 of them meaningless crap. The first one that was worth reading - if I can go as far as saying that! - is from my sister Kate, who I haven't seen or spoken to since she came to visit me in hospital when I had my little bender ages ago. She bleats-on about forgiving me for all the things I said back then and hopes that: "We can both move on with our lives". Well, no we fucking can't actually. I never want to see her again, or that fucking mongrel kid of hers and that is exactly what I say in my return message - fucking amazing!

The second non-junk mail is equally incredible, it's from Steve, the guy I was seeing before I hooked-up with Amanda. He proceeds to inform me that not only has he got married - to some girl called Charlotte - he's had a daughter with her that he's weirdly named Sarah! He then goes on to ask me if we could: "Meet-up for a drink sometime?" What a bloody cheek! I really can't believe the nerve of some people, what planet is he on? He even has the gall to add a smiley emojis at the end of his message! I email him back, telling him to: "Fuck off" and "Never contact me ever again" and then I delete and block his email address as well as Kate's. Un-fucking-believable!

* * *

I transport myself using the Madjick power of *Alter* and *Initiate* and stand naked in all my natural beauty in the shape of a cross before him. I am wet. I lift my head from its bow and smile a smirk at his shock at my sudden appearance in the living-room of his flat, almost giving him a heart attack in the process - poor old bastard! He stands and stares at me with mouth wide open and eyes out on stalks as he gazes at my glistening nakedness - my perfect breasts, my smooth vagina, my long toned legs, my tattoos, and then into my face as he screams at me in his nightmare fake upper-class accent:

"WHAT ARE YOU DOING HERE? GET OUT OF MY FLAT OR I'LL CALL THE POLICE. HOW DID YOU GET IN HERE?"

I laugh at his useless words as I drive him insane and mess with his head:

"What happened to your car John?" I ask him sarcastically.

"HOW DO YOU KNOW ABOUT THAT?" He shouts.

"Because it was me that set fire to it that's why you stupid ignorant old cunt." I counter and smirk back at him.

With that he lunges at me at his old speed. He aims to grab my neck and strangle me but fails pathetically, instead both his hands going straight through my body and he collapses to the floor like the joke he is. He can't touch me as I'm simply not here. I am an apparition. I am a ghost. I am a projectional hologram of my shell and I vanish into thin air, leaving him crumpled on the floor in terror and bewilderment.

I reappear at my old place of work, in the departmental office. I order the lights to be switched on and I scan the large open-plan room. Nothing has changed, nothing at all, everything is still exactly the fucking same as before. My desk has changed a little though as it now has a new occupant, obviously female judging by all the cliched girly items placed all around it.

Over at "His" desk I steal some of his pens, a photo of his crappy motorbike and one of him when he was in the Army when he had hair - I burn them both later in my kitchen sink. I swap his "special" chair for someone else's and pinch other items, all to fuck with his mind when he comes in tomorrow morning - at his regulation 3-minutes late obviously! - as yes, he's still working here! He must be 73 by now and he's still chained to his desk and this pathetic company - what a waste of life. I change his calender to a different month and tear his notepad into a thousand pieces, leaving the remnants in the shape of a pyramid on his desk. I spit on his computer screen and smash his stupid glass coffee mug against the wall. I shit in the top-draw of his desk onto his calculator and pour my handful of piss I've collected onto his keyboard, hoping it will fail and even ignite when he turns it on. I daub *"SEE YOU ALL IN HELL"* in blood on the main wall with my hands and then stand back to admire my handiwork.

Suddenly I feel something tugging on my left-arm but I can't quite make out what it is. I open my eyes and turn my head to the left to see Eva sitting there staring at me like the little love she is. It was her tapping me through the duvet that has woken me from my lovely dream. I say "Hello" to her and she replies the same back to me in her own special feline way. I roll over and stroke her head, making her purr like a little engine. Oh well, I guess I'll have to get up now and give her some breakfast, and for myself also. The time on my bedside clock reads 9.25am, not that that makes any fucking difference to anything.

✳✳✳

I've been spending much of my time trying to do the outline of the book that I'm writing. It's taken an unbelievably long time to get going but I think I have it now at long bloody last. I've written loads of individual sections for it, really throwing myself into the task. It's all I seem to do these days, spending my waking-hours - and quite a few nights - scribbling-away burning myself out. Writing is my life now and my life is writing - there is nothing else.

Now all I need to do is bolt them all together to form some sort-of semblance of chapters. Hopefully when I've done all that I can then begin to create my vision - my dream. I honestly didn't realise how bloody difficult this was going to be writing a book, I really don't know how people do it all the time, they must be mad? It's a ghostly-quiet, solitary existence, locked in thought, remembering all the shit from the past and putting it down on paper. I have absorbed myself in my writing to the point that my hand and the pages have become moulded together to become one single entity, consisting of nothing but letters and words. My ability to create is beyond your imagination. You have to live to be able to tell a story, and as you very well know, I've lived! A bit too much in some areas it must be said, but that's life!

My mind, my hand, the pen, the paper, have all fused together, telling a miss-mash story of one woman's existence on a small planet called Earth and her struggle to survive upon its surface, with lurid reflections of her past life. The writing feeds my neurosis as it feeds my imagination, churning my mind of past experiences, most of which are rotten, making the hallucinations in my fractured brain drive my madness.

I want it to stop but I can't let it, I must go on.

Once again I have to suffer for my art as every word shatters my mind into a million fragments and I can see no end to my pain.

Why am I putting myself through more crap yet again? What is the fucking point? Why do I waste so much of my precious time?

I have sacrificed myself to it and have gone beyond destruction, although all this angst does seem to fire my mind and my imagination, creating some really juicy scenes in the book. I'm just not sure that anyone is going to believe it though, believe the life that I've had? What if nobody is interested and it doesn't sell? Pangs of self-doubt haunt me like spirits. When will it end? When will it all be over? Now that I've created this monster I have to stand by it to the bitter end. I have faith in myself that it will all turn out OK, I have to, or I will cut myself, cut myself off further from society - and cut myself physically.

***

I'm out on the prowl, up to my usual tricks once again. It's 5pm on a Wednesday, it's cold, dark and it's pissing down. I'm sitting here in the RS in the car-park listening to the rain bouncing off the roof of the car as I await my target. She shouldn't be too long now as I know that she comes out of work at 5.15pm so I reckon she should be back here at her flat somewhere around 5.25-ish at a guess? Clothes-wise I'm wearing my black v-neck jumper from Bluefly, a pair of black combat-trousers and a pair of black trainers both from Blacks - without socks. My underwear is in sexy red lace from Figleaves that makes me look super-hot, even though I'm naturally hot anyway! I'm also wearing my black bomber-jacket from Jacketvests, this of course negating the use of a clutch-bag - not that I really need one for this mission in the first place. I've also got a pair of Andy's old black leather gloves on as I don't want to smash my beautiful hands up when I smack that fat bitch Linda in the mouth. My hair and make-up I leave as is. My perfume is *Kenzo Flower* by Kenzo that I've put on as an in-joke.

It's 5.27pm when I spot her car through the distorting rivulets of rain as they run down my windscreen. I watch her park and switch-off her cars lights and I'm already behind her, poised to strike. She extricates her fat arse out of her seat with her back towards me and locks and alarms the car with one blip of her key-fob. She turns to face me full-on but she doesn't see me - I am invisible - the rain obscuring her vision and my black baseball cap doing likewise to my beautiful face. I punch her in the mouth with the most powerful right-hook I can muster and she falls backwards to the soaking-wet tarmac with a thud and a dull moan. The stupid giant bag she was carrying flies into the air as she falls, ejecting and spilling its contents over the wet surface of the car-park - a book, a half-eaten bar of chocolate, a packet of *TENA LADY* panty-liners (HA HA HA!), and other crap. She clutches both her hands to her mouth in pain and shock as I then give her a really nasty right-kick to her crotch, making her scream into the early-evening gloom.

Within 30-seconds I'm back in the RS and away. I know she didn't see me - I know it - and I'm back on the A29 heading South to Foxhill and home to Eva and the crazy little World I live in.

As I strip my clothes off the belt I was wearing - a beautiful old leather one of Andy's that smells glorious - snaps in 2 as I remove it. I feel a sudden loss come over me, almost as if Andy has just died in front of me for a second time as I stand there perplexed, holding each broken piece in my hands. Is this some sort-of mysterious omen warning me of my actions? Is it a message from beyond the grave? I don't know but I must carry on - I must.

I laugh out loud at my life as I guzzle gin naked in the living-room and say a big "Cheers" to fatty Linda. She really is as think as shit!

As the saying goes: "Don't get mad, get even."

I'm already mad.

And now we're even.

Bitch.

***

Mind.

My mind.

In my mind.

Things in my mind.

Many things in my mind.

So many things in my mind.

There are so many things in my mind.

I cannot breathe.

2

Sleeves

As I've told you a million times, I'm used to getting plenty of looks when I'm in public or out driving around, especially in the Lamborghini, but today I've noticed that everyone is staring at me more than usual - and I mean EVERYONE.

I'm out in the Lister, the big fat yellow and green monster that Andy bought years ago from some guy in America who had had it converted into a race-car. Andy subsequently converted it back to road-spec, including the colour. And so here I am, rolling-along at a steady 50 in a 30-zone.

I'm on yet another mission - one which will last the best part of all this week - as I'm having both my arms and both my hands tattooed! Now, before you start asking yourself "Why?" and all that shit, I have to tell you yet again that this is my choice and that I will do whatever I fucking want with my body. There are multiple reasons for this decision, I have no need to work ever again and so obviously having all this work done on me is not going to affect any future job prospects are they? Plus of course I'm not getting any younger, I'll be 37 this coming November and if I'm going to do this properly then now is the time to do it. I've thought about doing this for a long time, certainly more so since Andy passed-away, and for the past several months I've been spending a lot of my spare time - and that's a lot! - drawing-up the artwork. I've decided to get both my arms fully covered - or "sleeves" as it's known within tattooing circles - as well as my hands - my beautiful hands. My creative skills know no bounds. My skin is the canvas of my life. My art and my body are one. My tattoo art is what makes me individual and unique. They are the story of my life, past, present and future. They will not hold me back - they will drive me on. I don't care if you like tattoos or my idea or hate it, it doesn't matter either fucking way to me. I am reinventing myself. I will become the new version of ME. My new tattoos will give me the inner strength to face the future and carry-on. They represent the inner me, the bit that you can't see and never will.

As per usual, it's John that's going to ink me and I've booked him exclusively for the next 5-days solid as from today - Monday - until the end of the week.

Today we're spending all day doing the outlines for the complete project, then the subsequent time adding-in a different colour each day. I can tell you here and now that this is going to be a long fucking week - mark my words! The recovery is going to be a fucking nightmare as well so I'll have to be extra careful with my poor old body, and that means taking it easy with the drinking - yeah right!

Bloody Hell this car is a bastard to drive! This is only the second time I've actually taken it out on the road so I'm not quite used to it yet. The sheer size of the thing is huge, it's so bloody wide I don't know how the Hell I'm going to park it! The power is bloody amazing though, almost as good as the Lamborghini, but the gearbox is a bit weird, it being 6-speed with sequential-shift, and when I get out onto a fast stretch of road and give it some beans, the car takes off as quickly as it looks. When I glance down at the speedo I see that I'm already doing 155 in a 70-zone - Fucking Hell!

I slow down at the roundabout as I have to do a right-turn here to head to John's studio. As I take my exit I notice a fucking cop-car lurking semi-hidden behind a large bush to the left of me, waiting for their next victim. I amble past them at the regulation 40mph and take a glance in my rear-view mirror - noticing the fuckers pulling out and slotting-in behind me - shit! The next second I see flashing blue-lights and hear a couple of blips from their onboard siren - fuck it - this is just my fucking luck!

I pull over into the next lay-by with the pigs pulling-in behind me. The cop in the passenger seat - a short, squat tosser with a face like a smacked arse - gets out of the car and starts walking in my direction. I switch my engine off and extract myself from the Listers bucket seat - not the easiest of tasks! - to face the officer and undoubtedly await more gobshite.

Today I'm wearing my black low-cut v-neck jumper from Bluefly that shows-off my bangers to the max, my leopard-print pencil-skirt from Polyvore - now you know why I had trouble getting out of the bloody car! - and on my feet my pair of grey suede ankle-boots from Ophelia. My underwear is in black lace from Autograph. My hair and make-up is the usual mix of classic and stylish with a few quirky extras thrown-in for good measure. My perfume today is *Poison* by Christian Dior.

"Morning Miss." Says the cop cheerfully, catching me slightly unaware because of his pleasantness and smile.

"Morning, what's the problem?" I bounce back at him.

"Nothing at all, we were just wondering what sort of car this was that's all?" He says, just as I notice the other cop in the Police car giving him the thumbs-up sign.

"Oh, I see! It's a Lister Storm." I inform him.

"Never heard of it."

"Well apparently they didn't make many of them."

"Bit of a rare beast then?"

"I guess so."

"What engine has it got?"

"It's a 7-litre V12." I tell him matter-of-factly.

"Bloody Hell, that's a big one!" He comes back laughing.

I'm then joined by the other cop - the driver - a tallish guy with a wonky nose and a beer-belly.

"Never seen one of these things before." He chirps.

"Its got a 7-litre V12 motor." Says his special friend.

"Blimey!" He exclaims.

"Listen guys, I've got an appointment to get to so if you don't mind I need to get on." I tell them.

"OK Miss, we'll let you get off. Drive carefully now won't you?" Says the shorter one.

I throw them a fake smile and a little wave as I clamber back into the car, buckle-up and then fire the massive engine back up. It bursts back into life with a roar and I stick it into first-gear. I get the sudden urge to smoke the tyres right here in front of the pigs as I pull away but I don't want to be stopped by them a second bloody time, it's not exactly a great start to the week as it is having already been pulled over. I drop the clutch quickly and give the engine some gas, making the rear-tyres chirp slightly and the exhaust emit a throaty roar as I go. Fucking arseholes, haven't they got anything else to do? I've been stopped by the cops several times before of course, but have always managed to wriggle myself out of being fined by using my superior feminine charm - this is the joy of being a beautiful woman!

I arrive at John's shop and park-up, taking the space of 2-cars as the Lister is so big and fat. I can't even see where I'm going let alone where I've been!

"Hello gorgeous, how are you?" Beams John in his usual manner and we hug and kiss cheek to cheek in his reception area.

"I'm good, and you?"

"Can't complain, busy as usual."

"I would have been here earlier but I got stopped by the fucking cops."

"Why, what have you been up to now?" He laughs.

"Nothing I could possibly tell you!" I smirk back.

"I'm really sorry to hear about your fella Sarah."

"Thanks, I'm pretty-much over it now but it still hurts to a certain degree." I confirm back to him. And it does.

We talk a little more shop and then get down to the business in hand. John already has my designs stencilled out and ready to go as I emailed them to him ages ago so it's just a matter of applying them and getting on with it really. The designs I've drawn out are all things that represent me and my life - a scorpion (as I'm a Scorpio), a cats face, mystical symbols of peace and death, Egyptian hieroglyphs, evil-looking skulls, musical notes, an English flag billowing in the wind, tribal-style black spines and other images, all tied-in with each other as one with crashing waves of blue water - Scorpio being a water sign - as the background. I will never be the same person ever again after having all this lot done and that is exactly what I WANT.

I peel-off my jumper and place it to one side as John looks at my body, my beautiful firm breasts, and then looks me in the eye and smiles. He wants to take me, just as he always has, and we both know it. I plonk myself down in his old dentists chair next to him and away we go, on another venture into the next phase of my existence, to alter myself into something else.

The sharp outline needle stabs my gorgeous skin and I momentarily jump, my pure red blood being replaced by black ink as John drills into my right-arm and I take it all without flinching or complaining as I overcome the physical pain with my extreme mental agility. The pain is a case of mind-over-matter, it's a difficult thing to master but I do and win it over.

I dream and wish and hallucinate as the onslaught of pain and the smell of my blood, the ink and the skin cleanser take command of my soul for the next 3 1/2-hours. We take a break between doing each arm to pee and drink coffee and eat a light lunch, John fetching us a sandwich each from the mini-store opposite the studio - a couple of BLT's.

After lunch we start on my left-arm next and I sit there looking at the thin lines that have scared my right-arm and hand forever. It freaks me out at what I've done and I start to question whether I've actually done the right thing? It's all too late now of course, there can be no turning back. The underside of my left upper arm stings and grabs me like fuck, it's way more painful than the right -arm was for some reason, like an electric shock shooting throughout my nerves and my veins.

What the fuck is happening, it literally feels like I'm going to have a heart-attack?

When I mention it to John he says that it's just the electrical impulses in my arm relaying to my heart and that there's: "Nothing to worry about girl." That's easy for him to say!

My left-hand is the last to do, with the words:

LOVE

HATE

inked under one-another on my fingers to juxtapose the words on my right-hand and across my fingers:

HATE

LOVE

You would not believe how fucking relieved I am when it's all over - I am fucked! Both my poor arms are a mess of red blood and black ink. To say that I'm sore would be the understatement of the century, but through the pain of the electric needle I am now stronger than ever before.

John cleans me up and wraps my oozing flesh with cling-film, taping it in place as I stand there topless apart from my sexy black lace bra. He helps me put my jumper back on, momentarily touching one of my breasts with the back of his hand as he does so. I don't know whether it was done on purpose or unintentionally, not that I care either way! We hug and kiss as before and then I leave, the time now being 6.13pm.

It takes me almost a whole fucking hour to get home, the traffic being really heavy for some reason? The Lister was great fun though, I'm so glad that I kept it and I must use her more often instead of using the Lamborghini all the bloody time. I strip naked and peel-off my transparent bandages in the bathroom and go to shower. I look down at the plughole in the wet-room and the swirling mess of red and black-stained water as it disappears clockwise between my feet and toes. I dry myself gently with one of my posh towels and then go to feed Eva, having a couple of swift vodka's as I do so to help me unwind from the day.

I push 2-fingers into my vagina as I squat on the floor in front of the curved-screen TV in the living-room. A DVD featuring Brazilian transexual porn plays its images before me as I love myself. A beautiful blonde TS-girl sucks-off some guys cock as she wanks her own cock to the motion of my fingers. I time it perfectly as the 3 of us cum together as one.

***

I get the awful gut feeling that the engine isn't going to fire as I turn the key in the ignition. The weird thing is though it only seems to start on the third turn anyway, and when it does it's like a bloody bomb going off, shaking everything in sight, including myself! I hear it turn-over, then silence, then a strange muted thud as then she catches. The whine from the enormous supercharger fills the car as the 7-litre Ford V8 engine thumps away. I'm using the crazy yellow Willys Coupe Gasser today, the first day of colouring-in my new tattoos. I've only ever driven this car once before, and that was only around the fountain on front of the house so this is going to be fun!

I clonk the 4-speed gearbox into first and we rumble away, the whole car shaking and vibrating as I exit the gates and head off up the road. The open side-exhausts are horrendously loud, even at low speed, so I have to take it a bit easy as I don't want a repeat of yesterday morning with any more hassle with the bloody pigs. Also, it being left-hand drive and mounted up so high, visibility is crap to put it mildly!

I trundle along minding my own business, concentrating on trying to keep the crazy bloody car in a straight line rather than watching people watching me. I arrive at John's tattoo studio unscathed and actually manage to park in a single bay this time. John and I greet each other in our usual fashion with a hug and a kiss as we settle ourselves down to another day of inking. Today I'm wearing a black t-shirt from River Island, my pair of grey slim-fit jeans from La Redoute and my pair of tan-coloured ankle-boots from AliExpress. My underwear today is in pale yellow - not dissimilar in colour to the Willys - from Ultimo. As for my make-up I've done my eye-shadow in coal-black to give myself a more wicked look, with my lipstick in cherry-red. My perfume today is *Mademoiselle* by Coco Chanel.

I remove my t-shirt gently as my arms are both still really sore from yesterdays drilling. Once again John stares at my breasts and I love it, I love having my body checked-out, either by a man or a woman, it's all the same to me. We then start straight away, the stab of the needle being so-much easier with the shading-in of the colour, in fact it can sometimes be quite therapeutic and has even put me into some form of trance-like state in the past. The blue is going in today as that is the biggest area of colour as John massages the ink into my skin and I drift away into tranquillity and beyond for the next 3-hours or so.

We break for lunch, coffee and a chat and then swap-over when my right-arm is done, now starting on my left and I fly across the sky over *Never Never Land* as I sit there and dream of an everlasting life with endless love and fucking.

At 5.30pm we're all done and my arms are horrendously sore and they both feel like lead weights, fuck-knows how I'm going to drive that stupid car home like this? John bandages me up as before and we kiss, this time softly on the lips, as he places one hand around my waist and the other lightly on my bum. I touch his cock through his jeans but have to tell him:

"We can't go any further." But in reality I really want to and he knows it.

I put my t-shirt back on and John helps me, cupping one of my breasts before I pull it down over my body to cover them. I kiss him on the cheek and then I go.

Fortunately the traffic is much lighter on my return journey today as driving the Willys home is a real pig. This is a car for short bursts of fun only, not for getting from A to B in comfort.

On the way back home I stop-off at a small convenience store on the A24. I've been in here a couple of times before for odds and sods - provisions and such. Unsurprisingly it's run by a family of Paki's. I don't know what they really are, they could be Indians or Sri-Lankans for all I know or care - in my World they're all bloody Paki's. I grab a basket and wander around the shop, picking out a loaf of bread, a pint of milk and a bar of chocolate off of their respective shelves. At the newspaper and magazine section I grab a copy of my usual paper and 2-others, one the local area newspaper and the other a small free magazine called *Challenger.* Whilst I'm there I also have a quick shufty through one of the beauty magazines from the shelf, I might buy and then again I might not, it all depends what's in it as something might catch my eye. I place my basket of goodies on the chest-freezer cabinet behind me and scan through the mag looking for anything interesting that I might fancy. As I while-away my time I suddenly spot the owner of the shop heading in my direction - he looks the spitting-image of Gandi but a younger version and without the nappy! I also notice that he's clutching a copy of *Asian Shopkeeper* magazine in his brown hands and I wonder to myself if there's a magazine called *White Shopkeeper* for the English shop owners but I doubt it - that would be racist of course!

"Do you have any intention of buying that magazine Miss?" He questions me.

"I might, and then again I might not. Why?" I fire back as I know exactly where this conversation is going to end up.

"This is not a library you know?"

"Yes, I know that. I'm not stupid."

"If you are not going to purchase the magazine you have to leave my shop."

I stand there in amazement at the fucking arrogance of this little shit. Who the fuck do these people think they are?

"And what exactly do you mean YOUR shop?" I say back.

"This is my shop. I am the owner."

"Really? And what is YOUR shop built on?"

"I own it."

"It's built on MY land. This is MY fucking country, not yours." I spit at him.

"It is my shop. You must leave now. I do not want you here."

By now of course I'm as mad as Hell and I want to shoot the bastard in the head and watch it explode but I have no weapon to hand. I drop the magazine on the floor and swipe my basket and its contents off its perch, they flying out and over the floor, enraging the Paki even more, not that I give a shit.

"OUT OUT OUT!" He screams at me, almost levitating off the floor!

"DON'T YOU FUCKING TELL ME TO GET OUT YOU FUCKING STINKING PAKI CUNT. WHY DON'T YOU GET OUT OF MY FUCKING COUNTRY." I scream back at him.

"OUT OF MY SHOP."

"OUT OF MY COUNTRY." I tear back at him, facing him off.

"I CALL THE POLICE."

"GO AND FUCKING CALL THEM THEN YOU FUCKING BROWN PIECE OF SHIT." I shout at the brown piece of shit.

The Paki then turns on his heals and heads to the back of the shop where his timid little Paki wife sits at the till in silence, presumably to call the cops. There's no-way I'm fucking hanging-around here waiting for the pigs to show up so I'm off out of here, exiting sharpish without my goods and quickly walking back to the Willys where I fire her up and speed-away with plenty of wheelspin and screeching tyres. I look in the rear-view mirror only to see the Asian standing there in the doorway of "his" shop on the phone - the little fucker really has called the Police! Not that I really fucking care, he's only a Paki after all. Although if he has clocked my registration number and passed it on to them then I really am fucked, I don't want them at my bloody door again.

I power home as fast as I dare, pushing the Willys to the max. The electric gates to my driveway click shut and lock in place behind me, closing-out this stupid twisted World. Eva sits and stares at me as I reverse and park in the garage, perched on the roof of the Mustang, poised for my return as ever. In comfort I clean myself up as yesterday although there's less blood and ink down the plughole today for whatever reason?

I down a bottle of chilled lager and then have another as I insert the neck of the first bottle into my fuck and masturbate with it as I watch Old Guy Cock porn on my computer and drink. I orgasm and cum into the bottle and lick and drink that to and I am fucked.

There is no sign of the pigs.

***

I seem to have gone from one extreme to the other this morning. Whereas the Willys I drove yesterday was really high off the ground, today's car is so bloody low you have to be a sodding contortionist just to get into it! I'm in the Ford GT40 MK1. I was in 2-minds whether to use it or not as its worth shit-loads - somewhere around £3-million! - due to its originality and its ex-racing history. It's also super-rare as they only made about 130 of them in the first place. I've decided I am going to use it though, cars are built for driving so I'm taking her out, regardless of her value or anything else.

As I've already said, getting into it is a bit of a mission, with the gear-lever mounted right in the way of entry, so I have to cock my left-leg over the top of that first, then under the steering wheel, slide my bum down and into the bucket-seat and then thread my right-leg in over and down - what a bloody performance! I also have to be careful with the drivers-door as the top of it also forms part of the roof so if I'm not fully seated I run the risk of chopping the top of my head off! Why do I do these things? The answer lies when I fire the car up, its massive 7-litre V8 engine bursting into life with an almighty roar behind my left-ear - the Ford being mid-engined. With no power-steering the car is difficult to manoeuvre at low speed, made worse of course by my arms, my muscles weakened by 2-days of intense tattooing. Once I'm underway though everything is great, the power of the engine behind me pushing me along like a missile and I love it. It sounds like thunder and goes like lightning!

Today I'm wearing my black boyfriend shirt from ASOS, my pair of white denim jeans from SimplyBe and on my feet my pair of white suede open-toe ankle-boots from Polyvore. My underwear today is in sexy red lace from Figleaves. My perfume is *Kenzo Flower* by Kenzo. My make-up I've done pretty-much the same as yesterday except my lipstick is in blood-red.

And it's red that is also today's colour of ink. John and I greet with a hug and a kiss - just a quick one on the cheek today for some reason? - and off we go yet again with more noise and pain. I strip my top off and sit in the dentists-chair with only my sexy lace bra covering the upper-half of my gorgeous body, my beautiful breasts overflowing and turning me on to myself. I WANT John to touch and caress and kiss them but he doesn't, he just stabs me with the scarlet point of his electric needle - fuck it!

For the next 6-hours - including a lunch-break of 45-minutes - he colours me in, filling my skin with the beautiful brightness of the red pigment. On my right-arm he covers-up the now almost invisible scar that I received from my horrible car crash last year, obliterating it from my skin but not from my mind. I will never forget that nightmare.

For some reason I start thinking about all the weirdos at the last company I worked for but I don't know why? How on Earth did I put up with all that shit? My mind must be incredibly strong - as is my will. How I survived all that shit without killing myself I will never know?

We finish earlier today at 4pm. It's been a much easier day today on my poor body and a bit of a relief I must say. I wonder to myself how much blood I've lost in the last 3-days, although it's probably not as much as I imagine it to be. We laugh and joke and piss-around as John bandages me and helps me redress, although this time he doesn't touch my body at all.

I miss the rush-hour on the drive home, the GT40 burning-up the road as I blast along. I get stuck behind some stupid bitch on the A29 heading South in one of those fucking awful BMW Mini's - a light-blue coloured one - barely moving at 45mph. I drop down a gear and nail the silly cow, leaving her behind in the wake of exhaust noise as I hit 110.

I am so fucking knackered it's not true. I hope and I must use all my willpower to make it through the next 2-days. I pour myself a massive glass of German white as I stand naked in the kitchen and inspect my arms and my hands and how they have changed in colour over the last few days. I'm still a bit leaky so I have to dab some kitchen-paper on my wounds to stop the drips of the ink and blood mixture falling onto the white-tiled floor. Eva avoids me as she doesn't like the smell my tattoos are emitting even though I had a shower as soon as I got through the door - she really must have an extra-sensitive nose!

I have to push really quite hard to get the dildo - my ribbed glass one from Lovehoney - past the barrier of muscles guarding my bumhole as I try to fuck myself. Suddenly it relents and in it slides and I wank it slowly and gently. I'm on my side with my right-leg in the air and my knee bent, laying on the smooth hard floor of the hallway. My laptop is before me, playing Gay Orgy porn from America at full-volume as I fuck my rear. Both my arms ache like crazy as I lean on my left one on the tiled surface and wank my bum with the other. There's at least 15-guys on the screen all fucking and sucking cock in a twisted heap of hunky, muscled men. I would give anything to be transported amongst them so they could abuse my body in any way they desired - fucking my mouth, my cunt, my arsehole - as they continue to gay-fuck each other. I change holes and fuck my vagina, not even bothering to wipe the dildo between fucks. I thrust myself harder and harder as I watch a couple of gays cum down the throat of another gay and he swallows their muck as I spasticate and cum myself.

***

After 3-days of clear weather, I awake to grey sky and rain - it's pissing down. There's nothing I can do about it of course, and it's not going to stop me or my mission. Today I'm wearing a Royal-blue sleeveless cotton blouse from Hugo Boss, my white leather skirt from French Connection and my pair of white suede open-toe ankle-boots from Polyvore. My underwear is also in white, a sexy lace set from M & S that makes me feel really hot and horny! Due to the crappy weather I'm also wearing my white woollen tasselled poncho from Peter Hahn. My perfume today is *Kenzo Flower* by Kenzo again whilst my hair and make-up is the usual old business although featuring pale-pink lipstick.

I'm taking the old Aston out today on my short trip. It's been a while now since I last drove her, and the power-steering will be a blessed relief on my poor arms, they both fucking aching like mad and are as sore as can be. I just know that I've pushed myself too far this time - so what's new! - and I just can't wait for Saturday when all this shit will be over.

I steam-along lovely in the car, the sound of the V8 thundering and crackling through the exhausts - I love it. I come upon a couple of workmen standing by their pickup truck parked by the side of the road, they fixing a broken drain-cover by the looks of it, one white guy and one black - how multiculturally/politically correct! - black and white unite! The black one gesticulates to me to slow down - I'm doing 70 in a 40-zone - so I gesticulate back to him, sticking 2-fingers up and telling him to: "FUCK-OFF." No-one ever fucking tells me to slow down - bastards.

I arrive at John's place bang on time and after our usual greeting and chit-chat I remove my poncho and blouse and sit myself down in his black-leather chair and await the first sting of the day. We're just filling-in today with other colours - yellow, white, green - as well as a little more black, blue and red and even some grey shading. Tomorrow will be left for the final overall tinkering with yet more filling-in and shading.

I lose my mind to the pain and the sensation of the tugging, pulling and pushing of the needle as it scratches and penetrates my lovely smooth skin. I think of Amanda and Andy and how we've all hurt and loved one another in our own unique ways. I feel myself start to well-up with tears of both sadness and joy and wonder why the fuck am I putting myself through all this shit? What the fuck is it all for? What is the fucking point? I want to run out of the studio right here and now and end it all but I'm pinned-down by John's grip on my sore arm and the nasty bite of the tattoo machines buzzing needle.

At lunchtime we pretty-much sit in total silence with our thoughts, I really don't have anything to say. We continue drilling into the afternoon, finishing at 3.25pm. John then wipes me down and bandages both my arms, they feeling heavy and useless, just like they're about to fall off. Yet again there is no touching.

Once back home I strip and shower in the en-suite bathroom and the beautiful warm water somehow seems to revitalise my melancholic mood. Maybe it's the loss of blood that's effecting my brain, starving me of the nutrients that feed my mind?

For dinner I cook chips with steak and kidney pie and French beans, all washed down with a couple of bottles of chilled lager. Eva has chicken in creamy sauce. We sit and eat and watch the evening news together, more fucking bullshit featuring yet more fucking immigrants coming into MY country - it doesn't matter whether they're "Legal" or otherwise, they're coming anyway. There's an endless fucking stream of them heading in my direction with each and every one of them as useless as the next. Are our politicians blind? Can they really be this fucking stupid? We don't have enough housing and other facilities for our indigenous people let-alone for all this scum coming in. My blood starts to boil and I have to turn the TV over, but with each turn of the channel I'm faced with yet more crap - channel after channel of niggers, Paki's, Slavs, queers and shit - FOR FUCKS SAKE!

I fuck and wank my vagina with my giant 10-inch realistic dildo from Ann Summers as I'm watching Massive White Cock porn on my laptop in the bedroom. I crouch on my bed as Eva watches me from the bedside cabinet as I masturbate the phallus in and out of my pussy - my vagina that is, not Eva!. There's some guy with a huge cock - it must be over a foot-long! - fucking some lucky girl in her minge as another female licks at his balls and cock and the other girls vagina at the same time. Every now and then she pulls his massive dick out of the other girl and sucks on it and licks at her gaping hole and then feeds his cock back into the girl - lucky whore! I lick my own internal juice from my fake cock and then return it back into my fanny as the guy on the screen cums his evil seed into the first girls vagina. The second girl grabs it out and swallows his meat and his milk and then licks out and swallows the oozing creamy mess from her sore and swollen twat.

I cum.

***

Finally, it's the last day of my inking. I just can't wait for it all to be over so I can get on with my life, wherever that takes me?

Today is going to be different I know for sure as I'm going to make it so. I know that as far as you're concerned everything might appear to be as intangible as the previous 4-days but I can assure you that today IS going to be different. For one thing I'm going to get John to re-pierce my nipples. As I've previously told you my dear and loyal reader, I had them done some years ago with rings through them and I always maintained that it's they that was the cause of them migrating out. This time though I'm having straight bars inserted so hopefully there won't be any problems. These new piercings will of course add to my collection of belly and ear piercings, bringing my total up to 25.

I'm driving the Mustang this morning, the big fat powerful beautiful American thing that she is - all 7-litres of it! And rare to, with less than 300 of these made in that year. I've decided to use this car today as its fairly easy to drive and has power-operated everything. As long as I take it relatively easy we'll both be fine, the only problem is of course it being left-hand drive, which once again, is a real pain in the neck.

As for my clothes I'm wearing my gorgeous pale-blue wrap-around mini-dress from Krisztina Williams today as:

1 - It matches the Mustang in colour.

2 - It's easy to remove.

3 - It makes me look even more gorgeous than I do already.

And that's about it for clothes really as I'm not bothering with any underwear as I don't bloody want to. The only other thing I'm wearing is my dear old pair of blue-suede Lola platform court-shoes - bless them! As for my make-up I've gone for my supermodel look today, featuring coal-black eyeshadow, plenty of blusher, and blood-red lipstick. My perfume is *Poison* by Christian Dior. I'm also taking my beautiful white leather Givenchy clutch-bag today as I've got to pay John for all his hard work - £3,000 in cash!

The Mustang purrs-along beautifully as I unleash its power through my right-foot. Its 4-speed manual gearbox is heavy and solid as I cruise-along without a care as all - at least most anyway - of my blues from yesterday have thankfully vanished into thin air. As I've already told you, today being the final day, we're effectively only doing touch-ups and filling-in the last segments of the project. I just can't wait for the end of the day - bring it on!

"I thought we could do things a bit different today, if that's alright with you?" I say to John in his waiting-room.

"OK, what did you have in mind?"

"I thought we could do it on the floor on the Japanese *Tatami* mat, the same as when you did my back."

"Yeah sure, if that's what you want. Why the change from doing it in the chair?"

"I just want the final day to be special." I confirm.

John unfurls the mat onto the floor, its beautiful odour hitting my nostrils at once and transporting my mind off to the

Land of the Rising Sun. I really must go there one day - another future adventure!

I take my shoes off and place them over to one side, treating them with the grace and care that they so deserve. I remove my dress, laying it over the back of the dentists-chair and stand before him completely naked. It's not the first time that he's seen me like this - if you've been paying attention you'd know that! - but it is the first time he's seen me like THIS - with both my arms now almost fully sleeved, not to mention my hands.

He looks at me and stares at my body, my perfect breasts, my smooth vagina, my beautiful long legs, my new art, and then finally into my eyes. He can read the message within them and we embrace and kiss. He runs his hands over my naked flesh and I want him to love me, to fuck me. I drop to my knees and tear at his jeans, undoing his belt-buckle, his fly-button and then the zip. He peels-off his t-shirt as I yank-down his jeans, exposing the pair of black y-fronts beneath. I start to rub my hand over his bulge and it feels so good, his cock growing in size to my touch. He moans as I stroke him and then I pull-down his pants to expose him fully, his dick springing out at me upon its release. I grab it with my right-hand and kiss its knob, running my tongue over and around its head. His breathing becomes heavier as I take his cock into my mouth and pull on his balls, making him cry out in pure pleasure. "Oh Sarah" he wails as I then feel his knob suddenly expand just a little inside my mouth as he suddenly and quickly ejaculates within seconds, squirting his cum down my throat. I release him and wank his cock, squeezing out the beautiful pearls of cum from his Japs-eye onto my gorgeous tits.

I collapse back onto the mat and lay there before him. He stands above me and gazes down at my gorgeous body. He knows what I want. He kicks-off his trainers and removes the rest of his clothing from around his ankles, chucking them over to one side in a heap. He goes down on me, between my already splayed-apart legs, and takes one long lick at my vagina. I scream "UH UH UH" as I feel the sensation of his tongue on my labia as I writhe and wriggle about on the floor like I'm fucking demented. My brain implodes and I see flashing lights and stars above me as John flicks in and out of my pussy and nibbles my lips gently. He inserts a middle-finger into my hole as well as his tongue and I'm in love and lose control of my mind and my body and I cum at him, spraying my love over his face and making us both laugh.

"Fucking Hell Sarah, what was that all about?" He says, wiping his face clear of my juice with his hands.

"I've known that you've wanted me for ages, and now you have." I tell him as I sit up and study his body, his own tattoo art and his dick.

"This has to be just between us Sarah. My wife must never find out OK?"

"Of course, I understand. You've got no worries on that score from me." I confirm to him.

We both go and clean ourselves up in the studio's small bathroom and joke and giggle and fool-around like a couple of teenagers. It's all harmless stuff and I want nothing more. John redresses as I stay completely naked watching him as we both then return to the business in-hand - finishing my ink. We decide to pierce my nipples first though and I lay on the floor as John sprays them with an anaesthetizer, although as he says it won't fully kill the pain - GREAT! I don't mind, a little pain sometimes is a good thing, I can take it all and more. He marks-up the needle entry and exit points, cupping each of my beautiful full breasts as he does so and I love it. He was certainly right about the pain though as the stab of the needle through my left-nipple causes me to yelp out loud - OUCH! John pulls the bar through and screws the ball onto its end and then repeats the same process on my other breast and then I'm done - both nipples pierced! - the whole thing taking no more than 20-minutes.

For the following 3-hours he needles me more, touching-up areas where the ink hasn't gone in correctly with small gaps here and there as I lay on the floor naked. Going over the parts from earlier in the week hurts and stings me like fuck, twice as bad as it was before and I shout and scream at him for all the pain he's inflicting on me and that I'm also inflicting on myself.

I hate it and I want to die.

We stop for lunch and sit and chat about stuff. I remain completely naked the whole time and I love it, I so wish I could stay naked for the rest of my existence but etiquette and the often cold crappy weather we have in England unfortunately dictates otherwise. We talk about his wife, his 3-kids and his 2-dogs and his cat and all that crap. His eldest child, a daughter, is coming up 20 soon with the others not far behind - bloody Hell!. It all makes me feel very alien as well as old.

With lunch over I find myself on my hands and knees on the *Tatami* mat. I look behind me and see John naked and dropping down onto his knees. I then feel the beautiful sensation of his smooth knob on my labia as then it parts to let him enter and we both moan in unison at our pleasure as it squeezes into my hole. He fucks me and plays and squeezes with my bum-cheeks and my tits as he bangs me doggy-style. I love his cock inside me and I want it hard. He keeps fucking me and I sense that he's about to cum and I tell him to: "Cum in me" and "I want your cum" and "Spunk me". Within 30-seconds or so he ejaculates his nasty within my body and I join him in ecstasy as he unloads. I turn on him and wank his cock and suck and lick his muck, it tasting sweet and salty and I love cock and cum and cunt and fuck it. We go and clean ourselves up for the second time and he kisses my cheek and touches my bum and my tits and my vagina and I love his attention and I WANT EVERYTHING.

We resume tattooing - there's actually not much more to do now, only about an hour and a half or so, with John chiselling into my wounded and bloody arms. Just when will this day end? He shades-in one specific section, using a mixture of grey ink and some of his sperm and my cum from when we fucked - it becoming a part of my body until the day I die.

We're almost finished now - the clock reading 3.05pm - when the front-door to the studio opens and in-walks some woman even though the sign in the door says the studio is closed. She's in her early to mid-50's with short mousy hair and carrying a few pounds too many, although she is attractive in her own way. She looks at me straight in the eyes and then scans my beautiful naked body as I stand there with John by my side, inking the last few drops of black into my left-arm.

"Hi, how's it all going?" She says to him, putting one hand on his shoulder and kissing his cheek.

"I'm almost done actually. How was your day?"

"OK I guess. Are you going to introduce me to your friend?"

"This is my wife Sarah. This is Sarah." He says amazingly!

We smile and shake hands and say "Hello" like 2-people with the same name do. It's weird isn't it, in all the time I've known John, not once has he ever mentioned that his wife and I share the same first name. Aren't people odd?

"Wow, that's quite a few tattoos that you've got there." She beams at me, simultaneously checking-out my gorgeous body, especially my perfect firm breasts, my long legs, my pert bum and my smooth vagina, the one that contains her husbands life.

"Thanks, John did my back some time ago and we've just spent all this week doing my arms and hands."

"Yes, he told me he had a big job on this week, although he didn't tell me it was on such a beautiful girl like you."

The air freezes around us at her masked bitchiness. What is her fucking problem? Maybe I should tell her right here and now that I gave her so-called "Husband" a blow-job this morning and that we fucked but I don't.

"Well, either you've got it or you haven't." I bitch back at her, wiping the smirk off her face.

John stops tattooing and silences the machine, the sudden quietness in the room making the situation even more edgy than it was before, although it's a welcome relief now all the pain is finally over. Without a word he then starts to wipe me down and covers my fresh ink with cling-film as the other Sarah slowly begins circling around me like I'm some sort-of prey of hers. I am a pure work of art.

I remain silent in my own little World as I let John bandage me up. She checks-out my back and reads out loud my Aleister Crowley tattoo:

"Do what thou wilt shall be the whole of the Law."

I say nothing and just stand there letting John finish off taping me up. No doubt his wife is having a good look at my body as I still can't see her on either side of me. She can take a good look at my beautiful legs, my pert arse, my gorgeous hair and everything else, I really don't care, she can look at my body until the cows come home, it really makes no difference to me one way or the other.

I redress myself under her close scrutiny and wonder what her problem is? Surely she must know that her husband sees semi-naked and even totally naked women all the time, that is the nature of his profession after all? Or maybe it's me? Maybe it's because I'm so fucking gorgeous that it's that that has knocked her sense of reality sideways and made her so jealous? Oh well - whatever!

I go to pay John my fee for all his work on me as he and his wife talk amongst themselves. When I offer him my bundle of cash - all £3,000 as we agreed - he tells me the cost is only £2,500 for some reason? I ask him if he's sure and he confirms that the job didn't take his as long as he had first thought, hence the reduced cost. I wonder to myself if that's the real reason or if the £500 reduction is hush-money to keep me quiet over us having sex? Whatever the reason I'm not bothered either way, life's too short to worry about him and his bloody wife - Sarah.

I say "Bye" to them both, giving John a kiss to the cheek and a small hug before I leave, but it's only he that replies. With that I'm out the door and away, I've got no time for any female bullshit from her or anyone else.

My poor fucking arms ache and sting like shit all the bloody way home and it's a good job the Mustang's steering is light or I wouldn't have made it, my skin feels as tight as a drum. I park the car in the garage, reversing it back into its designated space, and enter the house my customary way through the adjoining garage/kitchen door. I have to laugh to myself as I open the door as Eva is sitting there erect and proud looking at me straight in the eyes as I enter. She is so beautiful - my love - and I rub her chest and kiss the top of her head as we both exchange "Hellos".

I strip in the bedroom and go to shower, catching a glimpse of myself in the full-length mirror as I pass by. I stop and stare at the vision before me. What the fuck have I done to myself? Look at my arms! Look at my hands! They're black with ink! I have ruined them! I remove my bandages and throw them in the sink in a mass of colour, blood and plastic. I wash-away all the mess in the shower and I cry, even more so when I notice Eva in the bathroom doorway wailing her tears along with me. I am destroyed.

It's just gone 8pm by the time I've calmed myself down since my little meltdown earlier and I'm sitting here eating my evening meal of bangers and mash with fried onions and marrowfat peas and a couple of bottles of chilled lager as I watch BBC News 24. The blonde newsreader - a really fit woman in her early-40's and dressed really stylishly - is going on about some so-called "Lord" who was exposed a few months ago by a national newspaper for using Taxpayers money to fund both his nasty drug-taking habit and the use of prostitutes. He was actually filmed snorting cocaine off of their tits! The upshot of this story is that the fucking useless Police have decided in their infinite wisdom not to prosecute the poor old sod, citing "Lack of evidence" as their excuse - fucking unbelievable! These tossers are getting away with murder - sometimes even literally! Is it any wonder this country has gone fucking crazy? We've got dole-scroungers earning more money than people with jobs, fucking Slavs who can't even speak English getting housing before our indigenous population does, people driving around out of their heads on drugs, fraud left right and centre, people in low-paid jobs struggling to make ends meet, Government Ministers ripping-off the constituents who voted them into power in the first place - the Government doesn't care so the people don't care, it's as simple as that - and then there's fuckers like this "Lord" and the self-righteous Police shitting on everyone in between. And don't even get me started on the poor bloody motorist!

There is no England any more.

It does not exist.

Everything is corrupt.

We are all fucked.

I have to switch all that shit off, I find it impossible to watch any more, it's all just driving me insane. I channel-hop from one disaster to another, eventually finding some weird old black and white film called *None Shall Escape* on a movie channel about a bunch of Nazi's who take-over some crappy little town in Poland, treating them with the contempt they deserve. They clear-out all the town's Jews, shipping them off in cattle-trucks to their smokey end. The chief Nazi - a real cool guy with a way with words as well as with the local girls! - confronts the local Rabbi when he refuses to leave, shooting the Jew point-blank between the eyes.

I dream that night tumultuous visions of England being governed by an iron fist with myself as one of their bitch Generals, blowing the heads off of anyone who doesn't fit-in with the ethos of the New England. I drown some nigger bitch in a tub of freezing water, watching her massive eyes pop out of their sockets as she dies and I laugh in victory.

I am a vampire, biting the neck of a Slav whore, making her part of myself as I am part of England - MY England. I fly over my enemies, dropping bombs on their heads and sticking 2-fingers up to them as I watch them burn.

I round-up all the old politicians and ex-Prime Ministers and laugh as I have them hanged by their scrawny necks from piano-wire until they choke and bleed to death.

I capture my ex-boss CJ and chop his arms and legs off and shit on his head as he wriggles and squirms about on the floor like a spastic.

***

I'm sitting at the living-room table writing my book. I am completely naked as I'm trying to dry out the ink from my aching arms as well as giving my new piercings some air to breathe. My mind wanders through my past as I tap-away on my computer, desperately trying not to make the story too leitmotif in its flow and construction. I have to get it right or it will come to nothing and I just hope that I'm strong enough to see it through to the end.

My self-imposed isolation has started to worm its way under my skin, just like my new tattoos. Although I thrive on independence, the double-edge of its sword also leaves me lonely and forgotten. Writing has made me even more of a recluse, shut away in the house without hardly ever venturing outside its grounds. The notion of being an author has given me peace but not peace of mind, my poor old brain digging-up nothing but nasty memories from its archives.

I continue writing, punching-in word after word from my mind and it kills me. I've been on this now for 5-hours straight this morning and I'm growing weary, noticing the computer getting slower and slower - or is it me? - until everything freezes and I get nowhere. I try to free the screen, attempting every known trick in the book but it's just no use - its failed - FUCK IT! This is just fucking typical, yet more shit I've got to sort out. Why does this have to happen now? If I've lost everything - my photos, my book, my life - I'm going to fucking kill someone. When is my pain ever going to stop?

As far as I'm concerned, there's no bloody surprise in guessing who - or what - is behind all this shit of course - my so-called "Guardian Angel" - my late-uncle Alf, trying to fuck me up the arse yet again with another one of his fucking tricks - and succeeding.

This is no good, I can't sit here pushing buttons and not getting anywhere, I have to do something and sort this bloody thing out, I really can't carry-on like this. I search the internet on my phone and find someone who does computer repairs, preferably someone who can come and have a look at it here rather than me taking it to them. I find some guy called Mack from Midhurst who reckons it could possibly be that the Motherboard has failed - whatever that is? - but he can't get here until 6pm this evening to look at it. I guess I don't have very much choice but to wait until then - bugger!

****

It's 5.50pm when the gate-buzzer sounds the arrival of computer guy Mack and so I let him in. Obviously I've dressed since earlier - greeting him at the door naked would probably have given him a bloody heart-attack! I'm only wearing 2-items of clothing anyway, a white v-neck jumper from Gucci and a pair of pale-blue stretch jeans from Zara and that's it, no underwear or anything on my feet as I don't need to. My hair and make-up I do as per usual although I've done my eyeshadow in coal-black to emphasize my beautiful blue eyes. My perfume is *Opium* by Yves Saint Laurent.

I let him in at it's all smiles and greetings all round as I then lead him into the living-room. He's tall, slim and quite nice looking and I would guess somewhere around 35-ish. He has a somewhat unkempt look about him, especially his straggly, wayward hair, but as I say, he is actually quite nice. Eva chirps at him as she sits on the back of the leather sofa but he doesn't go to stroke her, informing me that he: "Doesn't like cats." He also informs me - quite bluntly actually! - that he's happily married and with 2-young sons - not that I wanted to know any of that shit. I guess that's him out of the equation then!

He sits at my table and starts fiddling-around with my computer - pressing keys, checking connections underneath and other such things - as I watch him from the sidelines, leaning over to see what he's doing. I catch him several times looking at my gorgeous unsupported breasts and I love it, it really turns me on and makes my breathing and therefore my chest heave more. I wish he would just stop looking at them and fuck them!

Just as he suspected, Mack seems to think that the Motherboard has failed and that he will need to take my computer away for further checks and analysis to confirm his suspicions - damn it! With that he gets up to go, not even touching the nice mug of tea that I made him - how rude, what is wrong with these people? He tells me that he'll be in touch by the end of the week and will let me know what the problem really is, that obviously meaning I've got no computer to carry out my work on - bollocks!

Later that evening I'm forced to masturbate watching porn on my mobile-phone - facial cum-shots porn from America featuring some young bitch of no more than 20 as she sucks on 2-cocks and then gets splattered in the face with a double-load of milky cum - lucky fucking bitch!

***

I'm going out tonight as I've arranged to go and see about buying a van, one being sold privately in the local paper by some guy over in Petersfield, West Sussex. It's a white one, as that's what I want, and with a petrol-engine as I need something with a bit of poke to it and not a fucking stinking diesel piece of crap. I'm buying it privately as when I eventually get rid of it, it will hopefully be harder to trace me than if I bought one from a dealer - private sellers ask less questions as cash is all they're after. The seller wants £2,000 for it so I should be able to get it for a bit less than that anyway.

As for my clothes tonight, I'm dressed all in black as I don't want to attract too much attention to myself. I'm also wearing a black t-shirt from Hugo Boss, black jeans from Gap, black socks from M & S, and my old black bomber-jacket from Jacketvests. It's my hair and make-up that is the real big difference. I'm wearing a short black wig that I bought from a market-stool in Horsham about 3-months ago. It's really strange looking at myself in the mirror with it on, it completely changes my appearance, it's like I'm a completely different person altogether. As for my make-up and perfume I'm not wearing any of either, that only enhancing my alien look - I'm just not me.

I'm driving to Midhurst in the Mini as that is the least conspicuous of all the remaining cars left in the garage. I dump the car in a quiet side-street and phone for a cab at a payphone on the corner, giving the cab firm a false name of course. The cab duly arrives some 5-minutes later and we speed across town to Petersfield without any drama, finding the sellers house easily.

The little Ford Fiesta Sportvan is parked in the front driveway, it looking perfect for what I need it for so I'm not going to argue with the owner too much regarding the price - I WANT it. He's an old guy of around 70 with a plummy voice not that dissimilar to that idiot John at the last company I worked for over in Horsham. I wonder if that old bastard is still alive? Not that I fucking care - the stupid old bastard. I try to avert looking at the owner of the van directly, avoiding any eye contact as I don't want him to scan my face too much for possible future identification. I also try to put on a fake Irish accent to throw him further off the scent but I fail in that miserably! There's no point in me taking the van out for a test-drive, he fires the engine and it starts and runs okay so that's good enough for what I want. I try to cut the price down to £1,500 but he says no, so in the end we settle on £1,750. I give him a false name and address for the registration document, dish-out his money, and then fuck-off. As far as insurance is concerned, they can fuck-off as well, I'll just have to be extra careful on the way back to the house that's all, obviously avoiding any stupid fucking Police in the process.

The drive home is easy enough with not a pig in sight, and I park the van in the garage all within 30-minutes of my purchase. I remove my stupid wig as I enter the house through the kitchen and make my way to the living-room, pouring myself a large neat gin as I cuddle Eva in my arms and think about the task ahead.

***

I bought half-a-dozen large cans of black car-spray from some cheap and nasty hardware store in Dorking several months ago, and it's these that I intend to spray the van with I bought last night. It doesn't matter if I make a shit job of it, no-one is going to notice it, not up close anyway, all apart from one person that is. I roughly mask-up all the glass areas as well as the wheels and tyres with old newspapers and then start spraying the white bodywork black. I'm wearing the very same clothes as I did last night as I don't want any paint on any of my nice stuff, that would be sacrilege. I start spraying away and really get into the swing of it, although the cans don't last very long and I begin to wonder if I have enough to cover the entire vehicle? If I don't that would be a real pisser.

I actually quite enjoy myself as I paint, bringing out the artist in me, and it takes just over an hour to complete the whole job. In the end it actually doesn't look half-bad, even if I do say so myself! Maybe I was a paint-sprayer in a former life?

I leave the paint to dry fully as I go and make myself some lunch, have a couple of stiff vodkas and to feed Eva. I have pasta in spicy sauce with Jalapeño peppers while Eva has tuna with shrimps - lucky cat! I watch one of my old porn films on DVD as I eat, the first part featuring choking porn from Australia that I find really funny, which is then followed by extreme lesbian 3-some porn where some hot blonde bitch of about 20 gets one hand from each of the other girls rammed into her pussy both at the same time, causing her to scream in pleasure/agony. Again I laugh at the visions before me as I finger my vagina and flick my clit with my thumb and cum myself. I suck my digits and down another vodka and then go and check my handiwork on the van.

The paint seems to have come out pretty good, certainly good enough for what I want anyway. I peel-off the masked areas to reveal the end result and no-one would know at first-glance that the van was white only a few hours ago. There's nothing else to do to it now apart from equipping it with a few essential items for my mission - basically just some thick cable-ties, several pre-cut lengths of duct-tape and a large dark blanket.

I spend the rest of the afternoon and the evening just fucking-around - a naked swim in the pool, about 1 ½- hours on the racing game in the games-room where

I crash at least 30-times, dinner of salmon with new potatoes, broccoli and a nice bottle of German white whilst watching a film from my collection - *Repulsion* - staring Catherine Deneuve. I order a cab to go and retrieve the Mini from

Midhurst where I'm there and back indoors within the hour flat. I then go and have a quick game of pool by myself and I win, and then fuck myself with my 8-inch realistic dildo from Lovehoney as I lean over the rear-end of the Lamborghini in the garage. I then finally have a long soak in the bath with loads of bubbles and more wine, feed Eva once more and then off to Bedfordshire.

***

I was up and about reasonably early this morning - it's now 7.45am, Sunday. I'm off to Ford Market in West Sussex, just South-West of Arundel and right next door to Ford Prison. How much I loath these sort of places I cannot tell you, if it's not the bloody scum it seems to attract it's all the fucking Slavs as well, selling "their" shitty crap to Joe Public, and there's no surprises in guessing where all that comes from is there?

I showered early and checked myself over for any problems - there were none. The last of my tattoo scabs have now also gone although I will continue using the protective cream on them for a little while yet just to make sure everything heals-up OK. As for today's clothes I'm wearing a black sleeveless ruff-blouse from Christian Lacroix, a pair of dark-grey stretch-jeans from Hugo Boss, and my old pair of black suede ankle-boots from Miu Miu. My underwear is in sexy white lace from Triumph. I've gone for a bit of an understated look to my make-up today - not that I know why? - with light-grey eyeshadow and pale-pink lipstick. My hair is as you can guess. My perfume is *Luxe* by Avon. I'm not taking a clutch-bag or anything else like that today as I'm wearing my black leather biker jacket, the second-hand one I bought online that has all the badges and patches on it, so I can therefore stash my keys, money, phone and other things in all its numerous pockets.

The whole reason for this little venture is to get a few chosen items for my next target, undoubtedly my biggest and riskiest one to date. If I'm going to achieve my mission I must prepare everything correctly, right down to the very last detail. There cannot be any mistakes. I arrive at the market relatively inconspicuously, having driven here in the Mini. Its been really great fun, hurling it around corners on 3-wheels and blasting it down the A29. It's actually not that fast but because it's quite low to the ground and the suspension is so bloody hard it feels faster than it really is.

I park-up easily amongst all the surrounding nondescript cars - the plebs of the car World - and head off on the short walk to the market itself. The stalls are basically set-out along the length of the old runway and I turn-left onto it and begin my search, desperately trying to avoid touching people as I quickly whiz around the corridors of tat as you never know what I might catch. Sure enough - just as I predicted - every other stall is run by a fucking Slav. Either that or it's a bloody rag-head of some sort or another. I just can't fucking win no-matter where I go or what I do - fuckers. I come across a butchers lorry selling a whole range of different fresh meats out of the big hatch in its side. The butcher himself is selling his stock via his head-mic as 2-young girls dish-out the goods and take the money from the punters down below on the runway. I buy a bag of 10-steaks from them for only £30 - bargain! - and then move on.

The amount of crap some people have on their stalls is unbelievable - worthless sun-bleached second-hand DVD's, knock-off kitchenware, fake handbags from China and all manor of shit. I find a stall selling toiletries and all that sort of stuff so I check that out. When I look closer though at the individual items for sale - all stupidly cheap - I notice that they're all nasty South African rip-off shit and not genuine products at all. I remember buying some of this crap off another trader at Kempton Park Market in Surrey some years ago and when I went to use it the toothpaste had the consistency of chalk and tasted disgusting! Needless to say I threw the lot away and vowed never to buy any more of this shit ever again. I give the stall a miss and walk on.

I buy myself a burger with fried onions from a fast-food stall for £3.50 and slather it in brown sauce, tomato ketchup and mustard. It's not the greatest burger in the World but it tastes okay and smells lovely. At least the stallholders were English, I wouldn't have bothered otherwise.

My attention is then caught by a bit of an argument at another stall up ahead of me to my left so I decide to be nosey and investigate. An old guy in his 60's - English - is shouting at one of the dirty-looking Slav stallholders, obviously without any success. It seems as though the old guy has bought something from the Slav who's then short-changed him - what a fucking surprise! The response from the Slav is just typical as he bleats in his evil tone:

"I speaka no Inglish. I no understand." Cunt.

Further up the row I come upon a stall selling second-hand tools and other hardware. This is just what I'm after. I scour his table looking for the things I need - a small crowbar that has plenty of weight to it and a few other essentials for the job in hand. The old guy serving is asking £20 for the lot but after a little bit of haggling and a fake smile plus a cheeky show of cleavage on my part we settle on £15.

I also buy a black peaked-cap off another stall - this one foreign run, some sort-of stinking Asian - for the sum of only £2. With that I'm all done and dusted, I can't stand any more of this place and vow never to come back here ever again as long as I'm still walking on this Earth.

I stroll out of the main market area and head for the car-park with my 2-bags of goodies. Passing through the middle row of cars I quickly scan the registration plates for foreign ones - just the scum Eastern European ones, not the genuine European plates like German, French, Spanish or Italian ones, not that there are any anyway. I soon spot a whole gaggle of them all together - Polish, Bulgarian, Lithuanian, Romanian and other shit. Making sure no-one sees me, I run myignition-key down the side bodywork of all their fucking sticking cars as I walk by them, gouging a deep line not only into the paint but the metal also - fucking bastards.

I load my bags and myself into the Mini with a smirk of deep satisfaction across my gorgeous face. I would have loved to have seen the faces of the Slavs when they returned to their shitty cars and seen the damage that I've caused. It's no more than they fucking deserve as you well know by now.

I pull out of the car-park, passing under the old Fighter-Jet mounted on its tall mounting-pole to my right, turn-left back onto Ford Road and then head North for home with a job well done.

***

Back indoors I suddenly begin to feel sick. I have a quick slug of Russian poison to try and dampen it down but it's no good, I just can't hold it within me. I puke into the kitchen sink an evil mixture of this mornings tea and toast, the burger, and the small mouthful of vodka. That does it, I am definitely NOT going back to that fucking market ever again - ever.

***

That night I'm back out in the Mini. I haven't eaten or drunk anything since being sick earlier. Getting on with the task in-hand is at the top of my spectrum, getting it done is more important than right or wrong. I'm not afraid to bend the rules and if this upsets others then tough shit. I'm staking-out my next target - the Big One. I have to get this right as everything depends on it, and if I make one little mistake then my life and my World as I know it will cease to exist.

***

I went back to see John again a few days later, this time to get my clitoris - the jewel in my crown! - and my outer labia pierced. He put a single-ring through my clit and 2 in each of my lips - 5-rings altogether, this taking my total number of piercings now up to 30. He also put his cock in my vagina and in my mouth as I sucked him off and swallowed his man-milk as I played with my new metal and I cum.

Over the last several months or so, I've also been having electrolysis treatment on my skin, over my entire body in fact - although not to the top of my head obviously, I don't want to be bald! - at a private clinic in London, to stop any regrowth of unwanted hair. This of course I've done to negate wasting any more of my precious time depilating my legs, underarms or my lady-garden and to keep myself smooth and gorgeous always and forever. The treatment was laborious as well as expensive at a whopping £55,000 but what the Hell, I can afford it and I'm worth it so who gives a shit?

3

Dark Entries

"THERE WILL BE NO ESCAPE FOR ME ONCE I ENTER INTO THE DARKNESS."

My life has been a well-trodden path, from anti-time until now. This is my year zero. I am desperate to exorcise the hate within me. I have faith that my self-preservation will see me through the next couple of days and beyond. It has to, as for some reason there is no turning back now - I have to go on. The future will be whatever the future will be and I can't change it even if I wanted to. This is the direction my life has headed to.

I am so far beyond despair that nothing exists any more. I've past through the pain-barrier and out the other side. As you all know by now, I suffer as only I can and do. You my dear reader, may argue that I'm somewhat idiosyncratic or even to go as far as saying that I'm somewhat otherworldly. The truth is I always have been and probably always will be disconnected from the human race. I never planned to be dissociative, it's just that I exist in a completely different dimension to everyone else on this Earth.

I also have to ask myself why am I risking my new-found status with this venture, and do I have the strength within myself to really do this? What the fuck am I doing? I don't have an answer as I honestly don't know why? I guess there must be something inside me that is driving me to do this, some kind-of self-destructive hysteria maybe? I don't know, it's all too much to comprehend most of the time. In the cold light of the day I have to keep pushing as what else is there to do? Even if it means risking my sacred blood I have to go on.

We are all Earthbound for such a short time so please don't fuck it up for yourself. Make the most of your life, and even if you do manage to screw some part of it up, at least you had a bloody good go, which is more than 99% of people do.

As for myself, I'm going to a place where the vast majority of the people of this Earth will never venture into. Not only is it beyond their capability, it's beyond their imagination also.

The stage is set. Everything is in place for the final phase of my project. All I need now is the key component and everything will be okay. Tomorrow is just another day. Except that it won't be. Tomorrow will be a day of true awakening.

THE NIGHTMARE HAS BEGUN.

***

THIS IS MY *ACTUS ESSENDI*.

I'm out in the van, following the bitch through the roads leading out of Horsham town centre. We're heading in the direction of Southwater, itself a town coterminous to the aforementioned, although the two are rapidly blending into each other at an alarming rate. I know she's heading this way anyway as when we were working together for that shitty company, it was part of my job to hand out the monthly payslips to everyone. Stupidly the company put each individual employees address on the front of each envelope as well as their names and as they all passed through my grubby fingers, getting hold of her address - or anyone else's for that matter - was a piece of piss - Hee Hee!

I stalk her like a primeval predator, keeping a small distance behind her car just in case she spots me. The chances are slim anyway, even though it's now 5.37pm the evening darkness is already upon us. Not only that, I'm wearing a cheap and nasty men's black jacket, a black cap, men's black combat trousers and a pair of men's black steel-toecap work-boots, all purchased from a charity shop in town - using cash of course. Because of all this no-one notices me as I'm simply not here, I am invisible to the human eye.

What little traffic there is heading this way thins out the nearer we get to Southwater. Turning into her road I follow several car lengths behind. She parks in the road outside her house, the one she shares with her black bastard, and I park-up behind her some 5-houses away. I switch my lights off but leave the engine running as I notice her kill her car completely, the fumes from the exhaust ceasing, but for some strange reason she just sits there and doesn't get out. What the fuck is she doing? Maybe she's seen me and is calling the cops? She's on her phone for sure as I can see it now, she fiddling about with it and touching the screen faster than anyone else can do as she sits there trying to look cool and sophisticated - fucking condescending arrogant cow. She's so fucking full of herself, the skinny-gutted bitch. She's nothing but hair on a stick. She doesn't realise what she's fucking playing with.

I decide to drive on a bit further up the road and park ahead of her car - an Audi A1 in a horrible dirty yellow colour - as I see her finally finish with her call and look to get out of her car, at long fucking last. With my crowbar in my left-hand I pull the handle with the other and I'm out and upon her like lightning, not even looking around to check if there's anyone about and jeopardising my mission without a single thought.

She's turned around in the opposite direction to me now and is starting to walk away, to the rear of her car. I'm like a pre-programmed assassin, everything is quiet and still, nothing exists any more except me and her and it feels like I'm in some kind-of trance-like state. Lunging at her I crack the heavy iron to the right-rear of her skull, hitting her like a clap of thunder, pole-axing her to the very spot. She falls to the ground without a problem in a motionless heap, without even a moan or a feint murmur, she smacking the front left-side of her head on the tarmac road surface with a thud in the process, knocking her doubly unconscious as her car keys clatter to the road with a metallic tinkle.

I stand over her for several seconds looking at what I've just done. I am perfectly calm and fluid in my actions, without panic or fear, even though I have now just stepped over into the dark side of wrong. I could have quite easily just set fire to her car as revenge but my issue isn't with her fucking car - it's with her. Reaching down to her I grab at her hair and pull her toward the back of the van and open its tailgate, dragging her motionless. Manoeuvring myself behind her I jump on her with animal-like dexterity and grab both her arms, crossing them behind her back. I tie her wrists together with the cable-ties from the back of the van and gag the bitch with the duct-tape also.

Picking her up is easy, she's just like a mannequin, the adrenalin flowing through my perfect body increasing my strength x 10 and she's safely in the back of the van within seconds. Nothing can quantify the phenomenal power I have at this moment. I tie her ankles together as her wrists and slam the tailgate shut. I have her now and she is ensnared. The larceny of her freedom. She is mine to do:

"WHAT THOU WILT".

Climbing back into the van I snick it into first-gear, switch the lights back on and I am gone. There can be no redemption. There is no going back now.

Using the main arterial roads I head out of Southwater with the coast clear, breathing a sigh of relief that this particular phase is now thankfully over, my mental and psychical strength and my sheer determination pulling me through once again. Out onto the A29 I head for Foxhill and home. I chill-out as I try to keep out of everyone's way and not draw attention to myself. I have control. Control is power.

Suddenly I hear movement in the back of the van, just as I turn hard-right onto the A272, with some moaning and groaning coming from the bitch. I guess the effects of the blow to her head are starting to wear off already? Within 5-minutes I turn into my driveway and open the automatic gates, driving through with them shutting behind me at my passing and lock. I click-open the roller-shutter door to the garage and reverse the van down the long line of cars flanking the walls on either side of me and then switch off the lights and the engine.

With the garage door closed I get out of the van and go to open the tailgate and there she is - my lovely girl.

***

She's in pretty-much the same position as when I shoved her in. She starts to roll about from side to side in a daze and doesn't react at all when I grab her legs and pull her towards me. Firstly I have to unlock and open the connecting door between the garage and the kitchen, therefore granting me an obstacle-free passage between here and the hallway - her final destination.

I take her in both arms from behind and semi-carry/drag her from the back of the van into and through the kitchen. My energy is spellbinding, there is nothing I cannot do. From there I drop the bitch to the smooth marbled floor and drag her by her fake blonde hair into the centre of the hall, her hair itself now matted at the back in small clumps and clusters of dried blood. Letting go of her she falls backwards and re-hits her head on the rock-hard hall floor, making her stir and moan loudly, her brain dislocated and delirious with pain.

Blood rushes through my veins at breakneck speed, driving me on. My adrenalin stabs me like cocaine and I hit her hard in the mouth with my fist, making it emit a sharp cracking sound.

I stand over her and look down at this bitch. I look at her with tears of sadness in my eyes. What has become of me to do this? Why did she drive me to this point? Why can't everyone leave me the fuck alone? It's too late now for regrets and if there are any ramifications then they will come later, as they surely will. She caused me untold misery and pain at a time when I was already low. And what a fucking shit year that fucking was, I don't and can't go back there ever again.

I kneel down to the right-hand side of her and stare at her face and her body, questioning myself:

What is she?

Why is she here?

What does she want?

I lower myself to her and grab her by the throat. Pulling her towards me I kiss the duct-tape that is still covering her mouth, then with the other hand I peel it off her face in one swipe of my wrist, virtually taking her lips off with it. I lower myself down further and kiss them, they're soft and beautiful and I give them a small lick with my pointed tongue, sensing a disgusting smell on her breath - a mixture of cigarettes and black cock.

I touch and feel her breasts with my right-hand, playing with them for a couple of minutes until I become bored with my action. I move down to between her legs and stroke her vagina under the covering of her clothes. I can feel her opening and she moans again but this time it's different, it's a moan of subconscious pleasure rather than that of pain and hurt as before.

She starts to mumble something so I stop fingering her and give her a small slap to her left-cheek. I can't make out what she's saying and she opens her eyes and looks at me. I don't think she can quite make out the fact that it's really me that she's looking at - the lights are on but there's no-one at home. I give her a mean right-hand punch to her face but it seemingly has no effect on her, she just keeps staring at me like the bitch she is. I grab her by the throat right under her jaw and shake her head from side to side in an attempt to wake the cow up.

"Mellis. Mellis. Can you hear me you fucking nigger-loving whore? Wake up you fucking bitch. Come on, wake up now." I say to her calmly.

I shake her a bit more vigorously and give her a dry-slap, noticing a feint glimmer of recognition suddenly appear in her eyes.

"Where am I?" She mumbles.

"Welcome to my house Mellis." I torment her.

"YOU! WHAT DO YOU WANT? YOU HIT ME. YOU FUCKING HIT ME!" She whines like a bitch and I can tell immediately by her physiognomy exactly what she's thinking.

She looks at me in total disbelief that it really is me - the beautiful, gorgeous and stinking rich Sarah Knowles that has her held captive. She starts wriggling and squirming about on the floor when she suddenly also realises that she is bound by both her hands and ankles.

"UNTIE ME YOU BITCH. WHY ARE YOU DOING THIS? WHAT DO YOU WANT?" She bleats between wails of pandemonium.

"If you have to ask me that Mellis then you're even more stupid than I thought. I'm doing this because I don't like you." I counter her calmly.

"YOU'LL NEVER GET AWAY WITH THIS."

"Oh yes I will Mellis, because I'm clever and you're stupid. This is justice Mellis. I know you don't understand the reasons why, but that's the way it is. You have to accept it, you have no choice. You and others like you have caused me so much unbelievable pain and anguish that it is impossible for me to put into mere words. What you are about to experience is not nearly enough in the way of compensation, but it is no more than you deserve - you fucking cunt."

"Please Sarah no, I'll give you money. How much do you want?" She whinges as she desperately tries to appeal to my good side but fails miserably - I don't have one.

"Money! Are you fucking joking? I don't need money Mellis. Look around you, does it look like I'm destitute? I've got more money than you could ever imagine."

She looks at me and then around the hallway with eyes of abject terror. I laugh at her fear and stare back into them. What is she thinking I wonder? What does she expect me to do, just let her go? Bury her in the garden? I'm not going to do either of these things.

I lean forward and over her and kiss her cheek, the right one. It's soft and feminine and it reminds me of Amanda - my love. I go to kiss her again but the bitch pulls to her left and I miss and kiss nothing but air. I touch and grope her right-breast and she screams. It's surprisingly firm although I think she's wearing one of those awful padded bras and that has tricked my brain into thinking she has more bust than in reality. She pants heavily at my action but she can't move, I have her right where I want her.

I let her go and stand above her. She continues to stare at me so I give her a nice powerful kick right between her legs and she screams again. I kick her once more, this time to her right bum-cheek and she moans as an injured animal would. I punch her in the face in exactly the same spot on the cheek that I kissed her and she reels-back and hits the back of her head on the marble floor with a deep thud, almost knocking her out again but not quite. It's just as well, I don't want her unconscious, I want her awake and alive.

I leave her and go into the living-room to get a bottle of vodka and a pair of scissors and then return to find her a little more compos-mentis, once again her bulging eyes following my every move. I toss the scissors at her body and they land on her belly and then bounce-off onto the floor with a clank. I stand at her feet and take a large swig of vodka from the bottle and swallow it down in one gulp, it burning my throat and sending flames shooting up and out of my nostrils. I take another large gulp and then put the bottle down over to one side out of harms way.

"YOU FUCKING WHORE." She screams at me again.

"Yes Mellis, anything you say." I sneer back at her.

"I'LL FUCKING KILL YOU, YOU FUCKING BITCH."

"Oh dear oh dear Mellis, is that the best you can do, threaten me with useless words? And how are you going to do that, look at you, you're not exactly in a position to do anything at all are you?"

"LET ME GO YOU FUCKING BITCH."

"No. And it's going to be a long night Mellis so you better save your energy."

"WHAT DO YOU FUCKING WANT? JUST LET ME GO."

"Just because your old-man is a copper you seem to think that you can do whatever you fucking like. Well, you're sadly mistaken Mellis, as you're going to find out. We're going to have some fun Mellis, you and me. Well, at least I am. I'm going to take you to Hell."

I stand before her like a praying-mantis. I undo the laces of my boots and kick them off to the right, in the direction of the dinning-room. I peel off my socks and chuck them the same way. As I begin to remove my clothes she starts with the shouting again.

"WHAT ARE YOU DOING? YOU'RE FUCKING INSANE?"

"No Mellis. I'm perfectly normal. You're the one that's insane." I inform her.

"WHY ARE YOU TAKING YOUR CLOTHES OFF?" She bleats as I remove my trousers and stand there in just my bra and knickers. She starts to scream once again, really having a go at the top of her voice.

"There's no point in screaming Mellis, no-one can hear you. There's no-one else here, just you and me."

"WHAT ARE YOU GOING TO DO YOU FUCKING MAD BITCH?"

I remove my bra first and she screams again at the gorgeous sight of my full, perfect breasts.

"WHAT ARE YOU DOING? LET ME GO."

I ignore her plea and remove my knickers and stand totally naked before her and I am beautiful. She watches me perplexed as then a wave of fear and dread suddenly sweeps across her tearful face.

"OH MY GOD, THOSE TATTOOS, ARE THEY REAL?" She says with her usual unrepentant sarcasm.

"No Mellis, they're iron-on ones. Of course they're bloody real you stupid bastard. I hope you like them, I had them all done especially for you. Look, I even had my nipples pierced for you as well, and my ears and my vagina." I tell her as I fiddle with my nips and then turn around slowly to show her the tattoos on my back.

"YOU'RE A FUCKING FREAK."

"No Mellis, wrong again. You're the freak."

"SARAH NO. WHAT ARE YOU DOING? WHAT'S ALL THIS ABOUT? WHAT DO YOU WANT?"

"Do you like my body Mellis? Do you like my tits?" I say, cupping them with both hands and squeezing them together.

"IF YOU DON'T LET ME GO ERROL WILL KILL YOU." She shouts at me.

"You can forget that nigger, you're mine now." I smirk back at her.

"WHAT ARE YOU TALKING ABOUT? YOU'RE FUCKING MENTAL."

"Do you like my vagina? Isn't it sweet?"

"YOU FUCKING DIRTY BITCH. JUST LET ME GO." She screams insanely.

"I'm growing a bit tired of this verbal combat Mellis, it's time to stop."

I look at her straight in the eyes as I insert my middle-finger between my labia and begin to wank myself slowly, making it wet with my internal mucus. I pull it out and lick and suck it in front of her face provocatively, making her grimace.

"THAT'S DISGUSTING, YOU'RE FUCKING CRAZY." She whines hysterically.

I laugh at her statement and push my finger back into my vagina. I play with myself, with the rings through my labia and my clit before I pull it out and move down closer to her, kneeling to the right of her body.

"Do you like my ear piercings Mellis? You can kiss them if you want?" I ask her coldly.

"YOU FUCKING KEEP AWAY FROM ME YOU FUCKING MENTAL BITCH. I'LL FUCKING KILL YOU." She screams, the words coming out of her mouth in a fusillade of viscousness as pearl-like tears roll down her tortured face.

"Shush shush shush Mellis. There there, be a good girl now. You're going to love this. It's nice and sweet, just like honey." I torment her.

I move my dirty finger closer to her face and she starts to wriggle about on the smooth hallway floor like a demented worm. I grab her bloodied hair on the back of her head and pull on it hard as I rub my vaginal fluid across her mouth. As I do she spits and I laugh as she now has the taste of my cunt on her tongue and I stand and watch her desperately attempt to dispel my flavour, without success.

"WHY?" She hisses at me.

"Why what?" I hiss back.

"WHY ARE YOU DOING THIS? WHAT'S THE POINT? WHAT DO YOU WANT?"

"Because I can. Because I WANT. I need to, to get all this shit out of me. It's people like you that have made me like this Mellis. You seem to think you can just take the fucking piss out of me and not expect me to retaliate. And as for screwing with that nigger, you should be fucking ashamed of yourself. You're a traitor to your race, to your country and to your blood. But do you know the worst thing? You have no concept of what I'm saying do you? That is the tragedy." I try to explain to the stupid bitch.

"WHAT ARE YOU TALKING ABOUT? YOU'RE MAD."

I squat down to her again and stare directly into her eyes.

"No Mellis. You're the mad one."

I pick up the scissors and point them at her eyes. She screams and tries to wriggle away but I grab her by the arm and start cutting at her clothes, the blades of the scissors making light work of shredding the material. She coils-up in defence of my onslaught but it's useless, no-one can stop me. She continues to scream so I have to punch her in the face again, using the handles of the scissors as knuckledusters. That shuts her up, albeit momentarily. I cut through her jacket and pull it off her, revealing her white blouse beneath. I cut-away at that also and it's only a mere few seconds before I have that removed and I was right - she is wearing one of those padded bras - I fucking told you didn't I?

There's not a peep from her now, I do believe that she's actually resigned herself to the fact that she can't stop me. I cut her black trousers to ribbons and try to pull them off but its belt prevents total removal. I unclip it and slide it out, taking the remains of her trousers with it to reveal her white knickers and the slight bulge of her pussy beneath. She starts to cry and whimper - pathetic isn't it? - as I chop her knickers off and there it is - her sweet vagina in all its glory. I chop her bra off in only 2-cuts and now I have her - naked as the day she was born.

I stand and admire the view as I swig some more of the poisonous Russian liquid.

I pour some over her body and she whines and rolls-over onto her front, showing me her pert bum. I squat down on my haunches and run my fingers between her bum-cheeks and she shudders and rolls back over onto her back in shock. I feel her small firm breasts amidst more irrelevant sobbing and the flowing of water, making them jiggle around in reaction to my touch. I start to finger my vagina as I fondle her mounds, pleasuring myself slowly. She tries to get away from me and attempts to stand up but I'm too fucking quick and strong for her and I grab her by the hair once more, pulling her back towards me. I hold her by her hair and force the vodka bottle into her mouth, ramming it in so far that she's unable to block its flow of flaming liquid down her throat, choking her. It empties steadily into her body and she becomes weak and passive with each and every glug. I remove it and take a hard swig myself as I let her choke and cough on the floor like the useless piece of shit she is.

I pour some of the vodka over my beautiful breasts - they are so-much better than hers - and then wipe and stroke them with her face, controlling her every move with a clutch of her hair in my tight grasp.

"There's a good girl. See, you can do it. I'm going to make you love me Mellis, cos, deep down, I think you always have. It's time for you to come out of the closet at last."

"Just let me go Sarah. I won't say anything to anyone, not even to Errol, I promise." She pitifully pleas.

"You're a fucking liar Mellis, just like all the rest." I whisper in her ear.

I lumber punch her and then punch her in the face yet again, as I then stand and kick her over and over - FUCKING FUCKING BITCH.

I grab both her legs and force them apart but she's stronger than I thought and resists me fiercely. I twice smash her in the face with the vodka bottle and she weakens for me. I insert one of my middle-fingers into her vagina and its warm and wet and she screams and so I push it in harder. I push 2 and then 3-fingers into her cunt amid more screaming and crying and intense wriggling and kicking out as then I push my whole hand into her body and then there is silence - she passes-out and all is quiet. I slap her face as I continue to penetrate her but there's no response, she's out cold.

I pull myself out of her and reposition myself between her legs. As I do she stirs and slowly comes back to life. I lick her vagina and her small throbbing clit and she moans with pleasure. I want to make her cum but I doubt if she's capable so I stop and insert the vodka bottle into her hole instead, pushing it right in up to the point where the neck widens. She moans louder as I fuck her but it's not really in pleasure - it's in fear and disgust. I bet if the bottle was a black one I would get a different response?

Removing the bottle I stand and look at her. I give her a full-on power-kick to her crotch and she cries in twisted excruciating agony and I laugh. I drink the last of the vodka down and sense the taste of her love in my mouth also.

Eva is watching me from the stairs and I wave to her. I can see her little brain working overtime, trying to decipher what it is her big blue eyes are seeing before her? It's evening now so I guess she wants feeding, although I'm not hungry at all. I give her a bowl full of food - rabbit in gravy - in the kitchen and then return myself to Mellis in the hall. She's still in the same position as when I left her, laying there with her hands tied behind her, pleading to no-one for help.

Standing with my long beautiful legs astride her, I piss on her nakedness and it splashes over her smooth skin and the black and white marble squares of the floor. She starts with the verbal abuse once again but I don't care so I squat down to her and start to wipe my minge with her hair and it feels so fucking good.

In the garage I unhook Andy's (my) large crowbar from its mounting on the wall. I can't believe how bloody heavy it is for such a small diameter piece of metal - it must be made from something other than ordinary steel. From the kitchen I grab one of Andy's (my) beautiful Japanese kitchen-knives from its magnetic holder on the wall. It's so unbelievably sharp it's scary - and gorgeous at the same time.

Back to the bitch, I place the knife on the floor over by the old black wooden German chest-cabinet. I take a swing at her with the crowbar and she screams and tries to move herself away from its trajectory but she's too slow, I hit her on the right-kneecap with a deep cracking sound that actually makes me wince a little myself. I scream and swear at the bitch as I beat her body and she reels back. I call her a: "FUCKING NIGGER WHORE", "DIRTY RACE TRAITOR", "JIGGERBOO LOVER" and "IT'S THE FUCKING GAS-CHAMBER FOR YOU BITCH" as I smash into her frame.

She screams the whole house down with the most bloody awful noise that you've ever heard. It's so bad that I have to hit her again, this time to her right shoulder-blade as she tries to cower-away from me. A third swipe to her spine as she reels in pain silences her to some degree but still she moans like a bitch.

I carefully place the crowbar on the floor, trying not to scratch or chip its surface, as now I WANT her. I WANT her love. I spin her over on her axis like a chicken on a skewer to face me. I go down on her, down on her body, holding and laying right on top of her nakedness. She tries to resist my power but she's wasting both her and my time. I kiss her face and neck as she swears and attempts to bite me and I have to fend her off. She tries to knee me in the groin so I position one leg between both of hers and intertwine ourselves together. I can feel the wetness of her vagina on my leg and her thigh between mine as I kiss her screaming mouth and squeeze her small breasts. I tongue her nipples, leaving a tiny rivulet of saliva trailing along the smooth silky skin of her tits. We roll-about on the floor as one as she tries to escape me but with her wrists still bound behind her back she has no chance. As I kiss and bite her tits she tries to headbutt me and I grab the crowbar and smack her across the face with it. She tries to reach up and cover her bleeding mouth and nose but with her arms tied she just falls back and hits the rear of her head on the marble tiles once again, stunning herself.

I grab possibly my one and only chance and eat her vagina, licking and sucking on its meat and juices. She tastes of woman, urine and cum and I love her and bury my face into her deeper, snorting on cunt. I lap at her lips and clit and she moans like the nigger-lover she is - FUCKING SLAG - and I continue to lick her until I become bored.

I remove myself from her hole and scoot upstairs to my bedroom to retrieve my old Doc Johnson 12-inch white double-ended dildo - the very same one that Amanda my love and I used to fuck ourselves stupid with - and then return to my prey. She's laying side-on on the cold floor, and I have to laugh when I notice Eva is now sitting down by her feet, sniffing them! What is it with cats and feet? I shoo her out of the way and sit myself down between the bitch's legs. She has another feeble attempt at kicking me but I slap her down and prise her legs apart. As I do I stab the dildo into her vagina with brute force, penetrating her labia with a squelch. She starts with the screaming and shouting again and I've really had enough of this by now so I kick her in her bloodied face with my heel but it still doesn't shut the bitch up. I fuck her with the fake cock and she moans loudly - I don't know whether it's in pleasure or pain or both, not that I give a shit either way - and then move closer to her, inserting the other end of the dildo into my own pussy. It feels so good to have cock in me and I wriggle forwards to get full penetration. I fuck us both as our lips meet and the effect of her vagina on mine and the dildo and the noise and the excitement and the alcohol and the blood all conspire to make me cum quickly as we scissor.

I grind for a while longer and then pull out - even that feels so fucking good! - pulling the dildo out of the bitch also. It's slippery with love and cum and difficult to handle so I grab it with a firm clench and force her own dirty end into her screaming mouth, holding her throat as I orally fuck her. She gags on plastic and her own vaginal fluid and I give it one massive shove right down into her throat, right into her windpipe, just like her dirty fucking nigger would.

She disgusts me. Look at her, she is pathetic. How could she go with one of them? It's abhorrent. Don't bitches like her realise that oil and water don't mix? They all seem to think that they're being clever - fucking a black or a Paki or a Slav - or that they're embracing the ethos of multiculturalism by spawning half-breeds. They have no sense of their own culture - even if they do they either don't understand it or hate it - so instead embrace those of the spear-chuckers or the curry-munchers. It simply has to stop, and for this bitch it's going to - today.

I slap her face to wake her up as I want her alive, to feel the pain, just like I have to every fucking day of my life. I torment her body with the sharp point of the knife, poking and jabbing her skin, making her flinch and yelp in annoyance and pain. I squeeze the cheeks of her face as I force her to look at me and gazing into her eyes I see nothing, not one fucking thing - she is empty.

The situation changes in a moment as I want to gauge her reaction to my power. I plunge the knife into her belly with all my strength and it goes in easily - my beautiful knife - its evil sharpness gliding into her meat and internal organs with glorious ease. Her eyes light-up and her mouth desperately tries to draw-in more air as she emits a silent shriek of terror at the same time - the silent howl of pain. She coughs and splutters and I hold her there, transfixed in time as she looks at me in horror, not believing what I've just done to her. She tries to talk but her words are muffled.

What did she expect would happen between us, that I would bake her a fucking cake?

I stand up and look at her, checking-out the vision of the blade still sticking into her naked body. I'm actually quite surprised by the lack of blood leaking out of the wound as I had imagined it would be pouring out all over the place but there's only a dribble. The look on her face is amazing, she simply cannot comprehend what has happened to her. She can do nothing now in the face of overwhelming horror. She looks down at the knife and then at me as I lean down and pull it out. It comes out so easily I find it hard to believe that this situation is actually real, that I've actually stabbed the bitch, that I've really fucking hurt her.

***

I don't actually think I've damaged any vital organs when I stabbed her. Although the blood that initially flowed from the wound at a nice steady pace now appears to be slowing down a bit.

She lays there sobbing from the pain, her teeth chattering like from being frozen and with a petrified look of horror smeared across her face.

I kiss her cheek softly.

I am beyond callous.

I am on a downward spiral with no end in sight.

I gaze in wonder at her naked body and her smooth pale skin. I touch her upper right-arm and she flinches with reaction and jumps.

I touch her hair and grab a handful with my left-hand. With a scything trajectory of the blade I lop-off the whole bunch and go to grab some more. She defends herself with all her might but it's useless, the pain from the knife wound, the beating, the vodka and this whole situation has nullified her strength. I pull some of her hair straight out from its roots - black roots that is! - in a great big chunk and scalp her hard. She screams the whole house down, making Eva run for cover back upstairs as I move closer to the bitch and laugh in her face.

Clutching the wad of hair in my hand I get to my feet before her and hold her fake blonde tresses in front on my vagina, pretending that her hair is really my pubes. I laugh my fucking head off as I start to dance about like a bitch in front of her crying face - although for some reason she's not laughing? Just what is her fucking problem?

Throwing her hair to one side I squat myself down by her side, right opposite her belly and her drying wound. A vision of terror appears across her face as I pick-up the kitchen-knife once again and place the point of the blade on her flat stomach - it actually looks quite attractive, like a work of art. My unadulterated quest for sensation fuels my mind as I begin to carve into the skin of her abdomen, cutting her a copy of the *Hakenkrauz* tattoo on my back. The symbol is my good-luck, not hers, she's going nowhere as she fruitlessly struggles in her suffering. Everything I do is carried-out with my usual atavistic bent. Her tears burst into heartbreaking sobbing as I cut her. But I have no heart, that was destroyed years ago by fuckers like this one continuously hurting me and damaging my brain.

I spin myself around and over the tears of pure horror emitting from the white death-mask that now is her face. I glide 2-fingers of my right-hand into my vagina and masturbate myself to distraction. My breathing is heavy as I push them in and out of my hole and love myself. The fucking cow tries to wriggle away from me as I wank but I hold her in place with my other hand as I quickly hit the spot and scream "OH OH OH" and spit my cum in her face, her features frozen in disgust.

I laugh at her action as I get off her and look at the mess I've left behind, her face no-longer pale and gaunt but somehow looking happy and at peace, it glistening from the splattering of my cum. I suddenly get the urge to pee so I stand over her and piss onto her body. I laugh with big chuckles as my warm urine splashes down onto her as she twists herself from side to side in slow-motion, looking directly into my beautiful blue eyes for mercy. I kick her in the cunt.

She screams in agony and retracts her legs in a vain attempt to protect herself and to warn me off. Spinning her over onto her front she yells at me more nasty words: "YOU FUCKING BITCH", I'LL FUCKING KILL YOU FOR THIS" and "YOU'LL NEVER GET AWAY WITH THIS YOU FUCKING WHORE", all crap that I've heard a thousand times or more throughout my life and will no-doubt continue to do so.

"YES I WILL MELLIS, I ALREADY HAVE." I spit back her in impending triumph.

"YOU'RE FUCKING MAD."

"YES I KNOW MELLIS, AND IT'S BASTARDS LIKE YOU THAT HAS MADE ME THIS WAY, DON'T YOU SEE?"

"LET ME GO." She pleads, like a pleader.

"NO. I'M GOING TO KILL YOU SLOWLY MELLIS, AND WITH MAXIMUM PAIN, JUST LIKE EVERYONE DOES TO ME. I AM YOUR CRUCIFIER."

I caress her bum-cheeks with both hands and her arse feels so beautiful to my touch, lovely and firm and so smooth. Once again she cries out to me: "LET ME GO."

But I can't hear her - I have switched myself off.

Grabbing one of her bound hands and squeezing her fingers together, I use a pair of Andy's pliers from the garage and grip one of her fingernails as tightly as possible and pull. She screams blue-murder as her nail tears-away from its mounting and I toss it to one side. The end of her finger has split itself open and is leaking blood everywhere, over her lower-back and between her bum-cheeks.

I stare down at what I've done and shout out loud to myself:

"FUCKING HELL."

I grab another finger and twist and bend it backwards. She goes absolutely crazy with pain and terror and wails like a banshee but I don't stop and break her finger, snapping the joint at the knuckle with a crack and causing her screams to hit eleven. She shakes and twitches in extreme, her whole body on fire with energy.

I move down to her feet and hold them both. She tries to kick-out at me and I momentarily lose my balance and I laugh. I slap her bum hard and grab one foot, the right one, placing the cutting section of the pliers at the joint of her little toe. I squeeze the handles together and it digs into her flesh and bone but it doesn't sever her digit completely, just leaving it hanging on by strands of throbbing gristle. I place the tool gently to one side and bite at the join with my perfect teeth, it tasting just like bone but salty and with a hind of cheese. It comes-away with a few chomps and a final tug and then I have it in my grasp.

Turning her over again I move up her frame and gaze into her eyes. They're dead and hollow and are as expressionless as her face so I give her a quick slap to her cheek. She turns to look at me like I'm the Devil herself - maybe I am? With her mouth wide open I plop her severed toe into her gaping hole and push it down her throat with 2-fingers. Shutting her gob I massage her neck, forcing her to swallow her own toe as she coughs and chokes, convulsing in spasmodic motion.

I get to my feet and look at the state of this bitch, laying there all bloody and beaten. How on Earth did this stupid fucking cow ever think she was going to get one over on me?

I spit in her face.

Kneeling by her right-hand side I touch and feel her breasts, squeezing them. Leaning over I kiss them and tongue her nipples in a circular motion. She sobs like a baby and I kiss her right-cheek as I continue to play with her mounds. I move to her right-ear and kiss and stick my pointed tongue down its hole and she hates me. I bite into her earlobe like a vampire and the taste of her blood on my lips and in my mouth drives me insane and I touch my vagina, fingering it hard like a fuck. The soft spongy lobe of her ear comes away easily as I continue to bite the rest of her ear as she screams and wriggles about in terror. My face is covered in her blood and it's sticky and disgusting and I pant and orgasm and cum.

I roll her back over onto her tits and bite her fingers, the bloody one now dried and black. I suck one of her thumbs like a cock and then position it in my mouth side-on. I bite down hard into its meat and she falls into unconsciousness as I chew her digit and then chop it off with the pliers even though she is incoherent to her surrounding nightmare.

I spit out her blood from my mouth and it lands on her bum. Slowly the mess runs down and between her cheeks to her cunt and I savour every beautiful millimetre of its descending motion. It really is a work of art.

Washing my mouth out with vodka I spit the first rinse into her face and swallow the second and third. The nasty liquid sets my blood alight and burns what is left of my heart.

From the kitchen I return to the hallway and plug the machine into the wall-socket over by the old German cabinet and give it a quick whiz. The electric carving knife whines into action and I have another one of her fingers removed in no-time. Still she remains out cold. It's probably just as well, the whole scene is a fucking bloody nightmare. I remove each and every one of her fingers one by one and throw them about the floor willy-nilly - it is disgusting. I have found my Rubicon. Switching off the knife I cut the cable-ties that restrain her wrists with the pliers and roll her over once more onto her back. She looks so peaceful in her stillness and yet there is something else - she has hands but no fingers or thumbs, just stumps of oozing blood.

I slap her face on each alternative side as I try to reawaken her. It takes at least 10 to 15 hits to wake the bloody bitch up when at long fucking last she stirs and starts mumbling more crap at me. I leave her be and just stand back and watch her, checking her reaction. Her movements are animated and disjointed, her confused brain seemingly having no control over her body, although she doesn't cry out in pain for some reason? Slowly it dawns on her that her hands are now free of fingers and she raises them to see. She holds them out and looks at them with terror in her eyes and they are completely bloodied, stained to death forever.

And her hands.

At her hands she stares.

Not believing what her eyes are telling her brain.

She has no fingers.

Her scream is indescribable, beyond terror and pain, beyond the agony of evil. She looks at me like death itself as if to ask me "Why?" I just stand there looking at her and her hands. What is going through her mind right now I wonder?

"WHY WHY WHY?" She sobs at me but I remain silent and just stand there watching her suffer.

She tries to stand up but fails once again as her ankles are still bound together. She leans forward and tries to untie herself but is stymied by the horror of her dilemma - she has no fingers to help herself. She screams and flails and holds her mutilated hands out to me. What does she want? What does she expect me to fucking do now - help her?

Picking up the small crowbar I crack her across the forehead with one blow as I lunge at her. She falls backwards and hits the back of her head once more with a nasty crunching sound that makes me wince once more. She's stunned but not unconscious and her eyelids flicker like mad as her vision is blinded by blood.

I lose control and smash both her kneecaps with the crowbar with deep thuds.

Everything is haywire and nothing makes sense as I'm swallowed by eternity and this moment of living execrable Hell. I throw myself into the fire and kiss the Angel of Death on her lips. The time now is the future and the past all rolled into one and I cannot escape its path.

"HELP ME PLEASE." I cry out but I am beyond any help.

I drop to my knees in tears and let go of the crowbar and it clanks and clatters to the floor, fortunately without damaging my beautiful tiles. I jump on her body and stab the bitch in the stomach with the kitchen knife once again, this time way deeper than before, right up to the hilt of the blade. Her blood-curdling scream echoes around the hallway and I stab her again. I puncture her skin, just a little at first, then thrusting the blade right into her belly as I tear her open.

"I'M GOING TO CRUCIFY YOU ALIVE." I spit at her as she recoils in excruciating agony, completely perplexed by the heinous crimes laid upon her as I cut. She grows tired and begins to expire as the blood flows from her body and pools on the tiled floor. She slips into peace as her destroyed self rejects the reality of its punishment and rests.

I rest also as I need to conserve my energy for the remainder of the night. The time is now 9.14pm.

***

My hands fit around her throat so nicely that it's almost surreal, it's like they were specifically designed for her neck. I squeeze her gently and it feels so good, so cool. I put more pressure on her and at last she starts to splutter and gurgle and I throw her a sinister smile as she chokes, just to let her know how much I'm enjoying myself. I am the audience of death.

"Look at my face for the last time bitch. It's time to say goodbye, so goodbye."

The dichotomy is too great and wide to allow both of us to exist.

She has to die.

She has to.

The hour of death rings out.

I reposition myself over her body to give myself a better angle of attack. I lose my smile and she tries to scream but no sound comes from her mouth as I remorselessly pile it on as her tongue screams in silence from between her teeth. Squeezing her throat ever tighter with both my thumbs on her windpipe, almost cracking her oesophagus and squashing her jugular, her face turns dark red and starts to swell and in an instant I have her totally.

I cannot really describe what is going through my mind at this present moment. I know what I'm doing and why but I somehow can't control it, the Devil within me has taken over my functions. The sensation of power I have over everyone on this fucking stinking Planet overwhelms me and I completely lose control. I don't give a damn about anything or anyone and I never have or will as all the stupid fucking events of my life - the Old Man, Mum, Kate, school, all the morons I've ever worked with, men, women, people in my fucking way, the Government, the Police, shit, fuck, love, hate, death, life, blood, cocks, cunts, breasts and cum - all flash across my vision at the speed of light and I die.

Using my full bodyweight I bear down on her with all the power and energy I possess as her torso twitches beneath me as she desperately clings to her pitiful life. My constraint on her becomes unbearable and I sense her slipping away from me as I starve her brain of oxygen. It is the slow drain into death.

The control I hold over her is all-enveloping, it's like the height of sex multiplied a million times over. She chokes and her face turns red and then blue as I strangle her of life. Her eyes bulge out of their sockets and there's a small cracking sound that stems from her throat as I squeeze her more and tighter followed by an awful gasping sound that emits from her mouth. Her breathing becomes slower and slower and she is mine to take - I own her right to live or die - I am her judge, jury, executioner and her Goddess. I am perfection and there is nothing she can fucking do to stop me. There can be no salvation now.

Her whole body relaxes its muscles as she fades into unconsciousness as she lays there completely motionless. She is not dead, although in reality she always was. Right from the very first time she pissed me off her days on this shitty Planet were numbered from day 1.

I climb off her limp body and lay down next to her, staring at her ghostly face. I stroke her cheek and it feels so soft and lovely. I whisper to her all the nasty, horrible and disgusting mindless things that I'm about to do to her body but she doesn't seem to care, she has no complaint.

On all fours I slowly make my way around my prey like an animal. My whole countenance has become bestial as I view my kill. I sniff her blood and paw and touch her body as I circle her clockwise. I hiss and spit at her like the despicable She-Wolf I have become. I am no-longer human. I snuffle at her face and lick her right-cheek, sensing the taste of her sweat on my beautiful tongue and my gorgeous mouth.

Her blood oozes from around the perimeter of where the blade has penetrated her stomach but not much. I twist its handle in the bloody slot and it begins to flow more freely, much to my delight. She lets out a small gasp of air from her broken mouth as I remove the knife and the blood starts to flow even faster. I insert one of my fingers into the hole and it's warm and wet so I push 2 in and feel around inside her body. I play with her sticky wound as I try to find something inside her to pull out but there's nothing, only wet slimy meat.

I lick her blood from my fingers and it's salty and sticky and it makes me want to retch but I just about take hold of myself and swallow the sick back down. I swipe her protruding collarbone with the crowbar, cracking the right-hand part of it in two. She stirs and moans and I punch her in the mouth. I lash the skin of her upper right-arm, slicing a nice clean groove of about 15-centimetres along its length.

She's half-awake now as I start to slice off her kneecaps with the electric knife, its stainless-steel serrated blades making light work of her flesh and bones, instigating instant paralysis. She screams a noise of pure horror, the diabolical black sound of death. Her scream is so fucking mad that I have to stop cutting and punch her again, this time in the side of the head to shut her the fuck up.

I puff and pant as I try to inhale more air. I am delirious with death and want to kill myself along with her. I want to slice my neck open and die alongside my bitch and be discovered by the pigs in a sea our intermixed congealed blood.

I chop around her ankles, severing her Achilles-tendons, sending a scything shudder of pain throughout her lithe body. Blood squirts out all over the hallway, covering my nakedness. I desperately try not to have any splash over the stairs carpet as getting that out would be nigh-on impossible, not to mention incriminating to yours truly.

I start to feel really sick again, the psychical kind, but this time I can't hold it within me any longer. I puke myself over her, over the nightmare horror that I've instigated, a diabolical razz of lumpy vodka splatting forwards into the wound to her belly. It is repugnant in the extreme. I wash my mouth out with the last of the evil Russian liquid and then wait a few minutes for it to reinvigorate me, at least to some degree anyway.

I stand over her looking like the dead shadow of my former self and she looks back at me and whimpers. I would love to know what it is she's thinking. This whole event is so unreal and as she stares at me I give her my final speech:

"You are nothing Mellis which is why you must die, so those more deserving can live in peace, like myself for instance. So if you believe in God, prepare to meet thy maker as I prey to the Devil in the hour of your death. If it makes you feel any better Mellis I'll even let you say a little prayer for yourself. Not that it's going to help you, there is no-one out there to hear your feeble words of mercy. So go now Mellis. Go now and enter into the dark. Hush now, do not fear the symmetry of death, the succour of ultimate oblivion. Complete the sequence unto the pattern of life and prepare yourself for death my bitch – you cow-cunt. You've had your chance, now it's my turn."

I am swallowed by destruction as the fear of my past, present and my future has frozen me to the spot. I know I have to go on, there can be no turning back from this point, not now. I laugh like Hell at her downfall and I cry.

Sitting on her pelvis I repeatedly jab the kitchen-knife into her small breasts, bursting their firmness. I stab and cut them as then I have the first one removed, detaching it with ease, and then the second. I cry in horror as I arch my beautiful body backwards, holding her severed bloody breasts in one hand and the knife in the other and I scream out loud:

"FUCKING CUNT IN HELL."
My entire head, including all my gorgeous hair, my hands, arms and shoulders are painted red from her blood, the horrid mess dribbling down my body to my beautiful full and firm breasts and beyond.

I am a nightmare vision in its purist form and I dance on her body with my trophies of hate as I rub my voracious bloodied cunt over her fuck.

I lob her tits behind me, leaving them for the maggots to feed upon. Slowly I crawl up her ripped torso, sitting directly on top of the leaking wound to her stomach. The wetness of the hole smears against my cunt-lips and it feels so fucking good that I cum in seconds - OH MY LOVE!

My eyes almost pop out of their sockets as I fall forward and in a frenzy I cut her face beyond recognition in a flim-flam of swooshing arm and blade. She recoils in agony but has no defence to my action. It's not like she can scratch my eyes out can she?

There must have been a sudden realisation that I was now actually going to kill her that raced through her feeble mind as suddenly she starts lashing out at me with her chopped and bloody stumps, striking my face and my beautiful breasts. Her desire and will to live conspire against me as she battles to survive, thumping me and thrashing about under the weight of my body. I smash the left-side of her face, her cheekbone, with the crowbar, knocking her senseless and quiet. The peace is beautiful.

I grab her top lip with my right-hand and cut her, it peeling away remarkably easy until I have it all in my hand detached - wiping away her smile, wiping away her face. The bottom lip is similarly removed and I joke with them, placing each lip on my breasts, glueing them in place with her sticky blood - it actually looks like my nipples are wearing red hats! I laugh on the outside that is my image and cry on the inside, the part of me that is not "someone" but "something" evil and terrifying.

I am possessed. I strike blow after never-ending blow to her head, destroying her skull into a gnarly mess. I hit her from side to side with the crowbar, inflicting massive internal haemorrhaging to her brain. I feel my own facial features becoming as distorted as hers as I hit her repeatedly, the destruction of the bitch mirroring the destruction of my sanity.

The air supply to her brain diminishes by the second as I crack at her and she slides into non-existence. With every blow comes an overwhelming sense of release and relief. After all the years of pain, torment, hurt, disappointments, arrogance, bullshit and death, maybe only now can I move on. I have to. I have to do something.

I stop and stand.

It is all over.

I look down at this "thing" beneath me. She is my creation, her naked body strewn before me in abstract paralysis. It lays there alone, its nerve-endings twitching their final death-throes before extinction as her whole frame gives-up its life.

She lays there motionless in death. And there. It is done. Life has turned into death.

SHE IS DEAD.

I have killed her. ME, no-one else. Not you, ME. I have taken her life away from her and it feels so fucking good and everything is clear now. She has passed on to eternity. As she dies a single tear forms in the corner of her right-eye and then rolls down her cheek, falling to the tiled floor below. It's a poignant moment in this time but also meaningless - I just don't care.

I desperately need a drink but I can't go into the living-room to get some more vodka from the bar as my feet are as bloody as Hell and I don't want to ruin my beautiful carpet. Instead I head to the fridge in the kitchen and crack open a bottle of chilled lager, taking a large gulp. The coldness of the liquid slides down my gullet like ice, spiking my nerves and giving me a renewed sense of being alive and I feel so fucking great - but also dead at the same time.

I am both a Queen and a King and you are all my servants.

I love you all to do with as I WANT.

I snap the cervical region of her neck, shattering her vertebrae and discs of cartilage, exploding them into fragments. I remove her head with at least 10-chops of the electric carving knife. It whines in protest as it hits bone but eventually it saws its way completely through. Surprisingly - once more - there's not much blood emulating from either her severed head or her neck, maybe due to the fact that her heart is no-longer pumping blood around her body - who knows? - who cares?

Switching the machine off I hold her detached head above my own for all the World to see my power. It starts to drip its contents over the floor and I bring it closer to me to make the droplets of blood and shit fall onto my beautiful firm breasts. I drop it with a thud onto the black and white - and now red - tiled hall floor. Just for a laugh I give it a good hard kick with my right-foot and it rolls across the smooth surface in a kind-of elliptical motion, almost over to the double front doors. The action is both hilarious and horrific at the same time.

This whole event was a meaningless death to a meaningless life - that of a race-traitor.

∗∗∗

My facial muscles twitch in reaction to the horror being fed to my eyes as I transform into death itself with the predilection of the eternal being. This is the madness of being me as I split myself apart.

I stand alone and naked, covered from head to toe in her blood, some of it now a darker shade of red due to it having already dried upon my body as my brain is caught in a maelstrom whirlpool of colour, light and noise.

I am no-longer human from this moment on.

My body is pumped-full of hyper-energy as it screams at itself. My mind is drugged to overload at the thrill of death, of removing another humans life from their soul.

The intense realisation of what I'm about to undertake next is suddenly activated. Can this actually be real? If it is then I must see it through, there can be no turning back now. It's a grisly and perverse task that has to be undertaken, there is simply no other way for it. Everything has turned red as the blood drips into my eyes and it's so fucking horrendous I don't want to think about it let alone talk about it and I don't know where I am or what's happening to me. The scene is as fantastic as it is unreal as I stand there gazing at her flayed corpse. The atmosphere is one of pure unadulterated Hell and there is nothing I can do to stop it going any further.

She looks down at her body as I hold her severed head above the hideous mess, a miss-mash of pure horror and pure joke. It is disgusting.

What is left of her face is frozen in petrified elegance. I gaze into her dead eyes and they stare back at me from Hell and I gasp. It freaks me and I almost collapse to the floor, down into the remains of her once pretty body. I run my fingers over the death-mask that was once her face. It just doesn't seem real, it's more like a lump of rubber than someone's head.

Kneeling down on the floor I take my knife to her skin and begin lacerating the connection between it and the meat below. Up under her jaw on either side I cut and detach and then peel back the skin to her face. It comes away surprisingly easy and within 20-minutes or so I have it fully removed. At arms length before me I clutch at her torn and severed skin and I sit there and admire my work as I have gone way above and beyond my own expectations. This ritual is not born out of despair or redemption, it exists because she tried to fuck with my life. I jiggle it about trying to make it talk but she doesn't answer back any more - she has no mouth.

I place her face over one of my perfect breasts - the right-one - and I'm shocked by how much my tit looks like her, the fullness of my peach giving shape and mass to her thin skin. I stand and hand the limp and lifeless mask over my vagina and laugh in horror as I see my beautiful cunt peer through the gaping hole that was once her mouth.

Obviously my next step is to put it over my own face, just for the sheer Hell of it, and it feels wet and sticky and smells of blood and makes me feel slightly claustrophobic. I dance and gyrate about like a fucking twat pretending to be her, coming out with statements like:

"Look at me, I is a nigger-loving white whore."

"I only suck black cock cos I is a fucking race-traitor."

"You want jerk-chicken brother?"

"Look at the way I walk, I can't walk proper in shoes man."

"Is it cos I is black?"

"I is a innocent nigger-bitch. I ain't done nuttin wrong see, know what I is saaaaayin?"

"You gotta respect me cos I is a big black jiggaboo innit."

I quickly to put a stop to this nonsense as I suddenly grow bored with all this racist black talk. It disgusts me down to my pure white bones.

I bend over and down and put my right-hand into the hole in her belly, right inside her body into the solidified mess and we become one. It still feels warm and somehow inviting, a bit like warm jelly, and it spouts a single tubular squirt of red goo from the wound as I press into it harder.

I crouch down on my haunches and push my hand into it further but I slip on the blood-covered floor and fall on top of her headless body with a splat - FUCKING HELL! My beautiful body slurps and squishes in her mess as I sink down into it, becoming immersed in a thick pool of meat and it's wet and somehow sexy as I'm suspended prone on her impermeably ripped torso.

I take the remains of her left-hand and place it between my legs, her wet meat against the wet meat of my vagina. I rub it against my awaiting labia and throbbing hot clit and pant heavily at the revolting degressive sensation of necrophilia. I jerk my cunt and cum a blind orgasm as we squelch together as one being - it is both beautiful and horrific at the same time.

WHAT THE FUCK AM I DOING?

Extracting myself from her shit I sit up and rest myself on her remains. A massive wave of power surges through my beautiful body and I revel in every second of this terrifying act, it driving me on to do more and worse and I can't stop myself, the brakes won't work. My bones start to ache violently as I squat there sitting in her red shit, the cold lifelessness of her body, quiet and still in execution. I am literally sitting in a pool of blood, it measuring some 2-metres in diameter - it's actually quite beautiful and I can even see my reflection in it clearly, the reflection of Hell in the form of the gorgeous young woman that is me.

I become embroiled with whatever manifests itself before my eyes. I fear that I have lost my mind and there is no-one to help me and with the middle-finger of my left-hand I write my name in the sticky red mess before me on the floor:

SARAH

A furious wave of adrenalin fires through my body like a high-speed ride to destruction, a nasty black rage of inner-turmoil that fuels the path of no return. I wreak havoc with her remains with lecherous depravity, my heart pumping on the verge of a conniption as chemical warfare explodes in my brain. I split her wide open down the centreline of her body and it is all so incredibly easy. I cut her down to her internal plumbing and retch at the vision of gore in the midst of perversity and bloody furore.

Between the remains of her breasts I expose her thorax. I smash and dismember her ribcage until there is nothing left. With my bare hands I start to rip and tear at her intestines and internal membranes, disembowelling her. I pull them and they come away with ease, all except where they join so I have to use the knife once again. I begin slicing her entrails and pull out a great big long length of it, there's fucking miles and miles of the shit - it's never-ending and it's disgusting.

I hold her eviscerated tubing aloft in both hands as it drips blood and goo onto my face in splashes. It goes in my eyes and my mouth and up my nose and I breathe-in the smell of her blood into my lungs. I stretch her entrails between my clenched fists and grip them in my teeth and scream like fucking and fuck and cock and cunt and cum and I am DEAD.

Tearing apart her insides - her stomach, heart, lungs, kidneys, liver, pancreas - I splatter her remains about all over the floor - my beautiful tiled floor - in a crazy mental illuminating fresco of blinding light, a pyrotechnical montage of colour that erupts within my mind like from a hallucinogenic concoction.

I have become lost in the maze of death. The cataclysmic atmosphere surrounding me has destabilized time itself and I no-longer exist in your dimension.

My perversity is my desire as I fuck her remains in a violent blitzkrieg of stabbing and horror. I spit at her my mouthful of human entrails and words of Hell on Earth:

"YOU FUCKING CUNT BITCH."

"CUNTING NIGGER SLAG."

"WHORE BITCH FUCKER."

"FUCKING SHIT CUNT CUNT."

Standing with knife in hand I survey the mess as its creator. I piss myself down my legs onto the floor, it tinkering on the surface and making funny small round yellow splashes in the sticky blood. I plod over to where I kicked her head and pick it up by the remains of her hair. Squatting down I let her kiss my perfect tits with the remnants of her mouth. Laying down in her blood I open my legs to her and let her lap at my vagina. I immediately begin to lose control at this mindless sensation and scream with both pleasure and terror, rubbing her broken head against my minge. I feel her nose against my clit and I yelp with love and ecstasy as it makes me cum - I LOVE IT.

Grabbing the knife I gouge her eyes out of their sockets but it's not as easy as it's made out to be, they're held in place tightly by tendons or whatever they are as well as the optic nerve at the back. I have to jostle with the knife to get inside it but eventually I make it and out they come with a squelch. They're actually way-bigger than you would expect them to be and they immediately start to freak me out. I play with them like a bastard, juggling them and making them look at each other for a joke. I insert them one after the other into my cunt-hole and leave them squished in there for safe keeping.

I try to smash her skull open by pounding it on the marble floor but I don't want to crack the tiles - they mean more to me than her fucking head does - so I reluctantly give up. Instead I hit it a million times with my crowbar until finally I win, splitting her cranium in 2, its sharp broken edges piercing the soft grey matter of her brain within. I pull her skull apart with my bloody fingers to expose her brain completely and it looks just like a dirty cauliflower - grey and beyond disgusting. I try to take it out but it seems tied-in somehow so I have to cut it out to remove it, slopping it out onto the floor.

With my knife still in hand I touch and finger and caress the soft outer folds of her labia. I pull at them the hardest I can, stretching them to breaking point as I then slice and cut around them, removing her outer lips as one. I lick and tongue at them, making a noise like I'm actually eating her vagina out. I stick my tongue out to a point and hang her severed labia upon it and try to twirl it around in the air but it flies off and lands in her pool of blood. Picking it back up I slide my right-hand through its opening and work it up my arm, upcycling it to become an armband - Ha!

Returning to the mess that I've created I proceed to remove the rest of her vagina, I don't know why, it just seems to be the next logical/illogical thing to do. I jab the knife into her meat and try to cut it out the best I can but it's so fucking hard - why is everything so fucking hard? - that it takes me ages to complete the task but eventually I have her entire reproductive organ in my blood-soaked hand, including its tiny little fallopian tubes et al as it drips its contents down my arm as I hold it aloft. I stab at it to rip it apart and it splits in 2, spilling more goo and stuff over my gorgeous legs. Suddenly I notice something weird within her womb, a dark shape attached to the inside.

OH MY FUCK - IT'S A BABY!

It's a human in miniature and dead before it's alive - a little black horror! - the fucking bitch was pregnant! That nigger of hers had impregnated her with his evil black seed! It's disgusting and I can't bring myself to look at it even though I do.

FUCKING SHIT AND CUNT IN HELL!

I kick out at the remains of this "thing" that I dare not ever call human - this mixed-race mongrel that would have spelled the death of my own race and I damn it to Hell for evermore. Fucking nigger-loving whore, she should have been fucking sterilised. Bitches like her should not be allowed to have kids, not half-breeds anyway.

I lunge at her and bite deeply into her right-thigh and chew her skin and meat. It draws little blood so I stab her and tear through her rectus femoris muscle to where her hole of glory once resided.

I attack the lower extremities of her body, slicing her thighs with the electric saw. It almost stalls as it grinds against her bones but I push on as is my WANT and I remove both her legs. I chop them again at her knees and throw all 4 extraneous pieces away over by the front door. The lower half of her body lays in total destruction, the difference between her and the floor now indistinguishable.

Light surges through my mind in a technicolor explosion that ignites behind my lightning eyes. I chop her up slice by slice in a ruthless barbaric frenzy of dismembering stabbing motion and cuts that are both frighting and hysterical at one and the same time.

I methodically remove each piece bit by bit until she is no-longer human, just pieces of meat on the floor - my poor fucking floor! Rigor mortis has no chance of settling-in now. My nostrils flair as I search for oxygen, inverting my brain. My lust for life is intensified as turbulence swirls throughout my head, my brain spinning in ultra-light as it disintegrates in ecstasy and dark theatrics.

I cut her amid anarchic pandemonium, it's almost a religious experience as well as being completely senseless as I saw her remains to pieces. I dispose of her deltoid muscle with pure ease, her pectoral cross-brace already destroyed. I annihilate her solar-plexus and destroy what's left, leaving the bits held together by paralysed veins.

The hard white point of her tail-bone protrudes from the end of her spinal column, itself broken to pieces, with her spinal-cord chopped-up like discarded elastic. Her pelvis sits quietly on its own over to one side, awaiting further adventures in future time.

There - I have finished.

My stomach starts to churn as I survey the damage and I can't hold it within me once again. I begin convulsing into the mess with gut-wrenching spasms as my insides eject themselves. I wearily rise to my feet, standing in her mess, the mess that was once Mellis. It is the nastiest vision yet to be conceived and she is actually decaying before my very eyes, the desecration of this thing that was supposedly once "human."

I stand in total and complete silence, there is not a sound to be heard - nothing. I stand amongst the apocalyptic nightmare of fragmented bones, meat, brain, blood, veins, sinews and sick. I want to puke again but I have no more within me as the smell penetrates my mind - she smells like shit. I pirouette on the ball of my right-foot in her blood, an abstract crazy-paving of colour - it is a sombre scene from Hell.

I desperately want to shower and to try and get this smell out of my nostrils but it would be a waste of time, I still have to clean all this mess up first, somehow? I try to tread carefully through the organs littering the floor as I need to pee again but I don't make it, I slip and fall arse-over-tit into the remnants of torn flesh, each piece indistinguishable from the next - Fucking Hell. Instead I piss myself in her blood and then play shapes with it using my fingers - Ha Ha Ha!

My beautiful hallway resembles a fucking abattoir rather than the splendid piece of architecture that it was before. I play with small lumps of meat stripped from arms and legs and toes and fingers that lay all around me, mixed-in with small hills of clotted blood. Her whole infrastructure has been butchered to pieces and totally destroyed.

FUCKING HELL.

WHAT HAVE I DONE?

***

It is getting darker by the second and I'm lonely, and as the Moon grows full, my lust for fuck grows stronger. I step outside into the garden, out into the solidified sunlight and the last remnants of the warm Summer night air and the rejuvenation if its freshness overwhelms me as I breathe in its love.

I am naked but I'm not. My skin is no-longer as it once was as tonight I'm wearing nothing but the dried-on splashes of HER blood. My make-up is destroyed by its redness whilst my perfume has also been replaced by the stench of her life-juice. My hair is still tied up as before but is matted with blood, goo and shit and I fear that it may be ruined forever.

I sniff and smell the air surrounding me, it is sweet and luscious as the breeze of the crisp night begins to move in. It reinvigorates my lungs and my blood - MY BLOOD. And yet there is death in the air, it surrounding me like the love I have for myself and I fuck it. I can actually feel the Earth moving beneath my feet and I love and then die once more.

The sense of relief that it's all over overwhelms me and I laugh and cry at what I've done. What have I done? Everything has changed. Nothing can stand in my way, not now. Things will never be the same ever again now that I've dipped my hand into cold water.

I call for my Mum to help me through this never-ending night but she doesn't come, her spirit has gone into hiding because of my action, ashamed to face me or even comfort me in my desperation to exist. As ever, my existence is purely solipsistic, trapped within the black shadow of myself, forever trying to dispel the spectres around me.

The night stars shine down on my skin and love me, gasping in wonder at my pulchritude. They twinkle their brilliance at me in the dead of night as if they are wishing me well, their beams bouncing off my body in perfect synthases as I give myself to the darkness.

The white-light reflects off the mournful Moon as the Sun disappears completely, leaving me encased in its magic glow. The sky turns as black as death itself. I have accepted the darkness as I have accepted my death. I am the supreme Earth Mother and yet I am nothing - not dead nor alive.

My action has left me standing on the edge of civilisation and has lead me to the dawn of a new age in my existence on this planet. It has strengthened my awareness of death. I don't fear it, I'm just no-longer scared of it as I bask in my new era of tranquillity.

I scream to my leader in joyous rapture, holding my arms aloft in celebration. I am alive and she is dead. I really can't believe that I actually did it, that that nigger-loving bitch is no-longer of this earth and that she's been vanquished - unto where?

But what will become of me now? I am lost to the World, stuck in eternal damnation forever. I am beyond human, banished into anti-time where no-one exists except myself. I have hereby resigned from the human race. I am number-1 on the podium. I am iconoclastic unto myself, the sole survivor of my own personal holocaust.

The bats come out to play with me, swooping about me as I love. I play along with them like I'm possessed as they brush against my naked body with their love.

In the night I am reborn, reborn with a new inner chaos. I accept it and run with it, literally. The Dragon of Death stands before me and holds out its clawed paw to shake. I take it and run but can never escape its chase, not now - I have gone too far this time. The spines and flapping wings of the serpent and his cunning ways are always behind me.

I run across the garden and laugh as I cry with the Moon reflecting monochrome my image as I shout:

"I'M ALIVE."

"I'M ALIVE."

"I'M ALIVE."

I am insane with being alive and I cry.

This night feels like a thousand nights long. Maybe it has no ending at all and that I'm stuck in my own time forever more, forever condemned to live in eternal darkness, coated in the blood of my enemy - HER.

I revel in nature as I crouch down and touch the grass, interacting with it, sensing the wetness of the early night-time dew between my fingers. It feels so pure and clean and I fall in love with it. I am nature and nature is me. We are in harmony. We have become as one.

The branches of my beautiful Willow tree reach out to me as my beautiful arms caress them back, honouring its power with Shamanistic love, my sylvan lover. Pulling at its leaves a few of them come away in my hand and I eat them. They're dry and bitter but I chew and swallow them anyway, absorbing the trees life-force spirit and its memories. It is the forbidden tree of knowledge.

I embrace the tree with my naked body and drink-in the love from its oxygen-giving life-giving trunk. The bark feels so good against my naked body as I melt into its surface, becoming a tree in anthropomorphic form, in appearance, spirit and in mind, strengthening my connection with Mother Earth.

The tree and I are one and the same - I become SARAHTREE.

I hug my Willow like a long-lost love, pawing and caressing and scratching its surface as it does to me. I surrender myself unto it with all my heart and soul - my love, my darling tree. I squeeze my firm breasts against the bark and wrap my right-leg around her trunk and fuck. The tree shakes as I make love to her, rustling its leaves until finally I tighten and cum in rapture. I feel the warm sensation of my juice trickle down my left-leg and drip onto the grass and fallen leaves below as we exhale a sigh of ecstasy together.

Crouching down I scoop-up a cupped handful of fallen wet leaves, engaging with life and nature. I embrace them to my body and love, they clinging to my skin with the glue of my cum. More leaves adorn my head as I throw another handful over myself as I laugh, they sticking to my face, my beautiful breasts, my body and my long beautiful legs - now is my time.

I'm suddenly startled by a noise behind me and I turn quickly to face its source - a gorgeous fox with eyes of fire and fur as red as the blood I've been soaked with.

I move slowly towards her to say "Hello" but the very second I flinch she's gone, away into the remainder of the night to be with her lover.

The hours pass as fleeting moments, traversing through the vagrancies of time as I dance and fuck and love, the warning of the midnight sky as it leads me into the start of another new day. The morning comes around far too soon as the day breaks and everyone awakes. Not for me though, I've been up all night, apart from the odd doze here and there. I cried myself to sleep on the hall floor. It was so hard - both aspects. I was unable to sleep proper in fear that the ghosts might rip my head off. That, and my dream of death, of meat, and of blood and horror.

The cool morning air recharges my soul - that's if I still have one? - and refills my lungs. The shadowy atmospheres of light touch my naked red skin, my whole frame camouflaged in dried blood, highlighting the thing I have become - anti-human. I am now different to other people, not that I was ever much like them in the first place! I fear the worst and the best is still yet to come. Fate will never be rid of me, I will always be its plaything, protected by my insular subterfuge.

I catch the new-day air in my nostrils, it's sweet and clean and pure and fills my lungs to maximum. I taste the saltiness of blood on my lips and shock myself of its origin - the blood of the dead bitch.

Can all this really be true? Just what have I done?

I bend over in all my naked glory to smell the roses at the edge of the mini-lake, their gorgeous heady fragrance hitting my brain in an instant and it is so glorious that I lose control of myself. I'm transported back to my childhood as a little girl running through a field of bluebells on a beautiful sunny day, laughing as Mum watches on, she heavily pregnant with my future estranged sister Kate. I'm so happy at the scene that a single tear forms in the corner of one eye, its purity turning to Hell as it becomes tainted with the rejuvenated blood of my prey.

I desperately need to cleanse myself, to rid myself of the smell of her. Slowly and carefully I walk from the edge of the mini-lake and become as liquid myself as I submerge into its cool water. I am immune to the chill and begin to wash myself in its fluid. I immerse my beautiful body completely and it feels wonderful as the water penetrates me and I shudder with excitement and almost cum as it takes me to heaven and I WANT it all and more and fuck.

I start to swim breast-stroke along its length, under the Japanese bridge and over to the other end. Clambering out up the opposing bank I rise and stand in vainglorious infamy as I laugh to myself at my fortune of being me in this time and place right now - HA HA HA!

I fall into the bottomless Great Pit of death and the lake of fire, surrounded by the purgatory of my own inner soul and incomprehensible chaos, corruption, anarchy and despair beyond all hope in this place of perfect misery and utter darkness, cast into this infernal pit of bondage. About me are the Damned, the passengers of Death - ethereal spirits swirling about my head, terrorising me with their bleeding eyes and malignant hanged severed heads suspended by bloodied hair. It is Pandemonium and the Palace of Satan and Death, a combustion chamber of Hell filled with dismal hate and wild love.

I become lost in the Dark Wood of Dante's *Inferno* and emerge into a new wasteland of the lost such as I where I find myself in Loves Lost Garden. There is no fear within me as I wander through the accursed dead as they all desperately try to spawn and spunk me, infecting me with their infection, all wanting to fuck me pregnant, the transgenders - women with cocks.

It is the dead that fear me as I am now beyond death and beyond life, surrounded by The Divine Comedy of my past, present and future.

A hideous cacophony of horror fills my eyes as the sweet pungent smell of fuck fills my nostrils but I stand firm amongst the blood and creeping impure flesh in this orgy of nakedness. My desire to live overthrows the touch of the dead on my person as they all grab my beautiful naked body with a thousand tongues licking me all over as I in turn touch the creeping things, the turgid and dismal wretches. My Guardian Angel guides me and tricks me at every turn, tricking me into betraying my England, trying to lure me with the sound of screaming nitrous engines - he is not to be trusted but I know him too well and win him over. He tries to take the remains of my soul and I laugh at his book of magic as I set it afire to ashes.

Crawling out from the darkness and my witch tormentors, Cerberus bites me with one of his 3-heads but he fails to stop me and I love him and fuck. His creeping sounds of passion turns to screams of ecstasy as I suck him and he collapses from within as he cums in my mouth - he is MY victim.

I leave this miserable place of Hell and join another, a new Hell in a new time of my existence, my beautiful body covered in the potent seed of death from Paradise. I feel no pain, the blood does not flow through my veins. The burning walls that surround me fall into the cold sea, a sea of cock and cunt, shocking my lifeless followers as they dissolve into dust and time and the everlasting flames of Hell on this Sabbath day.

I abandon this diabolical veil of tears and despair as I am reborn from time analogical. I am a butterfly transforming from my chrysalis, emerging out into a new World ever more powerful than before, ready to face whatever it may bring and nothing. And yet I am still Sarah, I am still me, under the guidance of the White God, the Fuhrer to my Queen self. I set him free and we embrace before the creation of a better World for the Master Race, my immortal soul protected by my kindred scorpions and Aryan Angels.

I stand naked as the hedonistic aberration I always have and will be. I am death in female form. I scream into the morning sky a scream of Death and Life as I am reborn as the reincarnation of the Goddess *Astarte.*

Dropping down on all fours onto the grass like a dog I insert 2-fingers onto my vagina and pleasure myself with frantic motion. I pant heavily as I breathe through my mouth, my breasts beneath me jiggling-around like crazy udders. My heartbeat tears-along at 1000mph as I feel myself about to explode and in seconds I freeze solid as I cum and ejaculate my love and moan:

"AH OH UGH UGH UGH UGH UGH AAAAAAH."

Slowly I get to my feet and try to regain some kind of consciousness, my head feeling light from the effect of masturbation. From the spiritual cleansing of the water I have homologated into a new me, a transcendental journey into a new time and era where negative reality has been put aside.

I am the new transmission in my own mind and body. I can fly and swim and love and sex. From this I will evolve into something else. I can be whatever I WANT to be once again.

My own self from the past meets me in the present to try and strangle me, to try and stop me reaching my future, my now, to stop me suffering any more pain but I fail and I love myself. I am killed by my own death and reborn into tranquillity as one.

The ground disappears from under my feet and I launch myself into the air. I am flying through the morning sky like a bird. I am a bird, an avatar, flying on the wind of perfect eternity, beyond the perfect green land of the Earth. Wherever you are, I am also. I am your God and your Devil intertwined in a nightmare vision of one. I am all around you in spirit as the spirits fly about me. I am YOU, and you are ME. Everything is distorted and twisted. I look around me and I see nothing, nothing at all - no trees, no sky, no ground, no water, no house, nothing - only myself.

I stand alone in the blackness of space, this girl, Sarah, alone in my fantasy World of visions of Hell and fucking and shit and cum. The Black Angels caress my beautiful body as the morning chill envelopes my nakedness. I love them as they love me, the spectral entities and the filthy lucre, running their evil hands and spunking cocks of sin over my gorgeous body, enticing me to return to death, to take the ladder down to Hell.

The Devil's Gatekeeper refuses me entry to Gate Number 9, forcing me to outlive my existence amongst the mortal, the likes of you dear reader - my special friend.

Satan calls upon me and I shout back at him and his Angel helpers and the brilliant Moon:

"TAKE ME IN YOUR ARMS AND HOLD ME. EMBRACE ME WITH YOUR HATE AND FUCK ME."

I don't fear him at all, on the contrary, from this moment on he must fear ME. On the day of exhumation and the resurrection of the dead, they will come to me for judgement as Death begs me to:

"COME AND SEE."

I join them, becoming the fifth horseman, a combination of the others as that is what I am, was, and always will be in this so-called "life", condemned to live on this Earth in the here and now to make the best of it in any way I see fit.

This seminal vision that is me is now forever stronger. I am above you all. I have survived the Seventh Circle of Hell. I have wiped clean the stigmata from my hands, setting myself free to roam the World in contentment and peace amongst the dead.

I was always dead.

I was always alive.

Hell and damnation surround my soul. My feelings for humanity were always atavistic at the best of times anyway and I laugh in the twisted face of the Black Goat of Hell as Satan grips my body from within and I whisper to him:

"Cum into me my Lord of Darkness your unholy seed of fuck."

My devotion to him knows no limit - I am the *SLIVED-ETACOVDA* with the body of perfection. I am the Queen of my hegemonic state, the supreme being in this twisted, inhuman World. I shall conquer this Earth and boil the sea and crack and split the lands in 2 as the so-called "worthy ones" kiss the feet of the graven image of their fake God full of eternal joy. I will now remain condemned to an undead state of eternal weeping, wailing and gnashing of teeth as punishment for my own doing.

By my divine right, as leader of the Fallen Angels and Sylphs, cast out of humanity for my sins, I am provided with the key to my own death, guided unto it by my love of *NUARDA*.

It is the prefect disaster, a quantum leap so fast that I once again meet myself on my return journey back to Earth a million parsecs away as I travel through the vortex of time, its spiralling waves spinning me out of control but I make it and love. I smile at myself as I come face to face with my own vision and we kiss and fuck as we make Heaven and Hell collide.

I fall from the sky into insignificance and here I am once more -

DER WEISSE ENGEL - SARAH

***

I break down and begin weeping and wailing in agonizing pain. I squat down on my haunches in her stagnated blood and destroy myself amidst 1-million uncontrollable teardrops.

What have I become?

How the fuck did I end up like this?

My lungs are filled with the acrid smell of her guts, the stench permeating the very core of my body and soul - it's fucking horrendous. I unstick myself from the remains and swagger off to the ground-floor bathroom, leaving her to rot in Hell. I gaze at the reflection of my disgusting self in the mirror and the shameful expression upon my face. My stomach churns and I get the horrible sensation of hunger within my belly. I really must eat something but I'm just not in the mood for any breakfast.

My mind and my evil thoughts collapse within itself as I degenerate lower than I ever thought I could possibly go. I begin to wonder what it tastes like, her meat? I know what her pussy tastes like but this is on a different level. But am I really that far gone that I could actually eat the flesh of another human? Am I really that fucking sick?

I shower like I've never showered before, scrubbing my skin raw to remove all the remaining blood from the hidden crevices of my beautiful body. I watch the swirl of red and black shit disappear down the waste-hole in the shower floor and strangely it gives me a renewed sense of hope in that what I'm doing actually means something. I dry myself off using one of my old towels, a shitty brown-coloured one, before I head back to the mess.

Picking up the remains of one of her arms I head to the kitchen and chuck her meat onto the central island work-surface. I try to peel her skin away from her upper-arm with my fingers but for some reason it's not easy, I pull at it but it slips from my grasp due to the blood. In the end I try to saw it off with a kitchen-knife but it's a mess and I can't do it properly and in frustration I stab at it. I run upstairs and back down again with a sharper tool but her meat still won't come off even with one of Andy's old cut-throat razors. What the fuck is up with it?

"They" say that human flesh supposedly tastes like chicken but I wonder? I fry some in a pan in the kitchen with a little rapeseed oil and feed some to Eva first and she likes it so much she wolfs it down like there's no tomorrow and calls for more - what a weird cat?

I throw her another piece and fork another for myself. I am numb to what I'm doing as I place the meat in my mouth and chew. I have no brain. No thoughts. No vision. I am nothing. It tastes like a cross between pork and lamb but not as salty, actually a little bit sweeter and with the fibrous consistency of beef, although not as tender or juicy as I swallow and have another piece. With the small piece of meat eaten between the 2 of us I add some water to the pan to soak and then return to the mess in the hallway, asphyxiated by the smell and taste on my buds.

I guess the question now is what to do with all this shit that's all over my beautiful floor? I start sorting through the detritus, separating the things I can use from the things that need to be destroyed. I collect a small pile of meat and her pelvis over to one side from the carnage before me, putting the rest of the remains in thick black plastic bin-liners. The next thing I need to do is clear-up all the thick blood somehow? I go and fetch a couple of buckets from the utility room in the basement as well as an armful of old rags and begin wiping-up the horror. It takes fucking ages to get anywhere and I wonder if I'll ever reach the end and get my beautiful floor back to as it once was?

Eva comes to be nosey once again, plodding her little feet and toes through a thin layer of residue blood and goo. She immediately backs away and runs off though, licking her wet paws over by the foot of the stairs. Seeing her do this injects yet more madness into my brain and I lean forward and down, placing my right-hand in a wet patch of her blood. I bring it up to my face and stare at it in amazement as it runs in smooth uniform rivulets down my hand and my arm to my elbow. It looks like I'm wearing one long red glove.

I rub the sticky redness over my breasts and it feels so good that it makes me giggle. I play with my nipples and my piercings and then rub some more on my face, marking my sharp cheekbones like an ancient warrior princess. I paint my belly with red lightning flashes and then move down lower, smearing my vagina with the scarlet juice. I insert 2-sticky fingers into myself and touch the bump of my clitoris and I pant like a fuck. I don't wank myself though and just play with my lips and my bean, using the blood of the bitch as sex-lube. Using my right-hand I wipe up another small pool of blood and lick it tentatively and then drink it - it's fucking awful - so salty that it makes me want to puke but there's something else in there that I can taste, I don't know what it is but its disgusting. I spit out all I can and flush the rest out with a cold lager from the fridge - what a fucking nightmare!

I return to the scene as bloodied as I was before, encased in gore and shit, and continue with the mopping-up process. I have most of it done by mid-morning but some of the blood has seemingly become ingrained in the marble, especially where the tiles join. Scouring around in the garage I find several cans of brake-cleaner amongst Andy's collection of cleaning, solvent, oils and other strange cans of stuff on the shelf. The cleaner works a treat but stinks like Hell, it smells like some kind-of nasty acid or something and quickly starts to make me feel a bit dizzy.

Finally the floor is back to its old self as the last residue of the bitch is wiped away. I chuck the soiled rags in the plastic bags, then hide them themselves in the garage for the time being - I'll deal with them later. I shower once more under the flow of warm water, not too hot as the temperature outside is already above average for this time of the year, making the air thick already. I don't bother with any clothes for the rest of the day, I no-longer have any need for them - they do not exist today.

Back in the kitchen I attempt to start stripping the remains of the bitch's meat from her bones although firstly I have to tackle her dirty bloody pelvis. I find the largest pot I have, a big copper one that the bone just about fits into. I try to strip the few strands of meat and muscle off of it but the time it's taking to remove all the flesh from the bones is bloody ridiculous and I can't carry on like this, I have to find an easier and quicker method. In the end I give up, it's just no use - it's too bloody difficult. I plop the bone into the boiling water and stick the lid on, hoping for the best but I don't think this alone is going to work either. I then start back on the flesh, trimming and sorting the various cuts and placing them in a sealed plastic container in the fridge, keeping some to one side as it's now 1.05pm and time for lunch.

I finish off the bottle of lager from earlier and crack open another as I prepare food for myself and Eva. I fry up another batch of meat and butter 2-slices of bread also as I make myself a sandwich. I give Eva a small plateful of meat, add some black pepper, brown sauce (*Daddies* - not that other shit!) and a smattering of English mustard to my sandwich, plate up and head for the living-room with Eva in tow. We sit ourselves down and watch a film on DVD together - *The Hunger* - staring the late great David Bowie, the beautiful and elegant Catherine Deneuve, and saucy Susan Sarandon.

By the time the film has finished it's gone 3.30pm and I guess I'll have to get rid of all the crap in the garage next.

* * *

From the garage I drag out the metal dustbin onto the patio area, away from the table and chairs, and over to near the edge of the stone slabs. From the shed I grab 4-bricks from a pile stacked up against one wall and place them under the bin so as it doesn't scorch the patio when I set it alight - that's my theory anyway! I go and grab all the plastic bags full of shit and a Jerrycan that is half-filled with petrol or whatever some other smelly shit it contains.

I chuck the first bag into the bin - not without some effort - and pour the contents of the can over the top of it. There seems to be some kind-of oily crap mixed in with it as well as it flows out in different streaky colours and consistency, not that I really care as long as it burns like fuck. Standing well back I throw a lit match into the bin. Nothing. I go to take a quick look at what's happening when whoosh, I almost get my bloody tits burnt off by the sudden vitriolic burst of flame that shoots up into the air - fucking Hell! A thick dirty plume of black smoke then wafts skywards as the contents of the bin spit and crackle to oblivion. I just hope that old Mrs. DeAngelis next door doesn't call the bloody fire-brigade or I'll really be for it!

I chuck the rest of the bags into the bin and continue to plod the pyre with an old broom-handle seemingly for ages until the contents turn to nothing but several pieces of charred bone and ash - ASHES TO ASHES. The smouldering embers are dealt with by a couple of buckets of water. I then empty the remains out over another black bin-liner and start sifting through the leftovers, picking out bits of bone from the wet dust. The bones I throw into the empty bucket and the ash I leave on the plastic for disposal later.

Back in the garage I put the first piece of bone in the vice - a leg bone I think it was? - and it crushes easily with the bits falling back into the bucket that I've positioned directly below. I continue on with my task and soon enough I get myself into a pretty fast rhythm, the jaws of the vice making light work of the bitch's bones as they disintegrate to powder. Her lower jawbone I first have to snap in half before destroying each side, and then start on her teeth. They're super-fucking-hard and are the worst bits to try and crush, especially the fillings. What am I going to do with them? I manage to save them all - 17 in total! - and then put them in a small resealable plastic bag.

By the time I'm completely finished it's bloody 8.25pm already and I'm totally knackered. Unfortunately I'm not finished yet though, I still have shit-loads to do, the next task being to get rid of all the ashes. This is relatively easy as all I have to do is mix them in with the few bags of fertiliser and compost that I can use on my vegetable patch and it's job done.

For dinner I decide to go the whole-hog and do myself a big roast - even though time is knocking-on as it's now 9.05pm. I roast some potatoes in the oven alongside some meat, leaving one final portion for tomorrow. On the hob I cook carrots and runner-beans - all the veg being my own produce - and let it do its own thing for the next 45-minutes or so while I have some fun with myself.

In my bedroom I lay on my back and fuck. I push one of my dildos - a 9-inch realistic one from Lovehoney - into my precious and moan and "OW" as my internal muscles are forced apart under pressure. I wank it in and out of my slot with my right-hand as I squeeze my tits and nipples with the other, crying and fucking shit. I swallow and eat cock as I place another dildo in my mouth, a vibrating 8-inch one from Ann Summers as I continue to fuck myself with the other and play with my perfect mounds. Using my tongue and my teeth I suck the rubber cock like a whore and push the other deeper into my love-tube. I cum and choke and shake like a fucking spastic as my orgasm takes control of my body and mind and I almost gag myself to death as my poor abused body gasps for more air. Pulling the dildo out of my fanny I suck and lick on both of them, tasting the juices of cunt and mouth. Cunt-mouth. Mouth-cunt.

I don't bother to shower again, I've had enough fucking water splashing on me already today that I'm sick of it. Instead I just wipe myself out the best I can and gargle and spit away the horrible taste of rubber cock from my mouth.

Back in the kitchen I check on how the dinner is cooking and all is well, even the pelvic bone that I left simmering-away has come up lovely! Using a pair of kitchen tongs I take it out of the pot and leave it on the draining board to dry itself before going back upstairs to get myself ready - after a quick sneaky vodka and a gin that is!

Dressing for dinner I put on my old white cotton mini-dress from Shanghai Trends that is super-short and just about covers my box and my pert bum, and also my old pair of blue-suede Lola platform court-shoes - the Chichester ones.

My underwear is in sexy red lace from Wolf & Whistle that turns me on so much that I have to touch my breasts and my vagina again through the gorgeous material of my clothes. I refigure my hair in my usual same old fashion, just adding my old skull hair-clip to it. My make-up I do in my special killer style featuring sharp cheekbones, orange lipstick and coal-black eyeshadow. My perfume is *Poison* by Christian Dior.

Actually, for the first time ever, even when Andy was alive, I'm using the dining-room to have my dinner today. I don't actually know why I've never used it before, probably because it always seemed a bit pointless sitting in there all on my tod staring at 4 blue walls.

I mix-up some gravy - instant - also using some of the elixir from the meat and then plate-up, giving Eva another bowl of meat to herself as well as adding a couple of spoonfuls of the gravy to it. We sit ourselves down together in the dining-room, surrounded by the blue and Andy's racing pictures, model cars and boats. We tuck-in to our respective meals and it's glorious, and it has been so long than I've had a decent roast dinner and it slides down lovely, eased on its path by a bottle of chilled white, not German this time but Niederosterreich Riesling by Markus Huber of Austria.

Once all finished I clear-away both our empty plates and return to the living-room, switch on the TV and settle down with the bottle of beautiful wine. It's just coming up to midnight now and its been a Hell of a long and weird day, full of craziness punctuated by moments of extreme pleasure. The weather report for tomorrow - read by a really attractive blonde woman in her mid-50's with fantastic breasts - is for more sunshine with a small chance of a shower later in the day. The main headlines are yet more misery - another wave of fucking Slavs heading for our shores, a married Government minister caught with a prostitute, some pension company ripping OAP's of their hard-earned cash, a British soldier being taken to court for shooting dead a rag-head in some shithole of a country even though he was actually doing the job he was assigned to do in the first fucking place! A Z-list celebrity announcing that she's having a baby - the only surprise there being that the father isn't black! - petrol prices are on the up even though oil prices are going down, some guy being done for throwing a banana at a black footballer, yet another car insurance scam is revealed involving immigrants making false claims - no, really? - an elderly lady of 92 is beaten black and blue in a care-home by her 2-Romanian carers, a convicted rapist is to star on a TV reality show and get paid 50-grand for the privilege, and then finally a report that apparently red wine is now no good for you even though last week they said it was!

And people wonder why I am the way I am when I'm constantly surrounded by all this fucking shit - and worse - all the fucking time?

By now the time is 12.21am and I need to complete my final mission of the day and then I'm clear. In my bedroom I redress in the same clothes as I used in the kidnapping and then make my way back downstairs to the garage. I don a pair of disposable gloves as the first thing I need to do is clear the van out of anything that is mine - the cable-ties and a few other miscellaneous odds and ends - and then grab the small packet of the bitch's fillings from the workbench. I lock the internal garage door behind me as when I go out I'm going to leave the main external roller-shutter open as I'm not taking the remote opener out with me in case I accidentally leave it in the van when I dump it - and knowing my appalling luck that's exactly what I'll do! Leaving the main doors open though is a risk I'm prepared to take, no-one can see the house from the main road and I won't be long anyway.

I turn-left out of my main gate onto the A272 and head towards Petworth. On the main road before the town I empty the contents of the plastic bag out onto the road as I whiz along - "Goodbye Mellis" - her fillings tinkling on the tarmac as they are lost to oblivion. There are few cars around at this time of the morning, in fact in the short time I'm out I only see 3 and they're all driven by nobodies. In under 10-minutes I drive into Petworth car-park and dump the van over to one side in a parking bay by the surrounding wall. Locking it behind me I say "Goodbye" to the van for its service in my mission and then walk away, taking the keys with me. Turning right out of the car-park entrance/exit I stealthy walk a couple of streets to where I left the Mini parked-up a couple of nights ago. I used that particular car because it's the least conspicuous one that I have, plus of course it's so small that I can squeeze it into the tiniest of gaps. It fires-up with a roar from the twin-tailpipes and I sprint off, traversing the one-way system in the town as I head for home.

Back in my garage I breathe a huge sigh of relief that it's all finally over. The keys to the van I destroy in the vice, squashing them into unrecognisable pieces of metal and plastic. I strip naked in the hallway near the kitchen door and go for a quick pee and wash my hands thoroughly in the ground-floor bathroom.

I find Eva asleep in the front-room on the leather sofa, seemingly oblivious to my presence but I know in reality the she doesn't miss one single trick. I down a large glass of gin quickly followed by another. I pour some of the third glass over my face and my breasts, rubbing the highly scented liquid over their full roundness.

Swallowing the rest of the glass I touch and finger my vagina with my right-hand as I play with my nipples with the other. I squat myself down on the other end of the sofa to Eva, facing the back of the seat and with my beautiful legs spread as wide as they will go. I wank and fuck myself with 2-fingers in and out of my hole. I think of Andy, Amanda, Steve, Jennifer, and everyone else that I've fucked and that has fucked me. I pant heavily and my breasts heave in unison and I start to squeal as I near my end and then I have it within my grasp - I cum. I spit my orgasm over my fingers, my hand and the sofa as I love myself and push my fingers in further. I scream breathlessly as my internal honey oozes out of my cunt and I lick it, it tasting so fucking good as it mixes with the flavour of the juniper on my tongue.

Eva looks at me with her big blue eyes, making me laugh. I love her so much, as I have all my cats, and I couldn't live without her. My life would be even emptier than it is right now.

I give her a little more food than usual, just for being a good girl, grab my clothes from the hallway and head upstairs to bed and sleep - at long last. I clean myself up, have another pee and then hit the sack - it's 1.55am. I think I'll have a nice long lay-in in the morning, I fucking deserve it.

* * *

It's the day after the day after that I put that bitch Mellis out of her fucking misery - and mine - as an immense sense of freedom overwhelms me now that that bitch has been filed-away for good. I did actually get some proper sleep at last night, and in my own bed no less!

It's so fucking hot out today it's unbelievable. Naturally I'm walking around stark naked, in fact I haven't worn any clothes proper for the last 3-days, there's just been no need to.

I'm on my second glass of chilled German white and I've skipped breakfast entirely except for a couple of slices of leftover meat. I've actually been quite busy this morning - masturbating whilst watching lesbian anal fisting porn on my laptop, wanking to my own masochism, followed by a quick sloosh in the bath in piping-hot water with loads of bubbles to try and ease my weary bones. I then made myself a pie for dinner with the last of the meat which is now cooking-away nicely in the oven.

I'm presently in the living-room sitting at the circular glass dining table catching up on a bit more writing. In the background I'm playing Bowie, the *Low* album from 1977, just sitting here letting the sweeping melodies rescue me from despair. I haven't got it on very loud as it gets in the way of my concentration, and anyway, Eva isn't a fan of too much noise as it freaks her out - even more so now after the last few days of mayhem!

I try to engage my brain in some serious thinking but after all what's happened this week and the effects of the alcohol and the self-pleasuring have each formed some kind-of barrier against me doing anything constructive. I desperately try not to think about what has happened but I just can't help it, the images are far too strong and I can't block it out.

Isn't the human brain a weird thing? I've risked losing everything but I just don't care. Why don't I care? Obviously I should but I just don't seem to have any real attachment to anything. No psychiatrist or psychoanalyst would ever be able to figure me out or all this shit in a thousand-years! My feelings for life has evaporated. How have I come to this? Why do these things have to happen?

I am the symbol for everything that is wrong with this miserable World - evil and with no morality. I am a pseudonym for something that has yet to be thought out. I always seem to be one step beyond life as well as death as with each passing tragedy another dead angel falls out of the sky. It was only a matter of time before I snapped and with the passing of every human event I am strangled just a little bit more. And yet the more awake I am the more tired I become. I always try to outrun my life, my existence, but it's no good, the Devil has one hand on my shoulder all the fucking time, pulling me back to him. There is literally nothing I can do about it, I am resigned to stay alive on this wicked planet forever. Sane or insane, what is the fucking difference? Who is to judge? Who is to judge me?

My imagination is suddenly halted by the sound of the front-gate buzzer ringing in the hallway just as I'm about to pour myself another glass of wine.

Who the fuck is this now, disturbing my peace, disturbing my freedom? I make my way to the TV-monitor in the hallway with glass in hand to check the images at the gate on the screen. There's a silver BMW there with 2-guys in dark suits standing by it - they look just like coppers!

OH FUCKING HELL NO! THIS CAN'T BE HAPPENING! WHAT THE HELL AM I GOING TO DO?

I couldn't stomach a life on the run, where would I do my hair and make-up for a start? Hesitantly I press the intercom button to see what they want.

"Hello, who is it?" I ask in my piss-taking condescending tone. That's the punk in me!

"It's the Police, we would like to talk to Miss Sarah Knowles please." Comes back the male cop as I suddenly notice on the monitor that one of them is actually a female.

"Yes, that's me."

"We would like to talk to you please Miss Knowles, may we come in? If you could open the gates for us?"

Should I really let them in or just tell them both to fuck-off? I don't like intrusions into my life, not from anyone, especially from the bloody Police. Will they dare to venture closer or keep their distance? I open the front-door to them still with my glass of wine in hand.

"Miss Knowles?" Enquires the male cop.

"That's right, come in." I say as I peer around the edge of the door and usher them into the hallway where I immediately notice that they're both looking at me in an awkward manner for some reason?

"Miss Knowles, I think we'd all feel a little more comfortable if you were to put some clothes on please." Says the male cop.

"What?" I exclaim, as then I suddenly realise that I've completely forgotten that I'm standing there starkers! Oh shit!

"Oh bugger, I'll just go and put something on, I'm really sorry." I say, excusing myself with some embarrassment although deep down I really don't care.

I put down my glass of wine on the big black ancient German sideboard and then turn and sachay my pert bum and beautiful legs and perfect body upstairs in order to find something to put on. From my walk-in wardrobe in my bedroom I select my gorgeous white silk mini-robe from LilySilk and glide it over my beautiful smooth skin, the sheer sensation of its contact almost making me orgasm by itself - it doesn't take much!

I make my way back downstairs in my own special unique manner, making 100% sure that both pigs get a fucking good look at me in the process.

"So, what's all this about then?" I quiz them, even though I know the answers to their stupid questions before they even say them, my psychic powers having no limits.

"Miss Knowles, I'm Detective Inspector Maynard and this is my colleague Detective Sergeant Murphy. We understand that you used to work with a Miss Mary Ellis at a company in Horsham?" Says the male cop, a guy of about 30 I would hazard a guess with a short stylish beard, not that I like beards I don't, I hate them. In fact I didn't think coppers were allowed to have beards, although I may be wrong?

"The name vaguely rings a bell, why?" I reply. I really should have been an actress!

"Miss Ellis hasn't been seen for over 3-days now." Replies the female cop. She's somewhere around the same age as her male counterpart although shorter, reasonably attractive but with a fat arse. Why is it all female coppers seem to have fat arses? Obviously she doesn't have a beard either, well, not on her face anyway!

"Really? What's that got to do with me?" I counter them. Can they really be this stupid? I mean, they're both standing directly on the spot where I slaughtered that fucking bitch - the murder scene. I know they don't have any comprehension of that but what the Hell - LOL!

"Well, according to our information Miss Knowles, it seems that you and Miss Ellis weren't exactly friends? Allegedly there was some sort-of psychical altercation between the two of you resulting in you being fired from your job, is that so?" Says the bitch copper.

"Yeah, so what? That was over a year ago."

"In fact Miss Knowles it was exactly 1-year to the very day of her disappearance." She informs me sharply.

"Really? I've got no idea what you're talking about." I say startled, although obviously I know precisely, I planed it this way all along.

They both look at me, into my eyes, both desperately trying to figure out if I'm lying or not. What can they tell? What can they see? Nothing, except for the beautiful woman standing before them. I can out-stare and out-poker face them all fucking day long if necessary so bring it on. How dare these "people" try to manipulate me - bastards. My powers of telepathy are so high that it would blow their feeble little minds if they really knew everything about my life, and as they speak I laugh at them behind the beautiful mask that is my face - my face and body of perfection.

"Does anyone else live here with you?" Says the male cop.

"No, I live alone. My husband died several months ago now."

"I'm sorry to hear that Miss Knowles. What was his name?"

"Andrew Clark. What do you want to know about him for?" I question.

"Just a routine background check that's all." He says as he scribbles Andy's name down in his stupid little notebook - idiot.

"So there's no-one else here at the moment?" Says the woman.

"No. I've just told you that." I come back sharply.

"So you won't mind us having a quick look around then?" She returns.

"Look around, what for?"

"No particular reason Miss."

"There's a reason for everything." I fire back at them.

"We would just like a quick look around Miss Knowles, that's all." Says the male cop, trying to diffuse the ever tightening atmosphere between the 3 of us.

I have to give in this one time, I don't want to create a scandal - even though I am a scandal all by myself! It goes against my grain to back down to anyone but what can I do, put an axe through both their heads?

I lead them firstly into the living-room where they have a quick scan around and say nothing, there's nothing to say as there's nothing to see. What do they hope to find? From there I guide them past the pool into the games-room and then back again. We wander down to the basement and they look around the gym, the utilities-room and the plant-room, again, all in silence. I don't think they're actually looking at anything at all, I think they're just being plain bloody nosey. From there I lead them upstairs to the bedrooms and Andy's old office, a room I rarely venture into in case I disturb the ghosts. They poke their snouts around, checking all the bedrooms and en-suites and then to my bedroom. I see their faces light up as they check-out all the erotic pictures and photos on the walls, as well as the erotic sculptures dotted around the room. It's a good job I didn't have any of my dildo collection out on display!

We descend back downstairs. Once again there's nothing to see in the dining-room or the ground-floor bathroom so we then head into the kitchen.

"Something smells nice." Says the female cop.

"Yes, I've made myself a meat pie. My cooking skills seem to be improving." I fire back at her quickly as I walk them straight through to the garage.

Suddenly something catches my eye to my left as we go - OH FUCKING HELL NO! HOW COULD I HAVE BEEN SO STUPID?

There on the draining-board rests the bitch's pelvic-bone, drying off after I scraped and washed it clean yesterday - OH SHIT! I feel my blood pressure starting to boil as the 3 of us reach the connecting internal kitchen/garage door. I prey to my fallen Leader and my Sungod to save me and they do, I don't think either of the cops see it - FOR FUCKS SAKE!

In the garage they immediately start quizzing me about the collection of cars sitting there before them and I have to go through the same old rigmarole of explaining that they were my late-husbands cars and that I inherited them all and the house when he died and all that old shit. I get the inkling they don't believe a word I say - just like everyone else - but I don't give a flying-fuck, I've had enough of all this shit.

Rather than go back through the kitchen and risk the pigs seeing something they shouldn't - i.e. the bone - I lead them out through the rear garage door onto the patio. Fortunately they say they don't have time to look around the entire garden and dismiss it there and then. It's just as well, we'll be here all fucking day otherwise! We enter the house once again through the large sliding patio doors and head back into the hallway via the living-room.

"Okay Miss Knowles, I think we've seen enough. If you happen to see or hear from Miss Ellis then you can contact us here." Says the male cop as he hands me one of his pathetic little Police cards.

"Well, I haven't seen her for ages so I don't think there's much chance of that, do you?" I say with my ever Sadean wit.

"Well, you never know. Keep the card handy anyway." Replies the smart-arse cow.

"Maybe her boyfriend has something to do with her disappearance?" I point out to them.

"We've already looked into that possibility and he has a cast-iron alibi." I'm dutifully informed.

"Oh well. There's probably a perfectly good explanation for all this." I say.

"We'll get to the bottom of it Miss Knowles you can be sure of that, goodbye." So says the bearded one.

I open the front-door for them and off they fuck, and good fucking riddance as well. I slam the door behind them as they leave me alone in my personal sacred World. What the fuck was all that about? Did they honestly think that she was here? They must be fucking mad!

Maybe they were testing me? Maybe they know? Maybe the house is surrounded by coppers and they're just waiting to pounce on me at any moment? If that stupid bitch had just left me alone in the first fucking place then none of this shit would ever have happened - COW.

***

After this mornings episode with the bloody Police I decide to have a quiet and easy end to my day.

To block the images and questioning by the cops out of my head I finish-off the bottle of German white I had started earlier and then hit the lager. After my second bottle I go back on the computer to masturbate to some porn, this time to massive cum-choking porn featuring some lucky bitch of about 20 with blonde hair (not real), a pretty face and a nice little tight body with lovely pert breasts, although they're not real either as I can see the implant scars underneath them. Her throat gets drowned in what looks like a gallon of hot white spunk from the cocks of about 20-guys - maybe more? - all wanking-off into her awaiting mouth. I really wish they they were all here with me right now, including the girl.

For dinner this evening I'm having the pie that I made earlier from scratch. As well as the meat, inside it I've also added a gorgeous onion from my vegetable patch that was so strong that when I was chopping it up it had me in floods of tears. I also added some diced carrots and a chopped apple from one of my many apple trees in the back garden - just to give it a bit of fruitiness. I serve it with roast potatoes, carrots and a parsnip - all home-grown - and smothered in onion and mustard gravy - instant - out of a packet that is! It's amazing how my culinary skills have improved since I've had this kitchen at my disposal. First it was gardening and now cooking, wonders will never cease! Whatever next - sewing?

As per usual I feed Eva first, giving her a whole tin of shrimps in sauce that cost me over 2-quid - lucky cat! I grab myself another lager to go with my dinner and sit my perfect bum down in the living-room so I can eat and watch the news at the same time. The international news comes on first, fronted by a lovely looking woman of about 50 with dirty-blonde hair and sharp features. She's wearing what looks like a light leather jacket in a dark mauve-colour that I must try and find one similar for myself - it's really cool. The news itself is the usual old bollocks - all doom and gloom about climate change, endless wars in the Middle-East, a Left-Wing nut-eater with half-a-dozen houses sending her kid to a private school - not very socialist is it? Yet more fucking immigrants entering what's left of this country when we're already overflowing with the fuckers and still they let more in - absolute madness! Then there's an article on some Government Minister that has been caught on the fiddle - this one has not only been caught screwing his female aid but her husband as well!

The national weather comes on next, presented by a dark-haired girl in her early to mid-30's with a foreign-sounding name - possibly Asian but she doesn't look it. She has a funny quirky manner about her which I find endearing, and really nice full breasts that I would love to lick and suck and rub my wet pussy over. Her weather predictions though are a waste of time as they're nearly always bloody wrong. I would get a more accurate forecast by having a piece of seaweed hanging from my front-door!

The local news follows on, fronted by another female, an Italian-looking honey with eyes like a cat and a hardbody that I would love to love. She starts going on about some woman that has been missing for several days and that no-one has seen or heard from. The next second the screen changes to an interview with some big black fucker who's built like a brick shithouse. His name is captioned below his wog face - Errol Mugabe or something like that? - as he bleats about his missing "love" with false black tears of "boo hoo hoo" and a stuttering voice of fake emotion. I sit and sneer at the black fucker as the screen changes once more to a photo and then a short video of his missing race-traitor nigger-loving white whore bitch - it's Mellis!

I almost puke my dinner as her face taunts me from beyond death, seeing her move on the TV screen before me as she looks straight into my eyes and laughs in my face - FUCKING BITCH. The video appears to have been taken at some party by the looks of it and I stare into her smiling face and then down at my dinner - they are one and the same.

I'M EATING HER!

I'M ACTUALLY FUCKING EATING HER!

WHAT THE FUCK AM I DOING?

OH MY GOD!

WHAT HAVE YOU DONE SCORPIO?

Now, don't go and roll your fucking eyes back or wince at what I do. Society - and therefore you - has created me. If you want to blame someone for my actions, for everything I do, including fucking men and women, then the answer is staring at you as you look into the mirror.

I raise my bottle of lager to her as a toast and tell her to "Fuck-off" - fucking cow. Her coon boyfriend then comes back on the screen with more pleading and a contact number for anyone with any information as to her whereabouts or anyone who may have seen her. I don't bother writing the number down, what would be the point? She no-longer exists, except in the memories of the few.

A copper appears on screen next, not your average pig, a high-ranking one with a flash uniform featuring plenty of silver bling - a Superintendent no less. It turns out the copper is none other than Mellis's father and that he's going to:

"Leave no stone unturned" until she's found! Wow, what big fucking words! He bleats on about her mobile-phone being found under her car, its screen cracked but still in working order. I'm guessing that she must have dropped it when I hit her but I really don't remember. Oh well, none of it matters any more now, it's all in the past. It's gone. It's over. Goodbye. Auf Wiedersehen. Arrivederci. Au Revoir. Fuck-off.

The death of Mellis was no loss to me, or in reality to anyone else. She was always as dead as I am, as we all are. She never existed as I don't exist as nothing is really real. Most humans have murderous thoughts about killing someone, coming out with crap such as: "I wish you were dead", "I'll kill you for that" and other such phrases. But how many of us actually realise these homicidal thoughts, or is it just me? Do you see what I mean, what is really real?

The remainder of the local news isn't even worth mentioning, some crap about fly-tipping followed by a report on a centre for immigrants being petrol-bombed and not much else, just some Left-Wing shit about teachers and how they're trying to educate (proselytise more like) their pupils on gay rights instead of teaching them real meaningful things like being able to read, write and count - bloody typical Left.

The local weather follows, fronted by some weird-looking young guy with a long face like a horse but I don't bother listening to it.

The meat pie was really lovely and it slides down beautifully. I take my empty plate back to the kitchen and grab myself another chilled lager from the fridge and then return to the living-room. Even though I'm naked, Eva still jumps up onto my lap as I channel-hop and she curls up and goes to sleep on me. Stroking her soft fur mellows my mind as I try to find something decent to watch next amongst the same old crap. The adverts between the so-called "programs" are even worse, especially one of them that features a video of some horrible starving nigger brat with bulging eyes and flies in its mouth from some shithole African country. I'm not and can't sit here subjecting myself to this horrendous shit and so change channels in an instant. I then stumble upon an old episode of the

American comedy *The Big Bang Theory*, one of my favourite shows, and I sit there laughing my head off at their crazy antics as they jump from one ludicrous situation to another - just like I do in my own life and worse.

It's just gone 9pm when the show finishes so I go back on my laptop searching for something weird and wonderful to masturbate to. Just like searching for a decent TV program, the amount of shitty Z-rated sites there are on here is mind-blowing. How the Hell does all this fucking crap get made in the first bloody place? Eventually I settle on a Brazilian site featuring transgender fisting porn which I find both funny and also a little sad at the same time, after all, these poor creatures can't help being born in the wrong body can they?

Slowly and gently I insert my dildo into my bumhole, the funny hand-shaped one from Lovehoney. My passage stoically resists at first as then in it slides against all odds. I ease it back and forth as I take-in the images before me as the 2 Latino-type T-girls suck each others cocks in a 69. They reposition themselves on their bed with one of them fucking the other up the arse as the other wanks her own cock to climax. Her cum spits out over her own leg and onto the bed as I finger my cunt with my left-hand, my other continuing to masturbate my rectum. The T-girls separate with the other girl - the giver - instantly squirting her cum into the others mouth as she sucks her off as I then cum and scream and moan like a fuck. I take a large gulp of vodka from the bottle on the floor beside me and pour some over my perfect breasts. Pulling the dildo out of my body I wank my pierced nipples with my fingers as I insert the plastic hand into my vagina and fuck myself with it. I push it in hard and fast and take myself to Hell once more as I cum-fuck.

***

I look at myself in the mirror and see the reflection of 2-different women looking back at me. One of them has the outside facade of beauty and perfection whilst the other is a murderer - a cannibal - and not human. This is where everything changes. This is the new me.

***

I am out of my mind. I drink my own piss, my own blood, my own life. I don't know what I'm doing or where I'm going. What is the fucking point of it all? Why do I bother with anything at all? Why do I bother with you, telling you the story of my life, my existence? Just turn the fucking page, or even better, close this book and go and fuck yourself.

Nothing makes any sense.

Everything is a con.

4

PJ

She's a funny-looking girl this one, strange, but at the same time mesmerizing. I just can't keep my eyes off of her, not in a sexual way you understand - she's not my type at all - but in an intriguing and hypnotic way. The way she sings and delivers her words into my ears is just captivating. Her mouth is also a little crooked but she wouldn't be who she is if it was straight would she? That's partly why I have always found her so fascinating, she's not like anyone else you will ever see or hear.

Her dress-sense though is terrible, I cannot even begin to describe what she's wearing, it looks like some sort-of up-side-down canvas bag, whilst on her head she has a plume of black feathers sticking-up out of her hair that makes her look like the arse-end of a turkey! I'm honestly not taking the piss out of her, she is what and who she is - individual - and I admire and love her for it.

But it's what got me interested in her in the first place that is her crowning glory - her songs, her voice, her power, as well as her independence. Her whole ethos to her work is also truly inspiring. She writes all her own material, as well as singing and playing different instruments on them, and then produces the end product as well. There is seemingly no end to her talent, there is no-one like her, or her music. There are no real bands out there anyway these days, simply because there are no real people to enjoy them - everything and everyone has turned to shit. The vast majority of all the crap you hear on the radio and the TV today - the shitty manufactured girl and boy bands - are not even on the same planet compared to her.

With the first song: *The Darker Days Of Me And Him* over, myself and the small select crowd burst into spontaneous applause. Her showcase continues with *To Bring You My Love,* triggering yet more clapping of hands and calls for more.

The venue for tonight's gig is the LSO St Luke's, an 18th-Century former Church in Old Street, London, chosen I'm guessing for its ethereal acoustical qualities. It certainly wasn't chosen for the location that's for sure, the nightmare part of London that is the multiracial/multicultural shithole of Lewisham - it's fucking awful. The stage and setting though are both beautifully lit in blue with strobe and spotlights in naked white, all adding to the ambiance of the show.

The audience themselves are mostly a hand-picked bunch - a few music execs, friends, acquaintances, fellow musicians, as well as a small gathering of fan-club members - myself being one of those. Tonight I'm wearing a black sleeveless cotton blouse from Prada, a black miniskirt from Chanel, a pair of black tights from M & S and a pair of black and gold Jacquard boots from Joe Browns. Tonight's underwear is in black lace from Obsessive. As for my make-up, I've gone for a dark and gloomy look to match the event, featuring coal-black eyeshadow, deep-red lipstick, plenty of blusher and black nail-polish. My hair goes without saying, except that I have my skull hair-clip in to finish off my look. My perfume is *Mademoiselle* by Coco Chanel.

I was going to get the train up to town but the logistics and the hassle would have been a bloody nightmare, so in the end I drove up in my new Focus RS, it goes like stink and handles like a racing-car and at the same time is small and nimble enough to park relatively easily. If I had used the Lamborghini it would have been a bloody joke!

As the music wafts around me there's some girl over to the right of me, a couple of metres away, who keeps looking at me as I dance and move my beautiful body to the sounds. She smiles at me and has the look of lust in her beautiful dark eyes. She's about my age - maybe younger? - with gorgeous dark brown curly hair, a fantastic looking face and a body to die for.

She's with some fella - a real smart-arse type - who clings on to her like she's his possession, his trophy. What does she want? Does she want to fuck me or fuck him? Or maybe she wants us both? I would be up for that as you well know! I WANT to stick my fingers and my tongue into her vagina and for her to give me her love. I'll take it all and run with it all night long.

The gig rolls-on through PJ's vast array of varied songs - *Oh My Lover, Dress, Victory, Naked Cousin, C'mon Billy, Long Snake Moan, Down By The Water, That Was My Veil, Taut, A Perfect Day Elise, Big Exit, Good Fortune, The Whores Hustle And The Hustlers Whore, Shame, The Glorious Land, The Words That Maketh Murder,* and the gloriously wonderful *In The Dark Places.* Each and every song is as different and diverse as the next - it's music to slash your wrists to - even so, I love them all.

After almost 1½ hours of bliss, she winds the show up with an encore of *The Wheel.* This has not only been one of the best gigs that I've ever been to, but one of the best nights of my life. I don't want it to end and I don't want to leave. I want her to sing to me all through the night and into dawn and wrap me up tightly with the experiences of her life in song.

As everyone starts to leave the building and file out, I scan around for the brunette honey but she's gone and I never see her ever again - this is my life.

Back in my car I sit there both elated and dejected at the same time. Elated in having seen and heard PJ live, and dejected at the thought that it's all over and I now have to face the long drive home back to Foxhill. I fucking hate driving in London, my dirty, stinking, immigrant-infested Capitol City. There are some beautiful and historic places of course, it's not all shit, but I never seem to get to see much of that these days for whatever reason. I have plenty of time but not the inclination.

I fire the car up and head South along Commercial Street and although it's gone midnight by now, the traffic is still reasonably heavy with other people out and about doing their own thing. I pull-up at a set of traffic lights in the left-hand lane of the 2-lane road as another car slowly glides to a stop in the right-hand lane next to me. I get the sense that I'm being watched so I cast a quick glance over to my right out the corner of one eye. I let out a deep sigh as there next to me is the not unsurprising sight of a couple of Paki's sitting there in their silver Mitsubishi Evo, it churning out a disgusting racket of Asian "music" at full-blast. Now, I'm faced with 2 choices here:

    1 - Burn them off when the lights change and have them race after me.

    2 - Bail-out and divert off to my left and avoid any confrontation with them and then double-back and rejoin this road when they've fucked-off.

I decide upon the latter as I don't want to even look at their shit faces let alone get involved in a bloody race with them, they're bound to catch me up sooner or later and I don't want any aggro from the likes of this fucking lot, I'm just not in the bloody mood. The lights suddenly change from red to amber and the Paki driver screams away and heads off straight down the road. I flick left and power-on for about a mile or so and then spin the car around and double-back to the same junction as before. I do a left again, thus putting myself back on the very same stretch of road as previously and I just hope that those dirty Paki's have gone.

As I drive on though, I seem to be surrounded by yet more bloody foreigners - blacks, more Paki's and obviously the obligatory fucking Slavs, all pootling along in their shitty Romanian/Bulgarian/Polish heaps of tin, not one of them with any fucking insurance or probably one bloody driving licence between any of them - CUNTS. The useless Police wont do anything about them either as they couldn't be bothered, not that there's ever any of them about anyway. I have to get away from them all, I hate each and every one of them, and so I put my foot down and leave them all behind. My heart sinks as there further up ahead I suddenly spot the 2-Paki's from before in the Evo, standing by their car on the curb outside a dirty stinking kebab shop, munching-away on what can only very loosely be described as "food." They stop eating and stare at me in unison, looking at me like they want to rape me but I'm not going to give them a chance. I roar away as fast as I dare and I'm gone. I don't see them again.

Once over the beautiful Tower Bridge I finally I get myself back onto the A3 and I can breathe a sigh of relief, for the next couple of miles anyway. Next I see some arsehole coming up behind me in a big fat Jag - not a sporty F-Type like Andy's old one but one of those big other ones, an XJ, and he tries to intimidate me when he sees that I'm a woman. Little does the old git driving realise though that I can beat him any fucking day of the week. I drop down into 3rd-gear and floor the gas-pedal hard, the RS accelerating away from the barge-like Jag easily as I leave it behind. Why do these people even fucking bother, as in my rear-view mirror I notice him flashing his headlights at me - what a twat!

Through Clapham, Battersea, Wimbledon, New Malden, Tolworth and Cobham, I turn left onto the M25 and head anticlockwise, aiming for Leatherhead at Junction-9, although no-sooner do I come off the slip-road onto the motorway, I have 2 fucking Herbert's in a little blue boy-racer Renault right up my arse - really? Are they fucking joking? They pull right alongside of me and egg me on to race them but this time though I'm not going to chicken-out so I drop the car down into 4th-gear and floor the accelerator hard. They desperately try to chase after me but they've got no fucking chance as I hit 150 and then 160. After a couple of miles of this I back-off and keep to a steady 90 until I hit Junction-9 and then turn off - arseholes!

Fortunately I get a hassle-free run for the remainder of my journey home with not a single turd in sight, or a pig for that matter - bliss!

***

That night Eva and I decide to sleep in the Summerhouse together. She's calmed down a bit now as she doesn't like it if I'm out late and it makes her wail like a banshee for ages.

I stroll down the garden completely naked with her following behind me. I'm carrying a box of select items for our nocturnal adventure - cat food, cat bowl, cat spoon, a bottle of expensive German white, crisps (prawn cocktail flavour), a bar of chocolate, my strange hand-shaped dildo from Lovehoney (again!), and some wipes. The air is so still and deathly quiet that I can actually hear my heart beating clearly and the soft brush of my bare souls as they disturb and crush the grass as I walk. Eva tucks-in to her bowl of tuna with shrimps as I guzzle on the German. I love her so much, as I have all my cats, as she munches-away on her fish.

I fuck my vagina with the dildo and it feels so beautiful inside me as I slide it in and out of my lover. I dream of the brunette with the hardbody I saw at the PJ gig earlier, that she's fingering me deep as I then start to shake and quiver as I cum and scream and scream and cum. I lick my own juice from my fake miniature hand as I use one of my own on my clit, rubbing and squeezing the rubbery velvety bulb with all my love. I really fucking needed that!

Eva sits there staring at me with her big blue cat eyes and gives me one of her little chirps, her feline way of asking me:

"Are you alright?"

"I'm OK." I tell her, adding "I love you so much" and she chirps back at me once more. I don't know what I would have done without her these last several months, life would have been damn near impossible.

I munch-away on crisps and chocs and sup more wine. It's nearly 2am the following morning by now and so we both settle ourselves down together to sleep and dream of the past and the future and I'm gone.

***

It's 2.45pm the following day - or should that be the same day? - when my peace is disrupted by the doorbell chiming, the actual doorbell that is, not the entry-gate buzzer. From the kitchen I head into the hallway and look at the CCTV monitor. I soon discover that I've accidentally left the electric main gates open all fucking night - bollocks! I could have sworn that I'd closed them after me when I came home from the gig. I also spot that there's another bloody Police car parked outside - a marked one this time - right outside the front doors. What the Hell do they fucking want now? I answer the door to them - 2-female cops both in there late-20's/early-30's, both blonde and average-looking.

Today I'm wearing a baggy v-neck jumper in salmon-pink from Monsoon, a pair of pale-blue skinny-jeans from Topshop and nothing else, not even underwear as I couldn't be bothered. My hair and make-up I've done as per my norm whilst today's perfume is *Luxe* by Avon.

"Miss Sarah Knowles?" Quizzes one of the pigs. I'm getting a little bit bored with all this questioning now aren't you?

"That's correct. What is it this time?"

"We'd like you to come down to the station with us to answer a few questions please Miss."

"Questions about what? You're arresting me?" I fire back.

"No, we're not arresting you. We just need to ask you about the disappearance of your ex-work colleague Miss Mary Ellis."

"Not again? What has all this crap got to do with me? I haven't seen her for over a year as I told the other officers last week."

"We understand that but we would still like you to accompany us to the station."

"This is ridiculous, what's the point?" I exclaim.

"Are you refusing to come with us Miss Knowles?" Pipes-up cop No.2.

"No, I didn't say that did I? Why can't you ask me here?" I say in exasperation.

"It would be better down the station Miss Knowles as you can have a legal representative there if you want."

"Why would I want that? I'm innocent." I stab them.

With the 2-officers permission - not that I fucking need it in the first place! - I quickly scoot around the house locking all the doors and windows, giving Eva some more food as well as a kiss and a cuddle, and then grab my keys, mobile phone and put on a pair of white trainers from Adidas and off we jolly-well go down to the cop-shop. What a pain in the fucking arse!

They take me off to Horsham nick, located behind the Fire Station on the opposite side of the road to Richard Collyer College. In the interview room, I sit my pretty arse down on a crappy wooden chair and lean across a crappy wooden table opposite the very same pair of plain-clothes coppers that came to my house last time - Tweedle Dumb and Tweedle Dee. They start questioning me, using exactly the same tired old lines as before about that bitch Mellis - "Blah blah blah blah blah blah fucking blah" - and I throw back at them exactly the same fucking answers as I did previously, belittling their arrogant attitudes to the point of sarcasm.

After over 30-minutes of bullshit the charade comes to an end and as per usual I've had my time completely wasted by these morons. If there was a point to all this, they didn't find it - again!

"Right, I think we're done for now Miss Knowles." Says copper "Dumb".

"Really, that's it is it? More of my time wasted and for what?" I snap at them.

"We'll be in touch if there are any new developments, you're free to go now." Says copper "Dee".

"Well, thank you so much. It's always nice to see that the tax-payers money is being spent so wisely. I don't suppose I get a lift back home either do I?"

"Unfortunately the tax-payers money doesn't stretch that far Miss Knowles. We're not a Taxi service." Says the first cop - FUCKING PIG CUNT.

"Great!" I smirk back at their piss-taking as I get up to leave.

How can they be so bloody thick? They must all go to a special school for arrogant thick bastards I guess? I crash my way out of the station, ignoring all their stupid comments like: "If you have any more information please pass it on" and all that shit. I turn right onto Hurst Road and walk the short distance up to Horsham Train Station to get myself a cab back home to Foxhill. Fortunately there are 3-vacant Taxi's waiting there so I grab one of those, eventually arriving back home at 6.31pm.

What a complete waste of fucking time.

Fucking useless pigs.

***

For the remainder of the day I continue with writing my book. Everything is in place now and it's all coming together nicely, with the story practically writing itself. The computer guy - Mack - couldn't fix my old computer, it was 7-years old to be fair, so he got me a brand new one, a Hewlett Packard, and even managed to transfer all my photos and other personal things over onto it, which was a blessed relief I can tell you! I sit there wondering if he went through my private photo file, the one that has pictures of myself naked and fucking - with men, women, and both together, and of me pleasuring myself? I hope he did see them, and that he masturbated over them.

The book has now got to the point of no return - I simply must carry on. If I have the power to create life - even to take life - then I must have the power to create this work.

The rage of writing overwhelms me, suffocating me to death. With each and every word I am immortalizing myself for future lives, none of which I can foresee will be parallel to my own.

An artists life is so deep, probably infinite, and it drives me ever deeper into my soul, blinding me with indescribable mental turmoil but I struggle on with it - I must.

5

FoS

That knob-head car dealer friend of Andy's - Craig or whatever his bloody name is? - the one that sold all the superfluous cars for me after Andy died, the one that I went to that stupid do with over at Petworth House that time, has emailed me several times over the last few months to see if I would like a free VIP ticket to a massive car show - the Festival of Speed (nick-named FoS) - the very same show at Goodwood in West Sussex that Andy and I were due to attend only weeks before he passed away.

I would have never have thought of going, it simply wasn't on my mind, and seeing as it's a VIP pass and free to boot then why the Hell not go? It's only just down the road from me anyway, held in the grounds of Goodwood House itself, not at the race track where Andy took me not long after we had met. I guess it's nice of Craig to think of me, but as I've told you before I know exactly what he's after - my body - and there's absolutely no chance of him having that!

Anyway, I've decided that I will attend, and by all accounts it looks to be a pretty big event so hopefully it should be a fun day out in the countryside.

***

It's the morning of the show and I'm up at the crack of dawn. Actually it looks like it's going to be a beautiful day - it's Friday - as the Sun is already shinning nice and brightly and the temperature is also up even though it's only 6am. I shower my gorgeous body under the warm water and then head downstairs to feed Eva and have some breakfast - just cornflakes for me today and no tea.

As for today's clothes I'm wearing a super-expensive white sleeveless blouse from Schiaparelli that I leave unbuttoned dangerously low so that everyone can see my beautiful breasts, and a tight white miniskirt from Moschino that really shows-off my gorgeous long legs. On my feet I'm wearing a pair of white Christian Louboutin Decoltish patent leather shoes that are to die for. My underwear is also in white, a lace set of matching bra and knickers from Ultimo. For my hair and make-up I've gone for my supermodel look today featuring super-sharp cheekbones, dark grey eyeshadow and light brown lipstick and I look good to fuck! My perfume is *Poison* by Christian Dior. The only other things I'm taking with me are my trusty camera and my white leather clutch-bag from Prada, containing cash, keys and of course my free VIP ticket.

I know the venue is only up the road a little way but I'm still going to take the Lamborghini there anyway - and why the fuck shouldn't I? Heading out of my driveway I turn left and head for Petworth on the A272 where I soon find the town already busy with traffic heading towards Goodwood and it's still only 7.10am. As I near the venue the Sun really begins to beam down, highlighting the glorious land that is my England. Passing the Sculpture Park on my left I join a small queue for the entrance to the car park - basically just a massive field - where I'm ushered into the VIP parking area. As per bloody usual I receive plenty of looks from everyone - my fellow car enthusiasts, the marshals, as well as the other punters - as I extract myself from the tight cockpit of the Lambo and then make my way up the hill to the entrance gate. My ticket is scanned by some nerdy-looking ginger kid in his late-teens with freckles who shakes like a leaf and stutters at my beautiful presence - poor little sod! - and then I'm through the door. I buy an event program from a lovely-looking girl on a stand - I guess she must be in her mid-20's and with long curly brown hair, gorgeous brown eyes and a hot mouth that makes my heart flutter. I want to touch her face, her breasts and tongue her sweet little vagina but now is not the time nor the place - unfortunately!

The first trade stand I see up on my left is from Porsche but I don't linger there as I've never cared for them much for whatever reason? Through a line of trees the event opens up before me - giant stands from most of the Worlds leading car companies, grandstands on both side of the track - actually the driveway for the house! - other trade stands, food and drink stands, and over to my right Goodwood House itself in all its splendour. It really is a beautiful place and even makes my own house look miniscule by comparison.

I follow the metal road to the left and wander around taking-in all the amazing cars and other things on show. I don't stop at all the stands, just the ones that catch my eye or that I'm interested in - Ford, Aston Martin, Lotus, Bentley etc.

There is so much to see and do that I doubt if I'll ever get around it all in just one day, although I don't really fancy coming back again tomorrow or Sunday, I think 1-day will be about all I can take.

By now the runs up the track have started so I watch some of that from the sidelines for a bit, those mainly being old racing cars from the 1920's and 30's. From there I venture across the track via the footbridge over to the same side as the main house. In the Supercar pits I ogle at all the exotic machinery on display from companies such as - Lamborghini, Ferrari, Aston Martin, Maserati, McLaren, Bugatti, Morgan, Lotus, and many other weird and wonderful cars, all of them beautiful.

Next I find myself in the old-timer pit that features cranky early cars with massive engines spitting flames and banging-away to themselves, some of them are really crazy and nothing more than death-traps on wheels! By the side of the house there's a section of classic cars as well as some bikes also, all under the title of *Style-et-Luxe.* They're all really expensive and rare stuff and all in fantastically beautiful condition - Rolls-Royce,

Bentley, Delahaye, Lagonda, Auburn, Tucker, Duesenberg - mixed-in amongst other strange vehicles from different eras.

I then head back up the hill to the Formula 1 paddock and other cars and bikes and find myself outside the Ferrari F1 marquee. The car is simply stunning in its scarlet red paint and just the technology involved in getting the thing started is incredible, involving at least 10-guys monitoring all its systems! The mechanics all look and lust at me as I stand there watching them work and as I take a few photos - Italian guys, I love them all, and just think what they could all do to me? The engine suddenly bursts into life with a high-revving wail that is music to my ears, it's gorgeous. I stand there watching both it and the antics of the Italians themselves as they tune the engine to perfection for the next 10-minutes or so before I move on to check-out all the other F1 teams and their cars, each one of them equal works of automotive art.

All around me are rows and rows of cars and bikes on display in all different classes and I literally don't know which way to look first - sportscars, Drag racers, Historic F1 cars, motorbikes, trucks, NASCAR's, Hill-climbers, sidecars - every conceivable type of car and bike on the planet you could imagine is here right in front of me and I am in Heaven!

I suddenly recognise the beautiful shape of the sleek black F1 car ahead of me, it's Andy's old Lotus 91 being prepared for its run up the hill. Standing by the rear of the car is Craig, talking to a woman in her early-50's who's wearing a racing suit and is just about to put her crash helmet on. Seeing the car once again brings a small tear to my eye as it makes me remember all the good times Andy and I had together. I miss him so much that I have to blot out my memory of him sometimes just in order to get through the day in one piece.

"Hello Sarah, glad you could make it." Beams Craig as I head towards him to say "Hi". He's all over me like a bloody rash but I'm just not interested, he really doesn't do anything for me at all.

"Hello. The car looks great." I reply.

"Yeah, it's just about to go out. This is Claudia, she's going to take it up the hill. Claudia, this is Sarah, Andy's widow."

"Widow" he calls me. Did you hear that? I really fucking hate that word. I know I am a widow but there's really no need to introduce me as such and rub it in. What a prick. She fastens up the chinstrap to her helmet and holds out her hand to shake mine as we both say "Hello" to one another. She then climbs into the tight cockpit of the car with one of the mechanics securing her racing harness for her. Ready to go, another guy starts the car up with what looks like some sort-of really long drill-type thing at the rear of the car and it suddenly bursts into life screaming its head off - it sounds beautiful and I love it, I could listen to her wailing-away all day long! Claudia snick's the gearbox into 1st-gear and hurries away out of the tent-like enclosure and I have to say that I'm a little bit jealous, when Andy was alive I never got the chance to hear the car run let alone have a go and drive her - lucky cow!

Craig and I then head off to one of the many track-side grandstands to watch all the cars coming up the hill, primarily Claudia in the Lotus. He starts to give me plenty of the usual old chitchat and chat-up lines as we sit there watching the cars hurtle past us but I don't take the bait. As I've said before, I just don't fancy him. Before long we soon spot Claudia and the Lotus on the giant TV screen before us waiting to go on the startline. She nails the car off the line perfectly and heads in our direction, I can even hear the car before I can see it! Within seconds the beautiful black shape appears as Claudia really gives the car some poke, she streaking past us at a huge rate of knots - what a fantastic sight and sound, it really is amazing! We watch her disappear under the footbridge and then follow her progress on the giant screen as she sprints up the remainder of the hill and over the finish-line - FANTASTIC! Even before she's reached the half way point another Formula 1 car blasts past us - a Ferrari from the 1980's being driven by its period driver - and I am truly in my element, what an amazing event!

At the end of the session Craig offers to take me for lunch at the VIP lounge and how can I resist - if it's free, take it!

We head back over to the other side between sessions, crossing the track this time through a gap in the straw bales and make our way to the VIP marquee. We show our special passes to the 2-guys manning the entrance and go and sit ourselves down on a small table smack-bang in the centre of all the other people taking lunch. Their eyes burn into my gorgeous self as I sit there with my beautiful long toned and tanned legs crossed, they all staring in amazement and jealousy at my hard body, my natural blonde hair, my beautiful face, my perfect breasts, my tattooed arms and hands, and my expensive clothes and shoes, all of them gorping at me in disbelief at my sheer perfection.

Craig and I order lobster and Champagne from one of the waiters, a young guy in his mid-20's with a really nice fit body, toned muscles to his arms, a tight bum and an OK face. I want him to pin me down on our table right here and now and fuck me with his hard cock right in front of everyone as they all cheer him on but it doesn't happen.

As Craig and I munch-away on our lobsters and sip our chilled Champagne he swoons over me like a bloody vulture looking for a kill. Why don't men realise that women aren't pieces of meat that they can just pick up whenever they feel like it, there is a lot more to us than that. I spurn his ridiculous advances in my own unique way, eventually having to tell him:

"If you don't fucking back off I'll slice your fucking dick off."

He laughs at me thinking that I'm not being serious but in reality you know different now don't you - my dear reader?

The action on the hill continues unabated with all manner of engine noises racing past us in the near distance. We finish our lunch and leave amid more looks from the snobs and the pseudo-snobs, all sitting there pretending to be something they're not - alive. Craig attempts to guide me back in the direction of the pit area where we met earlier, placing one hand on my arm to do so. I back away from him in disgust, how fucking dare he touch me, who does he think he is? I snarl at him with daggers and he backs off quickly, saying "Sorry" as he does so. I have to inform him that I don't like being mauled and that I'm going my own way and that it's all over before it's over - twat.

I make my way back on my own over the footbridge to the other side once more and go for a quick pee before continuing my wander around. I suddenly spot the Lamborghini stand so I make a detour to that first. The stand itself is fenced-off all round for some reason - probably to stop any riff-raff getting in? - with the entrance gate guarded by 2-gorgeous honeys, both stunning supermodel types. The one standing to the right is a blonde - not natural like I am - and in her mid to late-20's with a beautiful face and has a fantastic figure. I can also tell that her tits are fake straight away but they're still gorgeous anyway, although not as big or as nice as my own. She's wearing a beautiful red dress that is super-tight and features a heart-shaped hole cut out at the front, exposing her lovely cleavage. On her feet she's wearing a gorgeous pair of red suede platform court-shoes that really emphasize her beautiful legs and slim figure.

The other girl standing next to her is a bit younger I would say, probably about 24-ish at a guess. She has light-brown curly hair that is beautifully done and a really pretty face that I want to make mine forever. Her figure is amazing - almost an equal to mine - tall and slim with perfect full breasts, a lovely round bum and gorgeous long legs. She's wearing a white wraparound dress that is to die for that features a sheer section over her shoulders and chest, exposing her girls. Her shoes are a pair of white strap-heals that are so fucking gorgeous that I must find a pair like them for myself - or maybe I'll just nick hers!

I sachay up to them with my heart pounding like crazy and I can't believe how fucking beautiful they both are - if they won't let me fuck them both I'll just die! All 3 of us say "Hi" in unison with big beaming smiles all around. I ask them their names, with the one in red being Jasmine and the one in white Laura - and tell them mine. I say how much I love their dresses and they both return the compliment. We chat about the show, the cars and the glorious weather and other crap and when I tell them I have a Lamborghini and show them my car keys they both invite me on to the stand although I find it increasingly difficult to keep control of myself as they're both so fucking beautiful. I WANT to stick my tongue and my fingers into their tight little vaginas and have them dildo me until I cum in ecstasy. I WANT to smother my face in their breasts as together they lick my honey. I give them one of my business cards each in the hope that at least one of them contacts me - in the hope that one of them is bisexual, in the hope that one of them is a lesbian, in the hope that I can have my evil way and have them love me and I can love them back but I never hear from either of them ever again. My sad guess is that neither of them are into girls and my heart shatters into a million pieces. It's such a shame and I would have loved to have them both as lovers, and the waiter guy also from the VIP marquee makes 3.

I head next over to the numerous tents and stands nearer the startline, wandering in and out at my leisure looking at all the different things they have for sale. One company is selling fantastic paintings of racing cars, bikes, aeroplanes and other beautiful machines, all of them signed by the original drivers etc. The prices are obviously equally fantastic with some of them well into 4-figures! I still have all of Andy's pictures dotted around the house of course, mainly hanging from the garage walls. I'll never part with any them for anything.

In another tent they're selling 1960's -style clothing, with the people on the stand all done up in their period gear - how groovy! There are also numerous book stands around but I don't bother with any of those as I don't have time. A huge stand selling wooden sculptures of horses and dolphins and other animals then catches my eye and so I pinch one of their fliers, there are so many things to see that I can't even remember most of them now - my mind is boggled!

By now it's close to 3pm and my poor feet are killing me and so I decide to call it a day and head off home. It's been a really wonderful event and it fills me with deep sadness that Andy isn't here with me by my side to see it all, we would have had such a great day together of that I have no doubt.

Seeing Andy's old Lotus tearing up the track was great - the noise of it was fantastic, as were all the other cars and bikes and weird and wonderful things - especially Jasmine and Laura - they were both fucking gorgeous!

***

Back at home I kick my shoes off and slump on the sofa with a large glass of German white - it's 3.46pm. Eva jumps onto my lap and purrs like crazy at my return and rubs her wet nose against my hand holding my glass, almost making me spill some. I down the wine quickly and have another before I then hit the shower. I strip naked in the bedroom and admire my perfect reflection in the bathroom mirror and touch my breasts, squeezing them together.

I shower under the warm water, washing away the day and the soapy bubbles that cover my beautiful body. I quickly dry myself in the bedroom before mounting the bed and touching my vagina as I lay on my back. I push 2-fingers into my pie and fiddle with my clit with my other hand as I pretend that it's the 2-hardbodies of Jasmine and Laura that are playing with me. I fuck myself harder and harder and I start to shake all over as I reach my final destination and I shudder spasmodically and scream "WAH WAH WAH" as I cum and spit over myself and the bed. I grab one of my dildos - a 7-inch realistic one from Bondara - from out of my sex-draw and lick and suck it like a fucking whore. I slowly ease it into my vagina as I dream of the fit waiter guy as I then begin to fuck it in and out of my body. I moan and pant as I shag myself stupid, the sensation of the fake cock inside my body turning me on more and more with each and every thrust as then I feel myself tighten once again as I orgasm and cum my fuck.

I yelp as I continue my loving until I can take no more, pulling the dildo out and licking and sucking it free of my honey-mucus. I push the rubber further into my mouth, to the edge of my throat, and choke on it like a cunt. I slap my fanny hard time and again to make it sore and sting as I cry in desperate loss for real love and affection. I hurt myself to the point of blood and death and then back off, my minge on fire and red-raw. To cool it down I pour some of the wine over it and it feels so fucking good that I laugh out loud with pleasure and sigh a big "AH."

On my knees I squirt my bumhole with some lube, rubbing a little onto my vagina as well to ease the soreness. I have to use major force to get the knob of the dildo into my anus, it resisting with all its tension. The rubber starts to bend under the strain so I have to jiggle it around to break the seal until eventually I have it and in it slides. It's thick and juicy and I feel my arse expanding as I push it in and start to wank myself. I moan like fuck and it feels so good that I want it to stay up my bum forever as I love my fuck and I cunt myself.

I then finger myself using 3, pushing them into my vagina as I continue to anal myself and it feels like I'm about to split myself apart but I carry on to the bittersweet end when I finally have to let go. I collapse down onto the bed totally knackered - the early start, all the walking of the day and now the wanking has all conspired against me and finished me off.

Reluctantly I pull the dildo out of my bum with a big sloppy squishing sound and then throw it to one side - it feels just as great coming out as it did going in! I hit the shower again to clean myself out and wipe off all the mess from my wanking. After drying myself in the bedroom I slip on my white silk mini-robe from LilySilk - nothing else - and head downstairs to fix myself some dinner, nothing fancy.

The remainder of the day is spent sat on my slightly sore arse in front of the TV watching a couple of Andy's old road-movies on DVD - *Vanishing Point* followed by *Two-Lane-Blacktop* - as there's shit-all on the telly to watch and it bores me to death - so what's new? As I loose myself in the on-screen action, Eva trots in from the garden, saying "Hello" in her own feline way as she passes. She suddenly starts to act strangely, arching her back and gulping. I know exactly what's coming next as this is an almost daily occurrence, and within seconds my fears are confirmed as she begins convulsing and then pukes over my lovely carpet. It's a mixture of grass, small leaves and other such greenery that she's just been eating out in the garden. I tell her every day not to eat them but does she ever listen - no!

That night in bed I semi-lay there with a big mug of milky frothy coffee watching the French comedy *Amelie* - one of my all-time favourite films. It always puts me in such a good mood and before long I drift off to the land of nod.

6

Emma

Once again I find myself looking out for love, even though I don't know what I really want - a fuckbuddy maybe? I WANT someone to be part of my life and to share my life with, someone to love and who will love me back. I know it sounds a bit corny but I don't care, that's the way it really is. I WANT something more than just to feed my unquenchable thirst for love and sexual gratification, someone like Andy or Amanda for instance, but not a liar and a cheat like Steve or indeed myself.

I've trawled through so many websites I don't know whether I'm coming or going, there is simply so much choice on offer that I don't know which way to turn - should I go straight or should I go bent? As you've probably guessed, I'm back on that very same crappy old website where I found that guy Steve in the first bloody place, in my first instalment ages ago, and where I also found those 5-guys in my second - the ones I had that wild and crazy night of passion with - even so I've decided not to go back there again for a third time, I've learned my lesson - yeah right!

Whilst doing my search though I discovered that very same site has an offshoot sister site that just caters for women only - a lesbian site - fuelling the forbidden desire for female flesh. My intrigue is readily piqued and so I take a quick look. Once again this site isn't free so I have to stump-up the £36 joining fee and fill-in all my details. My profile and pictures are accepted almost immediately thanks I'm guessing to the crossover between the 2-adjoining sites so I'm quickly able to peruse as to whom and what is on offer.

I key the search location for West Sussex and press "Enter", making sure I only have profiles with photos appearing on screen. Amazingly, there are about 2-hundred females listed for my County alone, ranging from girls from 18 to their early-20's, some in the 20's/30's bracket, with the vast majority though being 40-plus, and out of that lot, very few of them light my inner-fire, although there are a couple of nice-looking ones but no-one really special - not like myself.

I extend my search to include profiles without photos as I remember from the other sister site that some of the guys on there had their profile photos hidden so that only fully paid-up members like myself could access them. After a good 45-minutes of digging I find 3-honeys buried-away in the group. The first is Lisa, a 27-year old brunette from Storington who looks really lovely. She's followed by Amy, a 36-year old from Horsham with amazing auburn hair like fire and a pretty smile. It's the third girl though that really grabs my attention - Emma - a 32-year old blonde from Worthing on the West Sussex coast. She's simply stunning and has a fantastic body, with about half-a dozen photos of herself in a white micro-bikini on a beach taken in what looks like some foreign hotspot somewhere. She is so fucking gorgeous and I WANT her, I WANT to fuck her with my tongue and have her fingers mess around inside my vagina. I think I'm in love with her already!

I message all 3-girls and await their replies. In a matter of only 2-minutes or so I receive 2-messages back in my inbox, the first one from Lisa saying:

"Thanks for the message but I don't like tattoos."

Oh well, fuck her then! The other is from some bloody black girl in central London who wants to meet up and calls me "Lover." Admittedly she does have a beautiful figure, not like a typical fat-arsed black as she has a more of a white girls body. The problem with her though is obvious - she's black - and therefore NO - I can't and will not go down that road. I don't bother to reply to either of them and block any more incoming messages from both. I don't ever hear back from Amy so I don't know what her problem is? Maybe she didn't even exist in the first place? Maybe she was really a guy in disguise?

Instead I scour around further afield, into Surrey, East Sussex and Hampshire, killing the next couple of hours of my life. I receive 3 more messages, the first being from some old bag in her 50's from Manchester of all bloody places, telling me how much she loves my body and all the dirty things she wants to do to my precious self. The second is from some horrible fat skinhead girl - a real archetypal Left Wing looking dyke with a face like a bulldog chewing a wasp! They're both fucking awful and I block the pair of them as well.

The third message though is from Emma, the honey with the gorgeous face and figure. She seems really nice, surprisingly even a little shy, and asks me to message her back with more info about myself. I do so straight away of course, attaching a smily emojis to the end of my words, although obviously I don't mention to her any of the nasty or stupid parts of my life - I don't want to scare the poor girl off! We chat for the following hour or so, talking about life and love and all that old crap, giving her my mobile number and she returning the same. She's so beautiful that I can't take my eyes off of her!

That evening I pleasure myself to her profile photos as I touch my breasts. I imagine her as naked as I am now, licking and caressing my entire body as I bring myself to climax and wet myself with my juice of love.

I have already given myself to her.

***

It's now over a week later and I'm meeting up with Emma today for the very first time and I'm so excited my heart is set to explode. We've arranged to have lunch together in Arundel but I'm not sure I'll be in a fit state to eat anything, my stomach and my nerves are both shot to pieces already in anticipation. I've been like this pretty much all week, I can't seem to concentrate on anything at all except her - I feel most peculiar.

It's completely unlike me to be this way, I guess it must either be lust or some form of pre-love that's causing it? I've also been masturbating myself to death as well, going stupid over Emma's photos that I've enlarged and printed-off.

After feeding Eva her lunch - duck in sauce with garden vegetables, again! - I leave her and the house in good time, it's 12.05pm. I'm taking the Lamborghini out once again as I just can't leave that car alone, we've become part of one another just like me and my poor old Fiesta ST. I turn right out of the drive and head along the A272 to the A29, neither of which are very busy fortunately. The few cars I do encounter in my way - about 10 or so, including a Porsche Boxter driven by some twat that I have to dispose of going up Bury Hill - are all easily taken care of. I do a left-turn at Whiteways roundabout at the top of the hill and head for Arundel along the A284. This is a great little road, twisty and undulating, and I power the Lambo along with the biggest grin ever - I love it! A quick flick to the left takes me straight into the town, past the magnificent Arundel Cathedral on my right, and I drop down into 2nd-gear as I head downhill through town, the low ratio making the engine note crackle and spit flames through the exhausts as I descend. Tourists and locals all stop and stare like they usually do, at the car and then at me, then back at the car again. They can all take a good look as much as they like, I don't really give a shit about any of them, they mean nothing.

At the small roundabout before the bridge over the River Arun, I do a sharp left onto Mill Road and then right into the towns car-park, parking almost dead centre in the lot. Behind me are a row of at least 8-coaches all parked-up, with one of them emitting a slow steady stream of olds, some of them really ancient and frail. As I extract myself from the Lamborghini I feel the usual sense of a mass of eyeballs on the whole being that is my gorgeous self, the old guys all staring at me in wonderment of my body while all the old girls just stare. I would really love to know what they're all thinking, these old-timers?

I get myself a day-ticket at the machine and walk off to the pre-arranged meeting place with Emma - in the middle of the bridge - how romantic is that! As for my clothes today I've gone for a real upper-class look. I'm wearing my beautiful white bodycon dress from Christian Lacroix that is just pure gorgeous and shows-off my beautiful curves to the max, and on my feet my pair of white suede open-toe ankle-boots from Polyvore. My underwear is also in sexy white lace from Figleaves. My hair and make-up are naturally both done to perfection, featuring a white silk bow in my hair - up, as per the norm - whilst my make-up is classic supermodel with coal-black eyeshadow, high cheekbones and strawberry-red lipstick. My perfume is *No.5* by Chanel. My clutch-bag is my white leather one from Prada.

As I strut past the ancient ruins of the Dominican Friary on my left I spy someone standing at the middle of the old stone bridge - a tall slim blonde beauty. My heart starts to pound like crazy and it skips a beat as I near her. This must be her. Please let it be her. I can't take much more of this and I already feel a little faint as I approach this vision of loveliness before me. I'm about 5-metres from her when she turns to her right to face me and fucking Hell, she is so fucking beautiful - striking is not the word! She starts to walk towards me with a big beaming smile across her perfect face and it's just like looking in the mirror, she looks just like me and I cannot contain myself any longer and I melt into a puddle on the pavement. She is stunning and vivacious in every way. She is so fucking sexy and her beauty radiates from every pore of her hot silky pearlescent skin. She has a gleam in her eye that I recognise at once - that she wants me - as she holds out her right-hand to shake mine and we touch each other for the very first time, hand to hand.

"Hi Sarah, I'm Emma." She says sweetly and kisses me on both cheeks - continental style - our first kiss. She's even dressed similarly to me in a beautiful, tight, figure-hugging white dress - that would look great on my bedroom floor in the morning! - and white suede heals - OH MY GOD! We exchange the usual first-meeting pleasantries when then she suddenly places her right-arm around my waist and pulls me nearer to her. She then plants another kiss to my left-cheek and I immediately fall in love with her - I just can't help myself and fucking Hell again! We chat a little more as we walk back over the bridge together and up the hill a little way to our lunch rendezvous at The Red Lion pub in the High Street. She is just so perfect that I can't keep my eyes off her - her figure, her face, her flowing blonde (real!) wavy hair, those long beautiful legs, her perfect breasts and bum. If I were to die right here and now I would be happy!

We enter the pub as one and I order the first round of drinks, a white wine spritzer for Emma and a large neat vodka for myself. My brain has turned to mush and I can't think straight as all the memories of my previous lovers pale into insignificance and evaporate into nothing. We sit our perfect arses down at a table and chat and giggle as we gaze longingly into each others eyes, the musk of her sex intensifying the transference of energy between us. She has completely melted all my inhibitions away - not that I had many in the first place! - and I WANT to have her right here and now in the pub, right in front of our fellow diners. I want to fuck her on this table and stick my tongue into her perfect vagina and make her cum at me. How the Hell I'm managing to keep control of myself is beyond me, although maybe someone else is keeping check on my emotions, someone from the other side - "HIM"?

We're approached by a young waitress - I think she had short dark hair but I wasn't really paying much attention to her as I only have eyes for Emma - and we both order the same thing for lunch - Arundel butchers sausages with mashed potatoes, ale-battered onion rings, all in a rich onion gravy.

While we wait for our food the conversation twists and turns its way around various subjects - previous lovers, interests, clothes etc. She tells me that she works for an electronics company out of town and asks me what I do for a living? I stumble and stare at her with a blank expression across my face like I've just been slapped by a wet fish. Our meals suddenly arrive just in time to break the flow of her questioning but she repeats herself so I decide to give it to her straight:

"I don't have to work. I have my own means." I inform her.

She laughs at my words and changes the subject, presumably not believing me, just like everyone else doesn't. She then tells me that she rents a flat down in Worthing, not far from the seafront itself, and when I tell her I have a country-house with a swimming-pool and a 20-car garage she almost wets herself laughing!

I'm not trying to be big-headed here as you know, I'm just telling her the truth. Why doesn't anyone ever fucking believe a word I say? Nothing ever changes.

With our lovely food and a second round of drinks all consumed, we decide to quit the pub and go for a wander around town. Arundel is a funny old place, with quirky shops and antique establishments secreted-away up hidden alleyways and behind other shops, the main attraction in the town of course being Arundel Castle, not that I've ever ventured in there I haven't as it's not really my thing.

As we make our way back to the car-park - Emma has also parked there - I notice her tendency to keep putting her hand on the small of my back as we walk, not that I mind I don't, she can put her hand wherever she likes!

"I'm over there." She informs me, pointing to her little dark grey BMW Z4 Roadster.

"Where about's are you parked?" She quizzes me.

"I'm over in the middle, over there." I say, vaguely pointing to the centre of the car-park.

"Which one?"

"The white Lamborghini." I reply with a coy smile.

"In your dreams!" She laughs back.

"It's not a dream, I'm serious. Come on, I'll show you."

Still not believing me, I walk her over to my beautiful Italian piece of moving art.

"This isn't really yours is it?" She questions me.

"It certainly is." I tell her, its doors unlocking themselves automatically as I approach and I swing the drivers-side one upwards and open to prove it to her as she swoons and touches my back once again and I love it.

I offer her my seat in the car and she gets in, or at least tries to as I have to take hold of her hand - her soft, elegant, beautiful, perfect hand - to steady her as I instruct her in the art of getting into one of these things.

"It's amazing, I love it." She beams as she settles herself in behind the wheel.

"I'll give you a ride in it one day." I promise her.

I help her to extract herself from the tight confines of the Lamborghini's cockpit and once out, we find ourselves both hand-in-hand and face-to-face. We look into each others eyes with a sense of longing and in a brief moment we are one but nothing happens - DAMN IT! We both look away from one another until in a split second we find ourselves gazing into one another's eyes once again and we kiss mouth to mouth. She tastes absolutely beautiful on my lips and is so soft and sensual that my heart melts away leaving me with a heady warm glow throughout my entire body - I am so in love. We embrace each other and kiss again and I just wish that time would end right now at this very moment so we could be locked together forever.

We both promise to meet up again soon and it simply cannot be sooner as I clamber into the Lambo myself and fire her up with a roar, Emma leaning down to kiss me once more before I shut my door. I select 1st-gear on the paddle-shift and pull away, both of us blowing a kiss to each other and I am gone.

Out of Arundel on the A284, I go to turn right at Whiteways roundabout to head North on the A29, when out the corner of my eye I spot a couple of road-workers to my left with their shitty white van who are supposedly repairing the road. They're obviously a couple of fucking stinking Slavs judging by their vacant expressions and they both stop and stare at me and the Lamborghini as I near them. Worse is yet to come as as I burble past when one of the cunts spits at my car, hitting the nearside door window with a stream of disgusting splats. I continue driving on in shock and horror as I take the entry onto the A29.

What can I do about it? They would surely just laugh in my face and humiliate me even more if I confronted them. I can't fight them, they would probably rape me and then kill me so what can I do? There's nothing I can do but just continue on and get myself home and try to clear my mind free of them.

But I can't, the image of them spitting at me has already burnt itself into my mind forever and the beautiful meeting between myself and the gorgeous Emma is destroyed and I want to die. They have completely fucking ruined my day - FUCKING SLAV SCUM.

***

Back at the house I destroy myself with the help from my old friend Vlad the Impaler. I don't know why I'm in such a fucking stinking mood, meeting Emma was one of the most exciting moments of this current year so far so why am I feeling like this? I even screamed at Eva to: "FUCK OFF OUT OF MY WAY" when she got under my feet and showed me affection and I've never done that ever before. I just fucking know it's those fucking Slav road-workers that have pushed me over the edge and I want to shoot them all in the backs of their heads - FUCKING BASTARDS.

I've lost count of the number of vodkas and gins I've had, not that it makes a fucking difference to anything anyway in this fucking World. In the bedroom I strip naked and fuck myself with my fingers, pushing 3 into my wet hole and then 4. I'm on my back on the bed with my beautiful long legs spread as wide apart as they will go. I imagine that it's Emma fingers that are playing around inside my pussy and I want her here so badly that I start to cry. Or maybe it's the gin that is making me sad?

As I fuck I begin to feel nauseous and my stomach starts to retch and I can't control it, I have to pull out and as I roll over onto my left-hand side I puke-up an awful grey mixture of vodka, gin and my lunchtime food. I feel like shit and I don't want to carry on. What the Hell is wrong with me? Why do I feel so fucking pissed-off, not just now but all the fucking time?

I stumble into the bathroom to take a shower, hoping that it might reinvigorate me into a more positive frame of mind? Then again, maybe it won't? I catch the reflection of myself in the bathroom mirror and I spit at myself just as those Slav fuckers did earlier. I can't stand to look at my beautiful face and I wipe the gooey phlegm over the glass with both hands to obscure my reflection, wiping away my existence.

Wild dreams and fantasies of suicide begin to swirl around inside my head. I want to kill myself but I don't want to kill myself, why the Hell should I? What the fuck is wrong with me? Why does life have to be so fucking complicated? I imagine drowning Eva and myself in the beautiful lake at Coniston, jumping off the pier by the cafe, and as we both sink into the murky depths we stare at each other in horror as our life-giving air is replaced by the icy water of death and we both die with silent screams of pain and freedom.

I'm only in the shower for a brief 5-minutes before I step out and dry myself off. I put on my white silk mini-robe from LilySilk and plod back downstairs - to what? What am I going to fucking do for the rest of this day? I have nothing to do except some more writing and I'm not in the right frame of mind for that right now. I check my phone to see if anyone has bothered to call or text me and I only have 1-message on the screen - it's from Emma, my darling. As I read her words my evil mood is turned on its head within seconds and I find myself on cloud number-9 as she wants to meet me again, not tomorrow or next week but now - straight away! I immediately text her back telling her how much I WANT her and give her the co-ordinates for her satnav - OH MY GOD! OH FUCKING HELL!

My schizophrenic mind runs wild at the thought of the 2 of us being together as my brain banishes all my previous miserable thoughts and images into its recycling-bin.

One minute I'm down and the next I'm up - my poor old heart.

***

Fucking Hell, she is so beautiful! She is the most beautiful girl I have ever seen - apart from in my own reflection of course! - with her perfect breasts and vagina all radiating pure desire.

We're up in my bedroom and we stand before each other naked. I reach out with my right-hand and cup her left-breast, our eyes aglow with the fire of ecstasy. Her mound is smooth and firm and is a perfect replica of my own in every conceivable way, except that hers aren't pierced. She pulls me closer to her and we kiss softly at first. She then begins to dart her tongue in and out of my mouth and I respond with the same. Nervously I run my right-hand between her sensuous thighs and it feels so soft and smooth and I venture up higher to her sweet vagina and she moans as I rub my hand between her legs, making it wet with her love. I insert my middle-finger between her lips and she pulls me tight to her so our bodies squish together as I play with her hole - her vagina is so bitch and sweet and I love it.

She cries in ecstasy as I give her 2-fingers and she wraps her left-leg around both mine. I flick her clitoris with my thumb and she collapses into my arms and screams and orgasms and cums. I lay her down on my bed and spread her legs apart, her beautiful oyster glistening its love for me and I can resist the temptation of her pouting vaginal flesh no longer. She screams at me: "OH BABE" and "LICK MY CUNT" and "LICK IT HARDER" as I probe the intimate surfaces of her labia. I fuck her with my tongue, flicking it in and out of her delicious hole, her throbbing golden slit as I squeeze and caress her beautiful milk-churns with my other hand making her pant like crazy, she grabbing my hair to pull me tighter into her body. She lets out a sudden sharp scream as she climaxes and ejaculates her juice of love into my mouth and I swallow her. It tastes like pure heaven and I lap at her oozing labia and drink it all down.

We swap positions and I move my body up to her head, straddling her face with my beautiful long legs. I lower myself down onto her and the sensation of her tongue inside my anchovy instantly make me yelp with unrestrained delight. I scream at her: "LICK MY CUNT LIKE A BITCH" and call her a "MOTHER FUCKING CUNT WHORE" and she laughs and laps me with increasing vigour. She parts my labia with her fingers and tongues me deeper. I sit on her mouth and I shake uncontrollably as I'm eaten-out by this vision of gorgeousness, it's like my whole body is shaking itself apart as her mouth and tongue satisfies my sensual delights. I order her to: "STICK 2-FINGERS INTO MY CUNT AND LICK ME HARDER" and she obeys my command in an instant. The suction from her mouth is incredible and I cum on her within minutes and I feel myself spit over and into her as she drives me insane. I touch my breasts as they wobble about as then Emma fucks my cunt, making me explode into orbit. I shout at her again: "PUSH YOUR FINGERS IN DEEPER" and "YOU FUCKING BITCH" as I collapse under the power of my orgasm and surrender my body and soul to her completely. I piss my love into her mouth as she licks me hard and I scream and cum my shit and Hell.

We kiss passionately like lovers as we roll-about on the bed, touching each others perfect bodies, our soft smooth female skin, our firm and full breasts, our beautiful wet vaginas. I wrap myself around her and feel her shape and form as we slide over each others hot bodies in a rhythmic motion, exploring them completely. I slither down her skin as she bleats out cries of "OH OH OH" and she loves me - we are both in love and I die.

As I try to extract myself and stand up our bodies squelch apart, making us both laugh out loud - it's hilarious! I place her on all fours and squirt some lube onto and into her bumhole. Taking my textured glass dildo from Lovehoney, I slowly push it into her and she cries "OW OW OW" as it penetrates and burns its way into her but I don't back off, I want her to feel the pain of my love inside her. I fuck her bum as I simultaneously finger her pussy and she collapses inwardly as I assault her with my passion.

I pull the phallus out of her tight hole and push it into her vagina with one long shove. She moans: "LOVE ME" and "LOVE MY PUSSY" as I tongue at her pouting rectum, the hole still wide and sore from its previous punishment. I continue to fuck the dildo in Emma's box as I then insert lubed 2-fingers into her bumhole, she shouting at me: "FUCK ME LIKE A WHORE" and "CUNT ME" as her beautiful body shakes and quivers with sex.

I order my new lover to: "FIST MY CUNT". I roll over and spread my legs akimbo and she starts to play with my vagina, poking me and fingering me hard, and then forcing her whole hand into my love-box. It hurts like fuck but I love the pain, shouting: "FUCK IT" and "FIST MY CUNT" and "FUCK ME HARDER" and other such obscenities at my beautiful attacker.

Laying her on her back with her legs apart, I bite firmly on my dildo and grip it further with my lips. As I position my face closer and closer to her twat she cries out to me: "COME ON, FUCK ME", "FUCK ME SARAH", "COME ON, DO IT", "OH COME ON", "FUCK MY CUNT NOW". She whines and pants as the glass knob touches her lips and I push it into her. Her fanny parts and in I go, fucking my head and mouth in and out of her vagina. She grabs my beautiful blonde hair with both hands and forces me in further, the blunt-end of the fake cock choking me as the business-end meets the resistance of her internal plumbing but I ignore it - I am gone. I fuck my head into her so far that her lips meet mine, the phallus parting the way for our beautiful sex. About to cum, I pull out of her hole, just in time to catch and savoir the sweetness of her female jism in my mouth and she screams as I eat her vagina, licking at its rare meat.

Both completely exhausted, we fall into each others arms and kiss and fondle. She bites my bum and I love her. She is so beautiful it's like I'm actually fucking myself and I just can't leave her alone. She runs her hands over my gorgeous body, caressing my breasts, my bum, my beautiful long legs, sucking my toes, licking my feet, kissing my armpits, tonguing my vagina. The bitch loves it and I cunt her, rubbing mine against hers. The connection is wet and oily, heightening the sensation of our love. We kiss hard and I tongue her mouth and it's beautiful. She returns the favour and I suck it like a cock. I feel my whole body is levitating off the ground and yet there is no ground as I am in Heaven.

I lay her beside me and kiss her breasts alternatively as I feed my right-hand between her legs, her sex oozing from her slit and she loves me more as I love her back and fuck.

* * *

It's Wednesday evening, actually the first Wednesday of the month. Emma arrived at my place at 12.33pm this afternoon as I'm taking her out tonight. I don't mean I'm going to kill her, I mean that we're actually going out somewhere!

No sooner had she gotten through my front door I had my evil way with her, fucking her on the sofa, the living-room floor and on the snooker table in the games room. She's so incredibly beautiful and I am completely infatuated with her. Afterwards we showered together, dried each other off, kissed and caressed, and then I made us both something to eat for lunch - a jacket potato each with lashings of butter, some cold turkey, and a side-salad with a few pickles, all washed down with a chilled bottle of German white. It was lovely and we both thoroughly enjoyed it.

Anyway, as I've said, we're off out tonight as we're going up to London to an old 1950's-style biker venue called The Ace Cafe, located in Stonebridge, not far from Wembley. They hold different events there all the time, not just for bikes but for cars also, all throughout the year and mainly in the evenings. I remember my late-husband Andy telling me about it, saying that we should go one evening, although unfortunately we never did due to his passing. Tonight though it's time to make amends, so that's where we're going. This evenings event is Hot Rod night so I'm taking Emma there in mine, the black 1932 Ford 3-Window Coupe with the flames painted over the front end. I've only ever driven this car about half-a-dozen times in total and it's completely bonkers, super-loud and actually pretty fast thanks to its massive V8-engine.

Tonight I'm wearing a white Bella bell-sleeved playsuit from Prettylittlething. com that is super-sexy and I leave the buttons at the front undone really low so that everyone can get a good look at my cleavage and my beautiful breasts. On my feet I have on my pair of white suede open-toe ankle-boots from Polyvore that really emphasize my long legs to the max. My underwear is in sexy white from Sensalle. My clutch-bag for tonight is my old chrome Art Deco one from Vintage Styler. My hair and make-up are as you would expect by now - moody and classic - featuring coal-black eyeshadow, plenty of blusher, and orange lipstick. My perfume is *Poison* by Christian Dior.

Emma is wearing a black wool cardigan that she's also left undone really low, also exposing her beautiful, firm, round breasts. She's wearing a pair of denim shorts that are so fucking short that half her bum is hanging out! Not that I'm complaining of course, I can't keep my hands off of her! On her feet she's wearing a pair of black suede heals that are so sexy, whilst her underwear is also in black - I think from Ultimo? She has her beautiful curly blonde hair down with her make-up also done in a classic style but not as hard-looking and sharp as mine. Her perfume is *No.5* by Chanel.

I fire-up the car and it bursts into life with a thunderous roar from the open exhausts, it really is crazy! It's 5.45pm by now as we join the A29 and head North. I didn't want to leave it too late to go or we wouldn't have been able to get in the Ace Cafe car-park and at the same time I didn't want to leave too early or we'd hit all the rush-hour congestion and that would have been a bloody nightmare, especially in this car.

The early evening heat is heady and oppressive as we make our way up the A24 through Dorking and the outskirts of Leatherhead to join the clockwise traffic on the M25. The traffic itself is heavy but flowing and we trundle along at a steady 60-70mph. Naturally we get plenty of looks along the way from all the drivers and passengers, not only because of the mad noisy car but also because of its occupants - 2-beautiful blondes, both with faces and figures to die for.

It's not long before we reach Junction-10 and turn-right to join the A3, where fortunately the congestion is considerably less so I put my foot down a bit harder, keeping the car at around 75. The Rod burbles-along as sweet as a nut, the only annoying feature though being that she's left-hand drive, making overtaking a bit of a mission. The poor rearward viability doesn't help matters either.

From the A3 we turn left and head for Sheen. I really hate it around this part of South-West London, in fact from now on the all surrounding areas get increasingly worse and worse the deeper we head into the Capitol. Along with the decrease in living conditions so does the increase in scum multiply - i.e. stinking bloody foreigners. I don't have to look for them, I can smell them!

Eventually we reach Kew Bridge and once over the River Thames to the other side we turn-right and head for Hammersmith flyover and then left again along the A406 Gunnersbury Avenue. From here on in it's pretty much a straight-line all the way to the Ace with the traffic by now virtually nose-to-tail.

Our journey through the once great Ealing along Hanger Lane seems to take forever before at long last we reach the madness that is the North Circular. Before we head to the Ace though we make a little detour for something to eat as it's now 6.05pm and both our belly's are beginning to rumble as much as the car's engine! We turn-left at the roundabout along the A40 Western Avenue just a little way as here on our left is an American themed restaurant just before the petrol station - Starving Marvin's. It's one of those big silver diners emblazoned with neon signs that has been transported over from the USA and plonked by the side of the road in this crap part of London - a bit weird maybe but what the Hell!

We pull-in and park in their ample car-park, right between a couple of other American cars - a huge red 50's Cadillac Convertible and an early-40's Ford Coupe in black, they both presumably heading to the Ace as well after a feed. We make our way into the diner where we're immediately confronted by one of the waitresses, a young thing in her early-20's with short blonde hair, a pretty face, and with a pair of massive breasts, way bigger than mine - they must be EE's at the very least!

Emma and I sit ourselves down at a small table opposite each other and gaze into each others eyes and hold hands with love. We order our food - steak and chips - with a Coke each as well to wash it down with as we sit there and chat amongst ourselves about life and lovers and love as we wait for our meals. They arrive pretty quickly from the kitchen, served by our sweet little waitress and I could easily fuck her and Emma both at the same time and I start to feel my juices flowing and my adrenalin pumping. The food is really great and the company is gorgeous and funny and we chat-away amid our fellow diners, mostly Hot Rod types with their slicked-back hair and dressed in their American-style garb. We finish up in under 45-minutes and I go and pay the waitress in cash at the till, giving her a tip of £5 also in the process that she accepts with a big beaming "Thank you".

In order to get to our next destination, the Ace, we have to head back in the opposite direction down the duel-carriageway and then spin the car around 180 at the next main junction and double-back. Fortunately it's not that far and little time is wasted. We pass the giant 1930's-style Art Deco Hoover building to our left, illuminated by its garish green lights. It really is beautiful although I also find it a bit sinister and somehow alien-looking at the same time.

We soon spot a couple of other American cars at the North Circular roundabout ahead of us - a beautiful blue Dodge

Charger R/T and a purple Plymouth Barracuda so I decide to follow them as hopefully they're both going to the same place as us. We follow them up the slip-road leading to the Ace and join a queue of about 30 American cars as well as some ordinary commuters in their crappy Euroboxes, and wait as we nudge-along. A gorgeous early Ford Mustang Convertible in pale-blue pulls-up alongside us, driven by a massive guy with a big ginger beard. Sitting beside him in the pure white interior is - I presume? - his wife, a little tiny woman a third of his size with crazy orange spiky hair. I laugh to myself that she has to go on top doesn't she, he would flatten her otherwise!

When they move up, their space is taken-up by a big yellow 1950's truck - I don't know what make it is, they all look pretty much the same to me - its driver leaning and leering out of his window at us like he's never seen a woman before in all his pathetic little life. He then shouts something across at us but I don't catch what he says.

"What did he say?" I ask my love.

"I think he said "Go large baby" or something like that?"

"What's that supposed to mean?"

"I've no idea."

"What a twat!"

"He said it in an American accent but I don't think he's American."

"He's probably never even been there."

"What a knob!" Says Emma and we both laugh at him - stupid old tosser!

At the traffic lights we turn-left and then immediately sharp-right but the idiot in the yellow truck chops my nose off as we round the corner so I give him a quick blast on the old-timer horn - what an arsehole! The car-park to the Ace is already pretty full by the time we get there but there's still enough room for us to park and maybe another half-a-dozen or so more cars to squeeze in after us. Unfortunately one of the Aces officials tells us to park right next to the idiot with the yellow truck, much to my annoyance, so that's what we have to do. Both

Emma and myself clamber out of the Rod, getting plenty of stares as we do so, once more from all the guys as well as the girls, it's a never-ending repeat situation.

I spot the idiot with the yellow truck gorping at me, he's some old guy in his late-50's, short, podgy, and with one of those stupid beards that only goes around the mouth and chin and with a 1950's-style American haircut that he's obviously adopted to make himself look younger - it's not working! We stare at each other for what seems like ages and something suddenly triggers in my mind, that I've actually seen this guy before somewhere, but where? We've definitely met before but I just can't place him and it momentarily gets under my skin.

Emma and I leave the idiot to himself and wander off to have a look around at all the weird and wonderful cars gathered. There's also quite a few bikes here as well and also some choppers - not the sort of choppers you're thinking about though! We head to the bar but the queue for drinks is a bloody nightmare and it takes us a good 20-minutes to be served. We take our drinks - a pint of lager each - and head back outside into the evening heat and have a proper look around at all the machinery. There's all sorts of crazy and beautiful cars here, featuring plenty of Rods like mine including Coupes, Roadsters and trucks, big fat American cars, muscles cars and some bikes mixed in also - mainly Harleys.

There's also a free live band on tonight - starting at 8.30pm - playing in the tiny area over to the left of the main building, so we decide to go and check them out next. We make it inside just in time as the band come on stage and I'm guessing by their name – Susie and the Greasemonkey's - that they're some sort-of 50's Rockabilly band and I guess right. The female singer, a young slim thing in her mid-20's, is dressed in big baggy blue denim dungarees and a bright-red check-shirt and huge black Doctor Martin boots. Her make-up and hair is typical 1950's, featuring a pancake face, bright-red lipstick and golden plaited hair. The rest of the band - all guys - are similarly dressed in outsized jeans and shirts. They start to strum at their guitars and big double bass as the drummer pounds-away his rhythmic beat. The singer - Susie - belts out quite a good tune for an amateur, some 1950's -style stomp that has a nice flowing tune to it, making the small assembled crowd all begin to bop and dance along, they obviously being more into this sort of stuff than Emma and I am. Their set carries-on for almost an hour and all in all they were actually pretty bloody good.

After their second encore, singer Susie announces they have a limited number of CD's of their music for sale at the bargain price of only 10-quid a pop so I decide to get one for a laugh when they finish - what the Hell!

"Hi, I'll take one of your CD's please." I say to her sweetly upon approach.

"Oh right, great, that'll be 10-pounds then please." She returns.

She looks at me and smiles, not because she's attracted to me - at least I don't think so anyway, she might not be gay or bi? - but out of thanks for buying her music. She's actually quite sweet and I try to imagine her naked, her laying on her back on my bed with my tongue in her pussy - that would really make her sing!

Emma comes back to me with a couple more lagers and we wander back outside into the car-park to see what's going on. The sky is completely dark by now as evening gives way to night and there seems to be some sort-of action going on out in the road, with lots of engine noises and the acrid smell of burning rubber wafting in our direction. A couple of muscle cars - actually the Charger and the Barracuda we followed in earlier - are both doing burnous in the street outside the Cafe and then blasting up the road Drag Racing each other to the cheers of the amassed crowd.

Next there's some guy on a bike - some Japanese thing - doing stunts in the middle of the road, causing the traffic in both directions, including a couple of double-decker buses, to stop and wait. Suddenly he jumps off the bike and lays it down on the ground with the engine still going, and then jumps back on it as it spins like a top beneath him, causing him to spin around with it - what a nutter!

Next up, some arsehole in a little Vauxhall piece of crap decides to push his way in on "our" night, attempting burn-outs and hand-break turns in the middle of the road, without much success. He's soon chastised by the crowd, including myself and Emma, with everyone calling him: "Wanker" and "Arsehole" and telling him to "Fuck-off" for gatecrashing our night of fun.

My joy and laughter is suddenly brought to a crashing halt as to my right I notice a couple of foreigners walking in my direction - both stinking Asians - dressed in their stupid fucking Muslim outfits and acting like they own the area, which in a sad way they unfortunately do. The sudden urge to push them both into the road under one of the continuous stream of buses overwhelms me but Emma's beautiful smile and her holding onto my waist thwarts my notion. My blood boils in having to look at them, at having them in my fucking country - FUCKING SCUM.

After another hour or so of antics out in the road, Emma and I decide to head for home. It's been a fun evening and certainly something a bit different to do. Back at the car I notice the yellow truck the arsehole was driving is still there parked next to us. It's starting to bug me now as to who he is, I just know that I've seen him before somewhere but I just can't place him. This is really getting on my tits! It'll come to me one day though I'm sure.

Firing the car up we burble out of the car-park and head back up the road. I give the engine some beans, instantly lighting-up the rear tyres, much to Emma's delight, making her shriek and then laugh. She leans across to me and kisses my right-cheek, placing her left-hand on my bare leg as she does so.

"Thank you for today Sarah, I've had a really great time." She tells me.

"My pleasure, although the evenings not over yet of course." I say to her with a glint in my eye.

She looks at me and gives me one of her beautiful smiles, one of those smiles that melts my heart and she kisses me again.

***

Emma moans deeply as I rhythmically fuck her vagina with 3-fingers, stimulating her sex-nerves.

"Do you like that?" I purr at her like a cat-bitch.

"Oh yeah, harder, fuck me harder Sarah." She sighs.

"You love it you dirty fucking whore." I tease her.

"Oh, push it in further. Oh fuck me you fucking bitch." She counters.

I suck her clit as I masturbate her and she yelps over and over. She starts to lose control as I bring her to her crescendo, she shaking and flailing like a mental bitch. She spits out her cum over my hand and face as I continue to bore into her love-hole and she dies at my wanking, the exhilarating sensation of having her juices sucked out of her vagina by my mouth.

We change positions with Emma laying flat on her back and me over her, my vagina inline with her mouth and my beautiful legs either side of her head. She inserts 2-lubricated fingers into my rear-end and starts to wank me slowly. Her fingers are quickly replaced by one of my dildos - the realistic 8-inch Doc Johnson one - as she steadily pushes the bendy object into my bumhole. It stings me like fuck at first and then she's inside me, completely filling up my rectal passage and I love it. She slides it in and out with a gentle fluid motion as I then feel her mouth and tongue on my vagina. She kisses my lips and then I sense her tongue inside my labia, swirling it around and about and I start to lose myself in her pleasuring.

I pant for air as my heart pressurises the blood around my body and I hallucinate in seconds with snapshot images of Emma's cleavage trying to burst out of her black cardigan, her pert bum in those tight shorts, the Hot Rod, the waitress with the massive boobs, the Ace Cafe, the face of the idiot with the yellow truck, Susie the singer, the burnouts, Emma's mouth, my vagina, Emma's mouth on my vagina, Emma's clit, the dildo up my arsehole and Emma's cum on my tongue as it then slides down my throat.

***

Work on the book is pretty-much complete now. I know I'm biased but I really do think that its turned out okay, although it does need several check-throughs to iron-out any bugs and stuff. The photo for the front-cover was easily sourced, it being one of myself laying on my bed with my gorgeous long fishnet clad legs towering above me. Emma took the shot on my DSLR camera and it's beautiful, as am I of course! She did photoshop all my tattoos out though - I don't want to scare people off!

It's been a real struggle to get the book done though, not only trying to fit it in with my lifestyle, but trying to fit my lifestyle around it - it has been a fucking nightmare! Just like every other artist, one is never happy with the finished work - it can never be finished - and that's the problem.

I was going to get myself an agent to do all my dirty-work for me and hunt for a publisher, but seeing as I have so much free time on my hands I thought:

"Why the fuck should I when I can do it all myself?"

Plus of course they would also want a slice of the action - the money that is - and I don't see why I should need to do that, so I'm going my own way as per usual. I've also sent preliminary copies off to several publishers - about 10 or so - but half of those didn't even have the common decency to reply, with the others just poo-pooing it, coming out with shit like: "Not realistic enough", "More like porn than romance" and other such bollocks. One of them even gave me a score of 3 out of 10 so they're no fucking loss - idiots!

Something will come up, I know it will, I can feel it in my water.

7

Jaime

I don't know if you remember but a little while ago I seem to recall myself saying something like: "I wish I was a transgender and then I would have the best of both Worlds - tits and a cock", or something like that? I'm really not sure why it is that I'm so fascinated by them, almost every time I watch porn on my computer I end up searching for them as well as all the other things - the straight stuff and the gay.

My wedding to Amanda is another case in point - remember all those weird and wonderful trans-girl bridesmaids over in Las Vegas? - weren't they great!

I simply cannot tell you how much I miss having a guy in my life. The problem is though, as ever, I need another woman in my life to comfort me also. I just can't seem to find an even balance. So what's new?

I've thought long and hard about this and I've decided that I want to meet a T-girl, not necessarily to instigate some form of sexual relationship - there's that horrible word again! - but maybe just to be friends with, we'll have to wait and see?

A quick Google search of Transgender Contact UK on my laptop reveals a secret World of strange creatures, all hiding behind masks of various descriptions. I click on one site based in London and I just cannot believe what I'm looking at - basically just contact adverts featuring what are reportedly transgender/transexual but are nothing than men in terrible-looking wigs! I laugh out loud at their photos, they're fucking hilarious - what a scream! One of them has even painted his face silver for some bizarre reason? He looks like a right nutter!

When I notice his location everything become clear though - he comes from Croydon - and that explains everything, enough said!

I click onto one site after another but I get nowhere as I realise that I'm going about this completely the wrong way. I change tack and stumble across an online noticeboard site - *Friday Ads* - selling everything from cats to the kitchen sink - literally! - and beyond. They also have a dating page that seems to be quite extensive, catering for anything one might desire, whether you're straight, gay, lesbian, bisexual, crossdresser, transvestite, and, lo-and-behold - transgender. I decide to check each genre out just for a laugh, I've got fuck-all else to do anyway, apart for some more writing and a ton of washing and ironing to do and I'm not doing any of that shit today that's for sure.

The guys on the straight section all seem like a right bunch of creeps, mainly old wankers and silly little boys - no real men. In the gay section there are tons of great looking fit guys to be had but that's just typical isn't it? Some of them are super-fit and I would love to get my hands on them but unfortunately they wouldn't be interested - what a waste!

The girls in the lesbian section are just as rough as the arseholes in the straight group. Some of them are real old dogs and there's not one nice little honey amongst any of them.

The bisexual section offers a little more hope, there's some really nice-looking and interesting guys and girls on there so I will have to keep this site in mind for the future.

I can't believe my eyes when I click onto the crossdresser/transvestite section as who do I see before me but none other than the old wanker from Croydon with the silver face again - what a twat! The rest of them on there aren't much better either! I scroll down through the transgender list, there's only 11 of them listed on here for the South East of England anyway and most of those look like failed drag queens! There is one particular girl who looks quite nice though, standing out amongst the dregs. Her name is Sally and she comes from East

Grinstead in East Sussex, which is a little too far away for me really but what the Hell? Her profile says that she's 29, blonde (not real), and is looking for either a guy or a girl - well, that's me isn't it? She has about 10-photos of herself online, including a few of her cock which looks nice and hot and it really turns me on. There's also a couple of her being fucked up the arse by some really old guy in his 60's - whatever lights your candle I suppose! I send her a message, telling her what I want, and await her reply.

As for the 3 other transgirls on the list they don't have photos but I take a quick peek at their profiles anyway. They're all older than me, 2 in their 40's and one in her late-30's. The 2-older ones I forget as one lives in Kent and the other in Essex, both too far away for my want. The third girl - Jaime - is 37 and lives in Cranleigh in Surrey, a nice little town that I even thought of moving to once upon a time but was put off by the influx of Pikey's - the fucking scum that they are.

She sounds really nice anyway and so I send her a message, attaching a nice photo of yours truly to it as well. I love being transromantic/panromantic and it increases my options for fucking.

***

It's 3-days later before I receive any replies from that dodgy transgender website. I say "replies" as I only get the 1 and that's not from the honey that is Sally but from Jaime, the one without a photo to her profile. Her message is short and sweet and she too has attached some pics of herself, and when I open her zip and take a look at them, I'm gob-smacked by her image, I cannot believe how gorgeous she is - she's fucking amazing! She has a beautiful round face, a mass of curly blonde hair (once again not real, I can tell a mile off!), and a figure to die for. She's dressed all in black in a sheer long-sleeve top with a lace bra on underneath that really shows-off her lovely breasts and cleavage. She has gorgeous wide eyes and a perfect smile and I'm intrigued by her hidden mystique and I actually think I'm a little bit taken! All 5 of her photos are really tastefully done and very professional-looking as I check out the room in the background which also looks very classy. I message her back to thank her for getting in touch and ask her: "Where do you want to go from here?" and "Maybe we can meet up for a drink sometime?" and await her reply.

***

Jaime and I have been emailing and texting each other for almost a week now. She seems really nice and even has a good sense of humour. Anyway, I'll find that out soon enough as we're having our first face-to-face meeting today for lunch. I'm driving over to her neck-of-the woods to Cranleigh, meeting-up at The Three Horseshoes pub in the main High-Street.

Once again I'm going for my full-on killer-look. I'm wearing my sexy white Bandeau bandage dress from Lipsy, underwear in white lace from Figleaves and a gorgeous pair of Fetish Peep Lace Gloss heals from Christian Lauboutin that cost me over £700! My clutch-bag today is my white leather one from Prada once again as I love it to bits. My perfume is *No.5* by Chanel. My hair and make-up is all done in my usual perfect style, featuring a white cotton bow in my hair and cherry-red lipstick and I look killer-hot!

Without too much deliberation I'm taking the Lamborghini out yet again today, sacrilegiously neglecting all the other cars in my fleet - poor cars! I blast out of my driveway and head East to the A29. I'm only going for a couple of miles when all of a sudden some old cunt in his 70's pulls straight out on me from his driveway as I head through Wisborough Green, chopping my nose off. How the fuck I miss him I just don't know and I screech to a halt in the middle of the road with the old fucker completely oblivious to what he's done and just continues to trundle off up the road without a care in the fucking World! I tear after the bastard as I'm not letting this one go, this fucker is about to see the wrong fucking side of me! I catch him up easily and overtake him on the wrong side of the road, he looking at me in disbelief as I pull alongside and then overtake, slotting myself in front of him and slowly coming to a halt in the road, blocking him off so he can't get past. Jumping out of my car, I go back to confront him and give him an earful:

"ARE YOU FUCKING BLIND?" I scream at him.

"Why? What's the matter?" He says, staring at me like the ignorant twat he is.

"YOU PULLED STRAIGHT OUT ON ME BACK THERE WITHOUT EVEN FUCKING LOOKING."

"I didn't see you, I'm sorry."

"I KNOW YOU DIDN'T SEE ME YOU STUPID OLD CUNT. YOU SHOULD GET YOUR FUCKING EYES TESTED. YOU SHOULDN'T EVEN BE ON THE FUCKING ROAD IN THE FIRST PLACE."

"Oh, I'm sorry." He bleats like a twat.

"DON'T KEEP SAYING YOU'RE FUCKING SORRY. IF YOU EVER FUCKING DO THAT TO ME AGAIN I'LL FUCKING KILL YOU, YOU OLD CUNT."

I clamber back into the Lambo and scream-off down the road like a scalded cat, the cars tyres leaving black lines on the tarmac as I do so, with the drivers of all the waiting backed-up traffic rubber-necking my actions. So what if I was doing 60 in a 30-zone, that's not the bloody point - the old fucker pulled-out on me, he could have killed us both.

The rest of my journey goes by thankfully unhindered, bypassing the A24 in favour of going through Rudgwick and then directly into Cranleigh itself. I park in front of the pub in one of their small parking spaces, being watched all the time by passers-by on foot and my fellow motorists in their crappy boxes on wheels.

The Three Horseshoes is really ancient looking - I think some parts of it actually date from the 15th-Century or somewhere around there - and is one of those traditional old-fashioned English pubs and I guess it has its own charm. Inside is pretty much the same thing, all old beams and the typical period fixtures and fittings. Thankfully there's only a few people inside, a middle-aged couple in the cosy snug to my left and an old guy in his 60's propping-up the bar, obviously a regular judging by his demeanour.

I order a pint of lager and a large neat vodka chaser and go and sit my pert arse down over at a table to the right and wait for Jaime to arrive. I wonder what she's really like? I hope that she really does look like her photos and not some guy in a dress or for that matter that old twat from Croydon with the silver face! I'll fucking die if she turns out to be him - fucking Hell!

As I sit there thinking to myself the old guy at the bar turns around and looks at me square-on - what the fuck is his problem? I look the other way, at the main doors, in the desperate hope that Jaime will walk through them any second and put me out of my misery. It's now 1.10pm and she's 10-minutes late.

"You waiting for someone?" The old guy suddenly chirps at me. Please don't let him be her and this is has all been one big bloody wind-up. I can't stand much more of this tension.

"Yeah" I reply curtly.

"Boyfriend is it?" He comes back like the nosey old git he is.

"It's actually got nothing to do with you." I cut him.

"I'm just being friendly." He returns.

"Yeah, well, I'm not a friendly girl." I hit back.

"Charming!" He quips, turning back around to take another sip of his beer.

"Bollocks" I mumble.

At that precise moment the main door opens and in walks Jaime, a vision of loveliness as she quickly spots me also and heads over in my direction. She's tall and willowy, dressed smart but casual in a white silk blouse, grey skintight jeans and grey suede ankle-boots. Her hair is big and wild and I think it's probably a wig but I'm hoping that I'm wrong. Her make-up is as impeccable as mine and her grey eyeshadow is superbly applied, maybe professional even.

"Sarah?" She says to me.

"Hi, you must be Jaime?"

"Hi, pleased to meet you at last."

"And you, what would you like to drink?" I enquire with a smile.

"I'll have an absinthe thanks." She tells me and I really can't stand that disgusting shit - yuk!

I get up to get her her drink and I notice her checking me out as I wait at the bar and I smile at her attention, loving the fact that this creature - this she-male - is attracted to me. I order another lager for myself as well as her green poison and then return to our table, sitting myself down right opposite her.

We chin-wag and laugh and gossip - you know the way it goes! - and she tells me of her work at a travel agent just off the main High Street here in Cranleigh.

We seem to hit it off really well but all the while we're talking I have to stop myself looking down at the triangle between her legs as I secretly try to spot any kind of bulge in her jeans - there is none. Is she really a pre-op or is her cock so bloody small its undetectable? Her face is absolutely flawless and even her facial features are seemingly those of a pure female with not a single trace of any masculine elements. There's not even any sign of an Adams apple to be found on her beautiful neck. Was she really born male or is she just winding me up? In fact when I really study her, every part of her body, I do actually notice a few strange misnomers - her hands are 2-different sizes for a start, her left being bigger than her right which is feminine and delicate whilst her left is more manly and slightly out of proportion. I also notice the tops of her arms are also very manly with well defined muscles, just like a guy would have, coupled with broad-ish shoulders. Her hips are also very slim, again just like a guys would be, which makes her bust seem larger than it actually is.

We chat about her life and how its changed dramatically due to her sexuality, telling me that according to expert diagnosis, she suffers from something called *Klinefelter Syndrome,* a condition that only effects transgender people like her. She also tells me that both her parents apparently disowned her when she told them she was really a woman trapped inside a man's body and that she was going to have a sex-change. Her older brother even beat her up and broke her jaw and one of her arms when she told him her news - what a bastard!

The really strange thing is, even though she's been through Hell in coming to terms with who and what she actually is - the hormone replacement, the psychological turmoil that no-doubt she's suffered, surgery for her breast implants, being cut-off by her family and all that shit - she doesn't want to be a complete woman. She doesn't want to go the whole way. She doesn't want a vagina and is keeping her meat and 2-veg intact! When I quiz her as to why, she can't - or won't - answer me and just dismisses the idea totally. What the Hell is all that about? Why go through all that trauma and still live like this - half man/half woman? It doesn't make any sense, not to me anyway.

We finish our second round of drinks and we decide to go, strolling outside into the fresh-air of the day where I blip the remote to the Lambo as she sits there dormant awaiting my command.

"Is that yours?" Enquires Jaime somewhat over-enthusiastically.

"It is yes, do you like it?" I ask her, trying not to be too pretentious at the same time.

"It's beautiful. I can't believe how low it is?"

"I know, it's crazy isn't it? Getting in and out is a bit of a pain but the driving experience more than makes-up for that. I'll take you for a spin if you like, if you've got time?"

"Definitely yes, that would be amazing!" She beams.

We both slide our way into my low Italian weapon and I fire-up the massive V12-engine with a throaty roar, much to Jaime's delight. I click the paddle-shift into 1st-gear and off we go, pulling out of the car-park and turning left into the High-Street. I blast the car through town, keeping it in 2nd-gear so that the higher revs of the engine generate more noise. Everyone - well, virtually everyone! - stops and stares at the car and us as it snorts and spits its way up the road, around the roundabout at the very far end where I then double-back and blast back down the High Street once more.

"Would you mind dropping me back at my place Sarah?" She asks.

"Yeah sure, where do you live?" I question her.

"Just down to the mini-roundabout and turn-right, is that OK?"

"Of course it is, is that where you live?"

"Yeah, I've a little cottage just down here." She says, pointing to her right as we enter her road - Knowle Lane - how appropriate!

We burble down the road for a short while until Jaime points to her house, a quaint little terraced cottage in white with some sort-of creeping plant winding its way over its facade and a gorgeous gleaming red Alfa Romeo C4 sportscar nestling on the small gravel front driveway. I park directly over her drive, partway on the pavement also as the Lambo is super-wide and the road is fairly narrow - I don't want some twat to side-swipe it.

"Would you like to come in for a coffee?" She says coyly, looking at me with those big green eyes of hers.

"Okay sure." I reply without hesitation, knowing full-well what "coffee" means, as do you.

She kisses me tenderly on the lips as soon as the front-door is closed behind us and I immediately sense the taste of anise on her mouth from her drink earlier. I love it and I kiss her back, harder. I feel myself being pulled toward her like a magnate and I'm her metal, pulled into this strange forbidden love. Her sensuous eyes are filled with sexual bliss that immediately sends my heart into mad palpitations and I melt.

We hold each other with hands on each others waists as we kiss and tongue and then embrace each other fully as we squash our bodies together. I sense something different about her as we fall in lust, something alien to all the other girls I've been in a similar position with - it's Jaime's cock - I can feel it, I can feel it against the mound of my vagina and it turns me on like fire. We stumble from the narrow confines of the hallway into the living-room, its vision triggering recognition in my mind from the photos she emailed me. It's decorated in total contrast to the outside of the cottage, it being modern and minimal in its execution, beguiling its very existence and heritage.

She touches my breasts as I flick my tongue in and out of her mouth and I start to pant with excitement and I'm hot. We sit ourselves down on her tan-coloured leather sofa and kiss and touch each other. She suddenly backs-off and on one articulate and fluid motion peels-off her top, revealing her perfect full breasts - whoever did her implants did a fantastic job, they're absolutely beautiful. We kiss again and I touch her tits, they feel so real no-one would ever know. She removes her black lace bra and flings it to one side and her exposed breasts are wonderful, firm and round and I suck and kiss and gently bite them. She lays back on the sofa as I caress and squeeze them, using my tongue to excite her small nipples and she moans as I love her with pure unhindered passion.

I run my right-hand between her legs but she stops me, grabbing my arm to forbid me any more attention. She kicks her shoes off and away and then undoes the belt to her jeans. I stand before her and strip completely naked in a matter of 30-seconds, lobbing my clothes and footwear I don't know where. She leans forward and touches my twat with her right-hand and it's wet with excitement and I feel it become engorged and beginning to drop.

Leaning back Jaime starts to undo her jeans, popping the top button and then pulling down the zip. Using both thumbs she removes them and kicks them away to her left, revealing her strange underwear, a white pair of what look like cut-down tight-fitting y-fronts. She wriggles her lithe body as she slowly removes them, the tension in the room becoming intoxicating to the point of suffocation.

I cannot believe what my eyes are seeing. This is unreal. She is amazing. She has the face and body of a woman but a cock instead of a pussy and I love her with all my heart. She is mine. My pleasure is all mine.

With her underwear discarded and dispatched to the floor, Jaime lays back before me, a beautiful vision of a woman so gorgeous she could be real. Her perfect body, her face, her hair, her lovely breasts, her long slender legs and her beautiful hard shenis. It grows as she wanks it and I drop to my knees in love. Without invitation I kiss her knob and run my tongue along its shaft, sensing her taste. I grab hold of it with my right-hand and take-over its masturbation as then I swallow it, taking its full length to the back of my throat, making her yelp with pleasure as I slurp-away at her/him.

She pulls my hair as I suck her cock and play and fiddle with her bollocks. As ever though I WANT MORE and I drop her out of my mouth and climb on top of her seated body. My brain becomes confused as to what she really is, although now I can somehow understand why she doesn't want to go the whole way and have her lovely cock and balls removed - they're too fucking good for that. I position myself over her, straddling her slender thighs as I sit on her legs. She touches my right-breast with one hand whilst keeping herself hard with the other as then I lower myself down onto her, feeling her bulb kissing my lips, my brain telling me "No" but my vagina telling me "Yes". I open myself to her and I wince and gasp as I take Jaime's bare cock inside me. Ironically it's one of the best cocks I've ever had - perfectly formed and thick and juicy as it hits my vaginal nerves, making me howl with lust. I ride her meat as she kisses and fondles my tits and we are both in Heaven as we fuck and it's so good to have a real cock inside me again, even if it is attached to another woman! I ride her penetration with rhythmic fucking, making me buck and moan and pant like a bitch.

I semi climb off of her and grab her tool with one hand as I do so. I squat back down once again, still with her cock-in-hand as I guide it into my puckered bumhole. It's fucking tight without proper lube but my vaginal juice helps a little but only slightly as I squeeze her into my rear-end as I fuck her cock up and down until it starts to get a little too tight and I have to back off.

I climb off and stand before her, her weird beauty freaking me but also driving me on. I drop to my knees once more and suck her cock ATM as I phlegm on it, simultaneously playing and pulling her man-conkers. In a moment I feel her tense as she starts to shake and moan loudly and with one hard tug on her sack and a long hard suck on her cock she screams a she spurts her cum into my mouth, a viscous orgasm that caresses throughout her nakedness as her muck ejaculates into my gob, the nasty white goo sticking to my tongue and my teeth as I hold it within my throat. I dribble it back out onto her cock, over her ball-sack, down my chin and onto my 2-girls as I wank her. I go down and lick and suck her dirty spent cock, making it mine to own and abuse. She strokes my hair as I lick her knob as she calls me "Baby" and "You dirty fucking whore bitch."

We swap positions and I open my legs to her. From this angle she appears to be pure woman as her man-parts are out of sight and I love her. She gives me one long quick lick to my labia and I pant heavily, making my breasts heave with excitement. She opens my shinning beauty with her fingers and I cry as she licks at my waiting clit, making it tingle and twitch. She finger-fucks me with 2-fingers in and out of my hole as she continues to suck on my bulb, making it pulsate with pleasure. It's not long before I feel myself go blind as my orgasm starts to overload my vision and I cum, spitting-out my love onto Jaime's face and awaiting tongue.

We kiss passionately and feel and touch each others bodies as we lay entwined on the sofa. She calls me: "My lover" and I kiss her beautiful lips as I wank her cock. We laugh and joke as we play and I suck her again, taking this female cock into my mouth. I wank her as I suck and yank her sack and it only takes a couple of minutes as I have her again and suck her jism out of her with all my strength. I swallow some down glug glug glug and spit the rest out onto her tits, rubbing the mess over their firmness with my mouth and tongue.

We shower together in piping-hot water and she anal fucks me as I spread myself flat to the tiled walls of the small shower cubicle. We are both in love and we will always have this moment forever etched in our hearts and minds until our final days.

"OH COME ON, FUCK ME, FUCK MY ARSE. TALK DIRTY TO ME." I shout at her.

"Love my cock Sarah."

"Cum in me, come on, fuck me harder."

"I'll fuck you like a bitch."

"Come on then, harder."

"I'll split your arse in two you fucking whore."

"Do what you want to me. Fuck it in me and finger my cunt. Fuck me harder. Finger me harder."

"OH OH OH OH, I'm gonna cum, I'm gonna cum."

"Cum up my arse. Harder."

"OH OH, I'm cumming OH OH OH."

"Oh that's it, cum in me, keep going."

"I don't have any more."

"Keep fucking me, just a bit more."

"I can't, I don't have any more, I'm done."

"Let me lick it." I say as I drop down onto my haunches, taking her into my mouth once more.

"Oh that's good, oh oh oh uh uh." She moans like a whore.

"I wanna eat your muck."

"Oh that's it. Oh my God. Oh you dirty bitch Sarah."

"You love it just like I do you dirty cow, you fucking bitch."

"Oh that feels so good, oh Sarah."

"Come on, stay hard for me and fuck my mouth, fuck it like a cunt."

"Oh go on, oh, oh come on, oh, oh my God, oh my God."

"No more?" I quiz her/him.

"No more, I'm done." She sighs.

"Now I see why you don't want this lovely thing of, your lovely cock. I love it."

"You're so beautiful Sarah."

"Yes I know, and so are you. Now lick my cunt like a fuck."

8

Emma & Jaime

Using my fingers I part Emma's lips, making her clit peek out at me, it pulsating like a miniature heart. I lick it gently and slowly, making her pant and whine as Jaime fucks my pussy from behind with her beautiful cock.

It's morning and the 3 of us are fucking on my bed and we are in love. Jaime fucks Emma's tits as I sit on her face as she licks my vagina and I cum. Jaime gives Emma a pearl-necklace and I rub it into her breasts and lick it, slurping some down as I do.

We continue to fuck for the next hour or so and then shower together, dry each other, apply each others make-up and do each others hair and then dress each other in our respective bikinis, all done with plenty of touching, kissing, laughing and general sodding about. My bikini is a skimpy white one from UjENA that also has a white sarong with it that makes me look and feel super-sexy and hot. Emma's is equally lovely, a yellow number from Blue Life Swim that is pure gorgeous, whilst Jaime's is in orange from Bed of Roses that also has a sarong to it and she looks as beautiful as ever.

After a breakfast of cereal, half a grapefruit each and freshly squeezed orange-juice with a splash of vodka, we spend the rest of the morning topping-up our tans whilst laying on sun-loungers in the garden over by the summerhouse. It's a beautiful sunny hot day with not a single cloud in the brilliant blue sky and I am so fucking happy that I can't stop laughing to myself! We rub each other with sun-cream all over our naked bodies and kiss and finger and suck and fuck and cum and I can count my lucky stars to be me right here and now at this time.

Not only do Emma and Jaime share my bed but they now also share my home, both of them having moved in with me a short while ago. Things seemed to have worked out reasonably well between the 3 of us and we all seem to get along fine, although I do have a strange gut feeling that it won't last forever. The 3 of us even sleep together in my bed, it being a Super King-size 4-poster there's no problem with space, even though sometimes it can be a bit awkward.

Eva doesn't like the situation though as there's now not much space left on the bed for her to snuggle down - poor old thing! She'll just have to get used to it, for however long it lasts. For me though, all I need and want at this moment is the 3 of us to be together - I WANT 3.

***

I'm in the kitchen with Emma preparing lunch. We're having salmon and cucumber sandwiches, washed down with a nice bottle of chilled MUMM Champagne from my collection.

From there I vaguely hear the buzzer for the electronically-operated entrance gates sound in the background as Emma places her right-hand on my bum and plants a soft tender kiss to my left-cheek - the cheek on my face that is! I respond to her love by touching and squeezing her lovely pert breasts whilst licking one end of the cucumber provocatively with my tongue, making us both giggle like a couple of naughty schoolgirls.

"Sarah, it's the Police at the front gate." Jaime calls out to me from the hallway.

Oh shit! What the fuck do they want now? I stop what I'm doing and join Jaime at the camera monitor by the front-doors and yes, it's the stupid fucking law once again. The buzzer buzzes for the 2nd-time so I reluctantly answer it.

"Yes?" I say curtly.

"Sarah Knowles?" Says the pig at the gates.

"Yes?"

"It's the Police Miss Knowles. We'd like to ask you a few questions, if you would let us in please."

"Okay. Come and park in front of the house."

I can't fucking believe this. What is their fucking problem this time?

"What is it Sarah? Why are the Police here?" Jaime quizzes me.

"It's nothing to worry about. It's probably just about that stupid girl that I used to work with, the one that went missing." I explain.

"Yeah, well, I don't wanna get involved with the fucking Police."

"Yeah, well, neither do I so just stay cool." I cut back at her sharply.

I press the button on the entry-phone and watch the front gates steadily open and the cops drive in and up to the front of the house. Emma comes to join us to see what's going on as I open the front-door to find 2-male Police officers heading in my direction. I stand back to let them in and close the door behind them, the taller one of the pair I notice having been here before, just after that bitch Mellis "disappeared."

They enter and momentarily stare at the 3 of us girls, each of us still dressed in our skimpy bikinis, there being no need for the use of imagination to see what beautiful bodies each one of us has as both Emma and Jaime stand there taciturnly in silence. I somehow start to feel strangely protective and concerned for Jaime, she not being a real woman, with the fact that the sarong wrapped around her waist doesn't entirely conceal the noticeable bulge of her meat and 2-veg, even though it has obviously descended in detumescence somewhat since our fun and games earlier!

"Miss Sarah Knowles yes?"

"Yes, that's right. You were here before, about that missing girl?"

"Mary Ellis, that's right."

"So what is it this time? Have you found her?" I say super-cool.

"No, we haven't found her. We were just wondering if you had any more information regarding her disappearance?"

"No, nothing. Why would I?"

"Do you live here alone Miss Knowles?" The other copper suddenly pipes-up. He's much shorter than the other one - and ginger - and with a sallow expression on his face that makes him look ill.

"No, I live her with my 2-girlfriends, and my cat."

"We all live here together." Jaime tells them bluntly.

"As lovers." I underline, placing an arm around both Jaime's and Emma's waists as I stand between them and pull them closer to me, although surprisingly neither of the cops react to my action and just stand there expressionless like the brain-dead pigs they are - typical.

"So how did you know Miss Ellis Miss Knowles?" Says ginge.

"We used to work together. I've already told you all this months ago so why the repeat visit?" I attack.

"We just wondered if you had any more information for us." Pipes-up the other officer once more.

"No, I haven't. I've already told you that."

There then follows a brief moment of silence that actually feels like an age. I even expected to see a tumble-weed roll past us through the hallway because of the tension but obviously that doesn't actually happen!

"So did either of you 2-ladies know Miss Ellis?" The smart-arse copper says to both Emma and Jaime.

"No, I've no idea who she is." Says Jaime.

"Me neither, I've never heard of her." Says Emma.

"So is there anything else?" I quiz them back, a little pissed by now obviously.

"We would like to have another look around Miss Knowles if that's alright?" Says the first pig.

"What for? You've already been around my house once so why again, what's the point? I can assure you that she's not here. What do you think it is that I've done, chopped her up and eaten her?" I coldly joke to them.

"No, of course not. We would just like a quick look around that's all. It's just routine, it won't take long."

"We're just about to have lunch." I snap back.

"It won't take long Miss Knowles." They bite back at me.

Reluctantly I'm forced to guide the 2-coppers around the house as quickly as I dare as Emma and Jaime depart to the kitchen to finish preparing lunch and then transporting it out to the gazebo in the middle of the mini-lake to await my return.

Once again I'm stuck in *deja vu* as both officers ask me the same tired old questions as before about the house, the cars, Andy, myself, and of course that fucking bitch Mellis. Just why are they here? Are they trying to trip me up? They've got no fucking chance of that, I'm way too sharp for either of them - idiots. It takes a good 30-minutes to show them all around the house, the garage and the garden. Just what they were hoping to find I just don't know - Mellis's head on a stick I suppose?

"Right then, if you're both all done then maybe now I can go and have my lunch, or what's left of it." I bitch at them.

"We're sorry we held you up Miss Knowles."

"Really? I doubt that for a start, so if you don't mind." I say sarcastically, showing them the door.

They both leave with plenty of shoulder shrugging and more eyeballing of my beautiful breasts. I watch them drive out of the main gates as I then press the button to close and lock them shut. Even though they've fucked-off, I know deep down that they'll be back again for more - I can feel it in my bones.

It feels like the net is closing in all around me and I'm not sure I can take it. I have to be strong, I have to, there is no other alternative. It scares me what I've done. What is it inside me that drove me to kill another human? If the Devil strikes me again there's no telling what I might do? If people didn't keep pissing me off then there wouldn't be any problem would there?

I make my way out into the garden to see my 2-lovers. They're both sitting in the gazebo supping champagne and muttering-away to one another and when I join them they both quiz me with question after question like I'm being interrogated by the bloody Police all over again and I have to warn them both to either: "SHUT THE FUCK UP OR GET OUT OF MY FUCKING HOUSE."

Jaime is especially harsh to me - she is effectively male after all, despite the hormone replacement treatment and the breast implants. Our lunch is ruined of course, not the actual food, but the atmosphere between the 3 of us has killed it stone dead.

I leave them to it and head back into the house and drown my sorrows on vodka. It only partially helps and so I head to the pool, strip naked, have another big slug of the Russian poison straight from the bottle and throw myself in.

***

I abandon myself to them as Emma begins licking my lips as I simultaneously suck-away on Jaime's rock-hard cock. I feel my mind losing consciousness and everything goes multicoloured as I cum and shake like a fucker. Emma comes to join me and sucks on Jaime's delicious cock also as I play and suck her balls. She can't contain herself any longer and screams out loud to us: "I'M GONNA CUM, I'M GONNA CUM", unloading several spurts of she-male seed into Emma's mouth, it dribbling out and down her member onto her balls and my awaiting tongue.

Jaime licks my vagina as I lick Emma's in a 3-way circle of love and fuck. She quickly starts to lose control and I have her, fingering her love-tube as she spits her honey over them. I take a while longer as Jaime's tongue is quickly replaced by her dick as she cums inside me and I scream and shit. Emma licks Jaime's semen from my oozing cunt as I suck on Jaime's dirty member, tasting both mine and Emma's love-juice on her she-cock as she tongues at Emma's hole.

I fuck Emma up the arse with my strap-on cock - the one from Lovehoney - as she swallows Jaime's real cock to the back of her throat and chokes and spits. Caressing my perfect breasts under the glare of the midday Sun I cannot think of anything or anywhere that I'd rather be or doing than being here right now fucking with my 2-lovers.

***

Success! After literally months of trying one bloody publisher after another, I've finally found one that is willing to take me on. They're called *Arachnid Publications,* and are based in Peterborough in Cambridgeshire.

They are in fact self-publishing affiliators, the next best thing to a real full-blown publisher, but even so, my book is going to be published - AMAZING!

It's been a long, hard road getting here of course but I've finally done it. I feel so elated my feet aren't actually touching the ground!

I just hope that it all works out okay - fingers crossed!

***

A soft wind swirls around my naked body as I masturbate myself whilst leaning up against one of the silver birch trees in the back garden. It's 3-weeks later and it's raining.

Neither Emma or Jaime live with me any more, with none of us on speaking terms with each other either. The 2 of them had a big bust-up - not for the first time I must add! - with Emma calling Jaime a "freak" and other such things, so in turn I had to put the brakes on our 3-way love. Jaime also turned nasty - transgenders can be viscous creatures - and kept going on about the fucking Police being here and the so-called "missing girl" and whether I did actually have anything to do with her disappearance and so in the end I had to tell them both to: "FUCK-OFF OUT OF MY FUCKING LIFE."

It's a shame as I really thought that Emma could be another Amanda but it wasn't to be. She said she loved me so why has she gone? I miss her so much, I had hoped that we would become inseparable lovers but no - once again everything has turned to shit.

Jaime was a different story though, she was the best and worst of both Worlds and quite messed-up in the head - even more so than I am and that's saying something!

I also knew for a fact that prior to the big bust-up, they were fucking each other behind my back, which was okay, I would have done exactly the same thing.

We live in a World of broken dreams and promises.

9

Ritual 1

I'm out for a drive with no particular place to go. Unusually I'm in the Ferrari today for a change, I don't know why, I just felt like giving it a blast! I'm on the A24 heading South to Worthing, having already gone up the A29 Northbound to Broadbridge Heath and then cut across to this stretch of road.

I've terrorised and picked-off so many cars already that I've lost count, not that I was actually counting in the first place! One particular twat - in a black BMW M3 so no surprise there! - tried to have a go at me going into the roundabout at Southwater. Needless to say I had to put him in his place and burn him off, much to his disgust - arsehole!

As I head towards Buckbarn Crossroads I suddenly decide to give Worthing a miss and so I take the left-turn onto the A272 and head to Henfield instead. I was going to do a bit of gardening this afternoon anyway so the trip to Worthing I'll save for another day - I'm pretty sure it won't disappear overnight!

I make my way along the lovely sweeping Cowfold Road and give the car some beans, that is until I come upon another bloody BMW, a shitty old 318i in silver being driven by some fucking Paki with his race-traitor white bitch sitting beside him in the passenger seat. The first bit of clear road I come across I nail them easily, not even bothering to look back at them in my rear-view mirror as they both fucking disgust me to the core.

Once in Henfield town I park easily in the car-park behind the small supermarket in the High Street. The small number of shops here are nothing to write home about, although there is one particularly nice farm shop where I'm an irregular customer so I decide to head there first. As per bloody usual I get plenty of looks from the locals, all eyeing me up and down as I strut and bounce along. It's hardly surprising really as today I'm wearing my gorgeous red sleeveless cotton blouse from Hugo Boss, a short white pure cotton mini-skirt from Prada and a pair of brown Paparazzi Lacey Booties from Joe Browns. As for my underwear I'm not wearing any, I'm having a "free" day today. My clutch-bag is my usual white leather one from Prada. I've done my hair in my usual style with my make-up being my dark and moody look yet again - that's the way it is. My perfume is *Kenzo Flower* by Kenzo.

After purchasing a couple of items - I don't have to buy much veg these days of course due to having my very own vegetable patch - from their varied selection of produce, I wander off back down the High Street. I head for the funny old spirit shop down on the left - *The Magick Circle* - the very same place where I had my future told by that psychic woman almost 1-year ago now. Stepping through the front-door I quickly notice that the layout of the shop seems somehow different from the last time I was here, it's not quite so crammed full of stuff this time around. There's also some big guy behind the counter, not the fat miserable hippy woman from before. He looks to be in his mid-50's I guess and bids me a cheerful "Hello" as I enter. I give him a "Hi" in return and go to start looking around the shop at all the weird and wonderful things on display.

"Haven't seen you in here before." He suddenly enquires.

"Oh, I've been here a couple of times about a year ago. I saw Susan Ford, the psychic lady. Does she still work here?" I ask him.

"No, I'm sorry to say that she moved down to Cornwall about 6-months ago now. Unfortunately I haven't been able to find anyone to replace her."

"That's a shame, she gave me a pretty accurate reading. There was another woman here also, a big fat hippy-type."

"That would be Karen, my wife." He informs me.

"Oh shit! I didn't mean any offence." I return without apologising.

"It's okay. She wasn't always the size she is now, she was as slim as you when we met some 25-years ago."

"Really? Wow!" I say back, finding it hard to believe that could be possible.

"I'm Max by the way." He says, holding out his right-hand to shake mine.

"I'm Sarah."

"So what sort of things are you into then Sarah? I can't help noticing all your tattoos."

"Yeah, I love my ink. I guess I'm into all sorts of art really. I've actually got an Aleister Crowley quote tattooed on my back."

"Oh really? A fan of "The Beast" are you?"

"Up to a point I guess. I just do my own thing in life. I have my own little rituals."

"Is that a fact? I run a Neo-Pagan group locally if you're interested in that sort of thing? You're quite welcome to come along if you like?"

"I'm not really sure that's my cup of tea. Is it like Devil worship?"

"No, not at all. Like you, we also do our own thing. We meet up a few times a month in a local park, at night obviously."

"Would I have to dress-up or anything like that?"

"We'll provide you with a robe to cover whatever you're wearing. Just come along and make up your own mind, there's no obligation at all. Here, have one of our flyers."

I quickly scan the A5-size piece of paper he hands me. Do I really want to get involved with all this crap? Do I really need to? No I don't, even though he seems like a nice enough guy and is really chatty, I don't think I'm really interested in getting involved with them, or with him for that matter. I certainly don't fancy him or anything like that, he doesn't light my fire at all.

I go and have a wander around the shop looking at this, that and the other, noticing that all the things on sale seem to have a somewhat darker tone to them than before. There's more of a sinister element to everything, amplified by the huge amount of skulls and other death-related paraphernalia on display. In the end though, I don't buy anything and go to leave, saying a quick "Bye then" to Max as I head for the door.

"Hopefully I'll see you at one of our meetings Sarah?" He fires at me.

"I'll certainly think about it. See ya."

Not on your Nelly you won't!

***

What a bloody morning! How can doing fuck-all be so fucking tiring? I strip naked in the bedroom in 30-seconds flat and head downstairs to the kitchen to make myself some lunch, it now being 1.20pm. I feed Eva while 2-slices of bread toast themselves under the grill. With the toast a nice golden-brown and smothered in butter and marmalade, I grab a chilled bottle of lager from the fridge and go outside into the afternoon Sun to eat and drink.

The heat feels fantastic upon my naked skin and I touch my breasts and my vagina as I swallow my food and drink. I really must do some gardening as I told you earlier, especially sorting out the vegetable patch as I need to pick some of the produce before it either goes off or having the bloody slugs attack it any more - bastard things!

With my lunch and lager consumed I pull a few bunches of potatoes out of the patch and give them a good shake to remove the dirt. They're beautiful and sweet and I think I'll have some of them for my dinner later. The onions are equally as nice as are the leeks - LEEKS!

After cutting the furry end off some of my leeks I run them under the outside tap around the back of the garage to wash them off. I position myself on my back on the grass section in-between the edge of the mini-lake and the patio with my beautiful long toned and tanned legs spread wide apart. I insert one of the leeks into my vagina and fall in love with it, it's only about 30mm in diameter and so it slides in easily. I pleasure myself slowly at first and then start to push it in and out faster and it feels so fucking good and I WANT MORE. I push a second leek into myself and I immediately feel my love-tube stretching under the pressure. I wank for a while longer until I feel myself start to peek and I hold it there under masturbation.

You know where this is going - I WANT 3.

I pull the 2-leeks out and bunch 3 together and fuck. It's cunting tight but I have to go on, if I back out now it will be a failure and I don't want that today. The pain is too much for my vagina to take so I just push it in really quickly with one hard shove. My mind goes white and I almost pass-out under the heat from the Sun on my poor body. With all 3 vegetables in my vagina I love myself and I think of giant cocks attacking me and what fun I could have if nothing else existed in the Universe except myself and cock.

I cum.

Pulling them out of my body I lick them free of my juice and I am so in love with my veg I bite and eat some raw. My vagina is also raw and red with pain from my wanking but it feels so good as I touch it with my wet fingers it makes me sigh.

For dinner I cook some of the potatoes I picked earlier along with 3-pork and garlic and herb sausages. I fry the 3-leeks (chopped) I also fucked myself with, mixed-in with one of the gorgeous onions (also chopped). I didn't even bother to wash the leeks, just frying them in my own cum-juice along with a splash of rapeseed oil - they were lovely!

***

The A281 is almost completely deserted. It's 11.40pm as I speed along in the RS. I'm heading to Parham Park in Storrington, West Sussex for my first, and probably one and only, meeting with Max and his followers. I'm using this car as it's slightly less - but not much! - conspicuous than all the others in the garage and I don't want to get pulled by the fucking stupid Police.

I really don't know what to expect from tonight. I just hope it's not some sort-of weird bloody cult that I'm getting myself mixed up in?

After a bit of searching and head-scratching I eventually find the place I'm looking for reasonably okay. There are some 15 or so cars here already parked-up and I spot Max and his fat wife Karen standing there at the rear of a black 4 x 4. Bloody Hell she's big, I'd hate to think what she looks like naked!

After a short and sweet exchange of pleasantries between Max and myself - the fat wife says nothing, not even when I look her straight in the eye to say "Hello." What's her fucking problem, yet more jealousy I suppose? Max hands me a folded -up piece of cloth made out of some sort-of rough canvas-type material, it being my robe for the evening - great, just my fucking style! I put it on over the top of my clothes, my old black v-neck t-shirt from ASOS, a pair of blue jeans from GAP, and my old pair of black trainers from Blacks. My underwear is also in black, a sexy lace set from Agent Provocateur. My hair is as well you know, whilst my make-up is light, flawless and at the same time stunning. My perfume tonight is *No.5* by Chanel.

The 3 of us make our way along a narrow dirt path for what seems like ages until we emerge out into a clearing. It's difficult to see anything at all in the moonlight, although I can just make out a circle of robed people standing around a wooden structure before me. They're a congregation of solemn souls, each devotee desperately trying to find themselves, trying to find some sort-of meaning to their lives and existence. And who can blame them in this day and age?

I then make out what the structure before me actually is, not a cross as I first thought but some kind-of star - it's a pentangle.

Max stands before us with his arms raised above him, reaching for the darkness of the night sky - it's now midnight - and the event is filled with mystery and awe as he starts to chant something but it's not in English. A sudden wave of icy air wafts its way around my body as I quickly realise that he is in fact speaking German! What the Hell have I got myself into now? Although I'm not the neophyte here, I'm not completely green to the situation either, or am I?

He points at me and all the other people turn to look at the author of this diary - now what? I quickly find myself being encircled as everyone else starts pointing at me in unison. What the fuck is happening, are they initiating me into their sect or is something else about to happen, something nasty? More incantations are heard, this time not in German but in something else - Latin maybe? I'm joined in the centre of the circle by Max and wife Karen. He asks me in English to join the circle and then calls-out to the night sky:

"BEHOLD THE POWER OF THE DARKNESS AND ALL ITS LOVE." Whatever the fuck that all means?

Out of the blue, fat Karen peels-off her robe to reveal her big fat naked body, closely followed by Max himself - OH HELL! She drops to her knees and grabs hold of Max's dick and starts to wank him to hardness and then takes him into her mouth - well I never did! No-one seems at all bothered by any of this and they just stand there watching her suck him in complete silence. She lets him go and drops onto her hands and knees with Max behind her and he starts to fuck her from behind doggy-style with her big flappy floppy folds of skin and breasts wallowing about like a giant jelly! It's terrible but at the same time hilarious and I can't seem to stop myself from watching it! Before long they both start to moan together as he cums his seed into her fat wobbly fanny and the show is over.

One of the collective group, a really old thin guy with a long grey beard and a bald head then comes forward. He lights a long stick at one end with a fag-lighter and its fuel-soaked rag bursts into a flame of orange and purple. He jabs the fire at the pentangle and it combusts in an instant. Max, now thankfully robed, then suddenly grabs me by the arm but I manage to pull away from him.

"WHAT THE FUCK DO YOU THINK YOU'RE DOING?" I spit at him.

"I'm sorry Sarah, but we've got to go now. The Police will probably be here soon and we don't want to get ourselves caught. We've had trouble with them in the past. You had better come on."

I certainly don't want to get caught by the fuzz either and so I follow everyone across the park and back to our respective cars. We all fire-up and flee as quickly as possible and the last thing I want is any more hassle from the pigs, they can all kiss my arse.

I tear back home to Foxhill as quickly as I dare, fortunately not seeing a single cop-car along the way - fuckers.

The time is now 2.27am the following morning.

* * *

It's absolutely pissing-down outside. I really wanted to do a bit more gardening today as well so I guess that's now out of the question, the grass is desperately in need of cutting as I've put it off for far too long. Fortunately I've got one of those big ride-on mowers so it's not the massive chore one would expect it to be, it's actually quite good fun.

I'm sitting on my arse having a quiet coffee and chilling-out reading the local newspaper - *The County Times* - as Eva sleeps beside me curled-up on the sofa. My eyes are then suddenly widened by the next news report I read, the headline being:

"Occultists Burn Cross in Park"

What the fuck! Obviously it's a report - and not a very accurate one at that! - about my little midnight meeting with Max and his special friends earlier in the week. It then goes on to say that:

"Devil worshippers have struck again in the area and Police are seeking anyone who has any information regarding the perpetrators."

Oh dear! What is it with these fucking journalists, it wasn't a bloody cross in the first place it was a pentagram. Why can't they get anything right? They're just as bloody useless as the fucking Police!

***

FUCKING CUNTS. Those fucking bastard publishers that I've signed with to publish my book - *I WANT* - have just emailed me to tell me that:

"Due to some of the content of your manuscript, we, as a company feel that we cannot go forward in publishing your work as it may damage our good name and reputation. If, however, you could tone-down some of the sexual scenes and omit the discriminatory racial language, we may be able to do something in the near future."

CUNTS - I can't fucking believe this, how could they pull the plug on me moments before my book is due to go into production? This now means of course that I'm back to square-one and I have to find another publisher to help me.

THIS IS NOT ON.

10
Ritual 2

I've got yet another email from Max, the guy from *The Magick Circle* shop. This is the seventh one this week alone, asking me if I want to go to another midnight meeting with his band of misfits? I'm really not sure about this sort of thing, I mean, do I really need this crap in my life right now? I don't think so, and so I message him back saying that I'm no longer interested.

I spend the rest of the day doing this and that, cleaning the Lamborghini - there's a hand car-wash place not far from me but it's operated by fucking Bulgarian scum of all "people" so I would rather do it myself than have their fucking paws all over it - and also some time in the gym trying to keep my perfect figure in shape, which amazingly it seems to do pretty-much by itself anyway!

I'm back on my computer once again, although by now it's just gone 8pm in the evening. I looked-up some porn to masturbate along to - gay anal fucking to start with, closely followed by bitch-slapping lesbians and then transgender fisting porn - but I somehow became bored with all that so now I'm checking my emails once more. Unsurprisingly Max has sent me yet another message, once again asking me to reconsider coming to another ritual meeting, this one set for in 2-days time.

***

I think this is only the third or fourth time I've ever driven this car, I don't even know why I kept it in the first place, the styling is pure pre-Second World War. I'm out in the Morgan Aeromax of course, giving it large as I head out of Petworth town and then right onto the A272 Midhurst Road. As you have probably guessed dear readers, I'm on my way to another of Max's meetings, this one being held on a private farm at Lodsworth in West Sussex.

It's a stinking-hot evening, even though it's now 11.46pm, and accordingly I've dressed light. I'm wearing a black playsuit from Lipsy and my old pair of black-suede ankle-boots from Miu Miu and nothing else, no underwear or anything as I don't feel like it. I'm not going to go on about my hair as you all know by now about that, whilst my make-up I've kept nice and simple featuring dark-grey eyeshadow and cherry-red lipstick. My perfume tonight is *Mademoiselle* by Chanel.

Finding the farm was a piece of piss, and fortunately the entrance to it is nice and firm, the intense heat from the previous weeks heat having baked the mud track rock hard. I follow the pentagram signs along the track as instructed until I come to a clearing where numerous cars are already parked, way more than at the last event. I spot Max talking to the old guy with the beard from the previous event and so after parking-up go over to say hello to them.

"Hello Sarah, good of you to come."

"Well, I was in 2-minds whether to or not."

"Well I'm glad you did. That's a lovely car you've got there."

"Thank you, it was my late-husbands."

"You remember "The Grey" don't you, from before?" He says, pointing to the old guy.

"Eh, yes." I stumble, as the old guy - "The Grey" - holds out his bony old hand for me to shake.

"I was telling "The Grey" about your tattoos and your fascination with "The Beast", Mr. Crowley."

"Oh, right." I say meekly, not quite knowing really what to say or where this conversation is heading.

"I'd love to see them, if that's alright with you - Spirit Girl." Pipes-up the old geezer to me.

"Why did you call me "Spirit Girl", my name is Sarah?"

"Because you have the power Sarah. You have visions of the future. I can see them in your eyes."

I freeze to the spot at his words, they being similar to the ones the psychic woman said to me last year at the shop during my reading. Who is this guy and what the fuck does he want from me? Silly question, he's a man isn't he? His age and his wrinkled knackered old body makes no difference to anything, they're all the fucking same regardless.

"We're inside tonight Sarah, we have usage of one of the farmers barns this time, for privacy. There is one thing I must tell you though." Exclaims Max.

"Oh yes, what's that?" I quiz.

"Everyone will be naked tonight. But don't worry though, as a newcomer you don't have to if you don't want to, the choice is yours."

"ARE YOU JOKING?" I say in horror.

"No, not at all. It's not a sexual thing Sarah, it's more of a spiritual nature that's all. If you don't mind."

"Well, I wish you had told me earlier rather than just spring it on me like this." I fire back at him.

"I'm sorry, you're right of course." He apologises.

So what would you do, the reader of my words - in or out? The answer is IN of course, you knew that all along as well as I did! Would you have been that brave/stupid to venture into the unknown inside that barn - I am!

There before me within the wooden building stands a ring of naked people, some old, some young - although the late-20's seems to be the youngest age - fat, thin, tall, short, you name it, it's all here!

I feel like a fish out of water as I'm the only one standing here with any clothes on, apart from Max and "The Grey" that is as they're both dressed in robes of black silk with flaming-red linings of fire. I sense a strange presence about me, like there's something or someone watching me from up above. A warm feeling starts to transmit throughout my body and I feel my skin begin to creep. What is it? My Guardian Angel calls to me and I feel his hand upon my lower back, pushing me forwards into the circle. Not only is he watching me, he's also reading my mind, my thoughts. I'm being guided by a ghost and I can't stop it and I don't want it to stop.

I stand before these humans in the hub of the circle, naked in all my glorious beauty with my arms above my head. They gaze at the sleek and graceful vision that is my body as the power of the Spirit World invades my mind, making me gyrate and spin on my toes like a ballerina. I can't control myself as I expose my love to my surrounding audience. They applaud my art, my figure, my beautiful hair, my gorgeous breasts, my lovely long legs, my firm round bum and the splendour of my smooth vagina. I love myself and I cum at the warped thoughts implanted in my mind of fuck.

I don't know where I am. I'm not actually sure of what I am, of what I have become. I don't feel degraded by my actions of love, nor are there any pretentious notions of desirability for anyone that surrounds me at this current moment in time.

This is my time.

This is my delight.

This is my WANT.

***

My fucking head! What the Hell happened last night? I awake to bright sunlight beaming in through my bedroom window - MY bedroom window. I don't even remember driving home or anything and yet here I am. Did I drive home or did someone else drive me? If they did where are they now? How could they even know where I live? Am I alone in the house or is someone else here? Fucking Hell I feel like shit and I pucker my lips at the awful taste in my mouth. What the Hell is that is that all about? What the Hell I've had in there doesn't even bear thinking about and I try to blank it out of my thoughts. The rest of my body feels okay though as I check my vagina and my bum and they both feel and appear to be normal. What the fuck have I done now?

My bedside clock reads 2.37pm. I try to stand but I'm dizzy and confused. I check my arms for any sign of needle marks but there are none, although it's difficult to see anything clearly amongst all my tattoos anyway. Maybe someone has poured something down my throat and that's why I have this horrible taste in my mouth? I stagger to the bathroom and gargle and rinse my mouth out with some mouthwash and it feels so much better I cannot begin to describe the relief.

I almost jump out of my fucking skin when I feel something touch one of my bare legs. It's Eva, rubbing her soft fur-covered body against me to say "Hello" - Bloody Hell! I pick her up and cuddle her. She's so beautiful and soft against my naked breasts, filling me with her love and restoring at least some sense of proportion within me - the fact that I'm still alive and seemingly okay.

I find the clothes I was wearing last night positioned on the *chaise longue,* the place where I usually leave them at the end of the day. I release Eva down onto the bed and put on my white silk robe, the one from LilySilk, and go and check-out the house and the garage for any sign of an intruder or anyone else, maybe even a lover from last night? A good half-an-hour later reveals no-one and nothing, not a bloody sausage. Even the Morgan was parked correctly back in its place in the garage so I must have come home by myself and yet I remember nothing. I hate not knowing, it's too scary for words.

* * *

I spend the rest of the day - what's left of it anyway - not doing very much. I'm so bloody confused I don't know which way to turn. I don't venture out either, at least not out of the grounds of the house anyway, I just don't feel like going out at all.

My mind drifts back to the events of last night. I remember the drive there to the farm, seeing Max and the old guy with the beard, what's his name? "The Grey", that was it, and that's about it really. I vaguely remember naked bodies and me being naked also and dancing around like I was possessed but that's about as far as it goes. There's nothing I can do about it now, except send Max an email to see if he can fill in the blank spaces of last night and this morning. It's with a small amount of trepidation that I fire-off a quick message to him as there's a little part of me that doesn't really want to know the answer. I feel somewhat sick of being in this position.

POSITION
The position I'm in should be one familiar to you all by now my lovely reader. I'm on all fours out in the garden over by the Summer House. I'm fucking myself with my giant 18-inch long dildo from Lovehoney that I've inserted one end into the ground to hold it in place and the other end into my lubricated rectum. I ease myself back and forth in a fluid motion, taking as much of the rubber inside my body as I see fit to use. I scream and moan as I love my bum, riding my big fake cock under the heat of the Sun. My perfect breasts sway and swing beneath me like udders and I touch their perfect shape, they're firm and luscious and I squeeze and slap them like a bitch. I finger my vagina, pushing 2-fingers between my labia, making me sigh with pleasure as I penetrate my hole. I squash the dildo deep into myself as I force my vagina to cum and spit my oily juice. I lick my honey from my fingers as I roll over onto the grass, the thick cock falling out of my arse as I do so and I love myself.

* * *

The reply from Max leaves me in a state of limbo. He says that I left alone along with him and everyone else all at the same time, each of us going our separate ways. So what does that mean? Was I followed home? And if so, by whom? Or did I really drive myself back, either under the influence of some hallucinogenic drug or guidance from the Spirit World? I really don't fucking know?

"We're looking for somewhere new for our next meeting, the farmers barn was only a one-off so we're looking for somewhere a bit more private if you know of anywhere?" He massages me by return.

"PS - Everyone loved you and your tattoos. Max."

I not going to fall prey to that old one. I'm not having a load of strangers in my house dancing around naked, I might not even have a bloody house left the following day!

Not a fucking chance in Hell.

11
Ritual 3

"WAAAAAAAAAAAAAAAAH!"

There's a girl screaming. I think it's her, it must be? I don't know who she is? Max is behind her holding her arms. Yes, it's him and they're both naked. "The Grey" comes to her and takes off his robe. My eyes must be playing tricks on me as his cock is fucking huge, like a horse, emphasized even more by his diminutive old body. He's as grotesque as he is eccentric.

I suddenly feel cum squirt up into my cunt but I don't cum myself. I'm being fucked doggy-style by a cock but I don't know who it belongs to. I lick at a cunt as hard as I can, pressing my tongue deep between her lips into the tight walls of her vagina. She shakes violently as she cums into my mouth as she sucks 2-cocks together. They then ejaculate their man-milk into her face and mouth and I lick her and suck cock and eat it.

The smell of sex and Hell is all about me, rampant cock and cunt and tongue and the visions of sexual perversion and my brain can't keep up with my eyeballs. The power of emotion feeds all those present, my beautiful garden a surreal field of depravity.

I WANT them all to ravage me, I don't care who or how many as I'm submissive to each and every one of them but can they keep up with me? Can any of them feed my avarice? I am obsessed with cock and cunt and become compelled to eat both - I can't control myself. What the fuck is happening?

I laugh and scream like the crazy fucking bitch I am at the wildness of this vision before me, my whole being exploding in a luscious orgasm of crystallized colour. A male fucks a female anally as she licks the vagina of another female as another guy fucks her mouth as another male fucks his mouth and I wank. I throw myself into the mix and suck on cock and lick cunt as I'm fucked up the arse by some guy as some girl laps at my vagina. There is absolutely no difference between a girl licking me or a guy, it's all the fucking same and I WANT EVERYTHING. I don't know who or what I have become or even what my fucking name is any more? Some guy cums into my mouth and I swallow half his sperm down my throat and spit the rest out onto the awaiting open hole of another girls pussy. I tongue the stringy mess into her wet fanny and bury my face into her love and fuck it.

Everyone is completely pissed and drugged out of their fucking skulls, heightening the experience. I don't even know what I've taken myself - some kind of stimulant I guess? They could have even hypnotised me, I just don't know, everything is as fucked as I am - although I'm pretty sure I'm still standing on my own 2-feet - just!

There must be at least 30-naked bodies around me, all fucking and sucking one another in my glorious garden - on the grass, the patio, in the gazebo in the middle of the mini-lake, up against the garage wall and everywhere as we all descend into communal madness and I'm caught up in the middle of this psychodrama as it swirls about around me like a typhoon. I am at its eye, controlling its direction like the Goddess I am. The vortex sweeps me up into the night sky and I fly like a vampire over my England, sucking on the juices of who and whatever I see fit. The energy fills the very ether of our surroundings and when I tap into it, it fills me completely and my heart explodes with power - I am heartless in the extreme. Magic flows all around me, soaking into the very core of my body as my new-found prophet calls out to me. I am under his spell. He can do whatever he wants with me - fuck me, anal me, suck his cock, eat his shit, drink his blood, kill me - and all because I am he.

Someone grabs my tits from behind, making me jump, and when I turn my head to see who it is I see that it's Karen, Max's wife. She laughs wickedly at her own action as I turn to face her. I move towards her and we embrace each others female bodies and we kiss and tongue with passion. We touch breasts and vaginas and we finger one another and we are wet for each other. She forces herself on me and we collapse to the grass in a heap of naked flesh. I open my legs to her and I shudder as she licks at my cunt. I lose control and orgasm and cum and spit my love - I am hers. We swap over and I push 2-fingers into her twat, making her cry and shake. I fuck her with my digits and my mouth and she pants heavily and screams as she cums for me. I lick her juice as she quivers like crazy as at once my vagina opens its doors to cock as some random guy starts to fuck me from behind. He bangs-away at me as I continue to lick Karen's hole. She spins around beneath me to 69 me and I lap her as she eats my vagina and his cock and balls. He cums his nasty gloop into my hole and she swallows the overflow, not all of it though as I want to taste it also. We separate and we both lick at his shaft together, sensing the tang of spunk, cunt and cock, her saliva mixing with the hot saltiness of his member. Karen and I kiss full-on, wrapping our dirty tongues around together. We touch each others bodies - breasts, vaginas, bums, arms, legs, hair and fuck as we lick his dirty knob. I am pansexual in the extreme.

I give myself to all of them with total commitment, even more so than they have to each other as they fuck. Everyone intermingles with each other as the women fuck other women and the men fuck other men. Anything goes and I'm stuck right in the middle of it, the chaos and the mayhem of ritualistic sex as human bodies fuck at any and every orifice they desire. I indulge in whatever is around as each of us has fallen under the spell and psychic direction of the Devil. They play with my spiritual essence as they play with my tits, mouth, arse and cunt. Wild emotion and passion surrounds my beautiful self as I fuck and cunt and cock and cum and shit and I am in love like never before.

A guy with a heavily pierced dick fucks me in the rear and I split and tear. He fucks my cunt and it feels so fucking good, the sensation of his piercings ribbing my internal love. I suck his metal cock and it rattles my teeth as I swallow his knob. I jiggle it around in my mouth with my tongue, it feeling so alien but I love it anyway. My eyes are on fire as sparkling and swirling flashes of light oscillate about me in the pure colours of the rainbow as I suck his steel cock. I wank him off in my face and let the splat of his muck dribble down onto my awaiting tongue and then my beautiful breasts.

The girl who was being fucked by "The Grey" is now mine. We stand opposite each other and touch one another's tits. She's tall and slim with long brown hair and a beautiful smooth cunt. Her mounds are small but firm and peachy and I drop to my knees and lick them, making her young nipples proud and hard and I suck them like a nursing baby. She fucks my cunt with 3-fingers as I suck cock as she sucks 2-cocks as the 2-guys/ gays/bi's kiss like bent lovers.

Max fucks my arse as I sit on his cock. We're on the edge of the water as I am on the edge of sanity - they have all possessed me. He sucks some guys cock as he lays there on his back. I lean forward as I fuck and lick and suck cock and kiss and swallow their love, devouring them both with my mouth. He cums his white shit and we both eat it and slurp on his discharge.

Some guy has his whole fist inside my cunt but there is no pain, only fuck. He twists his hand within me to match my mind as the brunette girl sits cowgirl on my face. I lick her anal passage and she cries like shit as another girl licks her tits and they kiss as another girl licks my cunt and the guys dirty hand and I am in pure Hell.

✳✳✳

I walk the lonely path to my death. They bind and gag me but I don't care, there's nothing they can do to me that will make any fucking difference to the World, not now. Everything will carry on exactly the same as before even if they kill me. Part of me even wishes they would.

"The Grey" fucks my cunt with his massive cock. It must be almost 40-centimetres in length and I WANT it all inside me. I scream like fuck as he penetrates my body and for a split-second I feel his cock so far within me that it may never come out. I feel my internal organs being pushed aside by its girth, making me retch. I can't look at him, he is repulsive to my beautiful eyes and I am blind. He touches my tits and I cannot move, the rope binding me rigid as I'm held by 100-hands to prevent my escape. I WANT this old cunt to fuck me to Hell and I don't care as he cums his ancient seed inside my gorgeous body, feeling his evil muck squirt and then splash against my internals and I cum and die yet another death as I am reborn, reborn into the same fucking Hell as I was before.

Nothing ever good will happen.

I seek refuge in the embracing wings of the Devil as he wraps his protection around me, shielding me from my fellow human-kind. I find comfort in his evil power, comfort that he will care for me in eternity and beyond the expanses of time. I dedicate all my love to him and give him my body and soul to do with as his WANT. He possesses me and fucks me in the night as I swallow his evil cum, drinking it down and ingesting it, it permeating my whole body as we become as one. My martyrdom is accepted by my Leader. I have become one of his many She-Devil disciples as I follow him into Hell.

* * *

The 4 of us stand before the animal. Max, with a curved blade. "The Grey" with his giant cock. The brunette girl - the carnal focus of the event and whom I'm guessing must be one of Max's female acolytes? - with her inexperience of life.

And then there is me, your one and only friend. I'm wearing a face-mask that I fashioned from the pelvic bone of "The Bitch", fastened in place with a lattice of plastic ties. It actually looks quite cool, as well as having its inherent sinister connotations of course, and everyone loves it as much as they all love and fuck me and I love and fuck them.

The air is electric with the power of the Dark One, the black mass of the demon, of death and perpetual existence in this time. We all follow the path of darkness as it leads us to our demonic sacrifice and we each lower ourselves in genuflection to the master that stands before us. Max speaks in incantations, using the tongue of the Dark Master:

"In nomine Die nostri Satanas Luciferi excelsi ave voluptartis carnis."

Not that I understand or care what any of it actually means, I swallow every word and feed on it. He chants the Shamanic prayers of death and blood, the Satanic and Wicca Magick ceremony of the Devil himself. Each of us are devoted to Satan and Hell and nothing else exists. I have no control over my untamed spirit as the convergence of sex and death permeates my being as my drug-addled mind, body and soul slip into the abyss of depravity once more.

"By the power of Klingsor behold this female and release her into our circle of sex-magick. Extol this ritual with the force and guiding light of the *Vril* so that she becomes cleansed from this time unto her dying moment. Let her be free of her Guardian Angel to wander her own path of life and death." So says Max, before ushering his followers into action.

I'm positioned behind the girl, holding both her arms tightly with my own although she doesn't struggle - she is hypnotized out of self-control. She is as drunk and drugged and as fucked as I am, as we all fucking are, as we await the ominous evil portent of our immediate future. "The Grey" holds the goats head as he straddles the animal, holding it up and back. With one clean arc of the blade the animal is dispatched, its blood of life spilling out from its fatal wound and into the awaiting sacrificial cup - the Chalice of Ecstasy. The goats slain body is released to the floor where it crumples in the surrounding silence.

Max orders me to: "Hold the girl steady" as "The Grey" fucks her cunt with his massive weapon and she laughs and loves his cock as it stretches and fills her tight vagina. Max pulls at her long brown hair, making her face the Sun and all its power, its blinding rays cancelling-out any vision of what is happening to her. He draws upon her breasts an inverted pentagram in blood, it featuring the head of a goat at its centre - the divine symbol of Satan and his followers for they are us.

He pours the warm red juice into her gaping mouth and she coughs and splutters and drinks it down as "The Grey" fucks her hard. Everyone cheers and cries at the girls pleasurable suffering. She loves cock and blood as both fill her to the brim. The life-giving liquid overflows her mouth and dribbles large scarlet rivulets down her chin onto her lovely breasts. I rub the red into her firm young tits with one hand as I continue to try and hold her steady with the other. The old fucker fucks-away at her cunt as Max now takes over holding her. I use my hands and my luscious breasts to rub the blood all over her body, painting her ruby from head to toe with love and fuck.

We lay the girl down onto the hard stone of the patio. I 69 her and lick her swollen cunt, tasting her love for my mouth and cock. Satan 666 looks down upon us as we fuck and fuck and I love the fact that he's watching us - that he's watching ME. I rub the awaiting hole of my labia over her face and it feels so fucking good that I moan in ecstasy of her tongue inside my fuck. Without hesitation "The Grey" cunts me from behind, his enormous cock filling my tube completely and then beyond. I wince and curse at the discomfort but I WANT the fuck. He must have been eating concrete to keep this bloody hard - the dirty old fucker! His saggy old bollocks swing about over the girls face, coating them red from the blood of the goat as he fucks me. I love his cock and her cunt and I fuck and shit and Hell. Max whips the bitch with his cat as she sucks the massive appendage of "The Grey", he simultaneously fellating himself with both hands. She desires her flagellation more and harder, the whip stinging its welts deeper and deeper into her skin with each crack as then the old bastard moans as he squirts his exquisite discharge from his Japs-eye, soaking her face, open mouth and tongue.

I remove my bloodied mask and suck Max's cock as I lick cunt. He alternately fucks the girls cunt and my mouth-cunt as I alternately suck cock and cunt as "The Grey" fucks my cunt and cums again, his spunk spitting out the end of his knob like a seismic eruption, filling me to overflowing. Max cums into my mouth and I eat spunk and cunt and blood and then I die once again as I cum.

I hear voices in my head, a single voice. It's the Master - Aleister Crowley - calling out to me:

"Do what thou wilt shall be the whole of the law Sarah."

But all I want is peace.

I just want to be left alone.

****

I awake at 4.47pm the following afternoon - it's Sunday. My usual Sunday routine of having a lay-in until 10 or 11-ish, followed by a lazy breakfast, sodding around with the cars, swimming, playing pool, playing on the racing simulator game and other some such crap has all but gone out of the window today, although my usual Sunday roast that I always try to do for myself and Eva I still very much intend doing - even if it kills me!

Naturally I kept Eva in all day yesterday, I didn't want her to witness all the strange shenanigans or the strange people doing strange things to one another in the garden, or in the house, so she stayed safely under lock and key in my bedroom with plenty of food and water, her cat-toys and her poo-tray. I love her so much, she is the centre of my World. I still can't let her outside even now as the remains of the dead goat are still laying out on the patio, although there is in fact less of it now this afternoon than there was last night as obviously the foxes or some other creature has pinched bits off of it under the cover of darkness.

I guess the first thing I must do is scrape it up and dispose of it somewhere, but where? I venture outside and put the bloody remains into a black plastic bin-liner and then put it in the garage out of sight and harms way. I hose-down the patio of blood, shit, cum and other detritus and then go and clean myself up. I guess I must have showered already last night/this morning as my body is clean but my hair is all over the bloody place and still a little damp.

After another quick shower and drying myself off I head into the kitchen. I feed Eva a light snack of crabmeat and then have a go at cleaning up my face-mask that I appear to have left bloodied in the sink. There is absolutely no telling what really went on here yesterday, it's probably a good job I don't remember much about it anyway or I might even shock myself!

I have a couple of quick vodkas to stiffen myself up and then start to prepare dinner - and no jokes about curried goat please, I'm not in the mood! I do roast beef with roast potatoes, runner beans, carrots and gravy. The small piece of beef I already had is resting on the side, whilst the veg of course are the products of my own fair hands - along with a bit of help from Mother Nature. I haven't bothered to dress either as there's no bloody point really is there? I just loll-around in my usual old white silk robe from LilySilk as it looks and feels so sexy against my naked body. I obviously haven't bothered with my hair, make-up or perfume either as there's only Eva and myself here - I'm not expecting anyone else - and I don't think she minds at all about how I look, all she wants out of life is food, love, warmth and peace - pretty much the same as myself really. I roast the beef rare as I like it nice and red and juicy in the middle. I've also cooked the potatoes around the sides of the meat as that way they soak-up all the flavour of the juices and makes them taste just divine.

Later, with my dinner all cooked and ready to go, I sit my arse down in the living-room in front of the TV with my beautiful food perched on my lap along with a bottle of chilled white, German naturally. As per bloody usual for a Sunday evening - it's now 8pm - there's sweet-F.A. on the box. There's some bloody boring antiques program on one side fronted by some stuck-up patronising old cow who obviously has BBC blood running through her veins. The news channels I also avoid like the plague as I'm no longer part of this World, I don't even watch the weather reports any more either as they're never correct anyway. How can this be in this day and age I just don't understand. In the end I stick a Blu-ray film on, *SOME LIKE IT HOT* from 1959 staring Tony Curtis (so gorgeous!), Jack Lemmon (so funny) and Marilyn Monroe, although I've never really been a big fan of her as I don't like her stupid dumb-blonde persona. I give Eva a bowl of beef for her dinner, along with a bit a gravy also, including some of the fatty bits from around the edge of the meat as she likes those, and we laugh along together at the antics of the 2-guys on-screen.

Later that evening I sit and ponder the events of yesterday. How fucking crazy was that? Once again my poor old beautiful body took a bit of a pounding and once again I came through it pretty much unscathed, although my thighs ache quite a bit for obvious reasons!

Now what the fuck am I going to do with that goat?

***

It's 4.00am the following morning - Monday. I'm heading towards Horsham on the A29 heading North in the RS as it's the least conspicuous of all the cars in the garage - except the Mini maybe? - for this mornings little job. The traffic is minimal to say the least as I take a right-turn and head through Slinfold Village, the old town where Amanda and I had our little love-nest, albeit briefly. I wonder how she's doing now and hope that she's happy in her life.

Out the other side of the village I turn left onto the A264 and head through Broadbridge Heath and the outskirts of Horsham. I try to avoid going too far into the heart of the town as these days there are bloody CCTV cameras everywhere and it's almost impossible to avoid them, I've probably been caught on several of them already without even knowing it. I take another left off of the Bishopric (or Bishops Prick as I call it!) and use the backstreets to get nearer to my destination. I park in a small side-road as I'll have to walk the rest of the way, fortunately it's not that far and there's still not a soul about apart from a milkman doing his rounds. Why do some people still have their milk delivered I wonder to myself, haven't they ever heard of supermarkets?

I heave the plastic bag out of the tailgate of the car - it's actually surprisingly bloody heavy! - shut the boot and off I go. I have to carry the fucking thing in both arms as my right-arm is still not 100% recovered from the car crash, and that was over a year ago now. I don't suppose it'll ever be the same again, I guess only time will tell? Fucking bitch.

Some old guy in his 60's passes me on the pavement, walking in the opposite direction. I try not to make eye contact with him so I don't know if he looks at me or not as we pass each other. He probably does, they all do, even though I'm wearing dark glasses and a black Baseball-type cap I'll bet you anything that he still looked. As for the rest of my clothes, I'm wearing my black v-neck t-shirt from ASOS, my pair of black jeans from GAP and my pair of black suede ankle-boots from Miu Miu. I've also got my black bomber jacket from Jacketvests on and a pair of blue latex disposable gloves so I hopefully can avoid leaving any fingerprints or DNA anywhere.

Several cars pass me on the busy road that leads past the Rail Station but I have to ignore them or I won't be able to complete my task. I empty the contents of the bin-liner out onto the steps of the building and then turn and walk away, letting as much of the congealed blood slowly drip its way out of the bag and onto the steps as I dare before I disappear into thin air once more.

I dispose of the blood-stained plastic bag on the way home, chucking it in a builder-skip outside someone's house near Five Oaks. It's their tough shit if they dare to look inside it.

I arrive back home at 4.57am and go back to bed to sleep and dream of myself and fucking.

***

The beautiful warm water feels glorious against my naked body as I bobble-about laying on my back in the pool. I lay there thinking about nothing as Eva sits right on the edge of the pool, just sitting there staring at me as I float. I wonder what she's thinking - funny cat!

My peace and tranquillity is suddenly interrupted by the sound of the front-gate buzzer sounding. Who the fuck can this be now? I walk up the pool steps and out of the peaceful water, grab a towel from the side-cupboard - one of my lovely white Egyptian ones that feels like a soft cloud as I wrap it around my beautiful skin. In the hallway I spy who it is that has interrupted my afternoon dip - it's the fucking Police - yet again! What the fuck do they want this time?

"Yes?" I say curtly into the intercom.

"Is that Sarah Knowles?" The female cop asks.

"That's right, why, what do you want?"

"If you could let us in, we'd like to ask you a few questions please."

"I don't see why not? Come up to the house." I tell her with my inherent sarcasm.

I release the gates and watch the patrol car drive up and park directly outside the house on the monitor and the 2-female pigs emerge. I watch them on camera, looking for the doorbell that isn't there, nor the letterbox for them to rattle either and I LOL at their searching - stupid fucking pigs! I keep them waiting and guessing for several minutes before I open the door to them and invite them in for, no doubt, yet another cosy chat - that being code for bullshit.

"Miss Sarah Knowles?" Enquires the cop, the very same one I spoke to just now and who was also the driver of the patrol car, a white BMW estate. She's in her late-40's, reasonably attractive with short brown hair but slightly overweight, not helped by her ill-fitting un-tailored uniform.

"Yes, that's me." I reply smugly.

"I'm sorry, were you having a shower?" She enquires, pointing to the towel wrapped around my perfect body.

"No, I was in the pool. What's all this about? Not more questions about that missing girl again?"

"Missing girl?" She quizzes.

"Yes, from the company I used to work for. Some girl went missing from there some time ago."

She looks at me somewhat confused. Have I just dropped myself in the shit or is there something else, something I've missed or failed to cover up? Or has my image intimidated her to such a degree that its actually clogged her feeble brain?

It can't be easy for these lesser mortals to come face to face with someone with my looks and figure, not that I really give a flying-fuck about them or what they're thinking.

"That's very interesting Miss Knowles, we didn't know anything about your connection to her. No, we're here about an incident that happened early this morning when someone dumped the carcass of a goat onto the steps of the very same company that you just mentioned." She comes back.

"Are you joking or what?" I snigger.

"I don't know anything about a dead goat. What makes you think I had anything to do with it? And who gave you my name in the first place?" I come back at her - cheeky fucking bitch!

"Your name was mentioned when we spoke to one of the managers at the company this morning."

"Oh really, let me guess - CJ? You shouldn't believe anything he says, that twat had it in for me from day-1."

"That's strange you should say that, he said exactly the same thing about you." Pipes-up the other copper, a younger female in her late-30's - at a push! - with quite a pretty face and a slimmer figure and a similar hairstyle and colour to the other officer, the one that's obviously been around a bit and seen some action in her time, hence her bolshy bloody attitude.

"Where would I get a dead goat from in the first place, Sainsbury's?" I quiz her back.

"You could have stolen it, or maybe found it and decided to play a trick on your old company for them sacking you?" Says the older cop.

"Really? So now I'm a thief as well as a goat murderer am I?"

"We're not saying anything of the sort Miss Knowles, we're just asking you if you had anything to do with the incident this morning?"

"NO." I return bluntly - super-cool or what?

The pair of them just stand there and stare at me like I'm from Mars - maybe I am? - not believing that I've actually defied their questioning and stood up to them. What do they fucking expect, for me to open-up about my life and admit my actions? They can both kiss my arse. Now there's a thought!

"Were you in the vicinity of Horsham this morning Miss Knowles?"

"No. I've been here all day." I lie.

"Are there any witnesses to that?"

"No, only my cat. You can ask her if you like?" I jest back.

"What is it you actually do for a living Miss Knowles?" The younger bitch asks.

"Nothing, I've retired from working." I smirk at them.

"What do you mean? You're too young to be retired." Says the older one, obviously jealous - and in more ways than one! - to the fact that I'll never have to work ever again in my life whilst they both have to do this shit.

"My late husband left me this house as well as his money, therefore I have no reason to work." I inform them, not that it really has got anything to fucking do with them or anyone else for that matter.

"Is that so? Well you can count yourself very lucky Miss Knowles."

"I do, every day. I'll never have to work in shit-holes like that crappy company in Horsham ever again."

"We understand that they fired you from you position, why was that?"

"That's right, I had a disagreement with the management over certain things, and in hindsight they actually did me a favour."

"So the dead goat on their steps this morning was some form of revenge was it?" The old cow fires at me.

"Don't get smart with me copper, that has nothing to do with me as I've already told you. Now, if you don't mind, I'd like to go back to my pool." I tell them both bluntly, staring them out for the second bloody time.

"Don't call me "copper" Miss Knowles. And you can be sure that we'll get to the bottom of this incident in due course." Exclaims the seasoned cop.

"Yeah, whatever. You can see yourself out, the doors there." I quip back, pointing to the door with one hand whilst desperately trying to keep my towel in place with the other.

Smart-arse fucking pigs, do they honestly think they can just come into my house and talk to me like I'm a piece of crap? Who the fuck do they think they are? I pay their fucking wages through my taxes after all. Well, I don't actually pay any tax these days but you know what I mean!

I watch them drive back out through the main gates and shut and lock them behind them. They've got some fucking audacity haven't they? Typical fucking coppers.

In the living-room I down a couple of slugs of vodka straight from the bottle in order to take the sharp edge off my mood. I drape the towel over the back of the sofa and stand naked and drink, next downing 2-large mouthfuls of gin. I climb onto the soft white leather of the sofa and masturbate myself, inserting 2-fingers into my growler and I push. I imagine that my fingers are the tongues of the 2-pig bitches flicking in and out of my hole as I hold a gun to their heads, forcing them to cunt me. I push myself harder and harder and touch my tits and I scream and orgasm and shudder and cum. I lick my juicy fingers and laugh at my love and my life. That bitch copper was right, I am a lucky girl and I'm gonna fuck and love and cock and cunt and burn the road at 200-miles-per-hour and no-one is going to fucking stop me.

What a strange few days these have been, what with the ritual, degrading myself yet again and all that goings-on, dumping the remains of the poor old goat on the shit-holes doorstep this morning and then the bloody Police at my door! I just know that they're going to be back to cause me more problems. Why can't everyone just leave me the fuck alone?

I give Eva a big wet kiss as I hold her against my naked breasts. The 2 of us are so alike it's uncanny! She is my best friend, my daughter and my lover all in one. I place her up on the work-surface - not very hygienic I know but what the Hell? - as I finish off cleaning my mask (the one fashioned from Mellis's pelvic bone) in the sink and leave it to dry on the draining board.

Maybe I should have gone to Worthing in the first place after all?

12

Supernats

I'm so exited. Today I'm off on my travels once again - this time to Bedfordshire, to a car show in actual fact. The event is called The Hot Rod Supernationals - or Supernats for short - held in the grounds of a country house in Old Warden Park, Biggleswade. According to their website and also some of Andy's car club friends, the show is a pretty good one, in fact the biggest and best of its type in the whole of Europe.

It's a funny old World, I'd never even been to a car show before I met Andy and now I can't seem to get enough of them! Somehow I feel duty-bound to carry on where he left off. It's strange isn't it?

I didn't particularly fancy going on my own and seeing as I'm not involved with anyone at the moment, I've hired myself an escort from a really classy agency in Brighton, East Sussex, one that I've used previously on several occasions. The girl I've chosen is called Spirit - not her real bloody name obviously! She's sweet, tall, slim and young - only 22! - and blonde (not real!) with lovely full and firm breasts (again, not real), lovely long legs, a pert bum, beautiful green eyes and very gorgeous. I've actually hired her for the whole weekend for the horrendous cost of £3,000, to do as I please with her, which is exactly what I did Friday night and all of yesterday - making love, having sex, fucking, licking, kissing, fingers, cunt, dildos, arse, bondage, tits, pain, love, cum, pleasure, vodka, goo, cocaine, shit, blood, horror.

I awoke her this morning at 6.35am - it's Sunday - and ordered her to: "Lick my pussy", which she dutifully did. I

cum into her mouth under my flailing orgasm as her tongue
fucked in and out of my vagina as I screamed for "MORE"
and "HARDER". It was then my turn as I fucked her with my
8-inch realistic dildo from Ann Summers as she shook and
shuddered on all fours with me simultaneously licking her
gaping bumhole.

We shower together and laugh and giggle as we wash each
others bodies and kiss and touch and finger. As the weather is
going to be another scorcher today, as it has been all week so
far, I'm dressing really light. I'm wearing a white Bardot cross-
over top from Shein that really shows-off my tatts - and my tits!
- and a pair of white sports shorts from Puma. My underwear is
in white lace from Wolf & Whistle. On my feet I'm wearing my
old pair of clear-plastic wedge-heals from Polyvore. In order to
keep my hands free of any clutter (money, car keys and other
crap) I'm wearing a snazzy bumbag also in white from River
Island rather than using a clutch-bag or anything else. I've gone
really full-on with my make-up as well - my supermodel look
- with sharp cheekbones, dark and dusky grey eyeshadow and
cherry-red lipstick and I look so fucking gorgeous and hot! My
hair is in my own usual style with my perfume today being
Luxe by Avon.

Spirit is also gorgeously dressed in a pale yellow bodycon
mini-dress that outlines her tight body beautifully, and has a
pair of yellow wedge-heals on her feet. I have no idea who
either her dress or her shoes or her gorgeous perfume are all
from but she looks beautiful anyway and we embrace and kiss
passionately and squeeze each others breasts as we tongue and
pant together.

***

The car I've decided to take to the show is the yellow Willys
Coupe Gasser - or "Coop" as the Americans pronounce it. It's
really crazy-looking and goes like the bloody clappers, not to
mention the noise it makes - it sounds like an old aeroplane

taking off! I'll really have to have my wits about me though as the noise is simply too much and is probably illegal, so I'll have to keep my eyes peeled for the bloody Police, especially on the M25.

Spirit loves the car, all of them in fact, and we hug and kiss and exudes her love and appreciation as we prepare ourselves to leave the house. I fire the enormous supercharged 7.6-litre V8 engine in the car and it begins throbbing and banging-away to itself like mad ahead of us. We pull out of the garage, through the main gates and head right onto the A272 and take the A29 North, being stared at all the while - the car and its 2-beautiful occupants by our fellow road users and everyone else. With the engine grumbling we head through Billingshurst, Five Oaks, Slinfold, Ockley and then Beare Green and out onto the A24. From there we pass through Dorking and then Leatherhead and hit the M25 - the Worlds largest car-park! - and head clockwise. As we head pass the junction with the A3 we spot some stupid blonde bitch in an Audi - what the fuck is it with bloody Audi drivers? - doing her bloody make-up in the fast-lane at over 80mph! - stupid fucking cow! This is how accidents happen, just like the one to my niece. These bloody people have got no common sense whatsoever and are as ignorant as they can be. It's near the junction for Sunbury that I say a quick prayer to baby Abigail as we pass the spot on the opposite side of the motorway where she was taken from me - "Rest in peace my love, my white angel."

The traffic is nice and clear for this time of the morning and we trundle along steadily at 70-80mph and no more as the Willys eats petrol at an alarming rate and I WANT to get there and back on 1-tank of gas if possible - even though I'm stinking rich there's no need to be stupid with my money. The only real problem we face is overtaking slower traffic, the car being left-hand drive and having no door mirrors (only a small internal one) making overtaking a bloody joke.

Spirit and I chat away the whole journey, with the subjects ranging from sex, women, men (like me she's also bisexual), clothes, shoes, holidays, food, drinking, cars, our past lovers and everything else under the Sun. We pass under an old bridge made of deep red-coloured bricks - almost black even - where some smart-arse has graffitied along the top with the slogan: *"GIVE PEAS A CHANCE."* How do they do that?

We laugh and joke around and Spirit kisses my right-hand like a lover. I touch her firm young breasts and she mine but I have to concentrate hard just to keep the fucking car in a straight line rather than get too excited - my love. At Junction-23A we do a left onto the A1(M) and head North towards Hatfield and beyond, with the traffic on this road fortunately considerably lighter as we power along. Through the Hatfield Tunnel we both open our door-windows for a laugh and I drop down a gear into 3rd and give the engine some stick, the beautiful noise from the open side-exhausts echoing and reverberating off the tunnel walls like never-ending thunder and we scream and laugh and she kisses my right-cheek.

We reach Biggleswade itself in another 20-minutes or so, swinging left at the second roundabout onto the B658. We pass an American Golf Centre - really? - on our left and then hit a queue of traffic with cars trying to get both in and out of a crappy Car Boot Sale on our right with people just pulling out everywhere willy-nilly - idiots! Next we pass an aeroplane museum on our left and then finally we reach our destination for the show. The people that are actually showing cars - like myself - have to enter the venue showground slightly further up the road than the ordinary punters do so that's where we head for. The time is now 10.20am.

***

The showground before us is littered with a fantastic array of cars, all in a variety of shapes, sizes and crazy outlandish colours. We park-up between a gorgeous blue 1932 Ford Model B Roadster with a white leather interior, and a white 1970 Dodge Daytona that has a crazy wing mounted high on its tail.

I switch the cars engine off to greet silence and relief at long last as we then escape the confines of our sweltering cabin. Spirit and I hold hands as we quickly survey our surroundings and have a swig of water each from one of the bottles from my mountain-bike. The showground of cars is encircled by trade-stands and stalls of various kinds with the splendour of Old Warden Park house standing behind us in all its Victorian glory. We decide to have a look around the stands first as the cars are still steadily filtering into the showground itself, although suddenly we hear over the showgrounds loud-speakers that the Wall of Death is about to start and that the first show is free entry and as we literally happen to be within spitting distance of the display we wander over to have a look-see. We climb the steps up the side of the big red wooden building - me leading - and once at the summit, we peer over the edge and look down into the cylindrical wall beneath us. It is truly scary as I don't really like heights at all and it gives me the shudders, as I take Spirits hand and grip it tightly for some sort-of reassurance. There are some 20-people or so with us around the perimeter of the viewing area by now as the guys and 1-girl - a nice looking blonde somewhere in her late-20's - prepare for the start of the show. At the base of the circular wall, a guy in his early-30's fires-up a really old motorbike and sets-off riding around the lower section of the wall. He's actually quite fit with a nice toned body and arms although he comes across as bit of a smart-arse to me. I still fancy him though and wouldn't say "No" to letting him eat me and fuck me like crazy! He whizzes around ever faster and higher, almost at the very top and it's really fucking mad and scares the shit out of me. Now back down at the bottom, the blonde girl climbs onto the front of the bike - right over the front wheel! - and off they both go hurtling around the wall together. Suddenly the guy lets go of the handlebars and holds his arms out to either side whilst still continuing to circumnavigate the wall at high-speed - is he fucking stupid or what? Next he grabs hold of his t-shirt and pulls it up over his head so he can't see where he's going, with the girl hanging onto the front of the bike for dear-life - they must be fucking nuts! After another 15-minutes or so of larking about, including 2-bikes going around together - which makes everyone in the audience somewhat dizzy! - the show is over and we all start to file out. We throw some spare loose change down into the pit as does almost everyone else, as suggested by one of the guys at the bottom, an old guy and obviously the boss of the outfit. I take a couple of photos of the surrounding showground from the vantage-point of being up at this level before Spirit and I descend back down the steps, back down to terra-firma and safety.

***

By now its gone 11.15am and the blazing Sun beats its rays down on our beautiful bodies. We kiss each other on the lips without a fucking care about anyone around us who may find our actions disgusting - I love her and that's all there is to it.

Hand-in-hand we wander around the perimeter of the showground looking at all the stands and their various wares. I buy a couple of t-shirts from one stallholder - both in black and featuring a biker-chic on one and a drag-racer on the other. Most of the other stands have car-related items for sale - obviously! - featuring all sorts of American and Hot Rod related ephemera. We both laugh at a small dog sculpture that someone has made out of car parts - including pistons for feet, a crankshaft for its body, and a brake disk for its face. It's so well done and funny and I take a lasting photo for my collection.

Another stand has numerous reproduction vintage metal signs - petrol signs, famous races, Hot Rods, bikes and others. I buy a really beautiful one that has a hot naked 1950's pin-up girl emblazoned on it with her standing next to a World War 2 American bomber. It's £145 but I don't give a shit, I WANT it and I make it mine forever.

From there we find ourselves on a stand selling the bloody craziest women's shoes I think I've ever seen - they're totally mad! Some of them are completely impractical - unwearable even! - but I need them and I WANT. In the end I buy 3-pairs for myself and 2 for Spirit, they're all relatively cheap anyway at around only £45 a pair. One of my crazy pair I'm buying is only for use in the bedroom anyway - shoes for sex/sex-shoes/ fucking footwear! They're made of some kind-of shiny black plastic material and are totally unusable for walking in, hence just for fun purposes.

At the top of the showground we head back to where we started, looking at other stalls as we wander. One of them is actually a walk-in hairdressing salon, doing women's hair in styles from the 1950's but both Spirit and myself pass-up on that as it's just not our thing. Another stand is doing pin-striping, with the artist sitting there painting an intricate design onto the boot-lid of a Willys Coupe similar to mine, although this one is a reproduction one in red whereas mine is an original car. We watch that for a bit and then move on, ending up on another stand selling vintage clothes, shoes, handbags and other stuff. Neither of us buy anything as this kind-of thing also doesn't suit either our of styles, although it is lovely to see the girls on the stand dressed up in their 50's outfits as it all adds to the essence of the show.

∗∗∗

The far-left of the showground is where the main food stands are located and with it now having gone mid-day we decide to indulge in some lunch and feed our inner-selves. We opt for a Coke and a hog-roast each - beautiful pulled-pork in a soft roll with stuffing, sauerkraut and Bramley apple and it's completely gorgeous - just as we both are!

We sit our perfect bums down at one of the vacant tables and eat, chat and watch our fellow humans as they swarm around looking at all the beautiful cars on display. Spirit starts to tell me of her troubled upbringing, of how her father abused her as a child and of her mothers heroin addiction and I desperately want to tell her of my own problems with the "Old Man" in my younger days but I don't, I just try to comfort her with words of sympathy and hold her hand.

With our lunch finished we head off to the beer-tent to drown our sorrows and ease our inner pain. I order us a pint of lager each from the barmaid - a girl in her mid-20's with short dark hair and numerous tattoos dotted about on both her arms and hands, all American Hot Rod-style ones and nowhere near as nice as mine. We stand around supping our chilled drinks outside the tent under the beating Sun, it being so fucking hot now it's almost unbearable. Obviously we both get plenty of looks from everyone around us but none of them dare speak to us, as is the norm. Spirit buys the second round and we head off for another look around the showground once more, taking-in the vast array of different types of cars, each one amazing - Hot Rods, Customs, American classics, Trucks, Pops and Gassers - and I count at least 20-Willys Coupes here, a lot of them painted in grey primer, with most of these being fake repro plastic copies like the red one we saw earlier. There's even a couple of Drag Racers on display as well as several Choppers, Bobbers and about half-a-dozen miniature Hot Rods for kids called Tot-Rods that are a scream to see being driven around by these little kids, not one of them over 8-years old! I capture the images of all we see on my camera, taking some 50-pictures or more throughout the entire day - pictures that I will treasure always.

A strange thing happens to me though whilst Spirit and I were walking around looking at all the cars. We stroll past this guy standing next to his chicken-shit yellow 1950's American truck - I couldn't tell you what make it was? - when I had this weird feeling suddenly sweep over me, like we knew each other, maybe even in a previous life? He's in his late-50's, short, greying, overweight, and yacking-on to his mate like he was talking for England, coming out with stupid statements like:

"There's only 3 of these in the World and I've got all 4."

"I've been coming to this show for over 20-years now."

"I love all things American even though I've never been there."

"I've got a gun-licence I have."

"I cook the best steaks I do."

"My daughter can speak fluent German she can."

"My wife has only been in her new job a couple of days and she's been made a supervisor already."

"Go large on that me old son." And other such shit.

I'm sure I've seen him somewhere before but I just can't seem to place him. He looks at me, directly into my beautiful blue eyes, but all the while it's like he's looking right through me and not actually AT me, apart from gorping at my tits and my legs that is, as well as Spirits - dirty old bastard.

***

As per usual the effects of the lager have gone right through me and I need to pee, as does Spirit. The toilets - if that's what you can call them! - are nothing but Portakabins stuck over in one corner of the event near the Fun Fair so we don't have much of a choice but to queue-up behind at least 10 other women all with the same urgency - great! - although the relief of finally getting into a cubicle and having a wee is overwhelming to say the least!

With that out of the way we decide to go for a walk up past the mansion house to the Swiss Garden a bit further along as hopefully there won't be many people there and we can have some fun together. As we walk I put my right-arm around Spirits waist and pull her close to me. I kiss her left-cheek and she turns to kiss me full-on under the mind-numbing heat of the Suns power.

The canopy of the beautiful trees in the Swiss Garden provide us with some much needed protection as we walk around its winding pathway entwined. Fortunately there is hardly anyone else here apart from a retired couple we pass heading in the opposite direction to the exit - good! We hide ourselves out of sight of any potential prying-eyes as we embrace and kiss with passion and tongues. Spirit runs her left-hand over my breasts with her right making a move down between my legs, causing me to pant heavily and lose control of mind - OH FUCKING HELL! I squeeze her bum and kiss her hard as she fingers me and I WANT it all. I release her and remove my top for her, she bending down to caress and lick and suck my gorgeous peaches. On her haunches she pulls my shorts and knickers down in one swift motion and starts to lick my vulva and I scream and I can't contain myself: "AH AH AH OW OW OW OW AH OW" and I explode.

I strip her completely naked and kiss and squeeze her lovely young firm tits as I insert 2-fingers inside her tight body. She moans: "Fuck me" as I fuck my fingers in and out of her wet vagina and she loves me, shaking like a spastic as she quickly orgasms and cums for me as I replace my fingers with my mouth and tongue, causing her to spit and cry: "FUCK ME SARAH, FUCK ME, OH FUCK, FUCK, FUCK, OH OH OH FUCK."

I stand and we kiss with passion, our love-honey smooching between our mouths as we embrace each others naked bodies and I have fallen completely in love with her.

We clean ourselves up the best we can and redress with more kissing and touching and giggling as we then start to walk back to the showground hand-in-hand, heading next to the small Fun Fair.

***

There are several amusements here over in one corner of the showground, no more than a dozen or so. I immediately spot the dodgems and beg Spirit for a whiz-around the track - in separate cars of course! I pay for a car each and we climb aboard our respective dodgems, mine being a white one and Spirits in fluorescent pink. There are a few other people joining us also - an old woman in her 70's with whom I presume is her niece, a little girl of no more than 5-years old, another car driven by a small fat kid with an angry look on his face that I just want to punch and so I decide to make him my first target! And in the last car a young sweet-looking girl of about 7 or 8 that I soon gather is the sister of the fat boy. The power is switched on and no-sooner do I get underway I'm sideswiped by the little fat kid and sent crashing into the line of parked cars at the edge of the track - BASTARD!

I free myself and chase after him but my plan is immediately thwarted as I'm hit yet again, this time up the arse by the old granny - what the fuck is going on here? The fat kid comes for me once again but I'm too fucking sharp for him, jerking my steering hard-left and then right, causing him to smack into his sister head-on, making her scream and then cry. The kids parents shout at him from the sidelines for causing his sisters tears as he just sits there dejected and forlorn, that is until I spin my car around and smash into the side of him at full-pelt. He looks at me in disbelief and I reverse away, calling him a "little cunt" as I race off back around the track. I catch up with Spirit who is chasing down the old woman, tapping her rear-bumper and trying to make her spin off. I catch Spirit in the side and we both end up ploughing into the edge of the track, just where the annoying fat kid was before he abandoned ship - game over!

We laugh and kiss as we clamber out of our cars, poking my tongue out at the fat kid as we walk pass him - little shit! Next we head off to another amusement, this one being a shooting game. Even though I'm not much of a shot I'm still willing to give it a go, although it's Spirit that tries her luck first, missing the target miserably and laughing at her failure. It's my turn next and more by luck than skill I just clip the edge of the target and win a prize - a big fluffy pink rabbit with enormous ears that I give to Spirit with a kiss and all my love. She's overwhelmed by my action and kisses me back, much to the surprised joy of the stallholder, a big fat tosser with no neck and a big fat greasy bald head - he's fucking horrible!

***

Both Spirit and I have had a really fun day and it's almost time to escape as I don't want to leave here too late and hit all the fucking return traffic on the M25. Plus of course I haven't paid for Spirit for staying at mine tonight and she also has to get home from my place and back to Brighton before the evening sets in.

We make our way back to the Willys only to find some guy sticking something to my windscreen. He's in his mid-50's and a typical Hot Rodder-type with a 1950's-style haircut, tattoos, a show t-shirt, Rockabilly jeans and big black work-boots.

"What do you think you're doing?" I quiz him as we approach.

"Is this your car?" He says back.

"Yes, why?"

"Congratulations, you've won a show prize." He informs me with a big beaming smile.

"Really? What for?" I reply in shock.

"For best Gasser."

"Oh wow, that's amazing!" I beam back with an even bigger smile.

"You need to line-up with the other show winners if you want to collect your trophy." He says, pointing over to his right.

I'm absolutely blown-away by this, I honestly never expected it in a thousand years! I laugh at my victory but at the same time I'm also crying, the car being Andy's creation after all. He would have been so proud, and maybe he is as deep down I know that he's standing by my side like the ghost he has become.

I tell Spirit that we need to line-up in the queue and so we both clamber back into the Willys. The heat inside the car is like stepping into a bloody inferno but we shouldn't really curse it, we've both had a wonderful day so far so I'm not going to knock it. We pull-up behind a couple of bikes waiting in line next to the beer-tent, one a Chopper and the other a Bobber, and await our turn. In no time we get called forward and I pull-up next to the events commentator - some guy called John. He makes a quick comment about the car being driven by: "Two gorgeous young ladies" that makes us both simultaneously give a little laugh - cheeky sod! It's true of course, we are fucking gorgeous and we both know it. I accept the trophy - a small statue of a Hot Rod mounted on a wooden plinth - from him as the surrounding assembled audience start to clap at our success and click-away as photos are taken. I'm really humbled by the whole experience and it must be said a little embarrassed also.

Both Spirit and I get back in the car and head back to the showground when out the corner of my eye I spot that idiot again with the piss-yellow truck, just standing there in the crowd staring at me, not joining-in with the celebratory clapping. Just who is that twat? What the fuck does he want?

We're forced to park in a different place as our original spot is difficult to traverse back to. We laugh and giggle and kiss at our - MY - good fortune and so we decide to go for one last drink at the beer-tent before we head off homeward bound.

***

We have one more lager each - Spirit paying once again - to celebrate our win before we hit the road. We chat and laugh about our day, our loving in the garden, all the beautiful cars and bikes, the people, the shoes we bought, the award, the glorious sunshine, and her - my beautiful whore.

At the last moment, just as we're about to leave, the very same guy I spotted just now in the crowd wanders past us with 2-women - both big fat lumps that I deduce are his wife and daughter. He stares at me yet again, just as before, but says nothing, as do the 2-fats. Fucking idiots, what is their problem?

By now my watch has just clicked past 4.30pm and if we're going to leave then now is the time to do it. The traffic on the M25 is notoriously bad at this time of the day on a Sunday and I just know we're going to have trouble.

***

Both Spirit and I wave and say "Bye" to the staff manning the exit gate as we leave and it really has been such a wonderful day.

We head home using exactly the same route as this morning only now of course - as predicted - the traffic is bloody horrendous. Out onto the A1 (M) the flow is steady but not great. Through the Hatfield Tunnel with more noise from the big V8 bouncing off the tunnel walls, we soon reach our turn-off and the exit-ramp for the M25 and as predicted it's absolutely stuffed! We don't have a bloody choice now of course but to queue-up between all the crappy normal boring cars on the incline. This section of road is a real bastard to navigate - I've been around it several times before and it's always shit! - with cars darting everywhere all over the fucking road - I don't think anyone actually knows where the fuck they're going! Fortunately the Willys has more power than all the crap surrounding us put together and I blast-away from each set of traffic-lights easily and get in front of everyone.

Eventually out onto the M25 and we're faced with a fucking nightmare - a sea of cars, vans and lorries everywhere. We trundle along at a steady 40-50mph all the way to the junction with the M1 where suddenly the sea opens up before us and I can put my foot down at last!

Our luck isn't with us for very long though as there's more traffic ahead, this time with warnings of an accident. We slow to a crawl and then to a halt in the middle-lane of the motorway, only moving up a couple of car-lengths at a time when we do actually get going. All of a sudden the engine in the Willys starts to make a funny noise and I hear the electric fans to the giant motor cut-in. Looking at the temperature gauge I notice that it's starting to rise ever higher and heading straight for the red.

"What's up with it?" Spirit asks me concerned.

"It's overheating."

"What shall we do?"

"Start praying I guess?" I joke back.

But this isn't a joking matter though as the gauge hits the red-zone and I start to seriously worry. Our prayers are answered almost immediately - someone out there must love me! - as the traffic suddenly begins to move a bit quicker and I manage to get into 2nd-gear and some much needed fresh air into the front of the car. We come upon the scene of the trouble just before Junction-15 and I cannot believe my eyes. There in the fast-lane looking forlorn with its rear-end all smashed-in sits a bright orange Ford Focus ST, exactly the same as the one I used to have, even the very same year and with white stripes down its flanks. The poor car has been rear-ended by some smart-arse cunt in one of those little Transit Connect vans, presumably at quite a speed considering all the bloody mess - what a bastard! The cops are already here attempting to sort things out, including trying to stop people slowing down and rubbernecking the accident. The driver of the ST is shouting at the van driver as one of the coppers desperately tries to calm the situation down, all without much success by the looks of it!

Over by the central-reservation wall an old woman in her 70's stands there in tears and obviously in shock and who I guess must have also been in the ST. She looks amazingly like my late mother and her resemblance freaks me and I have to look away. She's the exact bloody spitting-image of her and I start to feel the blood draining from my face in shock. What does this mean?

Once past the incident the traffic thins-out as it speeds up once more and we cruise along now at a steady 70-80mph with the engine thumping-away to itself and the temperature gauge returning back to normal - as is my blood-pressure!

10-miles on we near Heathrow Airport and the traffic once again starts to build up as an overhead gantry-sign flashes ahead of us warning that there's yet another incident and further congestion. Not wanting to risk overheating the engine again I take the decision to turn-off the motorway at the next junction for Sunbury and risk going that way instead, hopefully the traffic that way being lighter.

We do a left at Junction-13 and left again onto the A308, heading East. This is quite a nice stretch of road so I put my foot down a bit harder, the Willys roaring its head off as I unleash its immense power. There's a bit more traffic as we reach the horrible town of Sunbury, not a place I like much at all as it's a bit shitty and scummy so I try to avoid it the best I can. At the end of the main road there's an underpass that goes underneath the M3 that features a multiple traffic-light system. It's a really stupid section of road and requires some navigating without getting hit but with the evil presence of the Willys everyone steers well clear of us. We exit sharp-left past where the old hardboard factory used to be and head onwards, passing Kempton Park Racecourse on our left and then into Hampton. From the imposing Water Works building, the walls of the narrow section of road through the town reverberate with the thumping of the Willys un-silenced exhausts, it's so funny that I have to give the car several stabs of throttle to induce more noise and laughter from Spirit and myself.

To our right now sits Taggs Island with its quirky river houses and then past the beautiful Chinese-styled house as then we reach Hampton Court Palace itself in all its 16th-Century Tudor splendour. Ahead of its main entrance gates lurks another stupid roundabout where one lane of traffic splits into 3-separate lanes. From previous experience I've found that it's always best to get in the middle-lane here as that suddenly becomes the main lane and road heading towards Esher once you navigate the roundabout. As per fucking usual I get some twat in the right-hand lane wanting to get into MY lane, and typically it's another fucking BMW! I give the idiot a blast from my exhausts to warn him off and he pathetically returns the same - knob-jockey! I have track position though and he has to back down as we go around the roundabout side-by-side, especially as he's now stuck behind some crappy people-carrier thing waiting to turn-right in his lane - Ha Ha fucking Ha!

We trundle along into Esher and pass Sandown Park Racecourse and into Esher High Street itself. This road splits into 2 at the end so I take the right-hand lane to go straight on for Cobham. Unbelievably (although it isn't really!) the twat in the BMW tries to push his way in front of us yet again at the traffic-lights - what is it with these people? No-sooner as the red-light disappears I floor the Willys and leave the knob-head standing in my wake of tyre-smoke - just why do these people fucking bother?

We then make our way into Cobham, over the A3 and then into the town. It really is snobs-corner around here, and I have to admit that even though I probably have shit-loads more money than anyone else living here I still wouldn't fit-in with these people - they all give me the bloody creeps! Through Stoke-De-Abingon and past the cemetery we thump our way through Leatherhead and out the other side onto the A24. I give the old car some beans when we reach the duel-carriageway section doing 80 in the stupid 50-zone. Do the idiot pigs really expect me to go that bloody slow? We hit Dorking in no-time and then onto another duel-carriageway section of the A24, passing Beare Green before joining the A29 through Ockley, Slinfold, Five Oaks, Billingshurst and then finally the sanctuary of Foxhill.

✳✳✳

Spirits legs flail wildly on either side of my body as I bury my face into her vagina. I lick and lap and suck and tongue and finger her sweet honeyslot as I bring her to climax and she cums for me and I love her lots.

I position myself on all fours waiting for my whore to pleasure me. I moan: "AH AH AH AH" as she fingers my bumhole with lube and then again louder as I feel the touch of one of my dildos - the clear-plastic ribbed one from Honour - on my exit. She pushes it into my body and I moan like a fucker as I sense the fake rubber cock slide within me. My legs turn to jelly and my eyes widen as she fucks me slowly as I simultaneously suck my thumb and then my fingers.

We roll around on my bed touching and loving each other - breasts, vaginas, bums, legs, backs, faces, hair. She pulls my belly-rings and I pull hers. She twists my nipple-bars playfully as I insert 2-fingers into her pussy, making her pant like a bitch.

I stand over her and order her to: "Lick my sex-shoes", the ones I bought earlier today at the Hot Rod show, and as she does I squeeze my breasts together and lick them with my pointed-tongue. We 69 each other as we roll about on the floor and giggle and laugh like the 2-beautiful gorgeous bisexual bitches we are. I fuck her pussy with my new strap-on dildo from Lovewoo, laying over her young naked flesh like a guy would, pushing it in and out of her love as she screams: "FUCK ME HARDER" and "OW OW OW" and "FUCK ME SARAH YOU FUCKING BITCH" and "I'M GONNA CUM, I'M GONNA CUM AH AH AH AH OH OH OH OH" as she does, ejaculating her love into my mouth as I go down to lick her cunt and I love her.

* * *

We say our "Goodbyes" at the front-door and we kiss one last time. I'm still naked from our duel shower as there was no real need for me to dress again for the remainder of the day, it's too bloody hot anyway.

"Maybe we'll meet up sometime again Sarah?" She says to me but I doubt it, I've already moved-on and looking forward to my next lover. Maybe I'll have a guy next as I'd really like a real cock inside me, or maybe another girl or even another transgender - who knows, I guess I'll have to just wait and see? I can fuck anyone I fucking like as that is my WANT.

As I watch her drive away in her white BMW Mini and shut the door to the World, it suddenly dawns on me the name of that mouthy idiot with the yellow truck. I'm pretty sure that it's "Wellington", or something like that? I still can't think of where I know him from though?

Oh yes I can, he was that idiot at The Ace Cafe that I parked next to when I went there with the gorgeous Emma - my love.

That's where I remember him from - what a twat! Maybe he was a friend of Andy's? But if he was, then how does he know me? Anyway, I don't want to think about him any more, it's been such a beautiful day and one that I will remember and treasure for as long as I live on this Earth.

***

Amazingly, after only 6-weeks of intense searching and nearly 100-emails back and forth, I've actually landed myself another publisher for the book, this one being based in London. I've suffered so many disappointments and had become so disillusioned with the book, I had to keep asking myself: "Why am I doing this bloody thing in the first place, what is the point?"

I really felt like just jacking in all in but I am not a defeatist and so pushed on, and I'm so glad that I did as here I am once again, with a publishing contract in my hand! Hopefully I won't get stabbed in the back for the second bloody time and things will finally work out OK for me with this new lot.

I got in contact with my solicitor Mr. Simpson to see if I could take legal action against the previous publishers for braking their contract with me but he went on to explain that the chances of success were pretty slim. Even though, I'm not going to let them get away with treating me like shit. You know me, I'll get them in the end.

13

Hedwig's Funeral

"OH NO NO NO NO NO NO. PLEASE TELL ME ME THIS ISN'T TRUE. THIS CAN'T BE HAPPENING. WHAT THE FUCK?" I shout out to no-one but myself.

I'm sitting at my computer dumbstruck. It's Saturday and 1.05 in the afternoon. I've just fed Eva and I'm sitting here reading my emails as I munch-away on a bacon sandwich with loads of brown sauce, English mustard and black pepper.

I prey to the "Great One" that my eyes are deceiving me and that the email that I've just opened isn't really there. It's from Hans in Germany with the devastating news that Hedwig - MY Hedwig - passed away 4-days ago, on Tuesday.

I don't know what to say. I am frozen in time. I down my glass of wine in one go. This just cannot be true, I only spoke to her the week before last and she seemed fine to me. We had kept in touch with each other via email ever since our first meeting nearly 18-months ago now and not once did she ever mention to me how ill she was. This all seems to ring a bell doesn't it?

I can't look at the screen any longer and so grab my glass and head into the back of the house for a refill, a refill of vodka that is. Why does all this shit keep following me around, there is absolutely no bloody escape from any of it. I pour myself another glass, a 50-50 mixture of white German and evil Russian, and sip heavily on it as the old photo of me and Andy in Berlin that Christmas burns its image into my retinas. It was then of course that was the one and only time I ever met the pair of them - Hans and Hedwig - with me taking an instant liking to her. My friend. How many times have you ever heard me say that word?

I begin to feel a little sick, the mixture of the alcohol, the bacon-butty and the shock of the news of poor old Hedwig's sudden departure from this Earth all starts to bite me.

I top-up my glass with more wine and head back out into the Sun, plonking my arse back down on the chair to the patio table. The message on the computer screen is still there, haunting me forever and there is no getting away from it any more. I go to grab the remainder of the last half of my sandwich only to discover some fucking dirty disease-ridden bluebottle fly - or Bulgarians as I call them! - has landed on it and has no-doubt spread its evil germs all over it. In horror I sweep my fist across it, knocking both the sandwich and the plate it was on onto the paved patio with a crash. The Bulgarian flies off, completely oblivious to all the fucking trauma that its just inflicted upon my brain, just like its stinking fucking namesakes do - BASTARDS.

So now, obviously, I have to go and fetch the dustpan and brush from the kitchen to clean-up all the bloody mess, whereupon my return I then spot Eva tucking-in to a piece of bacon from the obliterated sandwich laying on the patio. I shoo at her and she runs away with it down the garden and eats it all up, brown sauce and mustard and all! I chuck both the remains of my lunch and the plate in the kitchen waste-bin and I am lost.

I'll have to message Hans back with my deepest condolences but not now, I'm just not in the mood. At poolside I strip-off my bikini - my skimpy white one from UjENA - and jump in naked. I swim backstroke and try to chill-out and clear my mind but it's no use, I'm too fucking pissed-off even for that. I clamber out and head back into the glare of the afternoon Sun, not bothering to dry myself as the heat will do that for free. I really don't know what to do. I don't want to go for a drive. I don't want to masturbate. I don't want to play pool. I don't want garden. I don't even want another bloody drink.

I sit back down at my laptop, still naked of course, to try and compose a return message to Hans, poor old sod, he must be heartbroken. I send him a short heartfelt note and give him all my love in his time of sorrow. I really feel for how he's feeling right now. I know as unfortunately I've already been there.

***

When I told you all before that I wanted to come back to Berlin one day, I never expected it to be under these circumstances. But here I am. I had to come of course, this is something I had to do on my own, for myself and for Hedwig, and for Hans of course.

I caught an early flight from Gatwick to Tegal Airport this morning, flying with Lufthansa once again. I'm staying at the Hotel Adlon in Berlin, the very same place that Andy and I stayed in for our Christmas break, and it's really good to be back here, despite the overall reason for my return. Obviously I'm not staying in the same suite as before, that would have brought back too many memories - all good ones I have to admit - and I think it would have also been a bit creepy if I had done.

With both my cases unpacked, I decide to go down and get a bite to eat for lunch in one of the Hotels restaurants. I'm wearing a gorgeous white sleeveless silhouette dress from Karl Lagerfeld that really shows-off my curvaceous figure. On my feet I have on my dear old pair of blue-suede Lola platform court shoes as they still look fantastic on me - as everything does! My underwear is in white lace from Victoria's Secret. My hair and make-up I've kept simple once again - classic and stylish - as is my WANT. Unusually my perfume today is *Opium* by Yves Saint Laurent, just for a change. My clutch-bag is my white leather one again from Prada.

The dining-room is actually quite sparsely populated for a lunchtime, I guess most of the hotels occupants are out and about somewhere doing their own thing. I order veal sirloin with mushrooms, macaire potatoes, pak choi and truffled hollandaise and just the one glass of the house German wine, I really don't want to get pissed today, out of respect of poor old Hedwig.

With my lunch all finished I just sit there for a while to contemplate the World and everything, thinking about my life and where the fuck am I going? Where the fuck am I going?

I desperately need some fresh air so I exit the hotel and grab myself a taxi, telling the driver - a little skinny German guy with a thin moustache and a black leather waistcoat - to take me to the Englischer Garten in the Grosser Tiergarten on Altonaer Strasse. Once there I wander around the beautiful grounds at my own pace, tying myself up in knots with yet more thinking, mainly about Hedwig and her funeral tomorrow - and I just hope that I can hold myself together. I spot a young couple - both about 20-ish - laughing and joking around like young lovers do. The girl jumps up at the guy and wraps her arms around his shoulders and her legs around his body and they kiss with passion. I smile at their love, it's beautiful to see but I'm not one little bit jealous. I have my own love, in my own special way. I find a nice quiet bench-seat to sit down and study the passers-by as the World revolves around them - the young, the old, the middle-aged, male, female - and all exactly the same but all completely different at the same time, just like you and me.

From there I catch another cab, this time over to the Kaufhaus des Westens department store that Andy and I came here to together the last time. Berlin looks so different this time around, with all the Christmas snow now a forgotten memory, and it looks just like any other major city in any country in the World. I make my own way around the store, checking-out all the wonderful things and all the beautiful people. I look as though I'm a part of their elite crowd but I'm not, I am way beyond anything they are now or ever will be - I am a Queen, a Goddess and the Devil all rolled into one perfect woman. They are all just like those stuck-up bitches I saw in the South of

France ages ago - fake. They disgust me and I want to kill them all right here and now, if only I had the chance.

I catch my fifth cab of the day - that's including the one I took from the house to Gatwick Airport - and return back to the Adlon empty handed. In the shower I just wash my day away, and although I touch myself intimately I don't masturbate, I just don't feel like it. I didn't even bring any of my dildos with me from my collection, for the first time in.................. ever.

I redress for dinner, it now being 6.25pm. I'm wearing a gorgeous petrol-blue mid-length dress from Thierry Mugler that is tighter than a ducks arse, sexy blue lace underwear from Curvy Kate and a pair of white suede heals from Christian Laboutin. My hair and make-up I've redone the same as before, partly because I couldn't be bothered to alter it as I look bloody gorgeous whichever I do to it. My perfume is *Poison* by Christian Dior. The evening dining-room is way more crowded now than at lunchtime, with hardly a spare table to be had. I'm placed over by one wall, out of the way from my fellow humans with - as per usual - all their staring eyes scanning every part of my good/bad self. I order Cote de Boeuf (rare obviously as that's how I like my meat!), seasonal vegetables and potato purée in a bearnaise sauce that looks, smells and tastes divine, along with another bottle of the same house white from earlier. I think about Hedwig and Hans and tomorrow as I eat, hoping that it all goes well. I've never actually been to a proper funeral - a real burial I mean - as the others I've attended so far have all been cremations. Maybe the Germans prefer burials, I don't know? I don't bother with a pudding and so make my way back upstairs to my suite. By now it's just gone 9pm and I decide to hit the sack early as tomorrow is going to be a long hard day and no-doubt I'm going to need the extra energy to see me through.

***

It's a beautiful sunny day in Berlin as the Sun shines its overpowering rays through the windows of my bedroom as I stand there in the nip and feed on its energy and power, gazing out onto the strong grey German city.

The funeral is at 11.30am this morning and it's now 9.35am. I decide to skip breakfast as don't I feel much like eating, and jump in the shower to try to kick-start my body into actually waking up. The water feels so beautiful as it cascades down my perfect body, my face, breasts, arms, belly, vagina, and legs down to my feet.

After drying myself off I dress for the day - all in black of course - wearing a short, tight long-sleeved bodycon-dress from Versace. My underwear is also in black, a really sexy lace number from Figleaves. My shoes are a pair of black suede open-toe platform court shoes from Jimmy Choo, with my clutch-bag a black leather one from Hermes. To cover my tattooed hands I'm also wearing a pair of vintage black lace gloves from Aprilsunrises as Hans hasn't seen my new ink and I don't want to upset or scare him off. Also I don't think it would be appropriate today - I'm not completely insensitive. I know my dress isn't really the right thing for a funeral either but even so I just know deep down that Hedwig would have wanted me to dress as I like, not as I'm expected to. If she were here then I'm pretty damn sure she would have done the very same thing, I just know she would, we had a connection. I do my hair and make-up as per the norm but with a darker overall look to it, featuring coal-black eyeshadow, cherry-red lipstick and a black silk bow in my hair. My perfume today is *Poison* by Christian Dior once again.

I've pre-booked a cab through the hotel and it's not long before my suite phone rings to let me know that it's here waiting for me and bang-on time - typical German efficiency! Oh well, here we go then.

The cemetery is the Stadtischer Friedhof III - the actual final resting place of German filmstar Marlene Dietrich - and I arrive there in good time, as I like to do. There must be a least 100 people here already, with a steady flow of new arrivals joining all the time. I slowly thread my way through the amassed mourners, all of them speaking German of course and all of them alien to me. I suddenly catch a glimpse of Hedwig's coffin in the near distance and an icy chill spears its way down my spine. Although it's beautiful - a white one with ribbons of black, red and yellow adorning it - at the same time I also find it truly morbid and somewhat sinister.

I then notice Hans, talking to a dark-haired woman in her 40's. He notices me almost at once and waves a small wave and gives me a smile and a nod. How can he be so calm and brave at a time like this?

"Sarah, it is so good of you to come." He says with another smile as he joins me.

"It's the least I could do. I'm so sorry about Hedwig, I liked her so much."

"Thank you. I am also sorry about Andrew, he was a good man and a good friend."

"Yes I know, thank you. I really can't believe that Hedwig has gone. She was so nice to me, and so sweet."

"She liked you also. She would speak of you all the time. She saw something of her younger-self in you I think."

My heartbeat start to quicken at Hans's heartfelt words and I feel tears of sorrow start to well-up in the corners of my eyes. We hug and I immediately feel myself starting to slide. Everyone stares at us as we do and I see them all question each other as to who I am but I am oblivious to their care. His embrace is wonderful, this big old German man that is filled with pain. Our hug is nothing sexual of course, it is just 2-people hurting and comforting each other in their time of need.

"Everything will be okay Sarah." He whispers to me softly.

"I somehow don't share your enthusiasm." I return.

"Hedwig knew of her breast cancer for some time now. She knew when her time was right."

"Breast cancer?" I question him back.

"Yes, she did not want people to know. It is the same as Andrew, he told us about his heart condition several years before he met you. I know this is hard for you to take Sarah but this is how things are."

I stand there stunned at his words. So Andy told them about his heart and not me - his own wife and lover. Why didn't he tell me? Why is it that no-one can ever tell me the fucking truth?

The funeral proceeds and we all gather around Hedwig's beautiful coffin. As the service is all in German I don't understand a bloody word the vicar is saying, although I obviously get the gist. I look around me at all the sad faces, at the blackness of everyone's clothes, at the white of the coffin, and I can't take it any more - I am surrounded by death.

I break-down and start to cry with big tears right there and then in front of everyone, the emotion is just too much for me to bare, all this continuous heartache is killing me more and more day by day. Some old woman next to me puts her arm around my shoulder to try and console me and offers me a tissue. I take it and thank her for her kindness as she says something to me in German but I have no-idea what it is.

I eventually regain some composure and before long it's all over - thankfully. I really don't think I could have taken much more of that. And how come I'm the only person in tears anyway, doesn't anyone else here have a heart?

Hans kindly invites me back to the house, offering me a ride in one of the big black Mercedes funeral cars. I squeeze myself in - not very elegantly in this dress I have to say! - in a car full of elderly Germans, none of whom say anything, not even to each other the whole way along - oh well!

Back at the house and once again everything seems so different this time around - the colour of the trees, the people in their late-summer clothes, and of course, Hans and Hedwig's house itself, surrounded by beautiful multi-coloured flowers and billiard-table flat lawns.

Inside, the house is packed-full of people - family, friends and hired staff handing out glass flutes of Champagne. I grab one and sink it in one big gulp, then immediately grab another. I wander around on my own between everyone, feeling like a fish out of water as I don't know anyone here, apart from Hans of course and I haven't seen him for ages now.

Suddenly I bump into the little old lady from before, the one that rescued me from embarrassment and gave me a tissue to stem my weeping. She says: "OK?" to me in a strong German accent and smiles. I say: "Yes, thank you" back to her as she then puts her wrinkly old hand on my arm and squeezes it gently. I look back at her and gaze into her beautiful clear-blue eyes. What does she want I wonder? What is she looking at? What is she thinking about?

She suddenly wanders off as Hans appears in front of me along with the dark-haired woman he was with earlier and a tall guy around 50-ish and 3-young kids, all girls and each one blonde and full of sweetness.

"How are you Sarah?" Hans asks with concern.

"I'm OK thanks. I'm really sorry about making an exhibition of myself earlier."

"There is no need to apologise Sarah, it is a natural thing to grieve. May I present my daughter Magda, her husband Glen, and my grandchildren."

Following lots of "Hellos" and the shaking of hands, I then recognise Magda from the photos Hedwig showed me back at Christmas time. She lives in the States somewhere with her American husband and their 3 US-born little girls.

"We've heard so much about you, from Mum." Says Magda to me in her American over-toned German accent.

"Really?" I say, somewhat surprised.

"She was very fond of you. She mentioned you every time we spoke on the phone or in emails."

I'm a little bit ashamed to say this but at this point I completely lose it yet again. I well-up and then sob my heart out for all the stinking rotten World to see, wailing uncontrollably into my hands as if there was nothing else on this fucking planet apart from the sound of my tears. Magda comforts me with the second embrace of the day as my mind collapses into itself, overloading with grief and emotion. How can I cry so much for Hedwig and my poor old cat Lacey but not when Andrew, Abigail or even when my own Mother died? What does that mean?

Hans takes over and puts his big strong arm around my shoulder and manoeuvres me between the crowd of gorping mourners and into the kitchen. He sits me down at the wooden central table and begins making me a cup of tea. We chat about Hedwig and Andy and life and all that shit. He tries to add some humour into the conversation and make me laugh but I don't want to laugh, how can I at a time like this? And how can he, on the very day that he's just buried his wife?

We're suddenly joined by the youngest of Hans's grandchildren, a sweet little thing of only about 5 or 6-years old.

"Why are you crying?" She says to me in her sweet little innocent - and also somewhat nauseating and sickly - American voice.

"Because your Grandmother has died." I stutter my reply.

"Why?"

"Because she had something wrong with her." Says Hans to her.

"Why?" She asks yet again.

"Because this is what happens to people darling." He tries to explain to her.

"Why?"

"That is enough questions mein Liebling, go and find your mother now." Hans says to her, bringing a halt to any more of her "Whys?"

The little girl runs off, back into the throng of people. Kids, why do they always have to keep asking Why? Why? Why? I only have a couple of sips of my tea before I make my excuses to Hans as I just want to get out of here and back to England. My return flight is at 7pm this evening anyway and I want to go, I've had enough.

We hug once more and I wish him well, he whispering something in German into my ear but I don't ask him for a translation. I think it was something about love but I'm not certain. I kiss him on the cheek and then I'm gone, walking out through the middle of the collective mourners like Moses through the parting sea, all without saying a word or even looking at any of them - I just want to leave.

Back at the Adlon and I'm in a mess. From the mini-bar I drink myself stupid so I don't have to think about this day any longer. I've already packed my bags and changed my clothes for the return flight home, a black sleeveless blouse in silk from Schiaparelli, my pair of pale-blue stone-wash jeans from BooHoo and on my feet my pair of black leopard-print peep-toe ankle-boots from Jimmy Choo. My underwear is left as is, the same going for my hair, make-up and perfume.

Now where is that fucking taxi?

***

It is the day after my poor dear old friend Hedwig's funeral. It's 11.27am and Eva is being a real pain in the arse. I'm still in bed of course, and the events of the last couple of days have taken its toll upon my weary body. Eva is desperately trying to get me off my arse for me to feed her, she running and jumping about like a thing possessed, although I suppose it is funny really in its own way.

I drag myself out of bed and both of us do breakfast - although it's actually closer to lunchtime by now! - cornflakes for myself and chicken liver pate for her. I'm so glad that yesterday is over, I really don't want to have to go through all that crap very often. At least I slept well last night for some reason? I think the long day knocked me out for the count.

I go to pick my mail from out of the door-box, there being only one letter in there, an A4-size packet postmarked from London. I return to the kitchen and sit back down on one of the breakfast stools to see what it is and my face lights up when I open it. It is the beautiful moment when my dream becomes reality and physically hold my book in my hands for the very first time has finally arrived - it truly is a special and magical experience. I am so proud of myself that tears well-up in my eyes and I cry, my emotions still stirred by all the events of yesterday.

My heart sinks though when I suddenly notice the first of numerous mistakes before me - the size of the text on the front-page aren't uniform, all the italics have been printed in ordinary font, the back-cover note has been repeated on the inside, and the title, my name and the publishers logo are all missing from the spine - WTF!

I phone my publishers straight away and tell them to correct all the mistakes at once. They seem very apologetic and genuinely sorry for all the cock-ups, saying they will issue me with a corrected version by the end of the week. Everything is always the same scenario, one second I'm up and the very next I'm let down again. Why doesn't anything ever fucking go right?

***

It's the following Sunday night after Hedwig's funeral in Germany and I'm preparing to go out. It's 12.21am so I guess technically it's really Monday morning.

I'm off out once again on one of my little missions, this time down to Brighton in East Sussex, on another one of my revenge excursions. I'm taking the Lamborghini out tonight as I want something fast to get me in and out of town. I know the Aston, the Ferrari and the Lister are all just as quick but the Lambo is my favourite as you know - my baby. I haven't dressed in anything specific for the task in hand, just regular clothes - although they are all in black - with a v-neck t-shirt from ASOS and stretch-jeans from Gap. My footwear is a pair of black walking-boots from LK Bennett. My underwear is in sexy yellow lace from Hanky Panky. My hair and make-up I leave as is although for some reason today I'm wearing "naked" lipstick - don't ask me why? My perfume is *Kenzo Flower* by Kenzo.

In the garage I load the passenger seat foot-well with a plastic can full of petrol, itself encased in 2 bin-liners to trap the awful smell. I also take with me a large box of matches, several pairs of latex gloves, a packet of antiseptic hand-wipes, and a street-map of Brighton that I printed off the computer as I'm not using my satnav just in case it could be tracked. I don't think I need anything else?

I head out into the night, making my own way across country, over the A29 and the A24 to join the A23 and aim myself South. The Lambo is nothing but pure joy as I pick off cars at my want, although I try to keep out of any real trouble just in case I come a cropper and slide off the road or get pulled by the stupid fucking Police. I seriously don't want any mishaps with a can of petrol inside the car right next to me that's for sure! From there I cut left onto the A27 and head East for Lewis, thus avoiding Brighton town centre itself and going around the back of it. At the junction at Falmer I take a right-turn onto the B2123 and head South once again where I decide to push the car a little harder, I don't know why, I just feel like I have to?

After a few miles I turn off the main road and slowly head in the direction of my target, guiding the wide Lambo down the narrow vehicle-lined back-roads of the little village of Woodingdean, Brighton. The bitch I'm targeting is that fucking junkie that slammed into me on the A27 2-years ago, thus writing-off my lovely little Fiesta ST and putting me in hospital with a smashed arm and concussion and causing me to lose my baby. I know I should have nailed her sooner but you know how my life has been since then - just one sodding problem after another.

It was the stupid bloody Police that actually gave me her details as last year they sent me a copy of their investigation statement into the accident which incredibly listed both her name and address on it! The cops really are fucking thick aren't they?

Traversing several tight roads and corners I find the road I'm looking for quite easily - Willow Close, a dead-end road, how appropriate! - and cruise past the fucking bitch's house as quietly as I possibly can. It's now 1.09am. I reverse back and park around the corner in Crescent Drive out of the way and prepare to sort myself out with gloves, the can - unwrapping it and adding the spout - and securing the car. Typically, just as I make my way back around the corner as stealthily as possible, a bloody box-van turns into the very same road where I've just parked-up. The 2-occupants - both fucking Slavs by the look of them - gorp at me and then my car as they pass, although fortunately they drive straight on and disappear into nowhere - Hell hopefully!

At the bitch's front-door I push the nozzle of the can through the prerequisite letterbox and I stand there in the chill of the morning, scanning around the vicinity for anyone spying on me or driving up the road. There is nothing. The air is quiet and peaceful except for the glug from the can as it empties itself between my hands. Once finished I strike-up the whole box of matches and shove them in the hole, it still wedged open by the end of the nozzle. It ignites in an instant with a giant whoosh in the other side of the door as an orange flame erupts from the ground upwards. I immediately pull the nozzle out of the letterbox and run with it back up the road and around the corner. With the passenger-door open and up, I place the spent can back in the plastic bag, shut the door and run around to the other side of the car, the Italian monster bursting into life and I am gone.

Back on the B2123 I head North for several miles, keeping the speed down so as not to be noticed too much - especially by cops in plain-clothed cars - and then turn off onto the A27 and head for Henfield and back home along my usual route when I'm down this way. I stop-off along the way, firstly to lob the empty petrol-can into a skip outside someone's driveway, and then later to shove the latex gloves and used wipes down a drain-hole by the side of the road and then I'm clear.

It is said that "Vengeance is sweet" and it's true, the feeling of having dealt a blow back at the fucking bitch for all the trauma she put me through is so immensely satisfying that I can't really translate it into simple words on a page. As I've told you all many times before my sisters, my independence is the key factor in my life and my cars are a massive part of that. That fucking bitch took away my freedom when she destroyed my car and now it's her turn to suffer - SHE CAN FUCKING BURN IN HELL. I have no thoughts for her kids or even if she has a husband or whatever, if they die as well then that's just too fucking bad, I simply don't care - Divina Platten is no more.

I reverse the car back into its parking space in the garage - it's now 2.02am - and I desperately need a drink. I down a mouthful of gin straight from the bottle as I stand leaning up against one side of the white leather sofa in the living-room. The gins heady aroma burns my nostrils and my throat and I swallow another mouthful. I burn from the inside as the alcohol mixes with my blood and I squeeze my breasts and then finger my vagina and I am so fucking hot. I strip there and then and run my beautiful hands over my beautiful body. In all my previous years I still cannot believe how fucking gorgeous I am - I am so fucking amazing! I do not have one single flaw on my entire body, not one. Everything about me is perfect.

I down another gin and go into the kitchen. I scan the contents of the fridge looking for things to fuck with. I notice that the cucumber has gone all soft and squidgy - what is wrong with cucumbers these days, they don't seem to last 5-minutes? - so that's no bloody good. Celery is the wrong shape so that's also a non-starter. The packet of leeks that I bought a couple of days ago then catches my eye - the ones from my own vegetable patch were devoured by the bastard slugs - and so I rip it open at once. There are 3-leeks in the packet - 2 small ones and 1 large - and so obviously I plump for the larger one! I trim the furry-end off and reshape the edges with a knife to make it easier on entry. Climbing onto the centre-island work-surface I position myself on all fours and slowly insert the leek into my vaginal hole. It feels so fucking good and I moan and love it and I fuck myself harder. I sit down on my perfect bum and spread my legs wide open and masturbate my vag with my veg. I pant loudly and my tits wobble to themselves as I fuck and I scream as I cum over the leek, my hand and the smooth marble surface of the work-top. Removing the vegetable I lick leek and swallow my love as I play with my breasts and tweak my nipple-bars.

In the living-room I have one more gin before I feed Eva - chicken in sauce - make myself a large mug of milky coffee with 2-large sugars, have a quick pee and then hit the sack. It's now 3.20am.

***

I don't rise that very same morning until 11.06am. I slept like a log as I was completely knackered, it being such a long and weird night. I have a pee and make my way downstairs to make breakfast for Eva and myself - chicken in gravy for her and tea and toast for myself. I switch the TV on to watch the 24-hours news but it's a disaster, the lead story being about the daughter of some soap-actor that I've never heard of and how she was found dead in the woods at a music festival somewhere after taking super-drug 2C-P on top of both Ketamine and MDMA, all given to her by her nigger boyfriend. Not only that, this bastard actually filmed her dying on his bloody phone as well - typical fucking coon!

I have no sympathy for this bitch of course, what the Hell did she expect from this black fucker, chocolates and flowers? If she wanted to jump into bed with a member of the tribe in the first place then she got exactly what she fucking deserved and paid the ultimate price for it - stupid fucking cow. Just to rub salt into her family's wound, the black fucker only got 8 ½ years in jail for this! He should have been skinned alive - slowly!

The following report is yet more fucking shit about immigrants, as apparently there's another 25,000 of the bastards heading our way! This is madness upon madness. Everyone turning a blind-eye to the truth won't make this problem disappear - we need to build the wall higher.

I turn the sound down to zero and click-on Teletext to block the sight of all this scum from my vision. Clicking on UK News I scroll down to see if there's any mention of any fires in the Brighton area last night, my curiosity burning within me. Page after page reveals nothing, although the very last page has a caption that instantly drains the blood from my body:

"Family of 4 killed in Brighton house fire."

I almost choke to death at the headline and I have to steal myself to click on the caption and read the following report. It goes on to say that a family of 4 have been killed in a house fire in the early hours of this morning with the Police suspecting arson, but the surname isn't right so this can't be the same one, this can't be anything to do with me, the surname of the junkie bitch was Platten, not Whiteford like these poor souls so it surely must be another fire, mustn't it? Switching the text off, I change channels to another news program, one that covers the South East, and wait to see if there's any mention of it on there. I don't have to wait very long as almost immediately the live images of the burnt-out house flashes-up before me as I sit there transfixed in numbed silence. It is the same house but it isn't the same family.

WHAT THE FUCK HAVE I DONE? I can only guess that the junkie bitch must have moved away or something, that's all I can think of, that has to be the explanation.

Eva sits there in front of me, staring me out with her beautiful big blue eyes. She knows that I've done wrong, I can see it in her face. I know exactly what she's thinking, clever cat. But what can I do about it? I can't bring them back from the dead, these people, these human beings that I've destroyed - 5 of them now.

Ask me how I feel?

How do I feel?

How can I have any feelings at all?

How?

I'VE KILLED 5 FUCKING PEOPLE!
WHAT THE FUCK HAVE I TURNED INTO?
WHAT?

***

It's almost 2-months now since Hedwig's funeral and the Brighton fire and you find me in a state of pure melancholy. I've had better times of course in my life and I've had worse - a lot worse.

I'm guessing that the postman has already been this morning and so I wander across to the postbox on the main gate to fetch my mail. I have 6-letters, 3 of which are from foreign aid scroungers so they can all fuck-off. Another is crap from a TV cable company, another is a bank-statement, and the sixth and final one is an airmail letter from America that fuels my intrigue. Who on Earth can this be from I wonder? I open it after the others, leaving it to last, out on the patio table with a chilled glass of Champagne on the go. Inside is a hand-written letter from Magda, the daughter of Hans and my dear old late friend Hedwig.

I am shocked and stunned by her opening line, that her poor old father Hans is also dead, having committed suicide only 3-weeks after the death of his lovely wife - the poor old sod, he must have been heartbroken. I really can't take it in that he's also gone, what a terrible tragedy. And how awful for Magda, especially with her being so far away on the other side of the pond. I wonder what's going to happen to the house in Berlin, as well as all those beautiful and rare cars? I guess that she will cop for everything now, and good luck to her if she does.

She concludes her short letter by inviting me to her fathers funeral, again to be held in Berlin as her mothers was. I decide here and now not to go, I just don't want to, I can't take any more pain.

FUCKING HELL - why does everything keep changing all the time, why can't I ever have peace and harmony in my life?

I find myself in an angry mood, angry at the passing of both Hedwig and now Hans. I am also angry at everything else, including myself for what happened in Brighton. I am angry at the state of my country as it is destroyed by those supposedly in charge. I am angry at the World as a whole for being so shit.

***

I'm out and about on the A24 heading South to Dorking. I've been to Leatherhead this lunchtime - not a place I visit very often as there isn't really much there in the way of shops, nothing that lights my fire anyway. My reason for going was to check-out a new burger-bar that has had really good reviews in the local press, a place called *PHIL YOU UP.* The food was really great and all handmade right there and then in front of you and to a high standard - handmade wraps, sandwiches, burgers, bacon buns and more.

I myself just had a plain burger in a soft bread roll with caramelised onions and it was really lovely, with a fresh home-made taste and a spicy kick. My only gripe was that I had to wait almost 15-minutes for my food but that's a minor detail really. Of course during that time I had to suffer the usual bloody scenario of being constantly stared at from my fellow diners waiting for their food. Today I'm wearing a halter-neck top in white from Olcaygulsen.com that is so minimal that I'm practically topless, especially as I'm not wearing any underwear at all, therefore exposing plenty of side-boob! My only other clothes I have on are my pair of white cotton shorts from Puma and that's that! On my feet I'm wearing a beautiful pair of white Formula RB-8-1 racing boots from Sparco, courtesy of Demon Tweeks, that are both super-sexy and super-comfy as well as being perfect to drive in - obviously! My hair and make-up are both sharp and gorgeous, featuring medium-brown lipstick and grey eyeshadow. My perfume today is *Poison* by Christian Dior.

With both my food and my Coke consumed, as I've said I'm now on the A24 heading South to Dorking. Past the turning for

Mickleham, I accelerate the RS - today's choice of transport - up to 65 in the 50-zone and overtake a couple of slow cars in the left-hand lane obeying the rules and all being the good/ boring citizens they are in their shitty cars. The first one I overtake - a very mundane Jap piece of crap, and in brown of all colours! - pulls out behind me a tails me from a distance. I immediately notice the driver - a woman of about my age, possibly younger? - is very precise and correct in her driving, professional even, but I quickly dismiss it as nothing and carry on without a care for them or their Japanese shit-box, motoring past Box Hill, *Ryka's Cafe,* the Stepping Stones and then into and through Dorking town and beyond to home.

***

It's a week later and I'm going out tonight - it's Saturday. I'm off down to a club in Brighton, East Sussex, to let my hair down a bit - not literally though as it's up as per usual! I've never really been into clubbing, for one thing I can't stand all that thumping monotonous music, mainly because it's nearly all black- orientated and that obviously goes against my grain.

As far as my clothes go - or as little in my case! - I'm wearing a beautiful white sleeveless crop- top from Missguided that is really tight and holds my full breasts, exposing plenty of front and side-cleavage as once again I'm not wearing a bra. My only other items of clothing are my skirt, a white mini from Charlotte Russe and my knickers, a white lace pair from Triumph. On my feet I'm wearing my old pair of white strap shoes from Raffi Scent as they're gorgeous, easy to drive in and also if I decide to hit the dance floor I want something I can move around in freely without falling arse-over-tit! My clutch-bag for this evening is my white leather one from Prada. I've also really gone to town with my make-up, it being my usual typical style - sharp cheekbones, coal-black eyeshadow, and cherry-red lipstick. My hair is as per usual - you all know the bloody score by now! - whilst my perfume is *Luxe* by Avon.

The car of choice for tonight's sojourn is the RS once more as it's reasonably small, fast and easier to park than the Lambo or any of my other cars - except for the Mini obviously! I give Eva a kiss to the top of her head and she repeats the same as then I go. The time is 9.45pm. I'm taking the scenic route once again, thus avoiding the main A-roads and hopefully the pigs. Fortunately there's not much traffic to speak of as I power on, even hitting 120 in a 50-zone at one point. I take it easier along the seafront road of the A259 with the build-up of cars stymieing my speedy progress anyway. Once through Hove I'm immediately into Brighton and I make my way to the underground car-park opposite the old burnt-out West Pier, my usual parking place whenever I'm down here. With the RS secure I strut my way to the exit doors and the tunnel under the main road where the awful smell of piss from the drunks, the junkies and the scum of the town all with no manners immediately infiltrates my nostrils. It disgusts me to the very core and I can't wait to emerge out from the other side into the fresh sea air and breathe freely once more.

There are several clubs along this section of seafront, all housed in ex-boatsheds, none of which I've ever been into before in all my days as I was never really a clubber *per se,* as the only real reason for me being here in the first place is to maybe pick up someone new - a new guy or a new girl, or maybe even a couple, who knows where it may end? My first port of call yields nothing, the place is practically empty apart from the bored-looking staff and a handful of punters, they too all appearing to be equally bored.

Another club further along is in the opposite situation as it's absolutely rammed solid, with a whole myriad of human bodies all squashed in together all trying to dance and pretending to have fun as the beat from the heavy so-called "music" thumps along, it actually making the pavement shake under my feet! I decide to give that a wide-birth also, stopping next at a club called *SEASHELLS* that for some reason entices me in. The attending crowd are the usual mixed Brighton bunch - men, women, gays, lesbians, bisexuals, transgenders, cross-dressers, white, black, brown, yellow, and of course the obligatory fucking Slavs. I order myself a large neat vodka from the girl serving behind the bar, a small sweet little honey of about 20 and of oriental origin that I fall for within seconds. Suddenly some guy appears from nowhere at my side and offers to pay for my drink. Even though he seems quite nice and is attractive, for some reason I decline his offer and move on. He's one of those smooth smart-arse types with a chip on his shoulder and I could have let him take me easily even so.

I have a little dance to myself as I sip my drink, scanning the room for love as I let the 1980's music take me to another level. I did a line of cocaine before I left the house just to sharpen-up my senses and it heightens the sound of the beautiful song that emits from the speakers as it literally lifts me off my feet - Soft Cell and *Bedsitter* - with singer Marc Almond's hypnotic voice and lyrics killing me as they bite into my heart and I die.

At once I spot a girl at the far-end of the bar, presumably just sitting there on her own although it's difficult to tell with all these people swarming about her. She's very pretty with long brown hair that has obviously been professionally cut and styled, and as I near her I notice her beautiful brown eyes and her kissable mouth and my heartbeat quickens and my mind races with thoughts of fucking her silly with my tongue and fingers. She's not in my league by any means of course, but even so she is attractive in her own way. I sidle-up to her and push my way in between her and some wanker with one of those awful long fuzzy beards that makes him look 50-years older than he really is. I catch her looking at me with glazed-over eyes and I can immediately tell that she's as pissed as a fart and vulnerable. She's wearing one of those strapless puffer-dresses - a bright yellow one - that I detest as they always seem to make a girls bum look twice as big as it really is. What's the bloody point of that?

I say "Hi" to her and she smiles and acknowledges me with the same greeting. I ask her if she would like another drink and she tells me: "Thanks, that would be great" and so I order myself another vodka and another large sweet white wine for her. We introduce ourselves with a small soft shake of hands - her name is Natasha - and I sit my perfect bum down next to her on a vacant barstool. We chat and talk about crap, just life and all that shit. Apparently she and her boyfriend had had a row earlier in the night as she wanted to go out clubbing and he didn't, not that I'm really interested in listening to any of her meaningless drivel. I have no idea what she's been drinking as her words come out of her sweet mouth in an incoherent muddle. Maybe she's taken some kind-of drug, I don't know, this is Brighton after all! She mumbles something about the fact that she comes from a Greek family - I guess that goes to explain her somewhat Mediterranean looks - and that her boyfriend doesn't get on with them. Her words waft over my head in a disinterested jumble as the vodka and the cocaine battle it out between themselves for supremacy in my bloodstream. I order us both another round of drinks from the yellow girl when yet again we both get hit-on by more guys, this time 3 of them, one of them coloured! Natasha tries to flirt with them but she's too pissed to really know what she's either doing or saying. I throw them a look of pure evil - as only I can do as you know my capabilities! - and my ice-cold stare pierces their bravado in no-time. They soon sense my horror at their stupid advances and they quickly melt-away back into the crowd, never to be seen again - knob-heads! I make more small-talk with my new friend Natasha and she laughs at my silly inane jokes. She asks me about my tattoos and I touch her left-hand and squeeze it affectionately but she doesn't back-off so I give her a harder one. I notice her pert young breasts peering over the top of her dress and my heart explodes into a million fragments. I catch a quick glimpse of her noticing my perfect full chest and it heaves faster at the thought of this girl wanting me, even though I know that she's probably straight. There must be a little bit of curiosity on her part I wish to myself, there must be?

I pour the third glass of wine down her throat and order round number-4 before we then leave.

***

I roll Natasha over onto her chest on my bed. Pulling down the zip to her dress I expose the lovely smooth skin of her back as well as her white strapless bra and the top of her knickers. She's only just about conscious as I help her up onto her bare feet with her dress falling to the floor in a crumple.

She has a nice figure, not as slim or toned or even as curvy as mine but then who is? I unclip her front-fastening bra to reveal her peaches before me. I touch and squeeze them and they're firm and beautiful and as I lick her nipples she moans like a lover, placing her hands on my naked shoulders to steady herself. Pulling down her knickers I have her completely naked although a small thatch of dark lady-garden springs out at me as I strip her - how I fucking hate pubes!

I stand and we kiss mouth to mouth. Her lips are soft and gorgeous to the touch and I tongue her. Looking into her eyes is like staring at a dead fish, there is no reaction or anything, she's just like a fucking zombie. I lay her back down on my bed and kiss her tits and bite them gently. She moans and giggles and she loves it. From the en-suite bathroom I return with a fresh razor, some soap, a glass of water and a fresh towel - a dark blue one. In under 10-minutes I have her depilated and her vagina is beautiful and smooth and I lick it, gliding my tongue over and around her labia and then penetrating her sweetness. She kicks out her legs as they spasm to my love as then I insert 2-fingers into her hole, she moaning: "AH AH AH" as I fuck her and she loves me as I quickly bring her to orgasm, making her scream and cum.

She lays there moaning at my pleasuring as I move up onto the bed myself, straddling her lovely Greek body with my long beautiful English legs. I position myself over her pretty face, semi-pinning the top of her arms down onto the bed with the lower-half of my legs. I start to rub my wet vagina over her face, over her nose, her chin, her mouth. She moans louder now at my action but doesn't pull away as instinctively she kisses my lips, making me pant with love. My breathing becomes more erratic as my alcohol/cocaine infused blood pressurises with excitement until I can take no more. My whole body shudders as I squirt my cum over her visage with some of the mess sliding down her throat from her open mouth. I fall off of her and kiss her beautiful wet lips, tasting my own honey. I squeeze her small breasts as I tongue her and she wraps her arms around me and kisses me and we are so in love.

We fall asleep together in each others arms with our female bodies entwined in their beautiful naked glory.

* * *

I'm woken by the sound of shouting. It's a female voice I don't recognise at first and it's close, right next to me in fact.

"WHAT THE FUCK? WHAT'S GOING ON? WHO THE FUCK ARE YOU? HOW DID I GET HERE?" Natasha screams at me as I lay naked next to her on the bed. It's 8.27am the following morning.

"Don't you remember anything from last night my love?" I question her as she clambers off the bed and onto her feet and starts putting her clothes back on.

"THIS CAN'T BE HAPPENING. YOU FUCKING BITCH. WHAT DID YOU DO TO ME? YOU FUCKING SHAVED ME. YOU'RE CRAZY!" She continues screaming.

"You really don't remember?" I quiz her back.

"YOU FUCKING DRUGGED ME?" She says, now fully-clothed but shoeless.

"No, I didn't drug you, you were pissed out of your head. We came back here to my place and we made love."

"WHAT? WHAT DO YOU FUCKING MEAN, YOU RAPED ME?"

"No, I didn't rape you, we had sex. You seemed to enjoy it as much as I did so I don't know what you're complaining about?"

"YOU'RE FUCKING CRAZY. I'LL GET THE POLICE ONTO YOU YOU FUCKING BITCH."

"No you won't. Everyone in the club saw you leave with me willingly last night so you don't have a leg to stand on." I tell her coldly.

"YOU FUCKING BITCH. I'LL FUCKING KILL YOU."

"But I thought you loved me?" I say to her sarcastically like the fucking bitch I am.

"YOU'RE FUCKING MAD. I'LL GET MY BOYFRIEND ONTO YOU, HE'LL SMASH YOUR FUCKING FACE IN YOU BITCH."

"There's no need for that Natasha. What happened between us last night was a beautiful one-off, nothing more."

"WHAT DID YOU FUCKING DO TO ME?" She cries, this time really crying, with proper tears, big ones.

"I told you, we came back here, we kissed, we had sex. We spent the night together in my bed and here we are. You have to accept it my love." I say to her quietly as I try to diffuse her tears.

"I DON'T BELIEVE YOU. YOU MUST HAVE DRUGGED ME. I'M NOT A FUCKING LESBIAN. YOU'RE A FUCKING NUTCASE."

"Well, the last bit is probably true but the rest isn't." I say jokingly.

"I'M GETTING OUT OF HERE." She bleats as she exits the bedroom and heads for the stairs.

"Natasha, there's no-need to feel guilty about what we did. It was just a bit of fun that's all." I say as I follow her downstairs still completely naked.

"FUCKING LEAVE ME ALONE YOU BITCH." She turns and screams at me.

"Natasha, come on. I'll make us a nice breakfast and we can sit down and talk about it."

"I DON'T WANNA TALK ABOUT IT, YOU'RE A FUCKING FREAK."

The double front-doors in the hallway halt her in her tracks - they're locked. I grab my spare set of keys from the old black German wooden sideboard and unlock them for her, not really wanting to stop her from leaving. If she wants to go then she can go, I don't have the right to stop her and keep her here, even though I could have killed her quite easily last night.

She's gone and away before I even have the chance to open the front-door fully, she pushing past me with a shove.

"OK, bye then! I don't suppose there's a chance of a goodbye kiss is there?" I quip as I also give her a little wave behind her back.

I watch her stride across the forecourt and disappear down the driveway as I stand in the doorway with the early morning Sun lighting-up my perfect naked body. Shutting the door behind me I follow her progress on the CCTV monitor as she makes her way to the big automatic entrance gates. Once there she momentarily stands there looking at them before physically grabbing hold of the metal bars and starts shaking them to open. It's no use of course, she's wasting her bloody time, she won't be able to escape like that, they're far too strong and secure to be able to be pulled apart with bare hands. She stops and scans her eyes around looking for a camera - clever girl - as she spots it easily, it being fixed up high on one of the many surrounding trees out of the way. I laugh as she gives me the finger and so I open the gates for her and then she is gone, back to Brighton and her stupid boyfriend, never to be seen or heard of ever again for the rest of my days in Hell. I wonder how she's going to get home? Not that I really give a fucking shit.

Anyway, we had fun, or at least I did! It's just a shame that she wasn't more receptive to her inner sexuality, we could have had a really good fuck.

I spend the rest of the day thinking about her, and poor old Hedwig and Hans also, and I hope that they can now rest in peace and that one day I will see them both again.

I make myself and Eva some breakfast - coffee and toast for me and prawns in jelly for her - and go to open my post from yesterday that I still haven't read. One of the letters is an ominous/official-looking one so I open that first. It's from the Surrey Police - who I also notice that they've spelt my surname wrong, can't these stupid pigs get anything fucking right? - informing me that I've been caught speeding - 63mph in a 50-zone, FUCK IT! - along the Mickleham Bypass. What a naughty girl I am! My mind flashes back to then as I recall that crappy brown Japanese piece of shit and its curious female driver and that it must have been an unmarked cop car as they were the only ones that had tailed me on that particular stretch of road - FUCKING PIG BITCH!

The letter - headed: *NOTICE OF INTENDED PROSECUTION* - goes on to say that as this is my first driving offence - yes, it really is, believe it or not! - I therefore have 3-options to take, these being:

    1 - £100 fixed penalty + 3 penalty points on my driving licence.

    2 - Attend a safety awareness course.

    3 - Request a court hearing.

What a fucking pain in the arse, I could really do without this shit on top of everything else in my life right now. I could quite easily just pay the fine and send my driving licence away but why should I when all I have to do is attend some stupid fucking awareness course? The course itself is being held at a hotel in Betchworth in Surrey at Hartsfield Manor, although I can pick my own time and day to attend. I decide to leave it for a couple of months before I go, booking my place and paying the stupid £92 fee online to the Surrey Safety Camera Partnership - whoever the fuck they are?

What a load of old bollocks!

***

What terrible things my beautiful eyes have seen.

What terrible things my beautiful female hands have done.

I've killed 5-people.

I ate one of them.

What the fuck is happening to me?

What is it that I have become?

14

Breakdown

It's Friday 30 September 2016. I'm sitting on the lounge sofa crying my eyes out. I've been like this for 2-days now. I haven't bothered to dress properly - I'm wearing a black silk robe from LilySilk and nothing else, black I guess because that's the fucking mood I'm in. I ask myself how much longer can I hide behind this mask of sanity?

I haven't even bothered with any make-up or done my hair either and both are a fucking mess, I can see no point. I haven't even been on the booze to try and fix my mood as I fear it may tip me over the edge and that will be it - the end of me. I did think about going to see my doctor, to see if he could straighten me out but what is he going to do, put me on drugs to see me through? That won't cure my problem, the problem of being me. Seeing a shrink won't help either, I would destroy them easily.

Unfortunately I can't erase all the memories of the past out of my head, I can't, they are locked in there forever, taunting me 24-hours every bastard day and every fucking night. I will always be eternally damaged by "Him" - the "Old Man." There is misery hiding in every corner of my soul.

Eva wails and moans around me like she's demented. I try to comfort her as she does so but we both just go around in circles and get nowhere. Everything has got out of control and it's all too much for me this time and I can see no future, what is the fucking point of carrying on? The strain and stress of not only writing that fucking book, but all the crap that goes with it - the stupid publishers, the red-tape, the bullshit, the lies, being conned - has built-up and led me to this point. I am emotionally constipated. I am physically drained. The added pressure of having all this money sitting in the bank, the house, the courts chasing me all the fucking time, the stupid Police on my back, idiots everywhere, has lead to now.

I'm struggling to take all the pressure and I think I'm about to crack. It's all too much. I've had enough. How can I carry-on under these circumstances? My inner-strength is fading by the day. How can I hold out?

Each and every day that passes I grow more and more dejected and full of despair, my mental balance is constantly on a knife-edge. Why do I have to keep being hurt by life? I have no-one to turn to, no-one to confide my inner turmoil, no-one to love. I begin to sob loudly into my hands as Eva paws at my arm - my little love. What can I do to stop my pain? I don't want to hurt her, I really don't.

I so wish I didn't have to go through this pain every day, the pain of being alive. What is it all for? Can anyone save me from myself? My heart bangs like a drum and I wish I was dead.

The big question is of course what is it that has caused me to relapse into this despair yet again? I have more money that I could ever have dreamed of, I should be ecstatic but I'm not, I am torn and broken like a discarded doll. Death means nothing to me, not even the final outcome of myself. I just know that it's that fucking book that had tipped me over the edge and I don't want it to fail - I don't want to fail. I have this terrible fear that if the book bombs then so will I. Why am I even bothering with it in the first bloody place? It's been the hardest thing that I've ever done in my life and an absolute fucking nightmare from start to finish. I've fractured my mind writing this shit and I hate it, it chewing and gnawing at my bones.

I find myself in a fucking minefield of endless computerised bullshit, tying me up in knots at every fucking stage. Why? Why are they doing this to me? Why am I doing this to myself, why do I bother? What is the cunting point of it all?

I try to disassociate myself from all the problems but it's no good, they're all still there, all the fucking time. I have more patience than most people, but that patience is now at an end.

My publishers ask me to answer their questions in my "Dropbox" but I don't have a fucking "Dropbox". What are they fucking on about? What does it all mean? They send me questions on my book schedule page and tell me to press the "Dashboard" key to access them but there is no "Dashboard" key. They ask me to "Unread" my messages but what the fuck does that mean? Do they want me to go back in time somehow? The whole thing is stupid. What am I going to do?

I have no-one to help me.

I am out of my depth.

I am out of my mind.

I talk to Mum on the phone even though I know that she's not there - she's dead of course, I know that. She nags me from death, from beyond the grave, bending my ear about shit. I shout back at her down the line, telling her to: "GET OFF MY FUCKING BACK" and "LEAVE ME THE FUCK ALONE" and "I NEED YOU HERE WITH ME MUM PLEASE" but there is no reply.

All my life I've been the outcast - because of my natural beauty, my political beliefs, my thinking, my loneliness. Hopefully, when my life has ended and I've gone to Hell, I will receive some kind-of answer to all the shit I've had to endure over the years. And so, I am in the hands of fate and what will be will be.

I am still young, but getting older every day.

* * *

It's no good, I can't take it any more. I hit the bottle and down a huge slug of vodka. The awful Russian shit stabs me in the lungs and I struggle for breath and choke and gasp for air.

The house is so quiet it's like a fucking morgue in here, the silence driving me even more insane. I drown myself in gin - Silent Pool - the super-strong flavour of juniper stinging my

taste-buds and adding to the nullification of my damaged brain
- brain damage. I lose control and sink down onto the floor in
a heap of female. I am shit and cunt and cock and fuck and I
am in Hell. I am as pissed as in drunk and pissed as in off. It's
unbearable and I WANT EVERYTHING. I crave for a million
things, but if I had them all I would still be bored in a matter of
minutes. If I plunge further into mania I will be no more. I hang
by anxiety. This is the narrow gap between sanity and madness.

I stagger into the kitchen, my eyes semi-blinded by their
swollen state and the overflowing of tears. I weep and sniffle
as I take my beautiful Japanese knife out of its wooden holder
and place the ultra-sharp edge of the blade at my throat. I pant
in horror at what I'm about to do, my heartbeat racing like fuck
and it's all too late - I don't want to carry on any more, it's a
catastrophe.

Eva suddenly appears at my feet and looks at me with her
big blue eyes and begs me to stop with a string of little cat yelps.
She has destroyed me, halting me in my evil tracks, saving me
from my own destruction. I throw the blade into the sink with a
deep metallic clanking that reverberates around inside my head
and I struggle to contain the turmoil within me, not knowing
whether to pick her up and hold her in my arms and kiss and
thank her for saving my life or grab the knife back and slice her
fucking head off for stopping me. I go for the former of course,

I could never hurt her as she could never hurt me. I'm not a
total fucking bitch - only sometimes.

***

I'm glad that fucking bitch Mellis is dead. I'm glad that I'm the
one that killed her, it was no more than she deserved. She is the
cause of all my problems even though she isn't. She is the one
that got me the sack from that shitty company. She is the one I
fucked. She is the one that ended up in a pie. I have no regrets.

***

I'm awakened from my floor-mounted coma by the entrance-gate buzzer sounding. I drag my fucked body to the monitor and spy the image before me on the screen - it's the fucking Police yet again! I stand and watch them like a cat does with a mouse, playing with its prey for fun. I don't bother to answer the intercom, I really couldn't be fucked today. They give my arse a headache.

****

I think it's Saturday afternoon although I'm not sure, it could be Sunday. Not that it really matters either way.

I phoned the escort agency earlier to see if they had anyone available for today - a guy - to come to my place today. They did and he's here right now, in the wet-room having a shower. His name is Chris. He's about 25 or so and OK-looking with a reasonably fit body. I did actually want a girl to fuck but the only one they had available at such short notice was an Asian girl called Priti so I had to turn her down, I'm not sticking my tongue into Paki-pussy - that would be disgusting!

My liaison with Chris though has already turned into a disaster. I can't bear to look at him as he has one of those awful fucking beards, one of those ones exactly like Abraham Lincoln, the old American president! It is truly terrible, and on such a young guy as well, what the fuck is all that about?

I've had to get myself pissed to have sex with him but that too has turned into a joke. I let him fuck me on my bed but I don't fuck him back - I don't want to and I can't - I just lay there in different positions as he fucks my vagina, my bum, my mouth, but I'm not really here, I'm like a fucking zombie.

I'm beginning to feel very old, like I'm in my 70's rather than my true age of only 36.

He fucks my tits and cums over my face, the mess splatting into my eyes, up my nose, in my hair and dribbling into my awaiting open mouth and I tongue and swallow his milk. There isn't anything that he can do to me that hasn't been done before as I let him discharge within me but it means nothing - I am not alive.

I fake my orgasm and don't cum.

***

I don't fucking believe this. Those fucking coppers are at my front gates yet again. How many bloody times is that now, haven't they got anything else to fucking do? There are plenty of scum around they could be catching but no, they have to fucking hassle me all the fucking time!

Once again I ignore the bastards, they can press my buzzer as many fucking times as they want, I'm not letting them into my house and conversing with them, they can all fuck-off.

***

I wake-up suddenly in the middle of the night and check the time on my bedside clock - it's 1.42am. I was awakened by something moving next to me on the bed that I presumed was Eva as she usually sleeps on top of the duvet alongside me, always to my left.

I reach across the bed and flick the bedside light on and look back to see what the Hell is going on and I gasp in horror and then scream as I'm surrounded by an assortment of severed heads, all laying there staring at me with big cheesy grins.

They are the heads of people and cats throughout my life, each one tormenting me - Mum, the "Old Man", my estranged sister Kate, baby Abigail, Lacey, my Guardian Angel, Andy, Heidi, Amanda, The Great One, Steve, Death, Tattoo John, Rachael, Suzie, Satan, the spirit woman, CJ, Mellis, Cagney, Emma & Jaime, the bitch that smashed my car, little Jennifer, the ex-boyfriend that cannot be named, Alan & Charlie, Bowie, Hans & Hedwig, John Fitzherbert, Mrs. DeAngelis and others. And there, on my belly, lays the head of my unborn child, laughing at me, mocking me, taking the piss, calling out to me: "MUMMY MUMMY MUMMY MUMMY MUMMY MUMMY MUMMY MUMMY MUMMY MUMMY MUMMY MUMMY MUMMY" in its hideous baby voice as it weeps tears of blood.

*****

BORED BORED BORED BORED BORED. As you can probably guess, I'm bored! I'm so fucking bored that not even alcohol can lift my spirits, although obviously I'm still giving it a bloody good try!

As I inebriate myself I flick through the latest copy of *Friday-Ads* to try and distract myself but nothing jumps out at me from the pages and pages of adverts. I scan the personal section for anyone interesting but that too goes over my head, that is except for one particular advert that suddenly springs into view from a couple in their 20's that are looking for a threesome. They're from Midhurst, not a million-miles from me here in Foxhill, called Jay and Tabitha, so I decide to send them a text message, I've got nothing to lose - only everything!

I tell them of my desires and my close proximity to them and await their reply. Within 2-shakes of a lambs tail I receive a message back, they telling me they haven't done anything like this before - so they say? - and could we meet-up for a drink later this same day? I answer back as a "Yes", despite my intoxicated blood. What the fuck, it's never stopped me before so why should it stop me now? I shower my beautiful body and change clothes. I decide to wear the minimal amount I can legally get away with as I just couldn't give a flying-fuck today, no-matter whatever happens. I slip on my gorgeous white mini-bodycon dress dress from Christian Lacroix, ignoring any underwear in the process. On my feet I wear my classic plastic wedge-heels from Polyvore. My hair and make-up I do killer - ultra-sharp with coal-black eyeshadow, plenty of blusher and super-pale lipstick. My perfume is *Poison* by Christian Dior. My clutch-bag is my beautiful white leather one from Prada.

Car-wise, I decide to take the RS out for my jaunt today as the Lamborghini is too big and pretentious for this deal? Midhurst is situated about 8-miles to the East of me and at the speed I drive it doesn't take me too long to get there. We've agreed to meet up in the Saint George pub, a name that rings a bell with me but I can't remember how come? It's not until I actually clap eyes on the pub that the memories all come flooding back back - that it's the very same fucking pub that I met-up with that bastard Alan a few years back, the guy who lead me willingly back to his grotty flat where he and his dodgy mate Charlie fucked me and beat me until I was black and blue. I wanted them both of course, there is no denying it, although I got more than I deserved or wanted that's for sure - CUNTS.

Just as before I park around the corner to the pub, it having no dedicated car-park itself. A sense of foreboding surrounds me as I enter the building, just what have I let myself in for yet again? Why do I put myself through this shit? I'm spied upon by all and sundry as I make my way up to the bar and order myself a pint of lager from the guy behind the counter, a big fat tosser in his 50's who has obviously let himself go judging by his enormous beer-belly. Not exactly a great advert is it?

I spy a young couple to my right, waving at me frantically as they try to attract my attention so I'm guessing this must be them. I saunter over and introduce myself and they both acknowledge themselves as my lovers. They're both in their mid-20's, Tabitha being very pretty with long brown hair, sweet features and wearing a very stylish blue sleeveless blouse that suits her perfectly. Jay is a different matter altogether, in fact he's just plain fucking ugly and I don't like him at all let alone fancy him. We sit and chat and drink and talk about love and fucking and shit for the next hour or so, just wasting our time.

The 3 of us agree to sex and leave, walking the 7-minute walk back to their flat - it located precisely opposite the block that those fuckers Alan and Charlie lived in from my first diary - crazy! Inside it's not actually that bad, the décor and furnishings being contemporary and clean and I soon relax to the point of being careless - so what's fucking new? Who fucking cares? I plonk myself down on their beige leather sofa and spread my legs for them, exposing my vagina for him and her. Jay drops to his knees and starts to lick my pussy and I sigh and moan as his tongue penetrates my hole. Tabitha just stands there watching us, not knowing what to do, this being their first threesome. I call to her to: "Come here and touch my tits" as she then sits herself down next to me on my right. I touch and squeeze her small, firm breasts with my left-hand and she laughs as she begins fondling mine in the same manner. I order Jay to strip and we both watch him and giggle as he does so, his dick standing proud before us as he stands there naked as the day he was born. Tabitha leans forward and sucks him as I play with his love-spuds as she gives him head as I strip naked single-handedly. They both stop and stare in amazement at my perfect body, my tattoos, my breasts, my long legs, my smooth wet vagina, my metal and my mettle.

I undress Tabitha as she sits next to me but she's very nervous, I can tell, her not having fucked another female before. I kiss her mouth and taste both her scent and Jays cock on her lips and I love her and want to make her mine forever. The 3 of us stand to strip Tabitha naked as ugly Jay wipes his cock over my bum and I kiss her again, forcing my tongue into her mouth. I sit her down on the sofa and prise her legs apart, exposing her beautiful shaved oyster. She's tentative to accept me at first but soon she opens up fully, especially when I stick my tongue into her wet vagina, making her flinch and moan with love as I lick her beautiful lips and the honey between.

I then feel Jay's cock touch my pussy as I lap her and then him pushing into me, causing me to pant as I eat and drink her love. He bangs me for the next 4 or 5-minutes until he reaches his peak, shouting at me;

"I'M GONNA CUM, OH, OH."

"Cum in me, cum in me." I slurp back at him as I continue to eat her gorgeous cunt.

"Your tongue feels so fucking good. Oh God! Oh lick me! OH FUCKING HELL!" Pleads Tabitha to me.

Jay's evilness explodes inside my body as I cum and bury my face into Tabitha's vagina, causing her to scream;

"AH AH AH AH AH AH AH OH FUCKING HELL OH OH OH OH OH."

We swap positions with me taking Tabitha's place and she mine. I spread my legs for her but she's hesitant to touch me, she not having tasted the delights of another woman's vagina on her lips. Jay eggs her on, using his fingers on me to open the gate to pleasure. Within an inch of my flange she smiles and gazes into my eyes and then she's all mine. I sigh deeply at the sensation as the light touch of her tongue hits me and I shake like a fucker. She goes in further and gives me one long lick after another and I love her lots.

Jay climbs onto the sofa to my left and I suck his rigid cock, taking it right to the back of my throat and I WANT MORE, ordering him to:

"Fuck my mouth and cum down my throat."

He tells me to:

"Suck my cock like a cunt" and I glug like mental as he fills my head with his member as the effect of Tabitha's oral pleasuring doubles my love. He cums in my mouth and I cum in hers as we all go to Heaven and I fuck and die.

I beg Jay to:

"Fuck my arse" but he refuses, he doesn't do anal and neither does Tabitha - what is their fucking problem? He fucks her on the sofa as she sits there and I slide myself under them both, playing with Jays ball-sack as he starts to fuck. I pull on them and tug them and kiss and lick them, making him yelp with pleasure and pain. I tongue at Tabitha's pussy as Jays cock penetrates it, tasting the intertwined juices of their love. I pull his meat from her slot and suck him and then lick her open hole and tongue her as I wank him with her mucus. I push him back into her with a squelch and she loves it and I shit.

Climbing back onto the sofa beside her I kiss her small but pert breasts, flicking my tongue over and around her nipples, sucking them into my mouth. Grabbing her right-hand I place her fingers to my labia and let them go to work, 2 of them inserting themselves and fucking my tube. I kiss her mouth and then his and then in an awkward 3-way. Withdrawing from her, Jay spunks over her tits, 2 long streams followed by a couple of dribbles. I go down on her, licking up his nasty muck and swallowing some. Tabitha kisses my mouth and licks off some cum for herself as I rub the remaining man-glue over her breasts and face as we love.

Jay disappears to shower, leaving us girls alone to fuck. She licks my vagina and I hers in a 69 on the sofa. I cum at her and she screams and laughs as I soak her face with my love as she continues to finger-fuck and lick my cunt. She orgasms for me and I catch her juice in my hand as she spits and I swallow it.

We laugh and kiss as we shower together, Jay being out by now and making coffee in the kitchen for all of us. We join him, both of us still naked, as we stand around chatting about life and fucking. He touches one of my beautiful full breasts and I say to him coyly to:

"Fuck my tits."

Tabitha then starts screaming at the both of us at our action, slamming her coffee down on the work-surface, almost breaking her mug in the process:

"NO, NO, NO, THIS HAS GONE FAR ENOUGH."

And it has. It's the end of our session of fun and frolics and time for me to make my escape as I've obviously outstayed my welcome. I decide to leave them to their own argument, I don't have the fucking time, patience or energy to get involved in this sort of shit, not for anyone.

I make my excuses, get dressed and then piss-off, I've had my fun. I don't know whether they have also or not and I don't fucking care anyway. It's a bit of a shame Jay wasn't a bit better looking although Tabitha was sweet enough, especially introducing her to the pleasures of lesbian fuck.

I'm back in my car soon enough, firing her up and heading home to Foxhill. I give it plenty of beans where conditions allow and again where they don't, scaring several fellow drivers in the process - plebs!

Once safely back in my cocoon I smash myself to pieces on vodka and gin and wine and I cry. What have I done? Why do I keep abusing my beautiful, gorgeous, perfect body? Not just with my drinking, but with this fake love that I do with complete strangers? What does it all fucking mean - what?

I go to bed and prepare myself not to sleep, but to die.

15

Launch Day

The launch of my book is only 2-days away and I am so excited, even a little nervous, which is very unlike me. I've enlisted the help of an independent company to organise and promote my work so at least that's a great pressure off my mind, allowing me to kick-back a bit. I didn't honestly think I had the commitment or even the tenacity to pull the book off. I guess it just goes to show what one can do when you put your mind to it?

It's 11am Thursday 7 October 2016 and I'm in my back garden with Ben, a male whore from Chichester that I've hired for the next 2-hours at the cost of £300. He's quite nice-looking, tall, well-groomed, smooth and with a nice toned body, several tattoos and a reasonably nice cock that is slightly above average in size and proportion. I'm laying on my back on top of one of my sculptures - the giant fibreglass penis-shaped one - as Ben stands behind me with his hard dick poised for attack. I grab it with my right-hand and lick the underside of his beautiful purple knob, running my pointed tongue around its meat. I order him to: "Move closer" and I swallow his cock, taking it down to the back of my throat and I choke on it. He fucks my mouth and I gag and splutter as I continue to suck him like mad, the smoothness of his helmet feeling glorious against my tongue and my teeth and I WANT to die right now with his cock down my throat.

I remove his fuck from my mouth and tell him to: "69 me and lick my cunt really hard" and he obeys like the slave he is. His tongue and fingers inside my pussy immediately fire me into Heaven like a rocket and I suck his cock like it's the last cock I'll ever suck ever.

We reposition ourselves and I have him on all fours on the grass by the mini-lake. I squat-down behind him and finger my twat with 2-fingers on my left-hand as I use my right to prize open his bumhole and tongue his ring. I spit on his arse and wheedle my saliva into his chocolate-starfish as I lick it deeper into his hole, tasting the foul tang of his scat. I un-wank myself and grab his cock from behind and start to toss him off, using my vaginal mucus as lubrication. He moans deeply but I shout at him: "SHUT YOUR FUCKING MOUTH YOU CUNT" as I pull on his todger with increasing force. I sense his arse-cheeks start to tighten so I drop down and spin my body around to face his Japs-eye, just in time for him to cum and splatter his evil muck over my face and in my mouth, slurping its slimy texture down my gullet as I ingest, draining his cock of seed.

On my back I open my legs as wide as possible and order Ben to: "Lick my cunt like a bastard" as I squeeze and slap my tits with both hands, making them red and sting. His tongue inside my vagina makes my mind collapse on the inside as I lose myself in ecstasy and I wince and whine and pant and moan as then I explode, ejaculating my cum onto his tongue and mouth with a gush.

We French-kiss and swill my honey between us around our tongues and mouths and it tastes so beautiful and I love him. He fucks my vagina and I moan with pleasure as his naked cock slides in and out of my body, the sensation is fantastic and there is nothing like a good old-fashioned fuck to make my day. Alternatively he penetrates my pussy and my anal passage, spending about 1 to 2-minutes pumping-away at each orifice until he cries that he's about to cum once more. He withdraws from my minge and shoots his nasty ejaculate out over my gorgeous tits and my belly - a few droplets also landing in my hair. I lean forward and let him wipe his dirty cock over my peaches, smearing his seed over their beautiful shape.

We shower together in the ground-floor bathroom, running our hands all over each others smooth and tight bodies. I dry him and redress him and then pay him his money, then telling him to: "AND NOW GET THE FUCK OUT OF MY HOUSE" and off he goes with his tail between his legs like the fucking whore he is.

Why have I been cast into this sin, this sin of defilement?

What have I done?

I spend the rest of the day just swanning-around doing shit - playing pool, swimming, fucking myself whilst watching porn on my laptop (this time lesbian orgy fucking featuring fisting, scat and dildos), sodding around, some light cooking, drinking, TV, and then off to bed at 11.05pm.

***

It's Friday and the day before the launch. I've just taken Eva next door to dear old Mrs. DeAngelis who has agreed to look after her at her place until I return on Sunday morning - bless her!

Today I'm wearing a yellow mini wrap-dress from De La Vali that looks super-sexy on me, as does everything. My underwear is in white lace from Hanky Panky. My shoes are a pair of yellow suede heals from Gucci. My hair and make-up is pure-killer (as am I) featuring dark-grey eyeshadow, sharp cheekbones and orange lipstick with 2-silver chopsticks mounted in a cross in my high-mounted ponytail - pure silver that is, not plated shit! My clutch-bag today is my white leather one again from Prada. My perfume is *Opium* by Yves Saint Laurent.

The reason I'm all dressed to kill is that I'm staying up in London for the next couple of nights at a top hotel, so therefore I absolutely want to look my best - impressions count for everything. I've booked an executive taxi for the trip to London - it should take less than an hour to get there by my estimate - and the driver is here loading my cases into the boot of his gorgeous red Jaguar XE HSE as I narrate my story to you - my special friend.

With the house all locked and alarmed, Richard - the driver - opens the rear nearside door of the Jag for me and in I slide, bum first, then my long beautiful legs, like the Queen of Death I am. He's somewhere around 60 I would say with heavily receding grey hair, beady eyes, a small beer-belly and a bit of a sarcastic bent about his manner that I counter easily and effectively with my acid tongue.

We cruise North along the A29, A24, M25 and then the A3 into London. Usually whenever I've been up-town I've always taken the tube and therefore don't see anything of it until I emerge from the station out into the light. Going by car one sees a completely different perspective of our capital city - the dirt, the foreigners, the cramped conditions, the pollution, the shit, all the famous buildings, the River Thames, the congestion, the stink. It really is a melting-pot of everything that is good and bad of my dear old country.

We make our way through Battersea and its former power-station with its 4-enormous defunct chimneys, over Chelsea Bridge, up along Chelsea Bridge Road to Sloane Square and across to Sloane Street. Once at Knightsbridge we turn right onto the Brompton Road and then left at Hyde Park Corner and into Park Lane, then finally right once more past Grosvenor Square with my hotel to our right - this now being the very heart of Mayfair.

I'm staying at Claridge's, arguably the best hotel in London - if not the whole of England - a beautiful 5-star establishment that's been in operation since the early-1800's. There's nothing fancy about the exterior of the building though, it looking just the same as many others of its type and buildings of the era, although the quality and the service is where the difference lies.

We park straight outside the entrance, taking the space just vacated by a giant chauffeur-driven Rolls-Royce, one of those bloody awful great big ones that are the size of a tank - I hate them! Richard opens the door for me and I slide out of the car pretending to be Lady Muck, greeted by one of the Hotel's concierge dressed in his top-hat and finery. He greets me like Royalty as Richard goes to the rear of the Jag to retrieve my luggage from the boot, a task immediately taken-over by another one of the Hotel's flunkies. After saying "Goodbye" and "Thank You" to Richard - I prepaid for his services online - I'm ushered into the Hotel and off he pisses.

I check-in at reception and then I'm guided up to my room by the Hotel porter. The Hotel itself is very grand inside - as I've already said - the quality being absolutely top-notch as one would expect. There are nearly 200-rooms available, all en-suite of course, a 1st-class restaurant as well as 2-bars.

Obviously none of this comes cheap, my 2-nights in the Superior Queen Room setting me back a stupefying £2,300 per night - BLOODY HELL! - payment for which I had obviously done in advance several weeks ago. My room is as beautiful as you would expect, all done in opulent Art Deco style.

I tip the porter as he then leaves me to my own devices. This is actually the very first time I've ever stayed here overnight in London, as you know I've been up to town a thousand times in my younger days but this is a new experience for me. After a couple of large swigs from the bottle of Vladivar that I brought with me, I decide to chill-out a little before doing anything else, maybe a wander down the road to be nosey and see what I can find?

I need a change of clothes first though so I strip-off and touch my body all over as I lay on the gorgeous bed. Spreading my legs apart as wide as possible I touch the wetness of my vagina and flinch at the beautiful pleasurable sensation as I fuck myself with 2-fingers in and out of my slot. I squeeze and play with my breasts as I masturbate and then reach my final goal as I shake and shudder and yelp and cum and I love myself.

I shower quickly in the en-suite bathroom, dry myself and then redress for my stroll down the road. I put on my red sleeveless cotton blouse from Hugo Boss - open low of course! - a pair of grey stone-wash skinny jeans from GAP and my old pair of black suede ankle-boots from Miu Miu. My underwear is in white from M&S. My hair and make-up I just retouch as I didn't get it very wet whilst in the shower, although obviously I add a few squirts of perfume for good measure - *Kenzo Flower* by Kenzo. The cash I take with me I stash into my jeans pocket, that way I don't have to carry a clutch-bag or purse or anything like that.

I step out of the Hotel into the mid-day Sun and strut my stuff in my usual confident style along Davies Street to the hustle and bustle of Oxford Street at my usual sure and confident pace, my body being scanned all the way by my fellow humans, each one of them wanting a slice of me but not succeeding. I window-shop as I go, not actually venturing into many shops at all as I don't really desire or need anything. I decide to get something to eat and so head into a posh sandwich-bar and grab myself some lunch, a chicken wrap with peppers, chillies, lettuce, dill, and all smothered in sour-cream - it's gorgeous! - that I wash down with a bottle of Coke - non-diet. I sit my arse down outside the bar by myself and watch the World go by - cars, vans, lorries, buses, taxis, people of all ages and denominations, snobs, scum, wankers, filth - you name it, it's all here!

The best part of an hour goes by as I sit there observing whatever passes me by and I can't help wondering what the fuck is it all for - the human race? Why are we here? What the fuck are we all doing? What is the fucking point of it all? I have to chuckle to myself as I sit there looking gorgeous watching these people. I know I've said this before a million times - the women looking at me with jealous daggers in their eyes and the men with lust. I just find it strange that one sex can hate me so much whilst the other instantly all fall in love with me - it's a funny old World isn't it?

My deep thoughts are soon brought to an abrupt end by a couple of suited arseholes on a nearby table as one of them - a young guy in his early-20's with a typical smart-arse attitude - tries in vain to egg his counterpart into saying something to me, whatever that may be? In the end I give neither of them a chance as I get to my feet and leave, slamming my empty glass Coke bottle down hard on their table as I walk past them, feeling all 4 of their eyeballs checking-out my perfect tight body as I head off further up the road - TWATS! If they both wanted to fuck me then why didn't they just say so?

I find myself venturing into a couple of high-class clothes shops but once again nothing catches my eye, apart from a few of the shop assistants - several horny hardbodies with faces and figures to die for, although none of them as perfect as mine of course. I then decide to head back to the Hotel - it now being mid-afternoon - as I'm bored, tired and soon in need of a pee anyway.

Back in my Hotel room I have a couple of mouthfuls of vodka straight from the bottle as I gaze out of the window at the people of London all going about their individual business. It's quite sad really when I look at them, at their blank faces.

I go to retrieve one of my dildo's that I brought with me from my suitcase - the 8-inch realistic one from Lovehoney. I strip naked, have another large swig of vodka, and touch myself all over my beautiful body with the fake cock, running its veiny length over my smooth perfect skin. I drop down onto all fours and run the dildo between my legs and up between my bum-cheeks and then over my labia, its wetness easing the direction of its path. I push it harder and harder against myself without actually penetrating as I then turn it back on myself, easing it into my love-hole and fucking it slowly but surely, making me buck and pant as my breathing becomes disjointed and wild. I love my cock as it loves me and before long I succumb to its pleasure and orgasm and cum.

I continue to wank beyond finishing until I can't take any more - it's just too fucking much - and I remove my phallus with a squelch and lick its gooey knob and shaft. It feels so sexy over my tongue and mouth and I laugh and giggle like a big soppy tart.

After cleaning myself up in the bathroom and having another quick vodka, I give Monica - the woman from the publishing company - a quick ring just to check to see if everything is still OK for tomorrows launch at the bookshop - it is. I also call Mrs. DeAngelis to see if Eva is alright and that she hasn't absconded back to my house, which thankfully she hasn't! I speak to Eva on the phone, telling her how much I love her and miss her and that I will be back home soon to continue our adventures together once more. She tells me she misses me also and can't wait for my return on Sunday - Meow Meow Meow, Purr Purr Purr!

I spend the following few hours sitting on the bed drinking and watching shit on the TV. The older I get the crappier the quality of the programs seem to be, 95% of which are just pure garbage - they're fucking terrible! The evening meals are served in the Hotel beautiful 1930's-inspired Fumoir restaurant and so I get myself ready to go down and have a good old feast. For tonight I'm wearing a gorgeous sleeveless and super-tight bodycon dress from Lipsy in white lace that is just to die for, it hugs my perfect figure perfectly and I look like a dream come true for any man or woman to have me. On my feet I'm wearing a pair of white suede platform court shoes from Jimmy Choo whilst my underwear is in sexy white from Agent Provocateur and my clutch-bag is my white leather one from Hermes. For my make-up I've gone for coal-black eyeshadow, plenty of blusher to accentuate my gorgeous cheekbones and matt-yellow lipstick. My hair I've let down for some bizarre reason - the very first time in public for years in fact although I don't know why? I guess I subconsciously felt like doing something different for a change - weird! My perfume tonight is *Poison* by Christian Dior.

The restaurant is located on the ground-floor of the Hotel, it's super-posh and as per usual I get all the usual bloody stares from my fellow humans as I make my entrance. I'm guided to my table and seated by the efficient restaurant staff - class! - with my surrounding diners staring at me like I'm from bloody Mars or something as they desperately try to take-in the vision before them - my perfect body, my beautiful face, my long legs, the fullness of my breasts, my gorgeous dress - and even so, despite all my many attributes, I think that it's the sight of my fully tattooed arms and hands that has tipped them all over the edge, as well as the crazy piercings in my ears, they simply cannot comprehend what they are let-alone why I have them in the first bloody place - stuck-up tossers! There is one old girl - she must be 90 by the looks of it but is dressed like a 20-year old! - who just can't take her eyes off of me. I decide to have a little bit of fun with her just for a laugh and so I shout across the tables to her:

"Good evening."

It doesn't do any good or make any difference though as the staring just continues as before, if not worse - stupid old bitch!

For dinner I order myself veal Schnitzel with duck egg, globe artichoke and spinach purée - and it is all absolutely beautiful. I don't think that I've ever had anything that tastes so glorious before, it is all perfectly gorgeous in every way - the service, the presentation, the taste, the texture, the smell - everything! For pudding I treat myself to a blackberry compote followed by a coffee, all once again the best that I've ever had.

Back in my room I have a quick pee before I fix myself a nightcap - another mouthful of vodka. Bloody Hell that meal was beautiful and I just cannot wait until the same time tomorrow evening for round-2 - bring it on!

I position myself upside-down leaning with my back up against the bottom end of the bed with my legs wide apart and resting on top of the duvet. I insert my special friend into my vagina and wince and moan as it parts my internal plumbing with pleasure and love. I fuck myself rhythmically as the rubber cock massages my inner muscles and pushes me on to its brain-overloading finale and I scream and cum.

I lay in bed thinking about Eva and tomorrow. I really hope everything goes OK but I also have a strange sense of foreboding that continuously screws with my mind.

I really wish Eva was here.

***

I'm up and out of my bed at 6.30am - I didn't realise that that time of the morning still existed! - and jump in the shower. After drying my beautiful body I dress for the big day - it's Saturday. Today I'm wearing my beautiful white bodycon mini-dress from Christian Lacroix that is pure gorgeous and enhances my perfect body and legs to the full. On my feet I'm wearing my old pair of white suede open-toe ankle-boots from Polyvore. My underwear is also in white, a little lace number from Figleaves. My hair I put back up in a ponytail, back in its normal position, and tie it with a white silk bow. As for my make-up I go down the tried and trusted classic route - black eyes, sharp cheekbones and cherry lipstick. My perfume today is *Luxe* by Avon. My clutch-bag is a gorgeous white leather one from Launer - makers to the Queen don't you know!

I have breakfast in the Hotels superb restaurant, ordering myself a full-English with scrambled Burford brown eggs, sweet cured bacon, middle-white sausage, grilled tomato's and field mushrooms and a cup of English breakfast tea. As one would expect, the food is once again perfect in every way and slides down without even touching the sides - it is Heaven.

Back in my suite I stand and stare out my window at the road down below as I wait for my taxi to arrive that the guy on the front-desk has ordered for me. I down a single mouthful of vodka straight from the bottle to stiffen myself up for the day ahead, even though it's not even 9am yet. I don't have to be at the bookshop until sometime around 9.30 at the earliest.

The phone in my room suddenly rings and makes me jump out of my bloody skin, it's the front-desk guy informing me that my cab is waiting for me outside. I have a little smile form on my beautiful face for somehow finding myself in this position - all my money, the house, the cars, my looks, my independence, my luck, my power. I've been treated like a princess and it's really no-more than I fucking deserve anyway.

In the cab we make our way to Charing Cross Road in the thick of the Saturday morning traffic, the distance of only 1½-miles or so taking us some 20-minutes to complete. My cab driver - an average guy of about 55 with a bald head and carrying far too much weight - stops directly outside the bookshop for me, a lovely-looking modern building in white called Bookworms. I try to exit the cab as gracefully as I can and then pay the cabbie in cash and off he goes out of my life.

There's a few people waiting inside the shop already as I scan around looking for Monica. We spot each other pretty-much at the same time and I make my way over to her, she standing there chatting to Claire, the owner of the bookshop, a short chubby woman in her mid-50's with grey hair and glasses - a typical bookworm-type. Monica introduces us to each other with handshakes all round followed by some general chit-chat and stuff before Claire escorts us to the rear of the shop where the signing is to take place. A small crowd of women are gathered there waiting in line behind a dividing barrier - all aged somewhere between their early-20's and early-40's I would guess - with some of them being very attractive, instantly putting my wicked mind into a spin. It goes without saying that I receive plenty of looks from everyone, all burning their eyes into me like lasers, not that I care, I love it all and I WANT EVERYTHING.

By now it's 10am and Monica and Claire give a small joint speech about my book and then it's all systems go with the signing. The first girl comes up to me and we start, signing my life away in some 15 or 20 books one straight after another. Out the corner of my eye I notice someone in the queue watching me intently and I have to do a triple-take as I cannot at first believe who it is standing there - it is the beautiful vision that is Amanda, my love, my wife (or ex-wife I should say!). She smiles at me a big beaming Australian smile and gives me a little wave as I smile back to her - I really can't believe that she's here, what does she want? I also notice that she's standing there hand-in-hand with another girl - of average height and build with dark hair tied-up as is mine, a pretty face and dressed smart/casual in a white shirt, grey jeans and tan suede ankle-boots. Finally it comes to Amanda's turn at the front of the queue and she heads straight towards me with a copy of my book in hand.

"Well, this is a bit of a surprise." I exclaim to her.

"Yes, I know! So you finally got the book published then?" She comes back in that lovely voice of hers, the one that melted my heart and still does.

"Yep, its taken a while but I did it. I've had to sell myself to the project in order to see it through though but here it is."

"Would you sign one for me, for old times sake?" She replies, setting off my memory-bank with the thoughts of our wonderful times together.

"Of course I will." I return, taking the copy from her sweet hand and signing it:

"To Amanda, with all my love, Sarah."

As I return my book to her and she reads my inscription, Amanda then introduces me to her girlfriend.

"This is Wiktoria, we're engaged!" She announces, beaming as only she does.

"Oh, right! Well, nice to meet you Wiktoria. I hope you don't fuck-up your relationship with Amanda like I did? She's too good to let go." I come back.

She holds out her right-hand and I take it and shake, although when she opens her mouth I'm once again flummoxed and confounded by the tone of her accent as yes, you guessed it - she's a fucking Slav!

I simply cannot believe it, what the fuck is wrong with everyone? Why is everyone so fucking attracted to them? They're fucking scum, every fucking one of them, the females included.

"Polish?" I enquire, not that I really fucking care.

"No. I am from Hungary." She replies in that awful tone they all have.

Not that it makes a fucking difference, she's still a fucking Slav, although the Hungarians aren't as bad as the fucking Bulgarians or the Romanians I have to admit. Come to think of it, when I study her face I can see it now, that certain look that all these fucking Slavs have - pale and gormless.

"We'll meet up afterwards if you like?" Amanda suddenly pipes-up.

"Oh, er, yeah, okay, if you want." I stutter my reply.

I really would love to chat with Amanda but at the same time what is the bloody point, what are we going to say to each other? What are we going to do, have a threesome back at the Hotel? I don't think so.

I sign a few more books and another girl comes and stands before me, she's in her mid-20's I would say, slim, with a nice figure and with short dark hair, a sweet round face and glasses. She introduces herself as Georgie and chats about nothing as I sign her book. She holds out her hand and gives me a card with her name and contact details on it and smiles at me with a knowing look on her face. I take the card with a "Thank you" amid more smiles and a "See you" from the little honey - I do believe that I've pulled!

As she turns and walks off - exit stage-right - I suddenly notice a disturbance at the front of the shop ahead of me with lots of shouting and bodies running this way and that. I see someone heading in my direction, straight for me, a big black fucker with an expression of hate and vengeance written across it. I recognise him somehow and from somewhere and then I suddenly click - FUCKING HELL! - IT CAN'T BE? - IT'S ERROL! - THAT BITCH MELLIS'S FUCKING HUSBAND!

He runs at me and I stand to face him, but it's only then do I see he has something in his right-hand as he raises it towards me and then shouts, staring my own mortality in the face:

"MURDERER - YOU KILLED HER!"

I have a vague recollection of a flash of fire, a loud cracking sound, a tremendous pain in my left-arm, falling and then...nothing.

***

I awake in hospital - how many bloody times is that now? - with my left-forearm in bandages and although I don't feel any pain, I can sense a dull aching sensation from it. I desperately try to remember the incident at the bookshop but I only have a vague recollection of what happened. I recall that black bastard Errol coming for me and then seeing the gun but that's about it really, after that there's nothing but darkness and silence.

I'm in a private room by all accounts, judging by its status. I press the hand-buzzer by the side of me and I'm soon joined by a Doctor - surprisingly an English one! - and a nurse. The Doctor is a young guy in his mid-to-late-20's and quite nice looking, tall and slim. The nurse is also young - early-20's I would guess? - small and pretty but carrying a few pound too many considering the roundness of her arse! He informs me that I'm in St. Thomas's Hospital in Lambeth, on the other side of the Thames, and that I had a single bullet wound to my left-forearm that had gone straight through me and out the other side. Unfortunately it had also smashed one of my bones in two as it passed through so he's had to screw the 2-pieces back together again somehow - FUCKING HELL!

I can't fucking believe this, I damaged my right-arm in the car accident ages ago and now I've been bloody shot in the other - this is bloody ridiculous! He tells me to get some rest as I will be here in Hospital for the minimum of 2-days - fucking great! The sooner I'm out of here the better, I don't want Eva to think that I've deserted her!

Suddenly there's a knock at the door and in-walks Amanda, along with her Slav lover. My ex-love beams at me and plants a soft kiss to my left-cheek. It's lovely and I want to kiss her back full-on the mouth but I don't of course. The 2 of us chat about what had happened at the bookshop as the Hungarian stands there in silence, which suits me just fine although it is a little awkward to say the least. She asks me who that guy was that tried to kill me and did I know him but I deny everything, suspecting a trap by the pigs who I imminently await with baited-breath.

Both the Doctor and the nurse leave as then Amanda offers to go to the Hotel and sort out my things and have them brought over to me here in a taxi, something which I readily accept and thank her for. She begs me to: "Take care Sarah" and kisses me again as before, much to the discomfort of the Slav - not that I fucking give a shit about her - as they then both disappear out of my room and my life. I never see either of them ever again.

After lunch - if you can loosely call it that! - my peace and quiet is disrupted by more visitors. This time though it's the fucking Police who I just knew would show up sometime - didn't I tell you? - it was inevitable. It's the usual old scenario with yet another gruesome-twosome, 2 bloody detectives this time, both men. The head-cheese copper is a right bloody smart-arse type in his early-30's with a sodding-great chip on his shoulder, whilst the other is one of our black friends with horrible black eyes like a horse and one of those really tight curly hairstyles that some coons have and I have to try to avoid looking at him as I just know I will puke. They quiz me about the shooting, asking me if I've ever met Errol before and my relationship with that bitch Mellis and on and on and fucking on. I question them back, asking the smart-arse pig;

"Has Mary has been found yet?" and "What are you doing about it?" but they seem more interested in that fucker Errol than Mellis's so-called "disappearance".

"Eyewitnesses claim that Mr. Ellis called you a murderer before he shot you, why do you think that was?" He says stony-faced.

"Why don't you ask him?" I return.

"You don't know?" Comes back the black pig.

"Know what?"

The cops then inform me that our dark friend fired 3-shots in total - the first one hitting me in the arm, the second missing me completely and hitting the wall, and the third going into and out the other side of his stupid ignorant black skull when he killed himself - class!

"Why do you think he killed himself? Maybe he killed Mellis, Mary I mean, and disposed of her body somewhere and then tried to frame me?" I question them.

"We're looking into that possibility Sarah." Says the dickhead.

"So it's Sarah now is it?" I snap back at them. Fucking idiot, trying to get bloody friendly with me. It is not going to happen.

"I'm sorry, Miss Knowles."

"What exactly do you think I've done, chopped her up into little pieces and eaten her?" I reply equally bloody smart.

"No, of course not Miss Knowles, but he must have had a reason to go as far as trying to kill you, don't you think?"

"Listen, for the last fucking time, I admit I didn't like her and the feeling was mutual, but all this was a year and a half ago. He obviously wanted someone to stitch-up and I was the easy target - that's all. You either arrest me or leave me alone to recover - got it?"

A good 30-seconds of silence ensues before smart-cop pipes-up one last time:

"I think that will be all for now Miss Knowles, we'll let you get some rest. We'll be in touch."

"Great." I reply curtly.

The pair of them piss-off and a sigh of relief exhales from my poor old beautiful body as it slowly slips back into tranquillity.

I have a quiet reflective end to the rest of the day. Monica makes a fleeting visit to see if I'm OK and to say that no-one else was hurt in the shooting - although the fuzz had already told me such - and that the shop will reopen for business first thing Monday morning, and a brief chat about the book and other stuff before she too disappears. I text Mrs. DeAngelis to see if Eva is alright, my luggage and things all arrive from Claridge's Hotel safe and sound, the Doctor has been to see me twice already for a poke and a prod (not of the sexual kind unfortunately!) and then dinner was served - some sort of potato mash that had the consistency of frogspawn, a horrible green mess that I think were peas and 2-burnt offerings that were once sausages - yum!

I hope and prey that this fucking nightmare will be over when I wake tomorrow but in reality I just know that it won't.

***

The following morning - Sunday - soon comes around and outside it's pissing down with rain, it beating steadily on my Hospital room window. It's 10.15am and I've already had two visits to my good-self - the first from another Doctor, an Asian female one this time, and then a second visit from the fuzz, the same bloody pair of idiots as yesterday.

Breakfast this morning consisted of 2-slices of incinerated toast, a cold mug of what was allegedly "tea" and half a glass of orange juice that tasted like liquid plastic! You would have thought that I'd gotten used to Hospital food by now wouldn't you but no - it's all shit.

My third visit of the day is the one that really knocks me back though, it's from my sister Kate, who not only brings with her her half-cast mongrel kid but her fucking Paki husband as well! I could really do without this fucking crap on top of everything else. She introduces her so-called "husband" - I can't remember his name, I think it was something beginning with "H" but I don't really care - and then the kid.

"This is John." She exclaims.

"JOHN! ARE YOU FUCKING SERIOUS? WHY DID YOU CALL HIM THAT?" I holler at her.

"I named him after Dad." She whines back at me in her blind ignorance.

"WHY NAME HIM AFTER HIM, AFTER ALL HE DID TO US?" I scream.

"Oh forgive and forget Sarah, it was a long time ago now." She bleats.

"ARE YOU COMPLETELY FUCKING STUPID OR WHAT?"

"Don't call my wife stupid." The Paki suddenly pipes-up.

"I'LL SAY WHATEVER I FUCKING-WELL LIKE IN MY OWN FUCKING COUNTRY, AND IF YOU DON'T LIKE IT THEN YOU CAN FUCK-OFF BACK TO PAKI-LAND WHERE YOU BELONG." I shout back at him.

"I AM NOT A PAKISTANI, I AM FROM INDIA." He shouts back at me.

"IT'S ALL THE FUCKING SAME THING AS FAR AS I'M CONCERNED." I counter.

"Sarah, what is wrong with you? We've come all this way up to London to see you. Why do you have to be so bloody nasty all the time?" Says Kate.

"IS IT ANY FUCKING WONDER? ARE YOU BLIND? LOOK AT ME, SOMEONE TRIED TO KILL ME ME FOR FUCKS SAKE!" I shout back.

YEAH AND WHY? WHO'VE YOU UPSET THIS TIME? YOU'RE FUCKING IMPOSSIBLE. YOU'VE GOT A SERIOUS ATTITUDE PROBLEM DO YOU KNOW THAT?" She screams back at me, really fucking mad.

"I DIDN'T ASK YOU TO COME." I bitch back at her.

"Come on Kate, lets go." Says "H".

"Sort yourself out Sarah for fucks sake." Kate says to me but I ignore her meaningless words.

In fact I say nothing as the 3 of them leave and shut the door behind them. It is the last time I see my sister Kate for a thousand-moons and more.

✳✳✳

First thing Monday morning and I'm being examined by both the Doctor and the Consultant. After another X-ray and a cat-scan they duly inform me that my arm is looking good and that there's no-need to keep me in Hospital any longer. I will obviously have to have physiotherapy - probably as I did on the other arm after Crash 6 - as I now have metal plates and screws in both bloody arms until my final days!

I still can't believe that this shit has happened. What is wrong with my life? Why does it always spiral out of control every 5 fucking minutes?

Just to underline what I mean, I'm suddenly faced with more crap heading in my direction as the Doctor then goes on to inform me:

"Unfortunately Miss Knowles there was also an anomaly with your blood-test results."

"Please don't tell me that I'm bloody pregnant again?" I bitch at him.

"No, you are not pregnant. Unfortunately Sarah you have a sexually transmitted infection. You have syphilis."

"WHAT! YOU'VE GOT TO BE FUCKING JOKING?" I scream.

"I'm afraid not, the test results were positive."

I sit there dumbfounded and with my mouth wide open by the fact that I've caught yet another bloody STI, this time a real bastard one. I try to think of who the Hell I got it from but the answer is a mystery, I honestly can't think who it may have been - it could have been any one of them?

Here we fucking go again!

16

Ende

This is probably my very last entry to you ever, my dear reader and only friend. Time moves on and things change, whether they are for the good or bad only the future will tell us. This is now the end of my journey with you as it's time to move on and do other things, whatever they may be? It is the overwhelming power of synchronicity that has led me to here and now.

I've been back home at Foxhill a couple of months now, convalescing after the shooting and my other little problem - the STI - it being cured pretty quickly with a course of antibiotics. I'm doing okay now, although I think the shock of what has actually happened to me has seriously affected me more than I first thought, more mentally than the psychical wound to my arm itself - broken bones can be mended, broken minds can't - with the scar and my disjointed tattoos being permanent reminders of that day for the rest of my life.

Obviously I need time to convalesce fully and fortunately I have plenty of it. I guess not many people can say that they've been shot, although in reality it's not something to be proud of. The bloody press had a field day with the shooting of course, especially when they found out that I'm stinking rich! In the end though the net result was more book sales, resulting in further injections of cash into my bank account, not that I wrote it for the money in the first place. I knew nothing of any of this at first as I was out for the count in Hospital, and it was one of the nurses - a small dumpy girl in her late-20's who was nice enough but I wasn't really attracted to - that saved me copies of several newspapers featuring various articles about myself and what had happened. Some had unfair and scandalous press regarding the fact that I'm bisexual - sausage or pie, it's all the same to me! - and that I had lost my baby in a car accident and that I had inherited all my wealth from my late-husband Andy and other such shit.

All this obviously lead to more intrigue from the tabloids, unearthing crap about my relationship with Amanda and even my first love with the ex-boyfriend who cannot be named - crazy! People I didn't even know suddenly came crawling out of the woodwork from nowhere claiming all sorts of stupid things, all trying to make a fast buck out of me. The Police even had to put a guard outside my Hospital room to stop the press and photographers talking to me and taking photos - fame at last!

As I've already said, the shooting did wonders for sales of my book generally, underlining the old adage: "There's no such thing as bad publicity." For some peculiar reason I've actually sold quite a few of my books in Japan. Quite why my darling Japanese friends have taken to it I just don't know? I know that I've said this many times before but why can't the rest of the World be more like them? They have one thing that is distinctly lacking in the Western World today - respect - respect for their country, their heritage, and more importantly, for each other. And in my fear - I love my audience.

Once again though I've been largely ignored by my English *Volk*. What is wrong with them? Why don't they like me?

Writing my book - the diary of my life - has taught me a valuable lesson in life, it has enabled me to really become myself, to be really free. It has given me greater intelligence than ever before and move into another dimension of existence. My books have become like birds and I their keeper, setting them free into the never-ending sky and I call to them:

"Take care my books."

And they love me.

*** ***

The hearing into Mellis's disappearance came and went. Apparently there was no need for me to attend the hearing so I didn't bother going - what would have been the point? The stupid Police had called for a further enquiry into her disappearance but fortunately for me the courts dropped it, stating that it was:

"Not in the public interest."

Even so, I still don't think that I've heard the last of this issue even now. At the end of the day a verdict of *"Misadventure"* was recorded and so that was that - no more Mellis - I'm as free as a bird! And what a bird I am. I really am something special, something else entirely, I know it and so now do the stupid Police. They even wanted to have a psychiatrist look at me to analyse my mental condition - fucking bastards. Why, what do they fucking know about me or my life? I bet it was that fucking bastard CJ - my ex so-called "Boss" - that told the Police that I needed mental help - CUNT. Hopefully now I'll get no more bloody hassle from them any more and I can continue with my life without them knocking at my door all the fucking time - stupid pigs - they will never break me.

The CPS (Crown Prosecution Service) decided that because her body was never found and there was no evidence that I was even involved, suspected or let-alone arrested, there was no further course of action. And as for her stupid coon, that also went nowhere, not that I give a shit about him - he's dead.

Of course the Police came to the house and searched it but found nothing - no bones, no blood, no teeth, no clothes, no DNA, nothing. I had got rid of her pelvic bone ages ago, smashing it to dust and chucking the remains in The River Arun. Why the cops were so fucking slow in all this I will never understand? And whichever way you look at it, it was all bound to end badly anyway wasn't it?

***

What I haven't told you yet my special friends, is that I have a new love in my life. Her name is Clarissa and I love her to bits. I've been waiting for her all my life and now I have her. I would walk through fire for her. She is one in a million.

We met at a party almost 3-months ago given by Craig - the car guy - at his house-warming do at his new place in East Lavant, near Chichester, West Sussex.

Our first encounter was the strangest thing, I saw her across the other side of the room and that was that, I fell in love with her the very moment she walked into my eyes! I have heart-eyes for her and straight away we were together - amazing! - my spell is cast! In actual fact, I was not sure I even had a place in my heart for anyone ever again, especially as my heart turned black and died years ago, living in a World of heartache. It all just goes to prove that one never knows what's around the corner.

She's a few years younger than me at 28, and brunette with beautiful shoulder-length natural curls. She's quiet and sweet and unassuming and with lovely chiselled features - a bit like that Australian actress Margot Robbie - and is lovely and slim with a nice tight figure, although nowhere near as curvy as mine obviously, but gorgeous even so. She's my angel lover and my sugar-tits!

Unlike myself she's actually 100% *bona fide* gay and has absolutely no interest in men whatsoever, which is fair enough. Also she doesn't ever want to get married - not just to me but anyone - or wants or even likes kids, which equally suits me just fine. I've got no intention of marrying again anyway, not for the 3rd-bloody time! Just imagine that, the bride of the Devil! But who knows what the future may bring? If things unfortunately don't work out with Clarissa and someone else comes along, someone special, I may take the plunge once more, we'll just have to wait and see won't we?

Although I have my own means and share it with her, Clarissa doesn't want to stop working - she's a Graphic Designer for a company based in Worthing - and I respect her for that. We all need our own independence and space after all, and that in turn I believe makes our love for each other stronger. If we were together 24/7 then we would probably drive each other insane!

We're also now living together, she having moved in just a few weeks ago. Things seem to be working out okay, although it is still very early days of course. We do get along amazingly well together though, we talk a lot, about everything under the Sun, and there's a real bond between us, even more so than Amanda and I had, maybe even with Andy also. I've actually told her more about myself and my life than anyone I've ever known, we are both that deep in love. She really stirs my senses and has hit my spot! Although I haven't told her absolutely everything about myself, obviously I must retain a certain mystery and keep some things secret, like "The Big One" obviously.

I WANT to feed off her, to breathe her air, to become one person with her and love her forever. She has even managed to control my tempestuous nature, I look at the World slightly differently now than I did before because of her.

My love for her has also made me re-fall in love with myself, and I love myself as much as I love her. And as I've said before, it doesn't bother me if I like other women as well as guys, you must never be ashamed of who or what you are - I'm certainly not.

I am super-intelligent, anyone can see that just from my poise, from my image, and so I can do anything I WANT.

∗∗∗

It's the stupid day of my National Speed Awareness Course at Hartsfield Manor in Bethworth, Surrey. I really find this whole episode absolutely pathetic. I mean, 63 in a 50 isn't exactly murder is it? - and I should know! There are better things I'm sure that the stupid fucking Police could do with their time, like catching real criminals for instance, particularly all those Eastern European Slav scum and all those dirty fucking Gypsy bastards that get away with everything rather than hassling the poor bloody motorist all the fucking time just in order to pay for their tea and biscuits.

It's an early start - the course beginning at 8am for some stupid reason? - and so I have to get up at 6am in order to grab a quick shower, get dressed and put my face on. Today I'm wearing a white long-sleeved blouse with a plunging v-neckline and a pair of black triple-pleated trousers with black braces, all from Louis Vuitton, underwear in black lace from Hanky Panky, and my pair of black leopard-print peep-toe ankle-boots from Jimmy Choo that are to die for. My clutch-bag today is a gorgeous white leather one from Lulu Guinness. My hair is my usual classic style, whilst my make-up is full-on killer with blood-red lipstick, super-sharp cheekbones and multi-tonal grey eyeshadow. My perfume today is *No. 5* by Chanel.

My choice of car today was easy - it's the Lamborghini of course! - and after kissing Clarissa "Goodbye" and she wishing me "Good luck", I head out at this unearthly hour onto the A29, the A24 to Dorking, then turning right at chicken (cock!) roundabout and onto the A25 to Betchworth. I find Hartsfield Manor easily via my satnav, the venue hidden behind the main road that runs through the small village, an impressive building and beautifully kept. I head down the ramp to the main car-park when suddenly the front end of the Lambo grounds-out as it hits the deck at the bottom - FUCK IT! - not the greatest start to the day! I park-up and survey the damage to the nose of the car, it fortunately being not too bad, just a small scrape to the splitter.

I then make my way to reception in the Hotel - it's now 7.45am - with the young girl behind the desk instructing me to head to the bar as that's where all those attending today's course are meeting - sounds like a good plan! There's only 1-person here before me, some boring old guy in his late-50's with an air of superiority about him. We exchange "Hellos" but not much else, only him telling me that he's a lawyer by profession and that he was done for doing 41 in a 40 - see what I mean?

Slowly and steadily more human bodies enter the room as the clock now hits 8am, including the pair who are fronting the course, an old guy in his early-60's called Ron - an ex-taxi driver - and a short smart-arse woman in her 50's dressed smart but casual featuring one of those awful cardigans that are twice as long at the front than at the rear - what's all that about? She really thinks that she's the bees-knees as she orders us all into the adjacent room like we're a bunch of 5-year olds - stupid old cow! I do have to give a little snigger to myself though when she informs us all that her name is Pamela Cockhead! - what sort of fucking name is that? - LOL!

We all sit ourselves down like the good little children we are in groups around our respective tables - 6 to a table with there being about 10 tables or so - fortunately with the boring lawyer guy sitting elsewhere. My fellow speedsters are the usual eclectic bunch I see everywhere I go - young, old, fat and thin - with the usual foreign element mixed-in as well of course; an oriental woman who can't speak English so has brought her daughter along to interpret - really? - about 6 Paki's, just the one Slav and a couple of blacks, one of which - a real fucking Zulu-type - that arrives by the skin of his gleaming white teeth and is given a ticking-off by the headmistress. Around my table - going clockwise - we have a van driver in his mid-20's (actually quite a nice guy to talk to and with a good sense of humour although I don't really fancy him, he's just not my type), some stuck-up cow of about 27 all dressed-up to the nines in her posh clothes pretending to be something she isn't who keeps looking at me with jealous eyes as she quickly realises that she's been massively outdone on the beauty stakes by yours truly - she's OK-looking herself but not that great. Next to her sits a guy in his late-50's - he's a Doctor - and he reminds me a little of Andy, having a similar look and demeanour about him. Another girl sits next to him, she's about 40 and only so-so looking, this being the second time that she's been caught and attended one of these stupid courses. Next to her sits Becky, she's about 25 with a pretty face and dark curly hair but is carrying far too much weight - she must be a size-16 at least! - and who lives with her boyfriend on the Goodwyns estate in Dorking, not a very nice place to be and I tell her to do herself and her fella a favour and get out of there - that place just breads scum. We hit if off really well and spend our morning together taking the piss out of our fellow drivers as well as the headmistress.

The morning drags on for the following 4-hours - yeah, that's right, 4-fucking-hours! - being bored out of my fucking skull watching a safely film fronted by an ex-F1 driver, questions, answers, writing notes down in the course workbook that we've each been given - although both myself and Becky don't bother as we really couldn't be arsed! - another bloody safety film, and listening to Left-Wing snowflake bullshit from Mrs. Cocksucker when she preaches crap to us like:

"If someone cuts you up out on the road, don't chase after them and have a go at them. Remember that someone somewhere loves that person - just let it go."

FUCK-OFF! Can you believe this shit? What a load of fucking crap! If some bastard cuts me up then I'll fucking kill them! What a load of bullshit!

At 12pm the farce is finally over, and with our driving licence details taken we all start to file out and go in our different directions and to our different lives. I offer fat Becky a lift home as she hasn't got her car here today for whatever reason but she declines my offer as her boyfriend is picking her up. I wasn't trying to get into her knickers or anything - although I would fuck her if I had the chance, you know me! I give her my mobile number anyway but never hear from her ever ever.

I fire the Lambo and head out of the car-park, passing the stuck-up girl from my table as she climbs into her pale-blue, blinged-up and slammed BMW M3 - yuk! - as I then gingerly exit without grinding the cars nose on the ground once more.

I pass Becky and give her a wave but I don't think she can quite believe that it's really me in this beautiful beast and my wave isn't acknowledged - oh well!

Back out onto the A25 I hit the gas and zoom along doing 70 in a 50 - some things will never change/some things cannot be changed. I park in Dorking and head around the corner to the Fish & Chip shop, ordering myself a small portion of chips, a saveloy, 2-pickled onions, a gherkin and a Coke all to go.

I sit myself back in the Lambo to have my lunch, watching the World go by as I do so. The same stinking Bulgarian car-cleaner I notice is still here, talking his Slavic shit down the phone to another one of his evil fucking brothers. He ignores me as I ignore him, not even getting the usual tired old line of: "Car washer, car washer" any more as I pass him both there and back to the chip shop. He knows that I fucking hate him - 100 times more than he hates me - simply because I'm pure Aryan and he's a dirty fucking Slav cunt.

I reflect on the morning and this whole episode, reflecting on what a complete waste of fucking time this whole thing has been - 4-hours of my life down the drain. There is no way anyone is going to slow me down, I don't have time to slow down, life is too short for that.

On the way back home I really push the car hard and on the A29 Billingshurst Bypass I hit 165. Speed limits don't apply too me.

✱✱✱

I've been such a naughty girl - again! - by spending my money on yet another car. Through Craig - Andy's car guy - I've bought myself one of those crazy/beautiful Ford GT's, a white one. It's basically a modern take on the old original GT40 from the 1960's, like the one I have already in the garage, another one of Andy's pride and joys.

The production run of these newer ones is limited and so they're pretty rare to see, and I now have a matching pair so up yours! This new one has set me back some £300,000 - absolutely stupid money I know but what else is there to do? All this cash sitting in various bank accounts doing nothing is a bloody waste so I might as well have some fun with it whilst I've still got it.

Talking of fun, I'm just off out now in the new car, to Cranleigh in Surrey to have a wander around the shops. Today I'm wearing a lime-green lace bodycon mini-dress from Goddiva, underwear in white lace from Victoria's Secret and on my perfect feet my old pair of tan suede ankle-boots from AliExpress. My clutch-bag is my old chrome Art-Deco shell one from Vintage Styler. My hair is up in its usual ponytail position although today I have a couple of genuine Japanese ivory chopsticks pierced through it forming a cross - just for a change. My make-up I've done really sharp featuring coal-black eyeshadow, dark blusher and black lipstick - really nasty, just like me - Ha! My perfume today is *Poison* by Christian Dior.

Firing up the 3.5-litre 650bhp V6 twin-turbo engine it bursts into life with a growl that instantly puts a smile on my perfect face. I click the crazy 7-speed PowerShift gearbox into 1st-gear and away we go, heading out onto the A29 left and North, giving the car some stick as it eats the road. I power past Five Oaks and Slinfold - sticking 2-fingers up to them all as I pass! - and then turn left onto the A281 Guildford Road and then right through Rudgwick onto the B2128.

This stretch of road out the other side of the village is a really good blast and so I open up the gas, the car hitting 130 in seconds with no fuss. The sweeping corners and tight bends that follow are a pure joy, the GT hugging the tarmac like it's on rails so I push it harder, scaring myself a little a few times and making my blood rush like a bastard - I love it!

Into Cranleigh High Street I slow to 45 in the 30-zone, keeping her in 2nd-gear so as to make the exhausts crackle and spit like mad. I park in the towns main car-park, away from all the pleb cars, get myself a 2-hour ticket from the machine and then wander off into town, all in my usual confident elegant style, my aura vibrating the surrounding air like my orgasm.

I have a quick nose around a couple of charity shops first but find nothing that tickles my fancy - no DVD's, books or anything else. I amble around a shop made up of various individually-owned and run stalls, purchasing a funny set of 3-wise-monkeys from a gorgeous brunette honey on one stall as she melts my heart the moment I see her. I WANT to have her right here and now in the shop, to have her lick my hot pussy and finger me and make me cum and I struggle to get a grip of myself, resisting the overwhelming temptation to kiss her beautiful mouth and squeeze her small pert firm breasts and I win - but only just!

I next make a stop at a newsagent further down the road to get a copy of today's paper. I'm a little startled not to find a brown face behind the counter as most newsagents have these days, even in more rural towns like this one as nearly always there's some sort of Paki running the shop. Instead I'm confronted by a beautiful young girl in her late-teens with blonde hair - I think it's real? - with a gorgeous smile that pleads "Fuck me." We exchange "Hellos" as I hand her the 55p for the paper and she smiles once again and I collapse inside, my black heart hitting the floor with a thud.

"Is there anything else you'd like?" She says to me in her not so innocent young voice.

I WANT to tell her: "Yes, I WANT you to fuck me with your tongue and piss on my tits and then I'm going to fuck your pussy with my largest dildo and make you cum into my mouth" but I don't of course, I just say "No thanks" and turn and head for the door like a fucking wimp. Not long ago I would have taken things further and made a play for her - Clarissa or no Clarissa - but now I'm older and wiser and more settled and I don't need her, all I need is Clarissa and that's that. And if you believe that then you'll bloody believe anything!

My next stop is the butchers, one of those really old fashioned ones that has dead birds hanging up outside and big glass display cabinets full of different meats, pies and other delicacies. I buy a couple of fillet steaks for mine and Clarissa's dinner tonight and a Cornish pasty for my lunch. The guy serving calls me "Young lady" - yeah fucking right! - even though I'm actually older than he is and as you know, I'm no fucking lady! Next door is an equally rare wet-fish shop selling all manner of sea food, all kept chilled on beds of ice although I don't bother to go in and just walk by the display.

I then venture over the road to another charity shop, buying myself a second-hand copy of *Hellraiser* on Blu-ray - the Directors cut/uncut version - for only a couple of quid. I wander around a small department store called Manns further up the road and buy myself a lovely German ceramic cooking pot with lid that sets me back £280. Following that I order myself a coffee - a Latte' - in the stores little tearoom and sit my perfect bum down on my own and contemplate life and all that shit. A couple of old girls in their late-70's sit at another table chewing the cud, going on about death and how all their friends and neighbours are all popping-off one by one. That must be awful and I can't even bare to think about it, not on top of all the crap I've had to put up with in my own life. As I sit there quietly thinking and looking gorgeous, one of the old girls suddenly pipes-up to me:

"I must say that's a beautiful dress you're wearing." She says.

"Thank you!" I return a little surprised.

"You've got a lovely figure." Says the other one.

"Yes I know, thank you." I say back, although trying not to be too sarcastic.

"We wish we were still in our 20's like you." Comes back the first one.

"So do I, I'm actually 36." I return.

"Really? You look far younger than that. What's your secret?" She quizzes me.

"I couldn't possibly tell you any of my secrets." I tell them both, giving them a fake smile in the process.

If I sat here and told them all about the horrible and disgusting things that I've done in my life and still do I would probably have 2-more deaths on my hands!

"I had a hip-replacement 3-months ago." The second one then informs me.

"That's nice." I say coldly as by now I've finished my coffee and so get up and prepare to leave. I'm not telling them or anyone else about my private life, plus I don't want to sit here listening to any more of their morbid crap.

I walk out the door without saying "Goodbye" or anything else to the 2-old dears, as they just sit there checking out my body, my tattoos, my perfect bum and perfect legs as I depart. I am perfect.

Turning right I head back up the High Street and window-shop the rest of the way as by now I've become a little bored with my venture. I cross the road by the War Memorial and head to the supermarket, only purchasing a couple of bags of crisps, some cat food and a small bottle of stain remover. From there I head back to the car-park, but when I near my car I notice some bastard in a black Audi Q7 has parked right up against my passenger-side door, meaning putting today's buys on the passenger seat impossible. Instead I therefore have to manhandle my bags across the interior of the car, much to my increasing evil temper. I decide I'm not letting this fucker get away with this so I walk around to the drivers-side of the Audi and let both its tyres down by poking one of my house-keys into the valves - Ha!

A middle-aged woman and her 2-daughters walk past me just as I finish and stand back up straight, all 3 of them giving me a funny look, not that I fucking care anyway. As they clamber into their car - yet another black 4x4 - I scratch the word "CUNT" into the drivers-side door of the Audi with my Swiss Army knife, that will teach the shit to park so fucking close to me - BASTARD.

I jump in the GT, fire her up with a roar and a small cackle from the exhausts, and head out of the car-park with the females

4x4 following behind me, the 3-occupants still whispering-away to themselves. I give the GT some right-foot in 2nd-gear going back down the High Street, making everyone top and stare - LOL! At the other end of town I stop at the petrol station for some fuel - £75 worth - also making sure that everyone there about me gets a bloody good look at both the car and my tight body in the process.

I then tear home back to Foxhill along the same route as earlier, giving the car plenty of throttle and being a general bitch to all the other road users, especially some stinking Paki in a black BMW 135i when he stupidly tries to outrun me, burning him off at 145mph in a 50-zone! He flashes his headlights at me as I streak away - what for I don't know, it was him that tried to race me in the first bloody place? What a knob!

Back home I settle-down in the living-room on the leather sofa to have my lunch, the beautiful pasty I bought earlier along with several glasses of chilled German white as Eva munches-away on her bowl of chicken in sauce and BBC News 24 plays on the TV. I sit there all afternoon watching crap until Clarissa walks through the door and we fuck on the living-room floor as Eva watches us perform with a big smile on her face and eyes as wide as saucers.

***

I order Clarissa to: "Lick me" and she buries her head between my thighs and eats me, my heart pounding-away as we lose ourselves in this moment of pretentious love. I feel my insides explode in rapture as her tongue flicks in and out of my vagina, sending me into orbit with flashing colours of light behind my eyes.

I moan "OH OH OH OH OH" as she laps at my oyster and I lose control and go mental and spasticate with her touch, my arms and legs shaking like crazy. I hit her with my love as I reach my peak, my honey splatting over her face and into her mouth. She comes to kiss it and we tongue and roll about on the bed entwined in each others arms like lovers.

We wrap our legs inside one another as we sense the wetness and heat of our sweet things squishing against our naked bodies.

"I love you Sarah." She says as I kiss her firm breasts and she pushes 2-fingers into my hot pussy.

I whisper "My lover" into her ear with passion and affection as she gives me 3-fingers and I scream for more and fuck them. I hold her throat as she cums me and I orgasm with lightning and flashes of fire as she touches my impalpable heart. We laugh and kiss and tongue with sensuality as we lose ourselves once more and I am gone as she captures me again and we drown together in the ocean of love.

On all fours I push 2-fingers of my left-hand into her punani and my index-finger of my right-hand into her pre-lubed bumhole, fucking her with my fingers and she moans:

"Oh yes yes yes. Oh Sarah. Harder. Oh my God. Harder. OH FUCK."

I kiss her bum-cheeks as I masturbate her and she starts to shake and then orgasms over my hand. We both lick her juice from my fingers with mutual passion and swallow and kiss and we couldn't be more in love ever in 1000-years. I lay on my back and open my legs for her and she plays with my labia and pulls me, positioning one of my dildos - the 8-inch realistic one from Doc Johnson - at my hole. She encircles my lips with the rubbery knob, making me pant and I love it and it drives me crazy. Suddenly she pushes the fake cock into my body and I feel my pelvis part to accept it within me. She fucks me back and forth right up to my limit and I hit the roof and scream with love. She kisses my breasts and then my pussy and sucks cock, pushing it back into me for more pleasure.

I stop her in her tracks as she fucks me and look straight into her eyes. I smile at her as I whisper:

"Show me heaven my love."

Pulling the dildo out again she places it at my mouth and I suck it, tasting my own love. Clarissa kisses my mouth and cock and we both suck it at the same time and tongue as I in-turn say to her:

"I WANT your body, your breasts, your pussy" and I kiss her beautiful firm peaches and push 2-fingers into her mouth and put my right-leg between her thighs. I knee her vagina with small thrusts as she sucks my fingers and plays with my girls and moans "AW" with each jerk. She cums for me and I feel her lover squelch over my knee as she cries with pleasure and I choke her with my fingers as she cums again as I kiss her mouth, giving head to her tongue.

We 69 with me on the bottom, licking and loving and penetrating each others vaginas with tongues and fingers as we roll about on the grass by the mini-lake stuck together with our glue as we kiss and fuck.

We go off to sleep together that night with Clarissa having one hand resting on my breast - she is so beautiful.

She is my saucepot and I love her.

***

I'm off out again this morning, just to do a bit of food shopping locally. Instead of going into Horsham this time I'm off to Sainsbury's at Pulborough for a change, it's a lot smaller than the Horsham branch but seems to be much nicer in its layout and appearance, probably because it's newer I guess?

I'm going on my own as Clarissa is at work all day - it's Thursday. Today I'm wearing a white lace bodycon dress - it's a party-dress really but so what? - from Lipsy that is super-tight and really enhances my faultless curves. My underwear is also in white lace, from Ultimo. On my feet I'm wearing my old pair of white strap shoes from Raffi Scent as they suit today's look. I've gone for a more pale-look to my make-up today to compliment my outfit, featuring pale-pink lipstick, light-grey eyeshadow and no blusher. My hair I do as per the norm but tied with a white cotton bow. My perfume is *Poison* by Christian Dior and my clutch-bag is my white leather one from Hermes.

I'm taking the Lamborghini out again today - so obvious! - as it's so crazy-looking and I hit the A29 heading South, blasting along the fast open stretch of road. At the Billingshurst roundabout I come up behind a slow car, one of those Ford Kuga mini-4x4 things being driven by an elderly couple in their 60's doing 50 in a 50. I can't get around it as the traffic coming in the opposite direction is heavy and there's no room for me to overtake and so I have to follow behind the old bugger for miles and miles - FUCK IT! Finally, at Adversane I get my chance and overtake the old git, blasting around him in 2nd-gear with plenty of noise from my exhausts. He flashes me with his headlights as they all seem to do as I zoom away so I give him the finger - FUCKING IDIOT. Why do I always get these old tossers in my fucking way every time I go out?

As I get near my destination I notice the car starting to feel a bit strange, like it has a lack of power or something? Or maybe it's just me because I'm not used to driving in these shoes? I park easily in the supermarket car-park, grab myself one of the smaller trolleys from the rack and head in. We don't actually need much food-wise, but even so I end up buying an organic sweetheart cabbage, a roll of pork with stuffing and crackling for Sunday's roast, cat food (again!), deodorant, a copy of today's newspaper, the latest editions of *Cosmopolitan* and *Top Gear* magazines, a bottle of plop (my code for vodka!), some chocolate, milk, lamb burgers, and a few other odds and sods.

At the till I'm greeted by a funny woman with a speech impediment - either that or she's been knocked-sideways by my gorgeousness! I pay my bill by debit-card and bag my items up into 2-bags, all the time being scanned by the till-lady and all those around me, including a young boy behind me in the queue of about 12 or 13 with his Mum, he standing there staring at my coloured hands and arms, my legs, my bum and my tits - cheeky little sod! - although I can't really blame him can you?

I place my shopping in the passenger-seat foot-well of the Lambo at she doesn't have a boot and then slide my perfect bum down in behind the wheel. I fire her up and select

1st-gear using the paddle-shift but nothing happens, I just sit there like a fucking lemon going nowhere - SHIT! I fucking knew there was something wrong, didn't I tell you? I try again several times more to find a gear, even trying reverse but to no avail, I'm not going anywhere - BOLLOCKS!

There's no other way for it, switching the engine off I'm forced to scroll through my phone-list for the number of the nearest Lamborghini dealership, I know damn sure that I put it on here as it was the very same place Andy told me he had bought it from a few years back and where she's always been serviced. I find the number buried deep in my phone and ring it, explaining to the guy on the other end of the line my situation, telling him that I'm pretty sure that it's the clutch that has failed but what do I know, it could be a whole myriad of possibilities? He tells me as he knew Andy quite well and of his sad departure, that he will send someone out to rescue me within the hour. Bloody thing, what a pain in the arse!

Oh well, there's not really much I can do at the present moment so I just have to sit there killing time by reading about all the doom and gloom in the paper - shit in the Middle-East, shit people on TV earning too much money for doing fuck-all, other shit getting away with murder (again and again), shit football players on stupid wages, and a report on ex-Prime Minister Tony "Cunt" Blair and all the properties he owns - not exactly very Socialist is it? How I'd love to shoot that grinning fucker right between the eyes - it wouldn't be a crime, it would be a public service!

With the paper read I then spend my time checking-out all the customers walking to and fro from their boring cars to the shop and then back again - olds, Mums with kids, guys in vans, men in suits, the occasional oddball - no-one that takes my fancy. Suddenly I spot a flatbed lorry entering the car-park, its driver looking straight at me. He parks-up and we have a quick chat about the car and Andy as he also remembers him from back whenever, and it's obvious now that I'm not going anywhere and so I have to resign myself to that fact. Tom - the lorry driver - offers to take me home after putting the Lambo onto the lorry and I thank him for his kindness in rescuing me. He's aged about 60 or so and not my type at all, and anyway, I'm way out of his league. Watching him winch my stricken car up onto the bed is a sad sight and it actually makes a tear form in the corner of one eye and I have to steal myself away from watching it being dragged up. I place my shopping and a few other personal items from the car into the truck and after strapping the Lambo down securely, off we trundle to my place.

Once there and with much gratitude and a quick shake of hands, I stand at my front-door as Tom drives away with my car. I cannot contain my emotions any more and I immediately start to weep as I have this strange foreboding that this is somehow the very last time that I shall see her - my car - as flashbacks of Crash 6 and losing my darling little Fiesta ST as then images of Lacey dying and other shit start to flood my mind in madness.

Indoors I hold Eva to my body as I down a couple of mouthfuls of the Vladivar I bought earlier straight from the bottle, its power blinding and stinging me like lightning. I call Clarissa as I put the shopping away in the kitchen, telling her of my crap morning. She laughs as I explain it to her but I don't find it funny at all, ending the conversation short. What is wrong with these people, have they no compassion? Don't they understand how much this means to me?

For the rest of the afternoon I just hang-out with myself and Eva, I'm in no mood to do anything but. The time now is 1.15pm. After a light lunch we spend frozen time together playing pool in the games room with Eva jumping around like a spring lamb on the green baize dodging and tapping the balls as I try to pot them - silly thing!

Later - it's now 3.30pm - the dealer calls me with news of the car, telling me that is was the clutch that has failed and that it's going to cost me the thick-end of £10,000 - FUCKING HELL! I tell him to fix it asap, a job he says will take the best part of a week to sort. Oh well, once again there's nothing I can do about it, if that's what it costs and takes then so be it, it's all completely out of my hands. It's not like I haven't got any other cars to fall back on anyway is it?

* * *

I received a strange email a couple of weeks ago, from Angie, the funny little Greek girl with the springy hair at my last company - the shithole that it was. Apparently someone there - she doesn't know who or either she won't tell me - had got hold of a copy of my book and has been spreading stupid ill-founded rumours that I wrote it about that idiot CJ and all the other creeps that work there! I know that in actuality it is true and that I did but I disguised each individual character well enough to cover my arse, and as I'm protected by Copyright Law and that the book is listed as fiction, there's pretty-much sod-all they can fucking do about it - Ha!

Anyway, 2-days later their company lawyers sent me a threatening letter promising court action if I didn't retract the book from sale - oh dear, big fucking threat! Obviously I wasn't going to do that so I sent the letter straight back to them with "FUCK-OFF AND DIE" written across it in big red letters - FUCKING IDIOTS!

That fucking arsehole CJ has got the knives out for me for sure. But I'm not worried, I can take anything and more that that tosser can bring to me. Who do these people think they are dictating to me like this? And all this bullshit just because I have independence, and now money, as well as some notoriety.

There hasn't been any word from them since then and I don't fucking care even if there is. This is not over until I say it's over.

* * *

I stand alone and naked in my bedroom and look at myself in the full-length mirror before me but there is no reflection, nothing at all, just emptiness and space - I do not exist. I crash-land in my own time in one long continuous nightmare, surrounded by shadows of people who aren't really there, images of the past stuck in the now.

My supernatural power over the living and the dead continues on and they all run from me when they look into my eyes, when they see my face, a face with hidden meaning. They cannot beat me, no-one can. I am a pure Goddess and everyone fucking knows it.

* * *

Clarissa and myself are here at the Lamborghini dealership in Kent, about to pick-up the car after its just had its new clutch fitted. We drove here in Clarissa's car, a white Lotus Evora that I bought for her as a gift of my love.

Today I'm wearing a black sleeveless jumper and a pair of black slim-fit jeans both from Hugo Boss, and on my feet my old pair of black suede ankle-boots from Miu Miu. Today's underwear is in black lace from Figleaves. My make-up is pure supermodel featuring purple eyeshadow, sharp blusher and purple lipstick.

My hair is in my own classical style whilst my perfume is *Luxe* by Avon. I'm not carrying a clutch-bag or anything else as I couldn't be bothered.

Clarissa is wearing a mesh-knit long-sleeved cold-shoulder top in lime - such a beautiful colour! - from Christian Lacroix, pale-blue skinny jeans from River Island, underwear in black from Wolf & Whistle, and on her feet my really old pair of blue suede platform court shoes from Lola that makes her stand almost as tall as me. Her perfume is *Opium* by Yves Saint Laurent. Her hair and make-up is simple, classic and beautifully done. She also isn't carrying any sort of bag, just a small white leather purse from Michael Kors.

We stroll around the showroom together looking at all the fantastic cars - Huracan's, Aventador's, and even an old Diablo in blood red, each one of them gorgeous. It's one of the

Aventador's though that really catches my eye, a brand-new "S" in a lovely blue colour with a black interior. The sales guy - Max - offers both myself and Clarissa a seat in the car and so we slide ourselves into its gorgeous cockpit. It fits me like a glove and straight away I fall head over heals in love with it, my heart and my mind doing battle over whether I should trade my own in for one of these monsters - what is a girl to do? Clarissa pushes me to buy it but I'm torn, the one I have now was Andy's pride and joy and I have a deep sentimental connection with it. Having said that, time does move on and Andy has gone, and I must move on as well. I guess it really is time to let go, and so after a good look around the car with Max showing me the massive 6.5-litre V12 engine and other new features of this beautiful monster, I therefore decide there and then - without even having a test-drive! - to take the plunge and order myself a brand new one from the factory, trading-in mine for one of these - in white with a dark-grey interior. FUCKING HELL, WHAT HAVE I DONE?

The cost of the new "S" is the best part of 300-grand, but with my old car as part-exchange I walk away with a good deal on my part. I don't give a shit anyway, I actually earn more money now in a single day in interest alone than I did in a whole year back when I was working at the shithole! What a crazy World we live in!

***

It's 9.30am on a Thursday some time later. I'm off to pick up the new Lamborghini today - the Aventador S. I'm going on my own as Clarissa is stuck at work and can't get away as there's some big flap on or some such meaningless crap.

Anyway, today I'm wearing a white bodycon mini-dress from Versace that is super-tight and super-short and a bit over-the-top just to pick up a car but what the fuck - I've still got it so I'm going to flaunt it! Just to be even more daring

I'm not wearing any underwear so I'll have to be that extra bit careful getting in and out of the cars! On my feet I'm wearing my old pair of white strap shoes from Raffi Scent as I can drive better on those - I don't want to crash my new car by wearing some crazy pair of stupid high heels! My hair is as the norm with my make-up done in the style of an ice-queen - pale as can be featuring purple eyeshadow, minimal blusher, purple lipstick and I look fucking gorgeous! Today's perfume is *Poison* by Christian Dior once again with my clutch-bag being my white leather one from Hermes - again!

I've actually got some mixed emotions about today, on the one hand I'll be sad to see the old Lamborghini go as we've had some really good fun times together, she's been an amazing car but time moves on as I've said previously. On the other hand I'm almost wetting myself with excitement of seeing and driving the new one, I just know it's going to blow my mind and I can't wait to own it - she is my new love, my baby.

In the garage I notice something placed on the windscreen of the Lambo as I near it, it's a red rose from my lover - OH MY LOVE, HOW SWEET! Out on the road I head across country heading East to the dealership. They did offer to deliver the new car but I turned them down, telling Max that I wanted one last drive in the old one, I owe her that at least. Our last journey together thankfully passes without drama, just a couple of idiots in my fucking way as per usual that I easily dispatch with the power under my right-foot - how I love this car! I'm pretty sure that Andy's spirit would agree with me in moving on with it even so.

I park-up easily in the forecourt of the concessionaire and say one last "Goodbye" to my love, giving her a little kiss as I exit the confines of the cockpit - I am so sad. Max comes out of the showroom to join me and we chat about inconsequential shit as he confirms how much more I will love the new car. We wander across the way together to where my new car is lurking, it sitting there like a sleeping dragon - it is so fucking gorgeous! It looks so much meaner and nastier than the old one and I fall in love with her in an instant, I just can't wait to drive it! He shows me around her, pointing out the differences between this and my previous one but I'm not really listening, I just want to get in it and go!

In Max's office we sort out all the paperwork for both cars over a lovely mug of coffee each, the money side of things having already been taken care of previously at our last meeting. We chat about cars, Andy, Clarissa, life and other stuff but I'm itching to leave and test the car - I'm like a dog with 2-tails!

Finally, with everything all signed, sealed and with the shaking of hands, it's time to go at last. I take one last look across the forecourt to my old car - my love - and say "Farewell" to her as here we go again, off on another adventure into the unknown! I slide into the drivers seat as carefully as I dare, trying to make sure Max doesn't catch a peek of my honey in the process! Several other guys have also gathered around - other salesmen, mechanics and other random guys - who have all suddenly appeared as if out of nowhere, all watching me, checking-out my body, legs, bum, tits, hair, face, tattoos, everything. I like them all looking at me and I ham it up more for them and snigger to myself as I watch them all squirm and whisper amongst themselves - just like guys do.

I fire-up the cars engine with the push-button starter and she bursts into an evil, throaty roar, it making enough noise to wake the dead - I love it! I thank Max for all his help and we shake hands once again with "Good luck" and all that balls. He shuts my door for me and I click the paddle-shift into 1st-gear and pull-away and out of the forecourt. A guy in a lorry lets me out onto the main road and I give him a little wave as I press the accelerator with vigour, the car taking off like a scalded cat with a howling wail from the exhausts as it propels me up the road amid more stares from pedestrians and my fellow road users in their nondescript boring crappy cars.

I try to take it a bit easy on my return journey back to Foxhill but I just can't resist giving the car some stick now and then on the M25 and the M23 - it would be rude not to! It feels like a completely different car compared to the old one, not like an updated version that is really is. This one even has 4-wheel steering, making the handling far more precise and sharper than the old Lambo, and heading back along the A264 from Crawley (Creepy-Crawley!) - a beautiful fast stretch of road I've driven many times before - I really give her some power, she accelerating like a fucking rocket with the exhausts howling and jetting blue flames as we blast up the road like shit off a chrome-plated shovel and I have to use all my skills and some more to tame her as she tries to bite me a few times at the roundabouts, but I love and respect her for it already. Needs must when the Devil drives!

I drive back home through Horsham town centre, laughing to myself for being such a lucky fucking rich bitch. I don't fucking care what people think or say about the car or myself as I power along making loads of noise, I fucking deserve it all and more for all the fucking shit I've had to put up with in my life, and so you and everyone else can all fuck-off and die.

***

I have a nightmare dream at 11pm about a huge black bedroom of black floors and black walls in the old house of my parents and sister as I open the black wardrobe doors to my far-right and take one of my books from a large cardboard box within and back to my bed to send fly-away to another land and then I shit and on the toilet there is so much where does it all come from as I pull the toilet-roll far away but it jambs as the towel surrounds the paper and I can't untangle either and I scream as the "Old Man" and Mum and Kate sit down to eat KFC in the kitchen "Dinners ready Sarah" calls number-2 but number-1 says "Stop running after THAT girl" and I'm covered in shit and I can't get it off and I hate being alive as the aeroplane crashes and continues to smash and it's not a dream it's reality and I really have shit myself in bed and I am in Hell and my dreams are all spiked with madness.

***

It's a funny old World isn't it? I've just received an email from my ex-love/ex-wife Amanda. Her relationship with the Slav girl - Wiktoria - didn't work out (good!) and so she's packing-up and moving back to Australia. Apparently she's landed herself a job working on a sheep farm in Tasmania as one their resident vets, and good luck to her, I really wish her well.

She also invited me out for a drink, for old times sake I guess, but I said "No." I explained in my return message that I'm with Clarissa now and that I didn't want anything to get in the way of our love and spoil it, even though it was only a friendly drink. Weird really, only a few years ago I would have said "Yes" and met up with her, had wild sex with her and not even thought anything about it. I guess I must be getting older and wiser? Yeah, fucking right!

***

It's Bank Holiday Monday today - not that it matters to me, every day is a Bank Holiday as far as I'm concerned! It's a scorching hot day - 82-degrees in old money! - and so Clarissa and myself are off out to a little fayre not far away from us at Wisborough Green, actually within spitting distance just up the road. They're having a little car show there as well as the fayre so we're taking the new Lamborghini and putting it on display amongst all the other cars, its public debut if you like.

Because of the heat I'm dressed accordingly - really light - in a white cotton sleeveless v-neck top from Karl Largerfeld that exposes my cleavage to the max, my pair of white sports shorts from Puma to show off my beautiful long legs, and on my feet my gorgeous pair of Sparco Formula RB-8.1 racing boots from Demon Tweeks. I'm not wearing any underwear at all simply because I don't want to or need to. My hair is in its usual high ponytail, and for my make-up I've gone for my usual high-class classic look featuring coal-black eyeshadow, super-sharp cheekbones and cherry-red lipstick. My perfume today is *Mademoiselle* by Coco Chanel. I'm not taking a clutch-bag today as Clarissa has hers. As for my lovers clothes, she's wearing my white waistcoat from Dapper - so gorgeous - and my white leather skirt from French Connection, a pair of dark-red suede court-heals from Gucci and she looks beautiful. Her underwear is in yellow lace from Triumph. As for her hair and make-up she's gone for her own look - neat, simple and gorgeous with her featured perfume being *Extrait de Parfum* by Alaia Paris - its musk turning me on to her, not that I need much persuasion on that score! Her clutch-bag is a small cream leather one from Givenchy, a gift from myself.

The event doesn't actually start until 1pm, and as it's less than 5-miles away there's no point in hurrying to get there. We spent a lazy morning in bed chatting, kissing and fucking, followed by a light breakfast of toast, grapefruit and coffee out on the patio and then showering together.

We pull out onto the A272 at 12.17pm and arrive at the fayre at 12.23pm - I told you it wasn't that far! There's about 20-cars there already, all parked together in one corner of the cricket pitch, with tents and stalls and other stuff dotted around the perimeter as well as in the middle. After showing the guy on the gate our pre-booked number we're ushered onwards to where the other cars on show are parked, slotting ourselves in between a huge silver Bentley and a Morgan+4, both cars from the 1950's.

All eyes are upon us as we extricate ourselves from the Lambo, with about 20-people just standing there staring at us and the car in amazement and envy. The car really does look amazing in the blazing sunlight, just as Clarissa as I do also, as we then wander off to have a look around the event. Some of the stalls and amusements aren't quite set-up yet, the flower show tent also being shut due to the judging taking place within. We walk around the whole pitch in no-time so we decide to go for a plod up the road to the church mounted on a small hill not far away - St. Peter ad Vincula. I've been past here a thousand times but never taken much notice of it really, me being an atheist why would I? As churches go it's actually quite pretty, with its tall spire piercing the lovely blue cloudless sky. The graveyard surrounding the church is so sad - as they all are - with row after row of ancient headstones, most of which have had their names and dates erased by time - nameless dead bodies with no-one to care for them. I can't even remember the last time I went into a church just to be nosey - maybe never? - and it's so quiet inside that you could here a pin drop, it's even a little bit creepy!

Clarissa explores the church, strolling around by herself as I stand alone in silence by the font. I don't want to look around as something is holding me back, something is stopping me. Is it because of what I've done, because I've killed another human? Is there pure evil within me and that the Devil has frozen me to the spot? Or maybe it's the spirit of my Guardian Angel, my Uncle Alf, that is holding me back, protecting me in his unique way?

I don't have the answers to any of these questions and I just want to get out of here and so I go, Clarissa following closely behind.

We then make our way back to the fayre, taking a small back-road past a little pond. I shoot a couple of ducks swimming along - with my camera that is! - they collectively lost in their own little Worlds. I wonder to myself who has the better life - me or the ducks? They seemingly don't have a single care in the World and just paddle around quacking and having a good time whereas I have to fight for survival every bloody second of the day just to do anything, including staying alive.

By now it's 1.20pm and the fayre seems to have livened-up somewhat in our absence. We're both a bit peckish by now and so we go and check-out the food situation, there being only 2-choices - fish and chips or burgers. We settle on the latter and my love pays for a couple at £4 each - a hamburger with fried onions for me and a hot-dog with the same for herself. The guy serving is quite fit and handsome, in his early-50's at a guess, and he reminds me a little of Andy in a way although I don't know why? My heart stirs as he looks at me and checks-out my beautiful face and gorgeous body, and I throw him a small cheeky smile as I read his mind of all the wonderful things he wants to do to me and me to him. Clarissa and I both grab our food, loading them with tomato ketchup and mustard, and make our way over to the seating area in front of the cricket grounds Clubhouse. We position ourselves on a bench-table with another couple - a man and a woman in their late-60's with a young golden Labrador dog. My love goes to get us both a drink from the Clubhouse bar, returning with a pint of chilled lager each. Tucking-in to our food we find ourselves both being watched all the time by our neighbours dog sitting there staring at us as we munch-away, shuffling himself in anticipation of us giving him something to eat but his "Mum" tells him "No" and then relays to us that: "He's not allowed any fatty food." I really don't see what the problem is, its never done me any harm, I mean, look at me, I'm fucking gorgeous!

As we sit and eat and drink I scan the showground looking at my fellow humans - young couples with their offspring's, elderly couples enjoying their retirement, general people soaking up the day in beautiful sunny England. It is all a joy to see and it makes such a big difference to go somewhere where one is surrounded by your own kind, such lovely beautiful people enjoying themselves in their own country. It is all so very English with not a single brown face or stinking bloody Slav in sight - what a joy! This is the way it should be throughout the whole country, not just in this corner of England here and now.

With our lunches and drinks consumed we head off to have another look around once again, making a beeline for the flower show tent - can you imagine, me at a bloody flower show! What is going on? How times have changed? An old couple look at us as Clarissa and I walk along hand-in-hand but we both ignore them, we love each other as much if not probably more than they do themselves so what has our love got to do with them? The flower displays in the tent are really beautiful - fantastic bright colours and in all shapes and sizes. I've absolutely no-idea what any of them are called but I admire them anyway, taking at least half-a-dozen pictures of them as we go - as you all know by now I haven't exactly got green fingers!

From the flower show we make our way around the rest of the fayre, starting with the stalls nearer the centre of the green. They're all mostly artisan, selling all manner of weird and wonderful things, none of which though takes either of our fancies, apart from one of them that features animal sculptures made from odd bits of scrap metal. Other attractions include face-painting for kids, a coconut shy, a dog show, Wellie-wangling, Morris dancers - although unusually they're all dressed in black instead of the traditional white for some reason? - one of those old-fashioned "Test your Strength" games with a big hammer and a bell that Clarissa begs me to try but I don't want to and so don't, a group of small animal pens featuring goats, pigs, a miniature horse, rabbits and a couple of strange tortoise with funny knobbly shells! We bypass a line of stationary engines phut-phutting away to themselves over to our left, their male owners looking as boring as their exhibits whilst their wives all just sit there beside them looking suicidal.

We've pretty much seen everything by now and so we head back to where we started and the little car show, there being a few more vehicles now than earlier and so we wander around looking at each of them in turn. There's a beautiful white 1931 Ford Model A Coupe that looks like it has just rolled off the production line even though it's nearly 90-years old. After taking a couple of photos the owner of the car comes over to me, an old guy in his late-70's and a real snappy-dresser in his period 1930's outfit. He starts to tell me all about the cars history, all the while gazing at my cleavage and I have to give a little smile at his brazen cheek! When I tell him though that I've got a 1932 Ford and that it was rodded by my late-husband he seems to take some sort of offence at this sacrilege and wanders off mid-way through my sentence - weirdo!

Clarissa and I continue browsing around all the cars - a lovely 1950's American Ford truck in red, a couple of Mini's (real ones, not that BMW crap!), a couple of bubble-cars from the 1950's that both look to me like death-traps, several nondescript English touring cars and sedans and also a few bikes, a couple of Harley's and a Triumph.

By now though both Clarissa and I have had enough and decide to head back home, back down the road a short blast. There are still plenty of admirers looking at the Lamborghini when we return to her, she sitting there like a resting monster waiting to pounce. All eyes burn into us as Clarissa and I swing its doors open and up and we climb in - all legs, bums, breasts and hair! I fire the car and give her plenty of right-foot, making the exhausts cackle like a cauldron of witches. The whole fayre appears to stop in its tracks as we pull-away and head out and back onto the A272. I give her full-throttle in 2nd-gear down the road and she barks and growls under my guidance as we break the speed-limit in a blink of an eye - I love it!

We're back at the house in no-time and I take charge, as is my WANT. I strip naked before my love in the living-room and place her hand on my right-breast as we drink neat gin - Silent Pool - and kiss mouth to mouth. I strip Clarissa of her clothes and give her oral-pleasure on the sofa, darting my tongue in and out of her vagina as fast as I can make it go, sensing her taste and smell. She cums for me and I drink her honey and we fuck with fingers and more tongue, the heat of the day intensifying our power and I WANT every day to be like this and hotter and harder with cock and cum and breasts and skin and cunt and fucking - all in my beautiful pure England.

I WANT to spend the rest of my life with her but it's not going to happen so what is the fucking point of it all?

***

A short while ago I was contacted by a charity affiliated to St. Thomas's Hospital in Lambeth, the one where I was taken to after the shooting - you remember?

They've asked me if I want to get involved in a charity fund-raising event they're staging at Brooklands Motor Racing Circuit in Byfleet, Surrey. I guess they're obviously aware of the fact - due to the papers no doubt - that I'm not without a penny or two and that I'm into cars and all that stuff and are trying to tap into my resources. Anyway, the upshot of all this is that I've agreed to take part in the event, offering free rides around part of the track in my new Lamborghini to sick children. Maybe this good deed of mine will release some positive waves into the atmosphere and free me of my pain and fill me with some good karma. We'll have to wait and see what happens on that score but I'm not counting my chickens!

Our Sunday morning lay-in together has had to go out the window today as Clarissa and I have to be at the venue by 10am - it's now 7.07am. We kiss and touch in bed and small-talk for a short while but we really must get our arses in gear as I hate being late for anything. We breakfast on tea and toast and ready ourselves for the day, although I'm really not sure I fully understand which way our day is actually going to go - up, down or sideways?

I've decided not to wear a dress or even a skirt today as it would be completely impractical for climbing in and out of the Lambo all day long, so I'm wearing a black sleeveless jumper from Schiaparelli, a pair of black slim-fit jeans from River Island, and my old pair of black-suede open-toe ankle-boots from Polyvore. My underwear is in white lace from Figleaves. My hairstyling goes without saying whilst for my make-up I've gone for my classic-look featuring grey eyeshadow, sharp blusher and pale-pink lipstick - I don't want to scare the kids too much!

My perfume today is *Poison* by Christian Dior. I'm also not bothering with taking a bag of any kind as there's no real need.

Clarissa is wearing a blue sleeveless blouse from Moschino, a pair of pale-blue skinny-fit jeans from GAP, and on her feet she's wearing my pair of tan-suede ankle-boots from

AliExpress. Her underwear is in yellow from M&S. Her make-up is more subtle than mine as she's not as adventurous on that score as I am - although obviously she still looks gorgeous! Her perfume is *Luxe* by Avon that she pinched off me this morning - a bit cheeky but I love her for it!

It's 8.55am when we finally drive out and head North for Brooklands. Through Dorking on the A24 we head left onto the A246 Young Street and the outskirts of

Bookham and Leatherhead and then through Stoke D'Abernon and into snobby Cobham. I know that I've said this a million times before about this town but it really does get on my tits around here - the massive houses, gated private roads, every other car a 4x4, and then there's the residents with their attitudes, each one pretending to be someone important when all they're doing is making themselves look a bloody laughing stock. And that's exactly what I do when I see them - LOL!

Over the top of the A3 we enter Byfleet, another posh area where a lot of the houses are buried deep behind woodland screens. Brooklands is located right at the end of this stretch of road - the A245 Byfleet Road - and we enter the gate down a short section of ancient metal road, a leftover from the 1920's. We're told by the old geezer manning the entrance-gate to park in front of the Clubhouse, alongside half-a-dozen other cars already here - a couple of Ferrari's, an Audi R8, a massive Ford Lightning Truck in yellow, a World War Two US Army Jeep and a Morgan 3-wheeler.

As per bloody usual I get all eyes burning into me, in fact we both do to be fair, when getting out of the Lambo. No sooner than we do, a woman from the charity comes over to introduce herself - Tessa - the same woman that I've been messaging back and forth with emails since the Hospital suggested me for this event.

"Hi, you must be Sarah? Wow, that is some car, is it really yours?" She beams to me.

"It is yes, I've only had it a little while." I reply.

"Expensive?" She enquires.

"Yes, very! But if you've got it flaunt it, that's what I say!" I return a little sarcastically.

"Well, yes, quite. I wonder if you would care to take Tommy for a ride around the track." She suddenly asks, producing a small boy hiding himself behind her, a really sickly-looking little kid with skin as white as snow and a bald head. His image takes my breath away and I struggle to answer her straight.

"Er, well, yes, of course I will." I stumble.

"Tommy has cancer as you may have guessed. Unfortunately it's terminal. Very sad at such a young age." She whispers to me.

"How old is he?" I enquire.

"He's only 9." Comes back her fateful reply.

DID YOU GET THAT? 9-YEARS OLD! 9 FUCKING YEARS! Poor kid. I WANT to wrap him in my compassionate arms and cure him of this evil viscous disease but I'm frozen to the spot in terror as I look into his eyes, the eyes of death. He gives me a little smile but I just want to cry but can't and mustn't. Why does life have to be such a bastard? Why has this innocent little boy got cancer and not someone who really fucking deserves it - like a rapist or Tony "Cunt" Blair for instance?

He politely holds out his right-hand for me to shake, his pale, weak, tiny hand. I touch it and shake it gently but it's like touching living death and an icy shiver shoots its way up my spine like the Devil has spiked me. I lead him around to the passenger side of the car and in he climbs unaided and as I strap him in he suddenly starts firing questions at me in his weak little voice:

"Is this your car?"

"Yes, it's my car."

"How fast does it go?"

"About 220mph."

"Cool. I've got cancer." He says, looking at me straight in the eyes and smiling a big grin.

"Yes, I know." I stutter back.

I close the door with a thud, blocking out his image whilst I try to regain my composure, take-in a large breath of air to recharge myself and then walk around the front of the car and climb in, shutting my own door down behind me.

"Ready?" I say across to him.

"OK, ready." He comes back with yet another smile and both thumbs up.

I fire the big V12-engine with a roar, click the paddle-shift into 1st-gear and we pull away, guided left by one of the officials towards what remains of a section of the old track - the famous banking. I click into 2nd-gear and give the car some gas, much to the joy of little Tommy as he sits there going "Wow wow wow." The track is really rough and I daren't go any faster than 60, although it feels more like 160 as the Lambo tries to ride the ancient uneven surface. We're followed out by one of the Ferrari's, a blood-red F40 giving a ride to yet another poor kid although all too soon we both come to the end of the short section of track and have to make our way back to the Clubhouse and park back up with the other cars once again.

Both Tommy's parents are waiting there for us, cheering and clapping for him as he sits next to me beaming like crazy. They're both in their mid-to-late-30's and seem like a really nice, average friendly young couple, although behind the scenes lurks this nasty truth, the terrible sad fact that their son has cancer and that his days are numbered - I can see it in their eyes as well as behind their smiles. We have a quick chat about the car and other inconsequential stuff as they both thank me for taking little Tommy for a ride, then letting them take a couple of photos of myself crouching down next to him with my arm around his fading waist in front of the Lambo. I just knew deep down that this day would turn out to be a sad one, and it has.

I give several more rides to other kids throughout the day - about 10 in all - including a little girl of 6 recovering from a brain tumour and a girl of 11 who had lost both her legs in a car accident and is now walking around really well on her pair of false ones. The bravery and courage these kids have just makes me want to shout and scream at the World for being such a fucking bitch and it all goes to prove that there is no fucking God - how can there be?

At lunchtime Clarissa and I go for a wander around the event ourselves, grabbing a really lovely hamburger each from one of the many stalls. There are plenty of other things going on all around us for everyone to do, not just the car-rides for the sick kids - a small funfair, clowns, a bouncy castle and loads of games and other attractions - all given free by their respective owners. It's all quite humbling and I feel somewhat emotionally drained. From there we both head off to go and see some of the cars in the numerous garages dotted around the track, from pre-war Grand Prix cars to more modern Formula 1 on display. There's also quite a few aircraft here as well, including a real Concorde, although planes don't really do anything for me, not like the cars do anyway. Around by the track Clarissa and I attempt to climb up the slope of the banking for a laugh but it's so bloody steep it's just impossible, especially in our shoes anyway!

We wander back to the Clubhouse hand-in-hand and go for a nose around the small museum and shop there, walking away with nothing but a fridge-magnet in the shape of the track as it once was back in its glory-days. There's also a few old cars and bikes in the Clubhouse museum, none of which really light my fire. We both laugh at a painting of some old woman hanging on one wall, she dressed in some bloody awful gaudy-pink outfit like an aged fairy or something - silly old cow! - what's all that about?

By now the crowd outside has grown massively, with hundreds of people all joined together in fun, all in the aid of sick children. We suddenly bump into Tessa once again and so stop to have another brief chat with her:

"How was your day?" She enquires.

"Its been really good, we've both enjoyed it." I reply.

"Yeah, its been fun, and a little sad too." Clarissa adds as Tessa stands there looking somewhat bemused, obviously taken aback that Clarissa and I are still holding each others hands like the lovers we are (I say lover and not "partner" as I hate that word, almost as much as the word "relationship" - yuk spit spit spit! - bloody political correctness bullshit!).

"I don't know how you can do this sort of thing all the time, working with sick kids I mean. Especially when some of them are terminal." I question her.

"It isn't easy I have to admit. Sometimes you have to switch yourself off from the nasty times."

"I couldn't do it that's for sure." I tell her.

"Neither could I, it's way too emotional." Says my love.

"I lost my own little girl to cancer at the age of 4. That's when I decided to do something and help others in a similar situation." She then shockingly informs us.

We both gasp at her statement. Even more so when she goes on to tell us that her ex-husband - the Father of the child - walked out on them both when they were told of the little girls plight - what a bastard!

She thanks us for supporting the event and all in all I have to admit that its been an absolute pleasure. In fact, its been a bit of an eye-opener to be honest and I've been well and truly humbled.

We wind our way back home to Foxhill in almost total silence, neither of us knowing quite what to say about the days events and what we have both experienced today. After a few drinks each - Silent Pool Gin - our minds aren't so numb and we sit and talk about life, hold each other, cry a little, laugh a little, and kiss. We fuck outdoors on the patio table and I tell her: "I love you Clarissa" as I lick her vagina.

"I love you too Sarah." She whispers as she kisses my breasts and sucks my pierced nipples and everything is beautiful.

***

It's 10.35 on a Monday morning and I'm still in bed, laying here all alone as Clarissa went off to work over 2-hours ago.

Eva lays next to me on the bed and I watch the hairs on her chest rise and fall as she breathes in and out and she is so beautiful it hurts. We are 2-completely different creatures that have evolved over thousands of years apart and yet we are so alike it's uncanny, it is truly amazing. How is this possible?

I get up and kiss her on top of her head as she sits there purring. In the en-suite bathroom I sit and pee, wipe, flush, wash my hands, and then check out my perfect face in the mirror - everything is clear. I know I'm vain in the extreme but looking like I do what do you expect, my skin is so perfect and smooth it looks like it has been polished by angels! I slide on my black silk Kimono robe from LilySilk over my naked body, it making me sigh deeply as it glides its way over my gorgeous smooth skin.

Eva and I make our way downstairs to the kitchen for breakfast. Even though Clarissa has already fed her this morning, being a typical cat she always wants more - just like me! I feed her first - chicken and salmon chunks in gravy - before I tend to myself, cornflakes and tea. Opening the cupboard door to fetch the cereal packet I discover to my amusement that Clarissa has left me a *Post-It* note stuck to the top of the box, it reading: *"NORWICH"* - a saucy code for: *"Nickers Off Ready When I Come Home"* as well as 3-kisses - cheeky bitch!

I don't really plan on doing much at all today, just lounge around I guess. I'll probably go for a swim, play some pool, check my emails, fiddle with the cars, and then sit on my perfect bum doing fuck-all until Clarissa comes home from work. I have breakfast in the kitchen with Eva, staring out the window down the garden, watching the birds pecking at the feeders that I put out for them and seeing them swoop about the sky with their inherent freedom. I wonder if they realise how lucky they actually are?

I leave Eva to continue to munch away on her food and lick herself clean as I make my way back upstairs to dress. My robe crumples to the floor as I head into the bathroom naked to shower when out the corner of my eye I catch a glimpse of a strange mark on the bathroom mirror. As I near it I notice that it's in the shape of a face, the face of evil - LUCIFER - and I freeze to the spot in horror.

Where the fuck did that come from? It wasn't there half-an-hour ago when I looked at it and Clarissa is at work so it wasn't her. Did I make the image myself? Am I going fucking insane? Is there someone else in the house and it's they that did it, maybe a burglar or even a rapist? The face stares back at me as I analyse it. It was definitely something psychical that has made the impression, something with form and function but what?

I rub it out with my towel and polish the surface of the glass, removing every last trace of its existence. It's all a fucking nightmare and I can't take it. I fuck myself on vodka until I blot it out of my mind and freak running out into the garden and scream at the crazy World and myself for being who I am - who am I? - as I'm spiked by the sanity assassin.

I think I really have lost it this time.

***

OH NO! WHAT THE FUCK! POOR LITTLE SOD! OH SHIT! I sit at my computer reading the email on the screen from Tommy's parents, the little boy that Clarissa and I met at the kids fund-raising charity event at Brooklands in Surrey a short while ago. Tommy has died, 2-days ago in hospital. Poor little boy, and only 9-years old. What a fucking waste. I am heartbroken.

His parents go on to thank me for taking him for a ride in the Lamborghini around the track, apparently he never stopped talking about it right up to his death - oh no, what can I say? They attach the photos they took of me and Tommy together by the car with him smiling away, pretending to be like every other 9-year old boy and so brave.

They invite me to his funeral that is to be held in 2-weeks time but I decline, there is no bloody way I could cope with that,

346

Abigail's funeral was bad enough and I sense that this would somehow be even worse. I thank them anyway and tell them that I will send flowers from Clarissa and myself, with both our love. I print-off copies of the photos and study Tommy's face for seemingly ages, trying to work out why it was him that was chosen to be a victim of this bastard fucking disease?

I smash myself on lager and then vodka until I'm physically sick on the living-room carpet, Eva watching every convulsion with her typical feline expression, one of destain coupled with intrigue.

Why does life have to be so bloody unfair?

R.I.P Tommy.

***

"AW AW AW" I yelp as Clarissa's pierced tongue licks against my clitoris as we step into the sexual fourth dimension together and turn to feather, my brain being attacked by rays of pure white light as I lose control, both of us radiating our love energy as we fuck with all-consuming love and devotion to each other. This is the passion of lovers - "For Death" she said.

After several minutes of this pleasuring I can't control myself any longer and scream and spit into her mouth my honeylove - my love. We French-kiss my juice between our mouths as we touch and fondle each others breasts as I rub my left-leg and then my foot against her vagina, making her pant like a bitch. She loves my sweetness with 2-fingers and I bite her bottom lip firmly and hold her in my power.

I tell her: "I love you Clarissa" in my most seductive voice and she responds with love: "Kiss my pussy and make me cum. Fuck me now. Fuck me Sarah. Make me cum my love" as we kiss and tongue.

I push her back on the bed gently and she spreads her legs for me, showing me her honey. I reposition myself at the foot of the bed and kiss her wet vagina and flick my tongue into her, making her button pulsate. She shakes like fuck as I take her to

Heaven, sucking her lips as hard as I dare without hurting her too much and then inserting 2-fingers into her body, blowing her mind as she cums her mucus for me. As I swallow her I pull her labia apart with the fingers on both hands and suck on the beautifully soft rubbery texture of her quim, making her scream out loud like shit and jump up and down on the bed like Regan MacNeil as I drink her cum and nuzzle my face against her hole.

Back on planet Earth we swap over, Clarissa tying my wrists around one of the bedposts with my sex-chain. She slaps my beautiful bum-cheeks, making them rosy, and then fingers my pert bumhole with lube, first with 1-finger and then 2. I moan like fuck as it burns me but I love it also, begging her to: "Push harder" and "Give me 3." It's fucking tight and stings like crazy but I don't complain, just moaning "UH UH UH" like the nymphomaniac bitch I am as my love pushes 3-fingers into my body and fucks. I lose my mind to the sensation and I feel numb and light-headed and I WANT EVERYTHING.

I am the perfect creation.

I am beyond beautiful.

I am beyond gorgeous.

It is so good to be perfect.

I love being a woman - and free.

Is it any wonder that I'm autosexual?

With her other hand she starts to bitch-slap my pussy and I explode at the abuse, my brain turning to jelly and I cry. After several minutes she stops and sits back, licking and sucking her fingers free of cunt and arse. I free myself from the chain and crawl over to her to help her task, tasting my own love on her fingers.

I take charge now and reposition her to sit over my face cowgirl as she squats plie', pulling her gorgeous bum-cheeks apart and flicking my tongue in and out and around her crack, making her breathing heavy and disjointed. I fuck her anally with my tongue and make her bleat softly:

"Oh yes Sarah yes, oh, oh, oh, my love."

I slap her bum and lube and finger her with 1, 2 and 3 and then 4 and my thumb in a roll, pushing her firm and hard. It takes almost 10-goes for me to break the pressure and get my whole hand inside her and she screams:

"OH FUCKING HELL SARAH" and "YOU FUCKING BITCH" and "OH NO NO NO" and "OW OW OW" and other such noises as I touch her chocolate and fuck it. I pull out of her with a humorous, plopping sound that makes me laugh and her sigh but I haven't finished yet, quickly reinserting myself back inside her body, this time into her vagina and she splits and spits and I enter her right up to my wrist.

"Do you like my hand in your cunt?" I say to my lover.

"Oh Sarah, please, no more. Oh, harder. Harder. HARDER. OH HARDER SARAH. FUCKING HELL. OH OH OH AH OW. OH FUCK."

I twist my wrist gently inside her vagina before pulling it out with a squelch but neither of us laugh this time. I rub her juice from my hand over my breasts and then hers, licking off the remaining honey myself.

The bedroom is filled with love, sex and fuck and I make her stand, facing away from me, tying her high-up to one of the 4-poster bedposts with one of Andy's old leather belts. Positioning her right-leg on top of the mattress and spreading her labia and bum, I crouch down and lick them both, making her moan and pant like a bitch. I lube them with my fingers and slap her bum hard and she loves me as all the others have and future lovers will also. Taking my lubed clear plastic dildo from Honour, I ease it into her rear with a push, forcing it beyond its stubborn boundary with cracked pleasures. She cries: "OH OH OH" as it hits her spot and I start to fuck her rhythmically. I carry on like this for several minutes before grabbing my 9-inch realistic dildo from Lovehoney and place its knob at her vaginal lips and play with them as I continue to anal her slowly.

"OH FUCK ME, FUCK ME SARAH" she pleads as I tease her and laugh. I slide the second fake-cock into her cunt with ease, making her gasp: "OH FUCKING HELL" at the pleasure of her double-penetration. I double-pump her alternately with one-hand controlling each fake penis and she laughs and cries as I fuck her and kiss and bite her bum. She cums for me and shakes like a fucker and I hold her there in a state of ecstasy until she shouts: "GREEN."

I stand and kiss and tongue her mouth, both cocks falling to the carpet with a twin-thud as I let each one go. Untying her wrists she collapses backwards onto the bed with a sigh of relief, that is until I open her legs and start to tongue at her hot pussy, it glistening at me like one giant sore eye - it is so beautiful and I kiss her cunt. She starts to shake like a whore as I eat her meat, her arms and legs flailing wildly as I take her to paradise with my mouth. I have her once again within 3-minutes as she fires her orgasm into my face and screams like an animal as I finish her off with one final lick to her minge.

I fall next to her and lay side-by-side with my love, both of us giggling as we touch each others breasts. Clarissa kisses my mouth, tasting her own honey on my lips and tongue and we laugh at our love for each other as our game continues. Rolling over onto my chest she kisses and licks my bum, tonguing at my hole. She massages and penetrates it with her lubricated fingers, rubbing and slapping me and making me laugh as she does so. Grabbing the very same dildo I used on her pussy, Clarissa rubs its knob around my rectum and then starts to push me. I try not to resist it but it's hard at first until finally it gives way as my barrier is broken. It slides into my body in one and I feel my lower organs moving out of its way as my lover fucks me. I sigh breathlessly with pleasure as Clarissa fucks my ass, it stinging me but I don't care as I order her to:

"FUCK IT. OH YES. FUCK MY ARSE. COME ON, PUSH IT ALL THE WAY IN. OH YES YOU BITCH. YOU FUCKING BITCH. OH, LOVE ME CLARISSA, LOVE ME, COME ON, YOU CAN DO IT MY LOVE."

We French-kiss as we fuck and she squeezes my tits, my nipples, and plays with my piercings as I suck her tongue like a cock. She pulls the fuck from my bum and we both lick and suck and kiss its length between us, savouring the taste of our endless love for each other as we become lost in time.

Clarissa fists my vagina with all her love for me as I accept her into my body, her whole hand inserted right up to her wrist and I think I'm about to pass-out as my brain spins around inside my skull. I moan "AW AW AW AW" as she parts my pelvis and fist-fucks my cunt with squelching and pain and pleasure and cum and love and I die. We kiss full-on and I lose control in a moment and soak her hand with my honey as I bite her neck. She screams as I scream as we become one person, one woman, just one single lover as she cunts me.

I cut a big line of cocaine for us both on our dressing-table top and together we suck the viscous white powder up our noses. I lick some and Clarissa tongues my mouth, exchanging the drug and our love for one another.

"I WANT your cunt." I whisper to her, making her laugh like the whore she is. I lay back on the bed and she moves over me, positioning her pussy over my face. I start playing with her lips, pulling them and sucking them, making her moan and love me more. Flicking my tongue in and out of her hole drives her insane and she begs for more and harder:

"OH SARAH, OH SARAH, OH GOD, OH GOD, HARDER, HARDER. LICK ME. OH OH OH OH I'M GONNA CUM, I'M GONNA CUM, OH GOD LICK ME AWWWWWWWW AH."

She shakes like she's made out of beautiful jelly as the cocaine and the orgasm bites her soul, her discharge spitting onto my face in several small spurts of love and I lick her lips and drink her.

"I'll be back in a minute. I need to pee and wash." She tells me between pants.

"Don't." I instantly jab back at her.

"I have to. I can't hold it any more."

"Piss on me." I tell her.

"What?" She exclaims.

"Piss on my tits and over my face."

"Oh Sarah really! Come on, I have to go."

She goes to climb off me but I grab her arms firmly, not in a nasty threatening way, but just enough to make her stop in her tracks.

"I really need to pee." She pleads back.

"Then pee. Piss on me here over my tits." I beg her.

"You're crazy, do you know that?"

"Yes, I know, that's why you love me." I smirk back.

She laughs as she sits up and then I feel it, the lovely warm trickle of her golden-rain splashing down onto my beautiful body - it is glorious.

"Oh, that feels so good. I really needed that." She says as she pees.

I move her further up my body as she continues to piss on me, over my beautiful breasts and then over and onto my face. I open my mouth to her and swallow her yellow, tasting the strange warm liquid on my tongue. I finger her vagina as the last flow of urine falls, making her jump momentarily but she loves it. I tongue her wet labia and make her yelp like a small dog - a bitch - as I continue licking her meat.

"Oh Sarah, no more, no more please, GREEN." She begs me and so reluctantly I stop.

We both take a couple of swigs each from the bottle of gin - Bombay Sapphire - that we bought upstairs with us, it numbing our brains along with the cocaine and the sex. We fool around with each others breasts, pouring the gin over them and licking and sucking it off.

Clarissa fingers my vagina with 2, making me sigh with pleasure as she masturbates me. I spin my body around so she has a full view of my beautiful cunt and she licks it, making me fly into orbit. I throw the tube of strawberry-flavoured Durex Play gel to her in silence, she has the imagination and the nous to know what I WANT without the use of any silly words between us.

The coolness of the gel on my bumhole is gorgeous as I moan a deep moan of love. Clarissa inserts 1-finger into me and wanks, then 2. The third is as tight as fuck but in she goes. Number-4 is a bastard but what the Hell? Her thumb is now inside the other 4 and goes in up to her knuckles. She pushes me and I cry as then she has me, splitting my bum as her whole hand inserts inside my passage with beautiful pain and pleasure. I moan as Clarissa moves her hand around inside my body and licks my cunt-hole and gives me 2-fingers of her other hand. 3 and 4 are a fucking tight squeeze with the less said about her thumb the better! Fisting my cunt wasn't as bad as my bum but with double-entry it is extremely difficult but Clarissa soon has me, she pumping me alternately and then simultaneously and then back again. I moan like a fucker as my mind becomes detached from what she's doing to me and I collapse from within and I don't know anything now - I am totally lost.

After almost 10-minutes of abuse I die again and shout: "GREEN" to my love. She withdraws both fists from my body and it feels like my insides are falling out as she disconnects from me - I'm done-for and breathe my very last breath on this Earth. We kiss and touch breasts and lick and suck my beautiful/evil juices from her fingers and hands and drink more gin and throw ourselves at each other as we destroy our lives snorting more cocaine from our breasts and more fuck.

We kneel before each other on the bed and gaze into each others eyes. We smile and we kiss soft and tenderly and it is so amazing that we've found each other, that I have found someone so perfectly suited to spend the rest of my life with and I for her also. The pure feeling of love between us is incredible, it is beyond reality, it is beyond existence. We have total and complete love and devotion to one another. We will do anything without question.

"Shit for me." I ask my love.

"Where do you want me my love?" She says as she squeezes my breasts and we kiss with tongues.

"On all fours." I reply.

"Help me push my love. Open my hole and lick it." She demands as she repositions herself on the bed.

Behind her I spread her bum-cheeks apart with my hands and begin to flick my tongue in and around her anal passage, making my love moan with desire:

"Oh oh oh. Lick me Sarah. I can feel it coming. OH MY GOD!"

I stop licking and move myself around to her left-side, pressing her belly underneath her with my left-hand as I separate her bumhole with my right. She squeezes and moans and I sense her sphincter changing shape as the turtles-head makes its glorious appearance. I let it extract only part-way before instructing my love to:

"Stop pushing my love, let me have it."

Clarissa obeys my command like my slave as I start to push her shit back into her anus, it squishing between my fingers like dough but I continue reloading her hole but the more I push it in the more it pushes out. In the end it just ends up in a big smelly brown mess of crap over both her bum-cheeks, her rectum, over my hand, down her legs, and onto the bed itself. I wank-shit her as I play with her left-breast with my other hand before forcing 2-fingers into her mouth, fucking it and making her choke but she loves it and sucks me.

I continue to play around with her sticky disgusting scat, spreading it around her arse and fingering it into both her arsehole and vagina. She cums down her legs as I fuck her with the brown and she screams between that and choking on the fingers of my left-hand.

We stop and laugh at the awful mess we've made, strip the bed of its destroyed sheets, and then go to shower together in the en-suite bathroom. We kiss as we wash-away all the detritus - the shit, the cum, the saliva, the piss, the blood - and then dry each others bodies in the bedroom with our finest Egyptian towels, kissing and caressing as we go. I position her over the end of the bed with her beautiful pert bum in the air, telling her to:

"Push hard. Push it out. Come on Clarissa, you can do it my love."

I clean her further with antiseptic wipes as she struggles pushing, her body now free and empty of the nasty. I move behind her awaiting the result as she continues to squeeze her internal organs out of her body as I push on her lower-abdomen with one-hand to assist her. I carry-on wiping her as she moans in discomfort as then it comes, her rear producing the disgusting red circular mound of her prolapse. I wipe it clean and then finger it, making her shudder and bleat: "OW OW OW OW" like a whore. I go down and lick the horror before me, making it pump and beat like a heart as Clarissa loses control and screams like fuck as I start to suck her prolapse with vigour. It's fucking vile but we're both so far fucking gone on love, sex, alcohol, cocaine, cunt, shit, tongue, breasts, skin, hair, legs, mouths, dildos, lesbianism, piss and Hell that none of any of this or that matters to either of us - we just do whatever we want to each other and fuck.

I tell her to: "Bite my hip" and she sinks her teeth into me, breaking my flesh and sucks. We scissor one another on the bed, rubbing our beautiful vaginas together and it is so pure and gorgeous that we cum quickly and kiss and touch breasts. We cut each others labia's - just a small nick with one of my scalpel-blades - and scissor again, entwining our blood together to become sisters forever as we melt into each others person and cunts.

I have her fly upon my wings - my love - and tell her:

"I give you my body and my life Clarissa - you are "The One" and I will love you forever my love."

***

Its been a bumpy ride hasn't it my friends? But even so, at long last we've both finally got there in the end. We've made it, and we have the scars to prove it - mentally and physically. I've been to the edge of the World - and I fell off.

I can assure you that I have suffered beyond your imagination in order to come to this point in my life - this nightmare - but I am richer for all the pain I have experienced, as hard as it was at the time. None of us were asked to be born and I am lucky to be alive - as are you - and over the years I have had both wonderful and horrible moments in my life. I have many precious memories as well as some that I can't even bear to think about. And yet here I am, bisexual psychopathic Sarah Knowles, still alive and still fucking gorgeous, still trying to beat the World, and at the end of my time I will jump into my grave laughing at the things I have done. I am my greatest fan and I love.

Well done Sarah.

All I ever wanted was to live in a World of love, peace, freedom, solitude and understanding. Instead though I found myself surrounded by hatred, conflict and bullshit where everything is not only up-side-down, it's inside out as well. All I WANT is tranquillity, and it is my choice to either fuel the fire or put it out.

I deserve to live the life I WANT after EVERYTHING I've been through as I stand and embrace my destiny. How I haven't had a heart attack after all my troubles I'll never know! 99% of all the people I've ever met couldn't handle half of what I've survived. I have more neurons in my body than anyone else. I talk to them and they talk to me. It is what drives me forward, drives me on - along with my independence, freedom, and vodka of course!

The omnipresent depression creeps over me and I cannot shake it off, it sticking to me like shit to a blanket and I hate it - I hate it all. I hate everything - including myself, even though I don't really. In my alcove - all alone - and in the hollow hills - so sad - the fear to touch. My struggle with anxiety haunts me from the very depths of my soul and I am on the fucking brink of suicide all the fucking time. I have got to the point now where I simply don't fucking care any more - this is the oblique image of myself.

I know that I'm a megalomaniac but what can I do? What I really do worry over is my mental instability and how far will it drag me down? Will it eventually destroy me? Will it destroy everything? I guess that it probably will. As I've said before, I cannot contain the contagion. I don't want to keep slashing my wrists every day just to ease my pain - I WANT MORE. There has to be a reason to live, a reason to believe?

I know that I'm a bit of a basket-case, it's true. The mental abuse I received from the "Old Man" over all those years has damaged me beyond repair. They were bloody hard times of course, but I won through and here I am - a masterpiece! Life isn't all sunshine and Spring-lambs of course, it's unfair and shit and we all have to deal with it in our own way, whatever that may be. Life happens, and every experience changes you.

I know exactly who I am and what I see, both on the inside as well as the outside. I am feral. I am liquid. And as such I have a deep understanding of death, and therefore life, and that is how I know exactly who I really am. My unique identity has transformed me into this stranger with the unnerving outward persona that I hold so dear to my twisted heart.

Life is a weird thing my friend and you have to make the most of it whilst you have the chance. The past cannot be undone so move on with your life and make it a better place to be. There's a great big World out there waiting for you, go and grab your slice of it. If you feel the need for change then change it. You don't need permission from anyone, you have the power, just do it and fuck anyone else. Always try to be 1-up on everyone, otherwise you will forever be No. 2 - and you know what that is!

Face your own image - I have, and do so every day. Have the courage to grab the nettle and ignore its sting, and at the end of your struggle you will find yourself, as have I. Get to really know yourself, and then you will see:

There is no light at the end of the tunnel.

There is no cloud with a silver lining.

There is no fucking God to save you.

You are on your own and you have to make the most of it the best you can, this is life - not everyone's toast falls butter-side up as you well know from my words.

Whatever path you choose, you must stick to it 100%. DO NOT deviate from it. DO

NOT take you eye off the ball for 1-second. Do it, and do it well. Search your soul to work out what you want from the future. Keep your feet on the ground at all times. Don't be so uptight. Be more free. And free yourself from the need for perfect acceptance - you are who you are and love it. Never run from anything, stand your ground and fight to the death. Control yourself at all times, especially in times of trouble - and laugh in the face of fear and adversity.

Do your job and do it well, but do it under protest. You are in charge, not the management - they can all go to HELL. Life is hard enough without them making it worse, but it's only hard because other people make it so - rise above them and fuck them all. Steering a pathway through life is as difficult as ever. No-one has the right to tell you what to do, not even your parents - and so under no circumstances tell your Mother anything, the least she knows the better!

Stop and look at the World around you and live your life the best you can - breathe the air, taste the food, drink the wine, see the trees, the mountains, the lakes, the sky, the Earth. Breathe-in their power and become part of their form.

Try to be positive and optimistic, living without hope, love and personal joy and private dreams is too miserable a life. Make something good happen. Have something exiting on your horizon and run with it to the end.

Don't be a hypocrite, and don't let anyone stand in your way. Be aware of your surroundings in order to fight and repel, and if you let people know that you will stand up for yourself and hit back, they will leave you alone. But if by some chance they don't - have them.

Don't let your life slip through your fingers - reject stagnation and a safe existence. Live your life and take the risks, otherwise everything will be boring and useless and you will spend the rest of your days in sad regret - don't let that happen. Do not allow yourself to rot within your own self. Clear your mindset and act upon calculated spontaneity. Be proud of your quality and let your quality define your soul. Empower yourself to greater things. Re-evaluate the priorities in your life in order to help you decide what YOU want and no-one else. I have a plan for my life - do you?

You know me, I'm not bitter at all! I am not, and do not, beg forgiveness from anyone. As ever I just do my own thing. I will always be bohemian. I will always be me. There is simply not enough space in my life for any crap, not on any level.

The philosophy to my independence is clear - be a loner, but don't be lonely. Remain in singularity. My attitude to life has been moulded by surrounding people and events - my parents, the stupid fucking people that I've worked with, people on the street - you. It's a fact that every day shapes the person we eventually become, for better or for worse.

That never-ending anxiety of feeling abandoned by my parents still hangs over me like a fucking vampire and I'll never shake it, no matter what I do. I just don't believe it, I don't believe in anything. Am I ever going to have a sweet and happy ending to my life? I don't fucking think so. You work hard all your days and when it's time to retire and relax your body then starts to fail and you either have a bloody heart-attack or you get some fucking horrendous disease like cancer or whatever and it's all over - you die.

I'm always searching for the truth but end up being surrounded by lies, and around and around we continuously go in a never-ending betrayal of empty words and meaningless bullshit. It all makes me want to cry.

I also want to get back at that arrogant fucking cunt CJ - and all the others as I have so many scores to settle - but as yet I haven't dreamt up a nasty enough way to do it. I will though, in time, and it will be the most evil one yet, even worse than what I did to that bitch Mellis, of that you can be sure. Maybe I'll set-fire to his stupid fucking caravan - with him in it - just for a laugh! Don't forget, people leave managers, not companies. Without sounding too pompous, incompetence breads dishonesty, and there is no-one more incompetent or dishonest than the fucking management, and the higher up the ladder you go, the worse they fucking get.

I am not like them - or you - and I never will be. I am special and I fucking know it, I'm a fucking star, and yet we only see the stars when it's the darkest.

Seriously though, what exactly do you expect me to do, seek revenge on everyone that has wronged me over the years? I would be here forever, battling against my foes and adversaries until the end of time. Everyone is my enemy - and vengeance and retribution will be mine. There is only so much I can tolerate, the bleeding sores of life, with people dragging me down and I am so tired of listening to all their gossip. Some day soon I'm going to spiral out of control and that will be the end of it all - there will be no more me.

But I just simply can't let it go however hard I try. Control is power and I WANT it all. I WANT EVERYTHING and I will never stop until I get it. I cannot be stopped. How can I even stop myself, I have to push all the time. I have to push my luck, what is the point otherwise? What is the fucking point?

The future is built on the foundations of the past, and with a past like mine you can see how unstable my future begins to look! I just want to be happy, whatever

"Happy" means? I can't help the way I am. Things go wrong in peoples lives and they have to readjust to their own situations, that's the way they are, especially in my case.

There is only so much sage advice I can bombard your brain with my dear reader, these words of bleak eloquence and unhinged Pathos. You have to be held accountable for the things you do, that's life, and you have to do your own thing as no-one is going to hold your hand and show you the way. You must be true to yourself, whatever the outcome, and there is only one person you can trust and that is yourself.

I can feel my life changing - I really can feel it - and no-one is going to get in my fucking way. I just hope and pray that it's all for the better, it has to be for everyone's sake or I will completely lose control forever. And yet what can I do to stop myself falling down further into the darkness?

There comes a time in ones life when you have to make a decision - Left or Right? It's the Right of course, as I continue to walk this lonely narrow path to my ultimate ending.

Things will change when we once again rise to power.

This will be the New Order.

With the power of my God - THE GREAT ONE - and the 14-words we can build a perfect new World.

* * *

It is now January 2017 and another crazy year has passed. Where all the time goes I just don't know? My 37th birthday last November came and went without anything of any significance happening, no-one wished me "Happy Birthday" except for Clarissa, Eva and dear old Mrs. DeAngelis next door. Christmas was the bloody same.

I am lonely even though I am not alone - the less people you have in your life the less misery you have to endure, the agony of friends, of ones family. I have an overwhelming desire to exist, but only for myself, an overwhelming sense of oneness, the relationship between myself and the Earth beneath my feet, that is the epiphany I have and you don't.

I WANT no further part in this so-called "Human Race", I've had enough - this is the final straw. I refuse to conform to society, and why should I when society doesn't conform to me? I have been born a thousand-times and have died as many also and there is nothing that anyone can do to me that hasn't been done already - as well you know my friends. And yet I am still here. I am still alive and kicking. Thanks to my pragmatic streak I am able to undertake my own dirty work, just as that stupid bitch Mellis found out to her destruction. And yet is what I've done really so terrible?

I WANT to live the rest of my days in peace here in this house with my loves Clarissa and Eva, but whether it will happen or not only the future will decide. I just hope that my future is not as lost as my past.

I know that one day I will have to pay for my actions and that will be the day I die, and as each day passes I am one step closer to death, the desolate abyss that she is. I am on the Dark Side of existence with all its miracle and wonder, being chased by screaming sores, the shadows of the dead, tattooed nightmares and voices from the grave as I continue as ever to be confounded by the dead-man's hand of fate - I am deathless. I don't want to be there but that is where I find myself. I can't do anything about it, I am stuck in this living nightmare every fucking day and I can see no way out, a World were everything is fake but I'm not fooled by any of it.

How do I get out of this trap?

How do I free myself from all this hate boiling-away inside me?

How long can I remain at liberty?

The fact is that I don't exist and I never have. I am a fantasy of the highest, yet lowest order. I am beyond existence. We all create fiction to hide our pain and I should know - I am fiction - created by the surrounding chaos of another where reality is nothing amidst the continuous total breakdown of civilisation and the stupidity of life itself. It is you that has made me so don't fucking complain at my words of HELL.

What really is in my mind - my real mind - you will never know as you're not allowed inside, it's for me to know and you not to find out. In future days my life will become a shrine to the last remnants of humanity. All the people will cry. All the people will die. But I will live on.

As I head along the path towards ultimate power and freedom, I will not have my master-plan thwarted in any way by anyone. Life has made me vicious and no-one is going to get in my fucking way, this is my obsessive despotic desire to survive. I will carry on and live my life unto death - my next great adventure.

I'm gonna fucking have it all and everyone is going to fucking suffer.

I WANT

I WANT MORE

I WANT EVERYTHING

I WANT YOU

Thank you all my cats, my only friends and loves - lady Suzie - funny Cagney - my Lacey - young Heidi - beautiful Poppy - and to Eva, a mixture of all the above, and to you my beautiful dear reader.

Sarah

"You must understand the whole of life, not just one little part of it. That is why you must read, that is why you must look at the skies, that is why you must sing, and dance, and write poems, and suffer, and understand; for all that is life."

Madjid Krishnamurti (1895–1986)